PRAISE FOR A

The Waning Moon: Honorable Mention (Urban Fantasy) in the 2018 Readers' Favorites Book Awards

"The Waning Moon is a can't-miss fantasy adventure with humor, snark, and fun banter. A must-read!"

LIZ KONKEL, READERS' FAVORITE, 5-STAR REVIEW

The Waning Moon is the second in the Eleanor Morgan series and I think I can pay Cissell no greater compliment than to say reading this book inspires me to read the first book in the series and to continue with the entire series, as it is completed. This is a winner and one of the best in its genre that I've read of late.

GRANT LEISHMAN FOR READERS' FAVORITE

"This [The Cardinal Gate] is a whole story with a strong female protagonist and superior writing! Brilliant and entertaining."

RABIA TANVEER, READERS' FAVORITES, 5-STAR REVIEW

"This [The Ruby Blade] is an epic fantasy and fans of magic and mayhem will lap it up, but the by-play and the strong, positive characters, especially the women, are so refreshing to read. This is one of those books that is impossible to put down as one exciting scene just literally drags you into the next, but for readers with a thirst for witty, sassy, dialogue, that's all here too."

"This book [The Broken World] was amazing! I so enjoy the characters and their quirks. I am very much looking forward to the next installment in this wonderfully unique series. I can't wait to see what happens next! Amy Cissell has now been added to my must-read authors list."

"Ms Cissell is a truly gifted writer. She has fun with her characters, just the right amount of sexy, and a solid understanding of how to write a series that you don't want to end. I find myself rushing to read the last chapters, to find the next twist even as I mourn having to wait for the next installment."

"Wow! I love, love, love this series! If you like Fae creatures of all kinds, magic, shapeshifters of all kinds vampires, a great love story or two, dragons, etc. Then this is your series and this book [The Iron River] does not disappoint!"

THE DARK THRONE

AN ELEANOR MORGAN NOVEL: BOOK SEVEN

AMY CISSELL

BROKEN
WORLD
PUBLISHING

The Eleanor Morgan Novels
The Complete Series

The Cardinal Gate
The Waning Moon
The Ruby Blade
The Broken World
The Lost Child
The Iron River
The Dark Throne

The Eleanor Morgan World Novellas
The Throneless King

THE DARK THRONE
Amy Cissell

A Broken World Publication
PO Box 11643
Portland, OR 97211
The Dark Throne
Copyright © 2021 by Amy Cissell
All Rights Reserved
ISBN 978-1-949410-24-2 (ebook);
ISBN 978-1-949410-25-9 (paperback)

Cover Design: Covers by Combs
Edited by: Christopher Barnes

For
Dad—thanks for always believing in me
Chris—for never giving up on me
Liana—for challenging me to be as brave as you

And for my readers—
Eleanor & I wouldn't have gotten here without you. Thanks for coming along
for the ride.

THE ROAD SO FAR

Eleanor Morgan had lived the first thirty-four of her years as a happily mundane human in the Pacific Northwest. She spent most of her free-time trail running, taking random classes at the fitness center (she'll always have a soft spot for Tai Chi), and working on her garden. Although she doesn't have a lot of close friends, she has her bestie Finn. Sure, he was once a one-night-stand that ended up spanning more than a few nights, but now they've settled into something more platonic. It is a nice, uneventful life punctuated by cheap food and expensive beer.

Of course, it wouldn't be much of a story if it stayed that way.

When Eleanor takes a mid-summer day to trim and shape Hedge Antilles, the laurel hedge on the north side of her property, her only expectations were getting hot and sweaty and wrestling an unruly shrubbery into submission. But when Hedge takes offense to the haircut and shoots up several more feet and a vampire shows up on her porch calling her Princess and threatening to eat her, things take a turn... It turns out Finn is not who he said he was, but rather a half-Fae servant of the Light Court sent to watch and protect Eleanor until it was time.

In THE CARDINAL GATE, Eleanor finds out that she is a

changeling child, sent from the land of the Fae to grow up as a human, connected to this land, so that when she's grown, she can trigger the magic and open up the once-sealed gates between Earth and the Fae Plane. Of course, those gates were shut for a reason—and it turns out the other supernaturals aren't as eager to return things to the way they used to be. She picks up another watcher—Isaac Walker, a sexy werewolf with not-so-hidden trauma and too many secrets.

With Finn's assistance, she finds and opens the first gate, releasing a flood of magic into the world that destroys technology and kills thousands of people. Eleanor, Isaac, and Finn travel to the Black Hills of South Dakota, looking for the second gate. Eleanor is learning to adapt to the new magic flowing through her and is determined to not let another disaster like Portland happen. To that end, she picks up another companion on the quest. Florence White Elk joins them to train Eleanor, help mitigate the damage the gate openings do, and to hold Eleanor to a promise—to help her find her twin sister who was kidnapped by the Fae when they were children.

Eleanor's first major Fae power is released when a Fae tattoo artist finds the dragon within and draws it out. Between getting used to her new powers, falling into bed and catching some feels with a werewolf, a kidnapping attempt by some Portland-based vampires who serve the deliciously sexy Raj—a thousand-year-old vamp whose origin story is told in THE THRONELESS KING, and the betrayal of her best friend, the road to the second gate is rocky, but ultimately successful. Only six more to go...and they head east.

In THE WANING MOON, Eleanor dodges assassination attempts from witches and vamps and kills the immortal Rasputin—kind of. Raj shows up to tag along for the ride to the third gate—just outside of St. Louis. In addition to locating the gate in Cahokia, she heeds Florence's warning and agrees to perform the mate-bonding ceremony with Isaac. She finds out that Finn has forged several links to her mind allowing him to follow her anywhere, and he reluctantly removes them, but only after losing an ear tip and a finger. After successfully opening the St. Louis gate, the crew heads south, stops for an interlude with a bobcat shifter in Appalachia who helps them get new identities, and ends up in Savannah.

Although Eleanor and Florence have managed to slow the effects of the magic waves at each gate opening, the magic is too strong to be contained. Technology is disrupted at each gate point, and Eleanor's crossed the entire country. Computers are down. Modern cars don't work. And most of the United States grid has been destroyed, leaving a tech-dependent country in chaos and causing the President, who turns out has been Fae this whole time, to declare martial law and reveal the existence of supernatural creatures to the public.

THE WANING MOON is a bittersweet journey for Eleanor. She gains a mate under the full moon in St. Louis, but instead of being able to celebrate with her new mate, Isaac says goodbye, opting to sacrifice himself to save the werewolf he'd thought dead at the hands of Michelle—ex-girlfriend, former captor, and unstable vampire. He walked through the fourth gate and into the Fae Realm to save Emma, a beautiful blonde werewolf, is deposited at Eleanor's feet right before our hero is shot by the human police.

THE RUBY BLADE, book three, takes Eleanor out of the hospital and on the road to Pennsylvania—in the winter—to find some magic rocks. Although Eleanor is still mourning Isaac, Raj is there with a shoulder to cry—or nibble—on. The confrontation at the fifth gate further proves that Finn and whoever he's working for are not going to let things go easily. Someone wants Eleanor dead, although Finn would prefer a different type of subjugation. After the fifth gate is opened, no thanks to Emma but definitely thanks to Petrina—Raj's gorgeous, Swedish, witchy vamp scion, the group heads down south again. They're heading to the territory of the Queen of New Orleans —the most powerful vampire in North America. Despite Raj's warnings that there is nothing he wouldn't do to retrieve his sword—an ancient weapon handed down from his father and his father before him, set with blood rubies—Eleanor still didn't see that betrayal coming.

She's traded to Marie in exchange for the blade, and Marie states her intention to make good on her promise to deliver the "head of the pretender" to Medb, current Queen of the Dark Sidhe. After an extended stay in her very first dungeon, Raj comes to her rescue. Eleanor is not impressed with him, nor is she pleased to find out that all of her companions were in on the plot to get Raj's sword back and let Medb—and Finn—think Eleanor had been hamstrung. Eleanor opens the sixth gate with an unexpected Fae army at her back—courtesy of Arduinna, who is not only an agent of the Light King and a double agent of the Dark Queen, but the chief of staff for the Fae President of the United States.

In book four, THE BROKEN WORLD, anti-supernatural sentiment is on the rise and humans are coming for the so-called monsters with tiki torches and pitchforks. Eleanor is forced to confront her feelings for Raj in Santa Fe and decide if she's going to forgive his betrayal and give in to her desire.

Bandolier National Monument, home of the penultimate gate, has been booby-trapped by Finn in a last-ditch attempt to halt the progress of the gate openings. It takes a lot of time, ingenuity, and care to remove the land mines surrounding the gate site, but they get it down and Eleanor opens the seventh gate. Before they have a chance to celebrate and regroup, Emma is shot—not by another supernatural in their continuing quest to stop Eleanor—but by a human whose hate and fear led him into violence.

Subdued and in mourning, Eleanor leads her diminished group northwest, dodging attacks by humans and attempts at either assimilation or assassination by the new human governments. Finally, they return back to where everything began—Portland, Oregon—to get their houses in order before the final gate.

The final gate is opened with a sacrifice—a Fae-made blade must open the gate with the blood of the world-breaker, otherwise known as Eleanor Morgan. Raj reluctantly agrees to use his recently recovered Ruby Blade on the woman he loves. Book 4 ends in death and fire—a silver stake in Raj's back, a ruby sword in Eleanor's gut, and the eruption of every volcano in the Cascade Range.

Book five, THE LOST CHILD, begins with Eleanor waking up naked (again) and alone in a dome of fire with Raj's Ruby Blade next to her. Six weeks have passed, Raj is nowhere to be found, and Eleanor is ravenous. It doesn't take long for Florence and Petrina to find her—Florence got a power boost when the final gate fell. Raj is recovered with a little magical high-jinx, but before Eleanor can get a handle on her post-apocalyptic world, Florence cashes in her promise. It's time for Eleanor to go home.

Eleanor is welcomed into the Light Court with open arms from the king, Eochid, and open hostility from his consort, Cloithfinn. It doesn't take long to prove that Eleanor is one of the most powerful Fae in the kingdom, something that doesn't open as many doors as she's hoped. Only after an exhaustive search throughout the Light Realm does Eo's chief advisor mention that the woman they're seeking is located in the Dark Realm—within the Dark Queen's court.

Eleanor and Connor use one of the rare, permanent gates between realms to travel to the Dark City to rescue a woman who isn't too keen on being rescued. When they finally convince her to follow them back—and Connor grovels for having abandoned her forty years earlier—they return to find an empty, blood-stained palace.

Cloithfinn attempted a coup, blamed the newcomers, and forced the king and his supporters into hiding. With the return of Eleanor, Connor, and Anoka—Florence's long-lost twin, Eo has the support he needs to regain his throne and force Cloithfinn into exile.

THE IRON RIVER opens with Isaac breaking free from the silver prison where he's been held captive by the rogue vampire Michelle. With the help of his former guard, Diane, they flee through a hidden gate and end up back on Earth—in southern Belgium. Isaac's mind, which had been deteriorating during his captivity, begins to repair itself even as Diane's health takes a turn for the worse the longer they're gone from the Fae Plane.

Eleanor, determined to keep her promise to save Isaac once she's done saving the world, follows him to Europe and across three countries, pulled by the force of his pain, her pledge, and their bond.

The magic that swept across the globe released power in the supernatural creatures that few were equipped to handle, and hordes of shifters, not tethered to an Alpha, vampires with no sire to keep them in line, and magic practitioners of all walks are out of control, turning Central Europe into a pre-industrial region too dangerous to navigate alone.

Everything comes to a head in a castle in southeastern Czechia when the vampires Petrina has claimed meet the shifters who've taken in Isaac, and they're forced to stand together against the worshippers of Chaos.

Just when they think they've gotten things under control, the unthinkable happens and Florence is felled with a single bullet hole in her forehead. Book six ends between light and dark, life and death, and madness and control.

Of course, there are plenty of puns, a few more appearances from Hedge Antilles, a lot of heat, and a few evil monks.

PROLOGUE

I hadn't heard a gunshot, but Florence was on the ground with a bullet hole in her forehead. Raj and Petrina knelt beside her having an urgent discussion, and Isaac took my hand as Diane turned a slow circle in the middle of the clearing. I should help—there must be something I could do—but all I could think about was finding whoever had done this and tearing them limb from limb while using my magic to somehow keep them alive. The sounds of conversation—of Petrina saying, "You owe me this, father," faded until all I heard was my heartbeat.

"There's no exit wound," Petrina said. The shrill hysteria in her voice was enough to break through the pulsing, red miasma of anger that'd draped over me. "There's no entry wound, either."

"What do you mean?" Raj asked, leaning in closer to Florence's prone figure.

Arduinna knelt on the other side and passed her hand over the bullet wound. "It's not real," she said.

"I don't understand," I said.

Arduinna pulled her hand away from Florence's forehead, and her skin was once again smooth and perfect.

1

Florence's eyes sprang open, wide and sightless, and she screamed, "Annie!"

CHAPTER ONE

"**M**y sister is dead!" Florence yelled. Frost spread across the clearing floor, wilting the small plants and sending icy spiral designs up the trees. The temperature dropped several degrees, plunging the forest from early summer into deepest winter. "There will be no debate."

Icicles grew from the branches above our heads, and I shivered. It was too cold for me—I wasn't dressed for it, and my dragon had a bad habit of settling into a torpor every time my body temperature dropped.

Florence grabbed my hand. "We're going now. If you want to come, hold on!"

Isaac still held my other hand, and an arm snaked around my waist. Something hard whacked my ass just as the ground dropped out beneath us and waves of nausea rolled over me. We were simultaneously stretched and flattened, like saltwater taffy, and the journey seemed to last for ages. This trip was nothing like traveling by gate between planes—it was the difference between luxury first class air travel and a two-seater with a novice pilot flying through turbulence in the Bermuda Triangle.

About the time I'd given up hope of ever arriving at our destination—any destination—my face hit something hard seconds before I tripped and fell. I opened my eyes to almost perfect darkness, felt around to make sure there was no one nearby, and emptied the contents of my stomach onto the ground.

I'd lost contact with Florence, Isaac, and Raj while we were traveling through the interdimensional meat grinder and didn't know if Petrina and Diane/Arduinna—ugh, I was going to have to figure out what to call her—had made the trip. I heard retching not too far from me, so at least one other person had landed in the same place.

"Roll call?" I asked. "I'm here."

"Here, and even more undead than usual," Raj said.

"I made it," Isaac said. "That was even more unpleasant than last time, and that trip ended in an icy river running through a vampire-infested cave."

"Eeee-hawww."

"Guess Jack made it, too," Arduinna said. Her voice, which had begun sounding stronger as she recuperated from her Medb-caused illness, was weak and exhausted again.

"Jack?" I asked.

"Isaac's monstrous donkey," Arduinna clarified. I guess I knew what had smacked my ass into the gate now.

"Florence and I are over here," Petrina said.

All six of us—seven if you counted Jack—had made it to the same place at the same time. If it turned out we were in the Light Realm on the Fae Plane, then I was going to call it a win, regardless of how terrible the trip had been.

"Where are we?" Isaac asked, sounding remarkably calm for a man who'd spent the better part of the last few years mad as a hatter due to our broken mate bond and his kidnapping and torture at the hands of a vampire and her Fae accomplice.

"The Dryad Wood in the Light Realm," Arduinna said. "We're in a root cellar."

"What should we call you?" I interrupted. "I knew you first as Arduinna, but Diane is how Isaac knows you best. Which do you prefer?"

"Arduinna," she said. "It reminds me of my first home, the Ardennes. I'd hoped to spend more time there, but it was not to be. This wood, however, is modeled on my Forest. It's where you first came into this land."

"We're a few days from the palace, then?" I asked.

"No." Florence said. She grabbed my hand again.

Goosebumps ran over my skin—her grip was icy, and it burned my skin. I snatched my hand back. "Florence, I understand your urgency, but I cannot make another trip like that so soon."

"It'll be better this time," she said. "Same plane."

"Florence, dearest," Petrina said in the low, soothing tones one uses to quiet a frightened animal or rampaging toddler. "If you are right, and she is dead, getting there sooner will do nothing to help her. You've already saved us so much time by getting us this far."

"Her murderer could still be there," Florence protested.

"That is unlikely," Raj said gently. "The murderer would've either fled immediately or been captured by Connor and Eochid. And if Connor caught the man who killed his love, there's nothing left for you to do."

The air temperature dropped another few degrees. As much as I wanted to comfort Florence—and I did, tragedy apparently brought out the humanity in me—I knew that hugging her would push me even further towards hibernation. I found the dirt wall I'd run face-first into and started tracing the perimeter of the room. If we were in a root cellar, there had to be stairs out somewhere. The sooner we got out, the sooner we could make our way to the palace and find out what had happened.

My feet found the stairs before I did. I tripped and landed on the bottom stair in an ungainly heap, wishing, and not for the first time, that my near immortality came with a generous helping of natural gracefulness as well.

"Found the way out!" I announced. I walked up the steps and pushed on the door. "It's absolutely locked from the outside."

RAJ MADE short work of the door, and we found a nearby empty cottage to spend the night in. Florence had argued vociferously, of course, but was outvoted. Arduinna was the only one who knew where we were and which direction we needed to go to get to the palace, and she categorically refused to lead us out of the woods and to the main road in the dark.

"I am exhausted," she pointed out. "We all are. A night to rest and regain our strength will not go amiss. I don't know anyone who could've ripped open a gate like that, pointed it where they wanted it to go, and pulled six people and a large donkey through without harming anyone. Florence, you must be exhausted as well."

Florence didn't answer. She sat on a chair with her back to the rest of us like a petulant child put in the corner as punishment. It made no sense for an adult to do this voluntarily. Humans were very peculiar.

Raj sidled up next to me. "Overwhelmed and inundated with Fae magic?"

"I'm drunk with it," I confessed in a whisper. "It feels so good to be home. I feel like...myself. Not so..." I waved my hands in the air dramatically to convey a sense of dark Galadriel power madness.

"Are those jazz hands?" Raj asked.

I heard the laughter in his voice and glared. "You can read my mind. You know what I'm saying."

Raj laughed. "I do. And I must admit, I'm looking forward to a stroll in the sun tomorrow. This place has grown on me."

I smiled at him, pleased and smug that he enjoyed the Fae Plane, even if my power eclipsed his here. Then I turned my attention to the whole group, Jack included. He was too big to be ignored.

"Before anyone else knows we're here, let's make some plans. It was always my intention to leave any decisions regarding the Dark Throne until such time as it could no longer be ignored, but recent events leave me little choice. Once we've secured the throne for Eo and determined who needs to be punished for recent events, I will be co-opting Eochid's forces and taking my throne.

"I've sure the Dark Bitch—nickname pending—was responsible for Anoka's attack. She's been behind most of the bullshit we've dealt with, whether directly or indirectly, and she needs to go already."

"I agree," Arduinna said. "The depravities she's visited upon her prisoners are terrible, and she enjoys it. But how will you, with Eochid's limited resources, defeat her?"

My lips curled up, and I felt a bit evil. "I have a plan...but you're not going to like it."

"I don't like anything that's happened in the last eighteen hours," Arduinna said. "Hit me with everything you've got."

I leaned in and started talking. Raj guided me in the background when I needed assistance. It was nearing midnight before we had a plan that everyone agreed to. I took the first watch, Arduinna volunteered for the second, and Florence the last.

After an uneventful watch, I talked briefly with Arduinna, then fell asleep next to Raj, secure in the knowledge that my plan was nearly infallible.

Florence woke me around sunrise with an unholy howl of fury and a sudden cold snap.

I rubbed my eyes. "What's wrong?"

"I thought your plan was foolproof!" she screamed at me. "How are we going to do this without Arduinna's ability to travel between groves? How are we going to find our way out of here?"

I sat up and stared at her. "What are you talking about?"

"Isaac, Arduinna, and that ridiculous donkey are gone!" Florence yelled.

CALMING Florence down had taken a lot longer than I'd anticipated. It was a friendship operation that had been considerably slowed by sudden onset torpor brought about by the cold front created by Florence's anger.

"Here," Raj said, handing me a blanket he'd found...somewhere. It was better to not ask too many questions.

"You know, for someone's who is always harping 'control' at me, you spend an awful lot of time giving people goosebumps when you're angry."

My jibe elicited another Arctic blast before she reeled herself in.

"You're right, of course," she said. "I had no business coaching you on control when mine is imperfect."

I held up my hands. "Whoa, whoa, whoa. That is not where I was going with that. At all. Just pointing out that we all have control issues from time to time."

Petrina glared at me from where she was standing to the right and slightly behind Florence. "She's just lost her sister and expended a great deal of energy to bring us all here. You need to cut her some slack."

I tipped my head back to look at the ceiling, took a deep breath, and counted to ten. "I am not trying to discount Florence's pain or minimize the loss that she suffered. I wanted to be able to respond—to offer reassurance—but I can't do that when I'm being buffeted with wave after wave of winter wind. Nothing that happened to me since I left Portland compares to what Florence is going through now, but if I learned anything, it's that control is necessary no matter what. We practice control of the little things, so we don't lose it when big shit happens. Florence knows that—she taught me that—and sometimes we all need a reminder to jerk us out of the pain or the anger or the self-pity and start moving forward again before we hurt somebody."

Raj's hand brushed against the small of my back when I teetered, worn out by cold and exhaustion. I didn't want to say anything else—didn't want to make it about me—but my control was wavering, too. The last thing any of us needed was a fire and ice battle in an old cabin in the middle of the Dryad's Wood. Although at least that'd probably garner us some royal attention and accelerate our trip back to the Palace. Being back home had flooded my whole being with raw, Fae power, and that power wanted nothing more than to be used.

The air temperature was warming up, and my subconscious decided that was a sign of spring. Glossy, dark green leaves pushed out of the ground in a semi-circle around us, then continued their upward trajectory until we were nearly surrounded by a six-foot tall...

"Hedge?" I asked. "What are you doing here?"

The laurel hedge quivered but didn't answer. Probably because it was a plant.

"This is Hedge? Your Hedge?" Petrina asked, staring incredulously at the shrubbery that hadn't been there five minutes earlier.

"I think so. It looks like Hedge Antilles. I don't know how I did it, but my control is apparently little better than Florence's right now, and with many fewer excuses."

Petrina stood with me and Raj as we examined Hedge. I knew beyond a shadow of a doubt that this was Hedge or one of Hedge's scions—saplings?—that had shown up in a moment of stress, just like when I'd inadvertently woken up Hedge when my magic first manifested on my porch in Portland. That day was so far in my rearview mirror; I seldom thought of it anymore except with anger, although whether I was angry at myself for not seeing Finn for who he really was or at Finn for worming his way into my life under false pretenses and ultimately betraying me, it was hard to say. The signs that he was up to no good had been there from the beginning. Finn had been cagey as fuck about who he was and what he was doing but found a way to be brutally honest about the things that hurt. I should've seen then that he was manipulating me into looking at one thing while he misled me about another like a creepier Vegas magician.

I ran a hand down the length of some of Hedge Antilles's new growth and relaxed into the raw, soothing Earth magic pouring off my newest successful gardening venture. Hedge's roots were burrowing deep into the earth, and through the slight contact I had, corners of the Fae Plane that I hadn't even imagined rolled out before me in a magical map. Eo's palace was a bright, sparkling point to the south, Medb's a dark, whirling spot far to the northeast. Smaller dots, equally important but with fewer powerful folk congregated in them, spread through both lands. I didn't know where the borders were, and they obviously didn't appear on the power map appearing in my mind, but there were a lot of pinpricks of light, and even some greater groupings, in regions that had to be beyond the Fae lands.

"I know where we're going," I said, pulling my hand away from Hedge. I was starting to feel the land in addition to seeing it mapped out in my mind. Not all of it was thriving, and I wasn't ready to deal with that. I might have to at some point, but not yet. Not here.

"What do you mean?" Florence demanded, taking several steps back and shrinking into her regular guise of the middle-aged kindly witch. She looked just old enough to start dreaming about grandchildren and young enough to keep up with the kids who inevitably found their way to her place. Partly for the never-empty cookie jar, and partly because she always gave the best life advice and never blinked no matter what you asked her. The epitome of World's Greatest Mother.

My breath caught in my throat. When we'd first met, before she left South Dakota to join me on my quest and teach me everything she could about magic, we'd had an encounter with her coven. I'd met her former partner as well as the maiden and crone. Florence had been the mother of the coven. I'd meant to ask, to investigate. But I'd forgotten. I'd been so caught up in myself, and my guilt and pain, that I'd never asked. And maybe it wasn't my place to ask—she'd never said anything about it at all—but I couldn't help feeling like I'd failed a friendship test.

"Florence—"

"I overreacted," Florence said. The temperature in the basement was back to normal, and all that remained of Florence's latest temper tantrum was damp spots of rapidly melting frost.

I closed my mouth. I'd meant to apologize for forgetting her past trauma and not understanding how it would affect the current. Of course she'd been obsessed with finding her sister who was forever a child in her memory, especially when she'd had a child of her own that was, for whatever reason, now absent.

"Don't," Florence said. "Don't dredge up the past. Not now. It's not a conversation I want to have, and those aren't memories I ever want to shine a light on. You will try to understand, but you won't be able to. Not now, and not ever. Let it be. Maybe someday that'll be something I want to share, but that will be for me to decide."

"Of course. I will never mention it, and I'll do my best to never think of it either. It's your story, and I will respect that."

Florence caught my gaze. "Thank you."

I gasped with the enormity of the debt she'd created. "No," I argued. "It is I who must thank you—for reminding me that even between close friends, there is no owing of secrets." The gulf between us shortened and the pressure her thanks had created lessened, allowing me to breathe freely again.

"If you can get us to the palace, then we don't need Arduinna and Isaac, although that stupid donkey might have been handy to ride. Arduinna's defection isn't surprising—if she ever stayed on one side long enough to form true alliances, I'd keel over with shock—but I'm disappointed Isaac chose to leave us so soon."

"I think he'd follow Arduinna anywhere, even after finding out who she really is," Raj said. "I've not seen a man so lovestruck since he mated with Eleanor under the full moon."

CHAPTER TWO

I closed my eyes again while the others made quick work of packing our few belongings. When I reached out to Hedge, the map of this plane surged into my mind's eye again, stronger than the last time. I found that I could zoom in on different points on the map if I focused, but the closer I got, the blurrier it was. It was almost like the map itself wasn't high quality enough to avoid pixilation at close range. The Dark and Light Fae Kingdoms were the clearest, and everything around the edges looked as though the mapmaker had smudged the drawing before the ink was dry. Trying to concentrate too hard on those areas gave me a headache between my eyes, so I backed off. I didn't need that information anyway. At least not yet.

I looked around and found gateways I'd used before, figured out what they had in common, and looked for one close to us. I'd work out how to get it to spit us out where we wanted to go when we got there. Hopefully.

After an hour and a half of walking through a surprisingly handsy forest, we arrived at the site I'd seen when I connected with Hedge. I'd immediately regretted trusting in my memory to get us where we were going and not sketching out a map. Taking a piece of Hedge with me didn't give me the same connection—I theorized that the root system was what connected Hedge with the land—and Hedge was either unwilling or unable to follow along. I tried getting angry every time I couldn't quite remember where we were or where we were going—I was never *really* lost—but other than making the dry, late summer wood around me smolder, I didn't accomplish anything.

"I need a break," I announced. I dropped my pack and slumped to the ground, leaning against the nearest tree.

Florence squatted next to me. "Is everything okay? Are we lost?"

I could tell by her tone that she knew we were lost. Raj wouldn't have given me away, so either my shields weren't as strong as usual, or my expression was betraying me.

"*It's your face, my sweet,*" Raj said. Even though his voice sounded in my head, my eyes were still drawn towards him. His dark, burnished skin glowed in the late afternoon Fae sunlight, and the twinkle in his brown eyes framed by ridiculously long eyelashes turned my thoughts to things other than getting unlost.

"Eleanor," Florence said with more patience than I deserved. Maybe someday Raj wouldn't turn my head, but I wouldn't count on it being anytime soon. Not much could distract me from him.

"We're fine," I reassured Florence.

"Tell me you're not lost," she demanded.

I plastered on a smile, turned it up to eleven, and said, "I studied the map in great detail before we set out, and I brought a piece of Hedge with me to help with any guidance-related issues we might run into. The paths in my mental map do not completely match up with the actual roads we're encountering, so I'm forced to make adjustments to stay on target." I dug my fingers into the soft loam at the base of the tree I was leaning against and searched for the words that would be reassuring, honest, and worthy of a leader. Power flowed into me like someone had turned on the hose. "Oh," I said. My thoughts weren't incoherent, but it felt like more effort than it was worth to speak.

The map spread out in my mind again, and this time I found the gate I was headed for almost immediately. We'd been going in roughly the right direction, although if we'd kept on in the direction we'd been headed, we would've bypassed it completely. "Paper?" I asked.

I heard rustling nearby and then Petrina thrust a notebook and pen at me. I shook my head, and Raj grabbed the paper instead. I opened my mind to him, pointed out the important landmarks, and then pulled my hands out of the dirt. He'd sketched out the best route to the gate, marked some nearby landmarks—a spring and a small village—and then added more details than I would've. He was a decent artist and did a much better job than I could've.

I smiled, sprang to my feet and took the map, then showed it to Florence. "We're here," I said, pointing out our current location. Raj had marked it with four small figures that looked suspiciously like the main characters from the Wizard of Oz. "Am I Dorothy?" I asked.

"Not at all," he replied. "You're the Tin Man. I'm Dorothy."

"I don't know if you've assigned me to be the Cowardly Lion or the Scarecrow, but either way, I'm not pleased," Florence growled.

Raj smiled at her, turning the charm up as high as it could go, until she rolled her eyes and turned back to me. "Your boyfriend is a menace," she complained.

"The gate we're headed to is here," I said, pointing at a spot on the map with an ornately drawn wrought-iron gate. "We're nearly there. We do need to leave the road we're on now, though, or we'll bypass it completely."

"What's this?" Petrina asked, pointing at the other elaborate miniature drawings Raj had added.

"A spring, a village, and an...anomaly," I said.

"What kind of anomaly?" Trina asked.

I wasn't sure if she was aware of how she posed in the middle of the clearing. Her long, blond hair streamed out behind her in the slight breeze, and her porcelain skin almost glowed in the sunlight. Her eyes were closed, hiding her cornflower blue eyes, but when she tilted her head up a little more, the tips of her fangs peeked out. Watching the vampires turn into sun worshippers every time we were on the Fae Plane was one of the highlights of the experience.

"I'm not sure," I confessed. I pushed my hands back into the dirt and let the map unfurl before me again. "It feels Dark. Wrong. Trapped."

"The anomaly is a trap, or someone is trapped there?" Petrina asked, opening her eyes and turning her regard from the sun to me, a downgrade for sure.

"I don't know." I wondered how many times I could say that before they decided not to follow me.

"*Confidence,*" Raj whispered to me.

I straightened my spine and tilted my chin up. "It's on the way, more or less. We should investigate."

"We don't have time," Florence protested.

"If someone is trapped, how can we not make time?" Petrina asked. "Annie is already dead. We cannot save her. But maybe we can save somebody else."

"And if it's a trap for us?" Florence asked. The acid in her voice wasn't nearly as caustic as I'd expected. Either she saw the wisdom in Petrina's words or Petrina got passes I didn't when it came to saying Anoka's name. Probably a bit of both.

"Then we walk in alert and ready," Raj said. "If someone knows we're here and set a trap for us, then they probably haven't had very long to perfect it. They'll have to take two vampires, one of the top ranked Fae in the realm, and the most powerful practitioner they've likely encountered without the element of surprise. There aren't many who could do that."

"You'd never forgive yourself if you found out you left someone to suffer," Petrina pointed out. "We'll take this detour, find the problem, then head to the palace to mete out retribution on anyone who deserves it."

Florence closed her eyes and briefly looked every one of her seventy-five-ish years. "Of course. We should take the detour. Whoever killed Annie—Anoka—will be long gone by now, anyway."

I handed the map back to Raj. My sense of direction was great—in the city. It wasn't even terrible outside of the city, provided I found the nearest interstate and had my GPS reading the directions to me.

But here? I didn't know which way was north, or if there even was a north. "Can you read it?" I asked.

"I think so, especially since I got a glimpse of the whole thing."

"All you people who got to live in a world without GPS are the lucky ones," I said. "Here we are, different world with no WiFi, and you can navigate with a crude map and the night sky."

Petrina rolled her eyes. "I'm sure you'd give up microbrews and pizza delivery to grow up in an era of rampant disease just to learn how to read a map."

"I don't need to have pizza delivery," I said as piously as possible. "As long as pick-up is available."

Raj swatted my ass lightly. "We'll follow this road a little longer then find a smaller path heading…eastish, for lack of a better term."

RAJ STOPPED SO ABRUPTLY that I ran into him. Petrina stopped just short of making contact with my back, thus averting a slapstick domino-like fall. I peered around Raj to see if he was teetering on a cliff. He wasn't.

He'd stopped on the edge of a clearing. It was a perfect—as near as I could tell—circle of the greenest, most storybook grass I'd ever seen. I looked up. The sky was blue. Sky blue. Marred only by one pristinely white fluffy cloud. The grass was dotted with red flowers. They were all the same size and shape and exact shade of red. Each flower had five petals, a curved green stem, and two leaves. Something about this was niggling on the edge of my memory, but I couldn't place it.

In the exact center of the clearing was an apple tree. The smooth, brown trunk rose up and split evenly into two large branches that disappeared into the green leaves that wreathed the tree. The leaves were the same color as the grass and looked remarkably similar to the shape of the cloud. The apples were nothing more than tiny red dots.

"It's like a child's drawing," Florence said.

"A child with no imagination," Raj muttered.

"Hey!" I said. "I'm pretty sure I've drawn this exact picture before. All it would need is some perfectly triangular snow-capped mountains and a spiky yellow sun."

"This is definitely a trap," Petrina said. "But who set it and why?"

I stepped out into the clearing, sidestepping Raj's hand trying to hold me back. The ground was springy, like walking on one of those in-ground trampolines. "I want to see the other side," I said. I walked a slow circle around the perimeter of the clearing, staying away from the tree. There was something about it I didn't trust. Again, I felt a tug at my memory strings, but couldn't put my finger on what my subconscious was trying to tell me.

When I got to the furthest edge of the clearing, away from where I'd started, I turned back towards the tree and shrieked. It had large, blue eyes with impossibly long eyelashes, apple cheeks tinged with red, and the biggest, widest grin I'd hoped never to see. The memory burst free. This was the recurring nightmare I'd had when I was six. Every night, I dreamed about this perfect fairyland with green fields, a blue sky, and perfect flowers. I could go into the castle and be the princess, but I had to pick an apple first. But every time I tried to pick an apple, the tree would open its mouth and show its fangs, giggle, and swallow me up.

I'd wake up screaming and refused to eat apples for several years, much to the dismay of my parents who lived smack dab in the middle of the Pacific NW's apple country.

This tree looked just like my nightmare tree. It *was* my nightmare tree. "You!" I screamed.

"Ho ho ho!" the tree laughed. "I wasn't sure if you'd remember me!"

"Remember you? You terrorized me as a child! You were a literal nightmare!"

The tree shrugged, although I couldn't quite see how. "It gets boring out here all alone. I wanted to see what you looked like and hopefully scare you enough to stay away."

"You're such a badass, scaring a six-year-old enough to cry night after night," I said. I didn't know why this was important, but it obviously was. I racked my memories for anything else that would help me. Questions! I snapped my fingers. "You have to answer three questions and do so with transparency and honesty."

"Ask away! I hope you've improved your interrogation skills. Although I guess I could tell you why I have such big, shiny teeth again if you'd like."

I shuddered. "How do you know who I am?"

"What makes you think I do?" the tree answered. "I've never called you by name or indicated you were anything other than a random misplaced Fae baby I decided to torture."

"That is not an answer," I replied.

"Your blood calls to the land, and I am tied to your earthly guardian. I watched you grow up as much as he did."

Fucking Finn. I squelched my anger, although I'd love to unleash some fire on this monstrosity.

"Who put you here?" I asked.

"I think you already know the answer," the tree said. "But I'll humor you. Cloithfinn planted me here at the request of her dear friend, the Queen of the Dark Realm."

"Will you give me an apple?" I asked before I could lose my nerve.

The tree looked shocked. "Don't you want to fight me for it? Pluck it yourself? You always fought when you were little."

"I always fought, and I always lost. I thought it might be more productive to simply ask."

"You won't win, you know," the tree said. It ripped an apple from its boughs and whipped it at me. I caught it, but before I could view my prize, the tree exploded into a storm of apple missiles and wooden shrapnel.

Once the debris storm was over, I raised my head cautiously. The clearing had returned to normal—all colors were natural again, and not a child's rendering. I looked down at the apple. It'd changed from the scribbled red circle into an apple-sized faceted ruby, banded with gold and topped with a gold and emerald tree.

"Holy fuck," I said. "This is the orb of the Dark Throne."

Now that our detour was over and the magical clearing returned to its natural state, Raj and I were able to get us back on track with zero issues. It was almost as if the pathway was opening in front of us. Less than an hour later, we stepped into a different clearing. This one looked completely normal—late summer flowers bloomed in clumps, a natural spring bubbled up against one edge, and the shrubs and trees that surrounded it were varying degrees of scraggly green. But this one radiated power in a way the last one hadn't.

"This is it," I announced unnecessarily. "I'll need some time to figure out how to use the doorway to take us where I want to go. It'd suck if we got spit out in the Dark Queen's boudoir, or in Texas, or somewhere we've never heard of. I can do it. I practiced before we left Eo's palace last time. But having practiced doesn't make me practiced. So I'll need a minute."

"No one would deny you the time to do it right," Petrina said. "Let us know when you're ready. In the meantime, perhaps I can prepare a snack for the food-dependent among us?"

I smiled at her, pushing all my gratitude into my expression. "That would be amazing. I'm incredibly hungry and would literally eat anything. Except apples." I patted my backpack where the Dark Orb hid beneath a pile of clothes of uncertain cleanliness.

"Cheese and bread and..." Petrina rummaged through the food sack Florence and I took turns carrying. "...cheese?" she finished.

"Those are three of my favorite foods," I replied. "Thanks for not making me choose between cheese and cheese."

I sank to the ground in a cross-legged position in front of the invisible gate and opened my thoughts to Raj. *"Can you help me?"*

Raj sat next to me and took one of my hands in his. "Tell me what you need me to do," he said.

"Anchor me here and let me draw on your strength," I said. "There are so many doorways in so many worlds, and if one has enough strength, any of them can be a destination. There should be only a few places this gate will gravitate towards naturally, and somewhere near the palace should be one of them. But I don't want to get trapped wandering, and it's all too easy to get curious and let the gate energy pull me along."

"It wasn't a problem before, when you were opening all the gates, was it?" he asked, holding my hand a little tighter.

"No. There was too much purpose behind what was happening, and not enough skill on my end. I had the raw power but didn't have the faintest clue how to use it. And since the gates were the original Great Gates, the only thing they were interested in doing was opening. It was possible to use them, but only at the original locations." I was barely paying attention to what Raj was asking and how I was answering. The conversation was enough to keep me grounded, to keep my consciousness from flitting about in the between-gate ether, and to remind me of my task.

"Have you ever gotten lost?" Raj asked, an edge to the question that pulled my mind back a little too far.

"No, but there was a close call," I admitted. "When I was learning how to link Eo's gate with Portland, I got carried away and roamed too far afield, peeking through gates to see where they led. In the ether, it's like walking through the star-spangled night. Everything is a deep, midnight blue speckled with twinkling stars and nebulas and galaxies. The doorways are faint outlines. If you're powerful and skilled, you can pull your consciousness along to where you want to go. Otherwise, you only end up in *maybe* the right vicinity and have to do some peeking out. It's fun to look at all the places and so many people. And I nearly forgot my purpose. But Connor had me tethered and was able to pull me away and back to my mission. But that's why I wanted you here. You ground me even better than Connor does, and there's no one else I've ever magically meshed with so well."

"Does it help if I talk?" Raj asked.

"Yes, and if I don't answer, a mental jolt would be appreciated." I settled in further and let the ether between gates take me. I knew what

I was searching for and pulled myself along towards the familiar feel of Eo and Connor. Their energy was bright and powerful, but not nearly as powerful as the Light Throne itself. It beckoned to me, and my longing for it felt...right. I was about to latch onto it and anchor myself when something even more attractive caught my notice. The next gate over pulsed with bright darkness, both oxymoronic and seductive. The Dark Throne. I took a deep breath in a place where breathing was unnecessary and let go of the Dark.

"I've got it," I announced, letting Raj pull me to my feet. Petrina handed me the bread and cheese and cheese she'd made for me and I scarfed it down, washing it down with water from the nearby spring. "I appreciate you so much," I told her.

"Are we ready?" Florence asked. She strode across the clearing and stood beside me, nearly vibrating with eagerness.

"We are," I said. "We should link arms, Wizard of Oz style, so we don't lose each other. This is my first time unguided, and I don't want us to be separated."

Raj hooked his left arm through my right, and I grabbed Florence's hand. She was already linked up with Petrina. Then I closed my eyes and pulled on the gate I wanted, willing it to fill the space in front of me, to become one with the gate here. An oval became visible before us and crackled with gate energy before clearing up and showing us the entrance hall of Eo's palace. The picture fritzed and fuzzed for a few moments, like an old-fashioned television with too much static, before the destination became clear.

"Go now," I commanded. "The less time I have to hold the gate, the better I'll feel."

We stepped through the gateway and into Eo's palace as one. I verified we'd all made it, and then I let go of both gates. It slammed closed behind us, shaking the earth we were standing on and causing dust to rain down on us from the battlements. Oops. Guess I should've been gentler.

I opened my eyes and stared into the business end of a spear. Eo'd replenished his guard. I didn't recognize this one. "Please tell his Majesty that his Heir has arrived and is seeking an audience," I said.

"And bring me a glass of wine. Preferably unpoisoned." I slumped to the ground as no fewer than a half dozen guards ran off in the direction of the palace entrance.

"You did it," Florence said.

"Yep," I replied as the world went dark around me.

CHAPTER THREE

I shook my head to clear the starry darkness from my sight and looked around, hoping I'd recognize the place we'd landed. The waiting area outside Eo's receiving hall was familiar, as were the large number of weapons pointed at my person. I scanned the faces hoping to find someone I knew. Finally, I landed on the centaur towering over everyone else—the only person, besides the dryad standing next to her, without a weapon pointed at us. The horse half of her was a shiny almost metallic sable, and her skin was ebony. She was wearing a chainmail shirt and the simple helmet that marked her as one of the king's personal guard. She had a long braid draped over her left shoulder that ended near her waist and dark eyes that surveyed the room.

"Alanna!" I called, waving enthusiastically. The tall, willowy, and grayish-green dryad next to her nudged her and said something to the centaur in sign language. My grasp of sign language was limited to the ASL alphabet and the signs for pizza, thank you, and the lyrics to "Love in Any Language," thanks to a middle school summer camp. It did not cover Fae SL. I snorted to myself. Fae SL. Heh.

Alanna must've recognized me or at least decided we were harmless enough to back off for a moment so she could figure out who was yelling her name from across the room. The guards lowered their various pointy weapons and took enough steps back that I was able to take stock of our situation.

"Hey!" I called. The dryad next to Alanna made the complicated hand gestures I recognized as sign language. I turned a little so they could both see my face, held my hands up non-threateningly, and walked towards them. I hoped my companions were all okay behind me, and I wasn't abandoning them to a surprise attack.

"We're fine," Raj said. "Just a little disoriented from the trip. I vastly prefer traveling under my own power."

"Same," I said. "This was way better than ley-line transport, though, right?"

The memory Raj sent me of what we'd done when left alone in a leyline conveyance had me suppressing a blush. I turned towards Alanna and her companion and tried to shove Raj's suggestive images to the back of my mind.

"My name is Eleanor, and I am the heir to the Light Throne and, with Cloithfinn's betrayal, the second most powerful ranked Fae in the Realm."

"My name in Tanwen," the dryad said. "I'll act as Alanna's mouth-piece. Everything I say, you can assume comes directly from her, unless I specify that it is my own commentary."

"I appreciate your service, Tanwen," I said, nodding my head. "I am ashamed of my lack of skill and would like to rectify it as soon as logistically possible."

"That's unlikely to be very soon, Your Highness," Tanwen said. "This is strictly my opinion, but I think you're going to be busy for a very, very long time."

I shrugged. "If everything goes as planned, I'll never be not-busy again. Which just means I need to make time for the things and people that are important. Being able to speak to everyone I work with is one of the most important things. What if you're unavailable or I meet someone else who speaks sign language and doesn't have an inter-preter? Once this—" I gestured around me to the guards who'd lowered their weapons but hadn't quite relaxed— "is straightened out and I've spoken with the king, can we talk about teaching me your language?" I had a sudden thought, and grimaced... "As yours and Alanna's schedule allows, of course. I'm willing to work around you if you're willing to teach me."

"How can I say no?" Tanwen said.

"You can absolutely say no if you want," I replied. "You're not my subject, and even if you were, I'm not much into forcing people to educate me against their will."

Tanwen smiled, and her golden skin—like aspen leaves in autumn —lit up. "Still speaking for me, but I like you, Your Highness."

Alanna reached down with one of her chestnut-colored arms and lightly thwacked Tanwen upside the head. Tanwen smiled up at Alanna and said, "Not as much as I like you, Queen of my Heart."

I grinned but tried to keep it to myself. I loved people in love. After I calculated that I'd given them sufficient time to make googly eyes at each other, I cleared my throat and waved. "As must as I'm enjoying this voyeuristic peep into your lives, I do need to get in to see the king. Do I need an escort, or can I just walk in and find him?"

Tanwen's attention moved from Alanna's eyes to her hands, then she turned to me. "An escort would speed things up. We'll send a couple guards who know you and your position here to take you to his private meeting rooms. He's not been in the throne room since..." Tanwen trailed off and looked expectantly at Alanna, waiting for her to finish. Tanwen's mouth made an 'O' of surprise, and the brief glance she darted at Florence told me what information Alanna had just shared.

"An escort would be much appreciated," I said, trying to push past the subject. "Do you know if Connor is with him as well?"

"He is usually attending the king," Tanwen said. "They are constantly in each other's company."

"Lead on, then," I said. "I would go to them."

Alanna whistled and got the attention of the guards. She spoke to them, too rapidly for me to follow even if I had understood their sign language, and three guards stepped forward.

I squinted at them, trying to place their faces, but drew a blank. I'd need to do better at remembering faces and names if I was going to be a good ruler, but generally speaking, all humanoids looked alike to me. I could typically single out the centaurs and sluaghs I met—although that might change if I started meeting more of them—but these guards, humanoid one and all, did not ring any bells.

Tanwen spoke, drawing my attention away from the guards. "These three were at Cloithfinn's Last Stand and recognize you and your companions. They were part of the former consort's household, but now serve the king. They will escort you to His Majesty's private meeting room and serve as your personal guard for as long as you are in residence."

I dipped my head towards the centaur. "Your aid is much appreciated, Alanna. I look forward to speaking to you more about the events that are certainly on the horizon."

She nodded back. "I would hold you to a promise to consult with me before plans are solidified."

I tilted my head and regarded her. I knew little about the centaur, but she was confident, and I did like confident women. She'd been made captain of the Royal Guard, which spoke to her competence as well. What the hell. There was no harm in promising to talk to someone. "You have my word that you will be one of the primary members of any War Council formed as a direct response to recent events."

"That will do," she replied.

ONE OF THE guards led us through the maze that was Eochid's palace while the other two brought up the rear. It made the area between my shoulder blades itch to know a heavily armed former member of Cloithfinn's house was in a position to put a dagger in my back, but I tried to trust in Alanna's system. I formed one of the clear, flexible air shields that had been the earliest magic I'd learned and encased each member of my party in a defensive yet unobtrusive bubble.

Yep. I was definitely trusting.

The lead guard swung open the door so violently that it bounced off the wall and nearly closed again in our faces. His face reddened around the ears and back of his neck, but he stepped into the room and announced, "Your Majesty, Eleanor Firestorm, Heir to the Throne of Light and her companions Florence the Free Witch and the vampires seek audience."

It was so weird to me that Raj and Petrina never seemed to get any sort of billing, although they'd both assured me multiple times that they didn't mind flying under the radar. Weird enough that I almost missed the "Firestorm" that'd been added to my name.

"Eleanor?" Eochid's voice rang out across the room. I looked around—I'd spent time here before. It was the "Royal Planning and Lounging" room. A large table with a map of the Light and Dark Realms carved into the surface dominated the room. Cabinets lined the walls, some made up entirely of little holes with more scrolled maps inserted. This was a room for diplomacy or war. Sometimes both at the same time.

I couldn't help but smile at my ostensible father as he speed-walked across the room. Eo spread his arms wide but stopped short of giving me a hug. I stepped forward and into his arms. He might not be my real dad, but he—and Connor—were the closest people I had to relatives since my parents had died fifteen years ago. It only took a second before Eo went from surprise to returning my embrace.

I stepped back and regarded him. He looked older than last time we'd seen each other, even though it'd only been a few months on either plane. His hair had bleached from blond to silver, and fine lines had appeared around his mouth and eyes. I bit back my questions but couldn't stop the concern flooding my mind. The Fae don't age once they hit adulthood. We stayed our prime for thousands of years, immune to age and disease and most injury. The only way we could fall is from external sources, and even that didn't always work. Fae could age, but it was rare and typically a sign of great age—over five thousand years, typically—and imminent death.

Connor appeared behind Eochid and held out his hands. "Eleanor. Thank you for coming back."

I clasped his hands in mine and studied him, afraid I'd find the same signs of aging on his face as I'd seen in Eochid's. He looked the same as always—dark eyes, smooth, brown skin, and elf-ears. I blinked. I was used to seeing through his glamour, but there was usually a shimmer at the edge of my vision when someone was glamoured. Connor had no shimmer. He wasn't bothering to mask who he was, which meant he was comfortable with the Light Court knowing he was Dark Fae. "Where's your glamour?" I asked.

Connor shrugged. "Enough people knew that hiding my true form would've been more detrimental and fueled harmful rumors. It's easier this way."

"What happened?" I asked. "What can we do?" My companions came up behind me and Connor froze for a moment when he met Florence's eyes.

"She looks so much like Anoka, especially now that her face compares only to the one in my memory," Connor murmured. He closed his eyes, took a deep breath, and squared his shoulders. "How much do you know?"

"She was shot. Here, on a plane with no firearms," Florence said. "How could you let this happen?"

"Come, sit," Eo said.

I looked at him and saw a faint tremor in one of his hands and the tell-tale shimmer revealing he was glamouring his appearance. He was hiding his age from everyone.

"That would be great," I said. "I'm exhausted from gating here." I strode to the table, careful not to walk in front of the king and breach etiquette. Eo caught my eye and smiled wearily. I stopped myself from grabbing his elbow and helping him to his seat.

When everyone was seated and drinks had been brought and orders for food and prepared rooms had been conveyed and everyone was fidgeting with impatience, we finally got down to it.

"We were in the throne room, listening to Alanna's proposals on how to increase the capacity of our armies. She was demonstrating her magic, which was most impressive—perhaps rivaling yours, Eleanor—and..." Eochid broke down sobbing. I was pretty sure no one else could see his true form, but several people, including

Petrina, rushed towards him. Servants were coming out of the woodwork to offer comfort and wine. He accepted both, allowing Petrina to put an arm around him and lead him to a seat at a nearby table.

I turned my attention to Connor, raised one—fine, both—eyebrows, and tilted my head towards a small table in the far corner. He nodded slightly and made his way over. I grabbed Florence's arm and pulled her along behind Eo. Connor and Raj were waiting at the corner when we got there, somehow having procured four glasses of wine already.

"Connor, I am so sorry for your loss," I started.

"And I am sorry for Florence's," he interrupted, reaching out a hand and clasping the witch's in his.

They shared a watery grin, and I looked away to give them privacy in their shared grief.

After a few moments had passed, I said, "If you're able, it would be great if you could tell us what happened. Had I known how close Alanna and Tanwen were at the time, I would've asked them to join us as well. They might have seen something you did not."

"It is possible," Connor conceded. "She is observant and intelligent, but unfamiliar with palace intrigue. She may not have made note of what she'd seen. Now, she has more experience and training in courtly politics and would be better poised to recognize a threat. Have you gotten all you need of Eo before you and I begin?"

His voice lilted with the same cool, steady dispassionate cadence I'd always heard from him; he always sounded mildly amused but mostly disinterested about everything. It was one way he lied without speaking any mistruths. It was easier for most people to believe tone than word, and someone sarcastically telling you they find your creation or outfit or existence "utterly fascinating" is an interesting way to play with the truth at the expense of someone's feelings.

But now, his eyes betrayed him. I wasn't good at reading people, but Connor looked like he was hanging on to his last thread of normalcy, and his hold was starting to slip. I wanted to put my hand on his free arm, to offer my comfort in addition to the commiseration he was sharing with Florence, but I didn't want to be the one who caused his grip to falter.

Breaking down was something you did in private.

I affected an ironic smile, hoping that one side of my mouth quirked up to give me a look of dry amusement. "I'm not sure there's much else I could get out of Eo. Has he been like that since—" I was hesitant to name the event that was the catalyst for our gathering.

"He has," Connor confirmed. "And although I understand that he's lost so much in a short period of time that having Anoka die in front of him must have been a great shock, I am surprised at the depth of his grief and guilt. I hope that your presence will help guide him back to himself."

I narrowed my eyes at Connor. Did he know what was under Eochid's glamour? Was the aging reversible? I had so many questions, but this was definitely not the right time and place to ask. "Tell us your version, Connor," I urged. "Then Florence can tell you ours."

"We were in the throne room. Alanna was dazzling us with her magic, doing her own version of a ranking test with the whole court watching. We were wearing the flower crowns she'd created. It was a truly delightful experience. The centaur's magic surpassed all expectations of the crown who heretofore had expected to see such power only in the nobility. I was about to advise the king to take Alanna's offer of service and accept her recommendation on how to recruit the rest of his realm when I felt Anoka stiffen beside me. I looked over and saw first the wound in her forehead signifying she'd been struck by some projectile." Connor's voice tightened and spread itself thin around the tears choking him and threatening to loose themselves. "Then she slumped over, and the exit wound became visible. She was dead before I even knew what was happening."

"A sniper," Florence said.

"But who?" Connor cried. "There aren't any guns on this plane."

"There *weren't* any guns," I said. "The gates are open to allow free trade between planes."

"They shouldn't even work," Connor protested. "The magic here is too strong to allow mechanized items from your plane to function."

"The magic isn't as strong," Raj said. "So much poured out when the final gate opened. The balance hasn't yet been restored. Now, it's like ocean waves going back and forth between the two planes until they're in balance. It's nearly imperceptible, but there is ebb and flow. We have several possibilities. Perhaps the assassin knew their firearm would be effective when the magic was at its weakest and had a way to track that. Perhaps they were just gambling. What I'm more interested in is why."

"The what and how matches what Florence told us," I confirmed. "I, too, would like to know why."

"There are two possibilities I can see," Connor said. "But I am too tied up in this to be unbiased."

I nodded at him. "We all are, to some degree. Continue."

"The first is that she was not the target, but collateral damage due to either a mechanical fault with the weapon and too much magic, or an amateur assassin. I do not believe this to be the case, especially after talking with Raj about the magical flows. The second is that the shooter somehow credited Anoka with more political power than she had. Perhaps they thought her in the running to be the king's new consort, or merely the head of his magic users, and assumed her death could destabilize Eo and thus the crown."

"That is truth, though, isn't it?" I asked. "She was leading the magic users, and her death has done...something to Eo. Has he held an audience since?"

Connor rubbed his chin. "He has not."

"I think there's a third possibility," I said. I didn't want to speak it and anger everyone in front of me, but it needed to be considered. "The assassin thought Anoka to be Florence and believed her death would be devastating to me. I hate the way that sounds, and I don't mean to center myself in this tragedy, but if the order came from the Dark Throne, I could as easily be the intended target. Emotional target."

"Why doesn't anyone ever just shoot the person they actually want to hurt?" Florence asked. Her voice was rough and raw with suppressed tears and anger, but the room temperature remained stable. "If someone wants to get rid of a king or a princess, kill them and not their friends."

"Politics," Raj said, though he must know as well as I that Florence wasn't looking for an answer. "Killing someone attached to royalty but who isn't royal means, to many who believe the right to rule flows in the blood of the nobility, that there are fewer consequences. Killing a king starts a war. Killing a member of the royal household who not only isn't noble but isn't even Fae is merely a message." He held up his hand to forestall whatever angry stream of words was about to issue forth from the inconsequential human's lover and twin sister. "This is not what I believe but would support Connor's theory that Anoka was the target—or Eleanor's theory that Florence was. It's not an admirable habit among the highly born—to use so-called commoners as pawns in their schemes—but it is common, at least on Earth."

"Here, too," Connor sighed. "Raj is correct."

"Now we must figure out the who," I said, before Florence could interject. "There will be justice. We need the assassin and whoever authorized it. Anoka wasn't Fae nobility, but she was openly a part of the royal court and the consort of the king's advisor...someone very high up would've ordered it. And in my mind, there are only two possibilities."

"Agreed," Connor said. "But figuring out which will be the real work."

The door burst open and a royal guard ran in, puffing and gasping. "Your Majesty! An army! We're under attack!"

CHAPTER FOUR

The Royal Planning and Lounging Room had been hastily repurposed into a War Council. Alanna and Tanwen took up one side of the table, reclining on red, silk cushions. Eochid sat at the head in a chair that looked suspiciously like a miniature throne. Florence, Petrina, and Raj sat facing Alanna, and Connor and I flanked Eo. The rest of the table was populated with Fae I didn't know well enough to name…except weren't those the judges from my testing? What were their names…"

"Cliodnah! Teagan!" Connor called. "Come, take your places."

The two Fae I recognized from my first trip to the Fae Plane made their way around the milling bodies and took the seats next to me. They'd been judges for my ranking test, but I'd thought them dead or on Cloithfinn's side. Their welcome proved otherwise, though, or they obviously wouldn't be here.

Our table was obviously the "command" table, but the room was full of Fae. I looked around again. I hadn't spent much time on the Fae Plane, relatively speaking, but I knew the look of the nobility—pointy ears, fancy clothes, and a general aura of insufferableness.

I leaned across the table and waved my hands in the air while calling, "Alanna!"

Tanwen glanced at me and nodded, then turned back to the guard Alanna was talking to. After wrapping up that conversation, they both looked at me.

"What was your plan? The one you were presenting to the king when..." I trailed off. I didn't know what to call Anoka's murder that wouldn't further stoke the fires of grief in Connor and Florence. And Eo.

"To invite all Light Fae to the midsummer celebration—a festival for everyone, rather than the few who usually participate. At that time, conduct a census of name, species, and a test of power levels. Allow anyone below a certain power level to volunteer for the army; we always need more ground troops. Anyone above the minimum power level will be conscripted into service with the caveat that if they volunteer, they'll have a choice in where they serve, and be rewarded with land, a larger share of the spoils of war if there are any, and a place in the court."

I gaped at her. "That's brilliant, Alanna! I can't believe no one thought of that before."

A corner of her mouth quirked up. "Those who hold power in this realm are not only reluctant to share it—they believe that power is finite and if others have some, they've given up theirs, but also have trouble wrapping their heads around the 'lesser Fae' having the same power they do. They firmly believe that the power elevated them to nobility and not that the nobility suppressed the powerful who they deemed undesirable. You'll notice that in this room, Tanwen and I are the only ones who do not appear elvish. Tanwen would be allowed to step up if she wore a glamour to cover the more treelike elements of her visage, but there are no other centaurs, no brownies, no beast-Fae at all. In fact, if you look at everyone in the palace, the only Fae who aren't elves of some sort or another are servants, and even they wear a glamour to appear bipedal and humanoid."

I did as she instructed and saw she was right. I'd never noticed before. "The palace isn't really laid out for centaurs, is it?" I asked.

She shook her head and switched her tail.

"Connor says you're nearly as powerful as I am, if not more so."

Cliodnah froze beside me and I grinned, pleased to have caught her attention. "Have you been formally tested?"

"It didn't seem urgent after..." Tanwen and Alanna both glanced towards Eo and Connor.

"I don't expect it matters too much," I admitted. "Except to them." I gestured at the other nobility, then turned to the women to my right. "How long would a test take if it wasn't the full spectacle I was subjected to?"

"If she's as powerful as you say, an hour at most." Teagan said. "Maybe less."

"And if we were testing everyone who stepped forward from the commoners?" I asked, wincing at the term.

"Five minutes to determine if they were powerful enough to be tested, an hour or two to perform the testing, another day to rank everyone," Cliodnah said. She was leaning around Teagan and splitting her attention between me and Alanna. "That is, if this was something we wanted to do."

"Tell me the reasons not to do it," I commanded.

"Nobles who are downgraded in rank may refuse to fight out of pique," Teagan said. "If it was just a one-to-one tradeoff—they left, but we received a new fighter in their stead, at least it'd be a net zero—but they would take their households with them, including the magic users who bolster their power."

"Are not most of those magic users slaves?" I asked. "They should be free to decide where to fight."

"Not most," Cliodnah corrected. "But yes, there are humans who serve via right of conquest rather than of their own free will."

"We don't have time to correct people's phrasing before this battle is fought, but you don't conquer children. Children are not the spoils of war, especially when that war is sneaking across the border and kidnapping children. Some things are going to change, and that is one of the first. No matter what it does to our numbers, no Fae is allowed into battle if he or she is still relying on the power of those who are there unwillingly and from this day forward, there are no slaves in the Kingdom of Light."

"Have you bumped me off the throne already?" Eo inquired. There was a tremor in his voice that I tried to ignore.

"Do you not agree with the pronouncement?" I asked.

"Whether or not I agree with you is immaterial when you issue commands in my stead." A hint of steel threaded through his quavering voice, and I hoped that my unintentional challenge would be what he needed to come back to his strength.

"Slavery does not become such a noble people," I said. "Nor does any bigotry. Free the slaves and call all your people to be tested."

I LOOKED out over the sea of people gathering in the Great Hall and sighed. Eochid was sitting on his throne, glamour in place, but behaving like a querulous old man. He refused to speak to any of the commoners as they received the results of the tests, leaving Connor and me to do all the heavy lifting.

I stepped onto the dais next to my supposed father. "If you don't sit up and start acting like you approved this idea, people are going to figure it out," she muttered out of the corner of her mouth.

He straightened up in his throne and said, "My posture is none of your business, nor is it theirs." He gestured towards the crowd but didn't deny that there was something to hide.

"I can see through glamour," I reminded him. "I'm probably not the only Fae who can."

Eochid shot me a sharp look and his true form shed forty years for just an instant. Then he slumped back down in his throne and the age settled over him again.

"Kinda makes you wanna look around for Gríma, doesn't it?" Connor asked, joining me and Eochid on the dais.

"If you tell me the army amassing outside the city's borders is primarily made of orcs, I will strongly consider fleeing," I said. "I am not prepared to take on Saruman."

"We're the pretty, pretty elves, though," Connor said. "We have glorious hair and perfect bone structure, and our people will always prevail."

"Please tell me that Cate Blanchett is Fae," I begged. "And that we have a way to recall her to this plane and make her our queen."

"Alas! As far as I know, she is a mere mortal. We're stuck with what you see here." Then he leaned in close and whispered, "Don't goad the king. We can't afford any more changes now…there's a lot to be done in the next few days."

"I was hoping goading him would affect positive change," I whispered back. "For a moment, I thought I saw his strength return, but he has no will for it anymore."

"Losing Anoka…" Connor paused, took a deep breath, and smiled brightly. "Losing the witch who was acting as one of his advisors seems to have broken him in ways I wouldn't have anticipated."

"Stop whispering about me like I can't hear. My ears are fine—better than either of yours, I suspect. I don't want to talk about it, nor do I want to hear about it. No one lives forever—not even when it begins to feel like you have."

I shook my head and looked back at the people beginning to form smaller groups. Most of the commoners tested had little or no ability, as everyone had believed. But about fifteen percent had power levels ranging from "qualifying for low level leadership positions or specialty roles" to "credible rivals to my power levels." It'd be interesting to see how the succession went. No one was going to be ranked higher than me, Connor, or Alanna today, but once this battle was won, there might be a few challenges to address. Or back down from. It all depended on how these people were going to hold the ideal of the right of primogeniture once they started talking about how meaningless assumed power was in a world that had been ignoring theirs.

Alanna walked forward, parting the crowds with her sable, equine body, and handed me a scroll. I looked at Eo, but he rolled his eyes and gestured for me to read it.

"One thousand Light Fae were tested today," I read as loudly as I could. Connor elbowed me.

"Speak normally. I'll amplify you."

Of course. Magic! I was making a great impression. I looked down at the words I was reading. They weren't in English, and the magic that allowed me to read them only persisted if I didn't see past the glamour. Maybe it would help all around if I could figure out how to program my glamour-piercing sight to be opt in instead of opt out. I grimaced, wrinkling my nose with effort, and did my best to forget I couldn't read Fae. If only that didn't feel so close to lying—it'd probably be easier. I smiled at the people massed before me. "Of those thousand, eight hundred and fifty have been referred to the King's army or personal guard. We ask for volunteers only, and no one will be penalized for returning home without signing up."

A grunt from the throne echoed throughout the room and it took every ounce of willpower I had not to roll my eyes at the king's childish behavior.

"The names of the remaining hundred and fifty folks are being posted throughout the hall. If your name isn't on that list, please head out into the courtyard to meet with the captains of the guard and military if you choose. If your name is on the list, find your presumptive ranking—we can finalize things with a full test once we vanquish the threat on our borders—and temporary assignment. If you choose to stay, you'll be working with a trained expert in your field as we head into battle."

"There's nothing by my name," something shouted. "No rank or assignment."

"If you have neither rank nor assignment, you will be working with the throne. We weren't able to rank you effectively because your power levels were so high that they came close to or even rivaled the top twenty-five ranked Fae in the Realm. If you choose to accept, you'll be working with the council on strategy and leadership. Now, find your places! Those gifted in short-term battle prognostication estimate the entirety of the enemy troops will be in place by nightfall tomorrow and will attack at dawn the day after."

"Shouldn't we attack sooner?" A woman asked, striding forward to stand in front of the dais. She was dressed in the short tunic and breeches of the common folk, and her height, bearing, and pointy ears signified that she was an elf. She had dark brown, nearly black skin, dark eyes that swallowed the pupil, and was completely bald.

"That's one of the things we'll decide on the council," I said. "There are arguments to made in favor of your approach or waiting for them to attack. What's your name?"

"Acantha, Your Highness," the woman said.

"Were you ranked?"

"No."

"Then come with me and lend your voice to the council."

She looked suddenly unsure of herself. "I am an innkeeper."

"Fantastic," I said. "You probably know a lot about organization, supplies, and dealing with cranky men who should be napping."

Acantha laughed. "That I do, Lady. I appreciate you taking the time to talk to me."

"Of course," I said. "After all, what kind of princess would I be if I wouldn't even talk to my peers?"

I stood on the wall of the castle and looked out over the battlefield. Connor stood on my right and Raj was on my left. The attacking forces were coming in waves, and although each wave looked cohesive, they didn't appear to know how to fight together.

"There are Dark and Light Fae down there," Connor said.

Raj looked at the enemy lines so intently he stopped pretending to breathe—a practice he kept up to make the rest of us more comfortable. I hoped he was checking in on Florence and Petrina. Neither of them would agree to stay out of harm's way. Much like Eochid, who was directing the Light Fae army from the ground. It should've been me. As the heir, I wasn't as important as the king. Plus, I was much younger, much spryer, and not a dotard. But he insisted, and I couldn't challenge him in public unless I actually wanted to challenge him. Which I did not. It was going to be hard enough to take and hold one throne. I didn't need to add the Light Throne to the mix.

Alanna was the real powerhouse in charge of the armies, of course, but the courtesy of taking Eochid's orders and trying to interpret them in the most advantageous way possible, was an honor being shared by Acantha, who'd turned out to be a powerful short to mid-range psychic, particularly when emotions were running high, and Cliodnah, who had similar talents in addition to her formidable water and earth elemental magic. Connor and I were supposed to stay out of harm's way. As the second and third ranked Fae in the kingdom, it was necessary to keep us alive.

I glanced at Raj. He was supposed to be keeping us apprised of the minutiae of what was happening below, but he was now going on three minutes without breathing. Something else had caught his attention. I reached out to touch his arm and get his attention, but before I could make contact, he disappeared with an audible pop.

"Where'd your bloodsucker go?" Connor asked. I don't know if he wasn't surprised or if he was just masking it well, but Connor sounded as blasé as always.

"No idea," I said. I peered down at the melee below. From this distance, it was hard to tell which Fae were on which side. I didn't recognize anyone except Alanna. There was a small figure astride her who I assumed was Tanwen, although she wouldn't need interpreting in battle. I shrugged and continued my ineffectual surveillance of the action.

If you'd asked me five years ago where I saw myself in the future, I certainly wouldn't have said, "Angry because I wasn't on the front lines of a supernatural battle trading blows with a satyr." Nor would've I said, "Inappropriately horny because I hadn't had sex with my vampire boyfriend in a couple weeks." Definitely not, "Worried about how I was going to take the throne from a woman who'd been ruling as long as I'd been alive." But here I was, anxious for my adoptive father, concerned about the outcome of a battle that had centaurs and dryads and elves and satyrs on the field, preoccupied with how much I wanted to jump Raj's bones at any given moment, and worried about how I was gonna plan and execute a campaign to take back the throne that was—somehow—rightfully mine.

Raj popped back into existence and dropped a person at my feet. I looked down at the tall man with red hair, pale skin, freckles, and a death wish. The last time I'd seen him, I'd thought he was dead. But somehow, once again, he'd slipped through my grip. But now he was right in front of me. I had the authority. I had the justification. And—I pulled my sword out of the hidden air sheath where I stored it when it wasn't in use—I had the necessary instrument with which to carry out the sentence. I pointed my sword at Finn's neck and tried to squish down the powerful sense of anticipation that was threatening to overwhelm me.

"You are guilty of treason and attempted murder of the heir to the crown. I suspect there are other charges we can add to the list later. The sentence for either of those crimes is death. Give me one reason I shouldn't carry out your sentence here and now." There was a slight tremble in my sword hand. Rage, I told myself.

Finn smirked up at me. I'd seen that expression on his face so many times, and the urge to knock it off his face with my fist was as strong as it ever was. I raised my sword above my head with both hands and prepared to separate his smirking head from his evil body.

"I know who killed the witch's sister," he said.

Connor caught my wrists a fraction of a second before I could stop myself. I stepped back, resisting the urge to kick Finn while he was down, and pointed at him.

"Explain, motherfucker, so I can finish the job."

"Why would I give you any information if the reward is death?" he asked. It was a reasonable question, but it still pissed me off.

"You're going to die either way," I pointed out. "Might as well delay it a few minutes, do some good in your last breaths, and maybe I'll develop some executioner skills I didn't know I had and won't botch your beheading. I might even have enough mercy on you to fetch someone who knows what they're doing."

I was pretty proud of my negotiation skills and grinned down at my one-time lover and current nemesis.

"If you don't tell us what you know, I can guarantee neither Eleanor nor an executioner will be responsible for your death. I will be, and it won't be fast," Connor said, rage vibrating his voice.

"I've escaped from your cells before," Finn said.

"You escaped because I left you for dead—prematurely," I pointed out. "You didn't get out of the locked cell. You got out of an unlocked cell—and you had help."

"How'd you know that?" Finn asked before clamping his mouth shut.

"Lucky guess," I said. I wasn't sure if it mattered at this point, but either Finn or Cloithfinn had placed someone in Connor's household. "Thanks for the confirmation."

Raj nudged Finn none-too-gently with his foot. "What will you choose, fool?" Raj asked. "Talk now and earn a merciful death? Or hold your tongue and find out the true meaning of torture."

"I'm pretty sure Raj has some dungeon techniques he's dying to try on you," I offered. "He has a thousand years of experience on both sides of the cell door to draw from."

"And I have even more," Connor said. "I'm certain that between the two of us, we can rob any trace of joy from what is left of your short, miserable life."

Finn laughed, and it didn't sound like he was quaking in fear. "I was going to tell you anyway," he said. "Why else would I let Eleanor's fuck boy capture me?"

I opened my mouth to tell Finn to shut the fuck up, but Raj spoke before I did.

"You spend too much time worrying about the strength of the men Eleanor loves when what you should be afraid of is her strength. The fact that she is stronger than me in many ways doesn't reflect badly on me or on her. The fact that you cannot stand it that she's stronger than you *is* the real issue. Your resentment of her strength and independence is one of the reasons why she was never able to love you, even when she thought you both human. It is not her strength that bothers you; it is your own weakness."

I wanted to applaud. Not only had Raj hit the nail on the head for why I didn't catch any feelings for Finn, he'd sliced Finn to the quick as well. The pale, redheaded Irishish Fae in front of me was splotchy and red from the tips of his ears—well, the tip of one ear; I'd docked his other ear years ago—all the way down his chest, setting off the pale green shirt he had open almost to his navel. I smiled down at my former friend.

"Are you going to tell us who killed Anoka?" I asked.

"Find out yourself," he sneered.

I heaved a great sigh. "I promise I won't kill you or direct anyone else to torture and kill you. Is that enough?"

"I want to go free," Finn said.

"Don't push your luck," Connor growled.

Finn's shoulders straightened and hunched up in a way that I knew meant he was getting ready to be stubborn regardless of the cost.

"After the battle is ended and the dust has cleared; once it is safe to release you, I will let you go. In the meantime, after you've shared everything you know about Anoka's murder, you'll be hosted on premises in a secure but comfortable location." I promised.

Finn sighed heavily. "If that's the best you can do. And if you swear you'll release me after."

"I swear, Finn. I will ensure you are released after the battle and will do no harm to you, nor will I order any harm done."

"Good enough," he smirked. "The killer was not acting of their own volition. Cloithfinn gave the order to have the witch killed, reasoning that it would sow discontent and chaos and remove a powerful resource from the king."

"I don't understand," I admitted. "Why not just order Eo killed? That'd be more chaotic and get her to civil unrest even faster, especially since I was on another plane at the moment."

"She wants to do that herself," Finn said. "Unlike your witch. She needed me for that—I'm the only one she knows with a cache of earth weapons that usually work."

"You?" Connor asked, tone mild. His jaw clenched so tight I worried his teeth would break, but his eyes and voice did nothing to betray his emotion.

Finn shrugged. "It was pretty easy. The security is shit here. I didn't even have to disguise myself to get into the throne room." He laughed loudly; the thread of madness that tinged his voice caused goosebumps to form on my arms. "By the way, Cloithfinn is disguised, but you'll recognize her by the ostentatious gown she insisted on wearing."

"Is she acting with Medb?" I asked.

Finn laughed again. "That question wasn't part of the deal. If you want to know the answer to that, you'll need to make another concession and let me go right now."

"I'm good," I said. "Time for your brief detainment." I wrapped bindings of air around him and called for the guards who were just out of sight. "Take this prisoner and lock him in the room that formerly held the vampires."

"Eleanor! Are you betraying me? Tsk, tsk, tsk."

"Of course not, Finn. I swore an oath, and I cannot lie. You'll be free when the war is over." The guards led him away. Just before they disappeared from sight, there was a loud bang and a clatter. Finn was gone, and the guard were unconscious.

A chuckle floated its way back to me, and I swore at myself for repressing the urge to decapitate Finn the moment he'd landed at my feet.

"Motherfucker!" I yelled.

CHAPTER FIVE

I spotted Florence through the crowd and ran to her side. Connor and Raj had convinced me that I shouldn't change to my dragon shape and swoop down on the battlefield looking for Cloithfinn. When I was queen—a phrase that always got my blood pumping—I wouldn't need to hide anymore for the element of surprise and could fly around as I pleased. Something that was definitely on my agenda. Just had a few things to clear up first.

I skidded to a stop next to Florence. "Cloithfinn ordered the hit on Anoka," I said to her and Eo who was on the other side of my friend. "Finn carried it out. Unfortunately, he escaped. Again."

"Where's Cloithfinn now?" Eochid asked.

"Somewhere out there," I said, gesturing at the battlefield in front of us, then had to resist the urge to sing the next line. "She's dressed up all fancy and is here to kill Eo."

"You should get back," Tanwen said. "Alanna will carry you to safety, Your Majesty."

"Don't be idiots," Eo scoffed. "She's not managed to get me yet. This is for my throne, and she is my fault. I will not back down."

"At least let us move you to a more secure place on the field," Alanna said. "Guard! Form a defensive line around the king!"

"To the king!" one of them shouted, and a group of royal guards started towards us.

"No!" Eo yelled. "I will, for once, stand on my own feet and not put anyone else between me and dan—"

An arrow sprouted from his forehead, interrupting his last stand. Four more followed in quick succession and found homes in his left eye, his heart, and both lungs.

Eo sputtered a bit, blood appearing at the corner of his mouth, then crumpled to the ground. "Iron," he said. "Ow." His eyes drooped until they were nearly closed, and his body went limp.

"Eo?" I cried, dropping to my knees beside him. "No! Eo!"

I couldn't find a pulse or any other sign of life. His glamour disappeared and he appeared to everyone as what I'd already seen: a wizened, elderly man with steel-gray hair and beard, deep wrinkles, and nearly translucent skin.

"I see her!" Florence said grimly. When I looked over, she was encased in ice with a snowy tornado spinning in front of her. "She will regret this." The tornado whirled away, picking up speed and debris as it sped across the field, pushing everyone else back and away from the battlefront. I pushed through the wind, letting it glide around me, and ran towards the storm.

Cloithfinn stepped in front of it and laughed. She held her hands up over her head dramatically and the clouds that were above us darkened with rain. Cloithfinn clapped once—she was bringing the show-womanship for sure—and rain burst from the clouds and soaked the field. Florence's ice began to melt, and the rotation of the snow tornado slowed. It stopped in front of Cloithfinn and began to dissolve.

Inside the tornado was a shape. It looked human—brown, ruddy skin. Long, dark hair liberally streaked with gray and braided down the center of her back. Taller than me but shorter than the former consort. I looked over at the Florence next to me, but she was gone. When had she disappeared?

There was something in Florence's hands, but I couldn't figure out what it was right away. Then Florence raised an arm over her head, and I realized that she had a long dagger made of sharp, polished ice. She brought the ice dagger down into Cloithfinn over and over until Cloithfinn was on the ground laying in a pool of her own blood and the dagger had melted into a barely visible nub.

I stood up and started forward. The ice wouldn't kill Cloithfinn. Even now, she was probably healing and getting ready to take her revenge on the second White Elk sister. I got within earshot in time to hear Cloithfinn say as much to Florence and picked up my pace.

Seconds later, I skidded to a stop. Florence's second dagger wasn't ice. It was iron covered in magical symbols. I didn't know what any of them meant, but it didn't matter.

Florence stabbed Cloithfinn once in the chest and left the dagger buried in her heart. Florence stood up, and with none of the theatrics of before, snapped her fingers. The dagger handle glowed blue, then white, and then the entire dagger exploded. Presumably. I saw the handle fly up into the sky, and Cloithfinn certainly blew up. I could only assume the dagger was the cause.

I looked down at my clothes. I had bits of Cloithfinn all over me. Florence walked back to join me. Her face and clothes were completely unblemished. Sound returned—soldiers on both sides were rushing forward now that there was nothing holding them back, but it'd be a couple minutes before any got close enough to interfere.

"Thanks a lot," I muttered, indicating the viscera and brain matter hanging off my left boob.

"I didn't know you'd be so close, or I would've warned you," Florence said.

"You did good," I said.

"It won't bring Annie back," Florence said.

"It won't," I agreed. "But it was justice."

"There's a little more justice that needs doing," she said.

"I know. He's on the list."

Alanna and Tanwen trotted up to us. "We need to get you out of here!" Alanna said. "The battle is far from over, and the Queen should not be on the front lines."

47

I opened my mouth to argue, then remembered that Eo had argued the same point and now he was dead.

"Fine," I agreed. "I'll head back to the walls to watch. Florence?"

"I'll stay here and see if I can convince Cloithfinn's armies to surrender. Or die." Her grin was bloodthirsty. She hadn't slaked her need for revenge yet, and I hoped Petrina was close enough to help temper the blood lust that'd been ignited and the rage that wouldn't fade. I was headed back to watch.

I turned toward the castle, but before I could walk away, I needed one more moment with Eo. I knelt beside him again, touched his face, and whispered, "You might not have been everything I was told you'd be, but I am delighted I had a chance to know you, to learn with you, and to find the bonds that run even deeper than familial bonds. Thank you for everything, old man. You have already been avenged."

The weight of my thanks rang hollow when there was no one there to take my debt. Tears slid down my face, and I dashed them away. Now was not the time to show weakness. I stood up and straightened my spine. I was the heir to the throne, and I would act like it.

Wait. Not the heir. Not anymore. Fuck.

I PACED BACK and forth in my bedroom—still the same one as before, even though the household staff had none-too-gently suggested I move into the Royal Suite. I wasn't ready yet. I wasn't sure I'd ever be ready.

I was still stiff and sore from running stairs to burn off extra energy. I was also pissed that I missed the end of the battle—which we won. After Eo's assassination, Florence and the others convinced me it'd be in my and the realm's best interest if I didn't also die on the battlefield. I'd spent the rest of the fighting time holed up in a secure room that supposedly even that snake Finn couldn't breach.

Alanna and Florence, acting on my behalf offered the same deal to Cloithfinn's remaining army as we had the first time we'd fought. Any common soldier willing to swear fealty to the throne and renounce their claims to any spoils of war would be pardoned. Any officer would have to give up their holdings and enter into service of the Crown for a year and a day, but after that would be pardoned. As for the Dark Fae…most of them disappeared as soon as Cloithfinn fell and didn't stick around to see if we would be kind.

Raj opened the doors and came in carrying a tray of food and a carafe of wine.

"Hungry?" Raj asked.

I stopped pacing. The aroma of beef stew and fresh bread wafted up from the tray. Raj handed me a glass of wine and I took a long drink before sitting down and digging in.

"I appreciate you so much," I said around a mouthful of food. Raj had been a little distant the last few days, and it was starting to freak me out.

"I was worried," he said. "Not distant. Anxious. The moment I saw the shots enter Eochid's body and watched him fall, all I could think about was the same thing happening to you. Now, I'm trying to give you space to come to terms with the throne. I wonder if this will be enough for you or if you'll need more. Will you still fight Medb?"

I stared at him, lost in thought. Did I need more? Was the Dark Throne too much? I hadn't even considered backing down and letting Medb keep her usurped throne.

"We both have much to think about," Raj said. "I must admit that the biggest subject on my mind is when you'll feel relaxed enough for bedsport."

"You're an incorrigible pervert," I said, body tingling with the beginnings of arousal. It was a welcome distraction from the grief that kept threatening to overwhelm me, but it still felt out of place.

"As are you," Raj retorted.

"I'm ready now, but the timing is terrible. Will you help me dress? Devin laid out clothes for me."

"I'm sorry you have to do this," Raj said, picking up the simple, flowing wine-colored dress and helping me into it. The skirt of the empire-waist dress swirled around my ankles, and the bodice was caught by silver rings on my shoulders, leaving my arms bare. Dark red was the funeral color for those who'd died unnatural deaths—which was almost always the case for a people who could more or less live forever. The bodies would be dressed in green and silver—the colors of the Fae and the Light Realm. They would be mourned, given into the embrace of their elements, and then feted. Raj's clothes were the same color and simple in style—burgundy linen trousers and a matching tunic. We both had on soft leather shoes that'd been dyed to match our outfits—kinda like 90s prom shoes—with a sole hard enough to tromp through the forest.

I slipped my arm through Raj's, and we walked out the door and out into the woods that backed into the palace to attend the funerals for Anoka and Eochid.

I stood beside Florence and Connor at the edge of the lake that dominated the center of an enormous clearing in the castle woods. Three biers were set up in front of us. Eochid was on the center, highest one. He was flanked by Cloithfinn and Anoka. I hadn't real-ized Cloithfinn would be a part of this. It seemed wrong, somehow, to include the murderer alongside the bodies of the people she'd killed.

The clearing was full of Fae, and the sea of dark red surrounding me was eerily reminiscent of a rippling puddle of blood.

I looked around for the priest or priestess, only then realizing I had no idea what kind of religion the Fae practiced, if any. But if they didn't have religion, how did they do funeral rituals? I let my brain follow that thought down the rabbit hole until I imagined up a high-ranking position of Chief Mortician and corresponding career days at school. The daydreams let me step back from my grief at losing my adoptive father and Anoka—I felt her loss both as a friend and through the grief of Florence and Connor.

Raj nudged me telepathically. *"It's about to start,"* he said. He and Petrina were somewhere behind us, helping coordinate the royal guards to ensure that I wouldn't join Eo today.

The crowd in front of us parted, and I desperately wanted to make a Moses joke. I didn't, and not just because I couldn't think of a good one. My sense of humor bordered on inappropriate at the best of times, but even I knew the importance of reining it in at a state funeral. A state funeral where I was the presumptive head of the state.

I straightened up as the Fae who'd been the catalyst for the parting of the sea of red mourners approached. She towered over most of the people she walked by. Her features reminded me of the Queen of New Orleans, if Marie carried a ten-foot-tall staff, had mossy green skin and juniper-colored braids, was eight feet tall, and had an additional five feet of height from her elaborate crown of living branches dotted with glowing burgundy peony flowers and dripping with Spanish moss. She was dressed in a gown of leaves ranging in color from spring green to the variegated reds, oranges, and browns of autumn; her belt was woven ivy dotted with the same peonies that were in her crown, and a living train dragged behind her, leaving a carpet of new grass and red wildflowers in her wake. An otherworldly glow of light and magic surrounded her, and the air around her wavered like a hot desert mirage. My heartrate elevated and my breath caught in my throat.

I wanted to drop to my knees; I'd never encountered anyone who'd inspired worship before, but this person did. I wasn't sure of the protocol and jumped back and forth between awe and irritation with Connor and everyone else for not warning me.

She stopped in front of the biers and looked at me. "Do you speak for the Fae?"

"No," I said. A collective not-quite-gasp rolled over the crowd. I'd obviously given the wrong answer. "I cannot speak for anyone but myself. I don't know if these people want a spokesperson, and if they do, that they want me in that role."

The dryad looked down at me for so long I had to fight the urge to fill the silence with an unrehearsed babblelogue about representative governments and my doubts about being queen of a land that still had legalized slavery.

She reached out and grasped my chin in her hand, tilting my head up to look into my eyes. "I am Jörð. This is my realm. None leave here but through me. And none rule here but through my blessing. You are here to ask me to take these back. You are here to ask my blessing to rule this Realm. So ask your favors and I will decide who is worthy and who will be cast back."

There were a lot of theological implications to her few sentences, but I was back on familiar ground. I had been briefed on what I needed to say to the officiant. I just hadn't realized I'd be dealing with an actual goddess.

"We offer these three, fallen in war. Take them back into their elements so that they might find peace until they live again."

Jörð stood in front of Eochid. "This man was your king. He ruled for centuries and was good to the earth. He observed the ceremonies at the turn of the seasons, gave deference to my children, and revered nature as is appropriate. Who offers him to me?"

"I do," I said. "As the heir to his throne and his power, I give his body back to the earth."

"He is worthy," Jörð said.

Vines rose out of the earth, wrapped around Eochid's body, and pulled him into the earth, leaving no trace of their passing behind. My jaw dropped a bit, and I felt a little dizzy.

Jörð moved to Anoka and stared down at her. "She is not one of this realm, but the children of Miðgarðr can be subject to my judgment."

Her stilted way of speaking simultaneously made my shoulders hunch in discomfort and my feet itch to walk forward into her embrace. I clasped my hands together so I wouldn't try to touch the goddess and watched her regard Anoka's body.

"This one was stolen from her family and raised to serve without question or reward. This practice was forbidden several millennia ago. How long have I slept that you felt empowered to resume this abhorrent practice?"

Jörð looked at me and waited for the answer. Her gaze burned through my head; I trembled before her. "I don't know, Jörð. Until today, I'd never heard of you. But I didn't grow up here and am still catching up on history."

The goddess turned her attention to Connor. "You cannot say the same. You are old, although not as old as you pretend, and you've never called anywhere else home. Tell me, how long have I slept?"

Connor bowed smoothly, and I vowed to make someone teach me how.

"Your Grace, your name is known to our people, but solely as myth. Our rituals invoke the power of the earth, but no one knows your name any longer. Any decrees you handed down have faded into legend, and from there into obscurity. The ritual kidnapping of human witch babies and keeping them as household power sources has been going on for at least two thousand years without stopping."

Jörð tilted her head and regarded Connor. Her blue-green eyes narrowed. "Two thousand years? That long?"

Connor shrugged. "At least."

She turned around to face the crowd behind her. The branches that crowned her wove together at the back of her head forming the roots of a tree of life.

"Do any of you remember me?" she called. The crowd sank to their knees, and no one looked up. "None of you?"

One figure stood and walked forward. When she got a little closer, I recognized her as Tanwen, Alanna's interpreter. She was a dryad and bore a striking resemblance to Jörð.

"I remember, Lady," she said. "I was here the last time you visited. That was for a funeral and a coronation, as well. It was almost three thousand years ago." Tanwen clasped her hands in front of her, hunched her shoulders, and looked down at the ground.

"I remember you," the goddess said. "You were a child. You wouldn't stop crying, though everything that was happening was natural."

"Natural doesn't mean there's no grief," Tanwen pointed out. "My mother had died, and I was only seven."

"You didn't want to take her place. You didn't want to be queen. When I asked what you did want, you told me you wanted to be like me, part of the earth and not the palace." Jörð spoke slowly as if the details were just coming back to her.

"You turned me into a dryad and took me with you into the forest after selecting a new king." Tanwen's voice was louder now as she gained confidence.

"I selected a king. An elf. I told him he was elevated above all people and to keep my decrees. He failed me."

"I don't know what happened to him," Tanwen admitted. "When I came out of the forest a hundred years later, he was no longer king. Someone new sat on the throne. Another elf. And the elves had elevated themselves above all others. The Realm had split into the Dark and Light—the only difference was whether the day elves or the night elves ruled. Not long after that, the raids to steal witch babies resumed. When you didn't return, people dismissed your visits as rumors. Stories. Myths."

"Three thousand years," Jörð said again. "Is anyone else that old?"

No one stepped forward.

"Most of us are less than a thousand," Connor said. "The fallen king you just commended into the earth was one of our oldest and even he hadn't yet reached fifteen hundred."

"Thank you, my child," Jörð said to Tanwen. She laid her hands lightly on the dryad's shoulders and bent over to kiss her forehead. "Is there anything else you would ask of me?"

Alanna stepped forward to stand at Tanwen's side. Tanwen turned to her and said something in the hand language they shared. Alanna replied in kind, and Tanwen looked at the goddess. "Nothing. My life is complete as it is."

Jörð nodded and looked back at Anoka's bier. "One simple question revealed so much," she said. "This woman's magic is of the earth, just not this earth. But she was powerful and connected to this realm and the people who inhabit it. Who gives this woman to me?"

It sounded so much like every wedding I'd ever been to that I had to blink rapidly to clear the cognitive dissonance.

Florence and Connor stepped forward. "We do," they said.

Jörð looked into their eyes. "She is worthy."

An almost-clear tornado dropped out of the sky slowly, almost reverently, over Anoka's bier. It spun around until she was completely encased inside, although she didn't rotate with the winds. The cyclone turned opaque—taking on the green color of Jörð's hair—then lifted and spun through the air until it was over the forest where it dissipated and disappeared.

Jörð walked to the final bier. "This woman failed to honor the seasons and the earth. She incited war and is responsible for more bloodshed in the last few years than this land saw in the last thousand years. Who asks me to take her?"

Connor stepped forward. "She caused the deaths of the others you have taken. We would never ask you to lower yourself to take one such as this. We would only ask your leave to give her back to the water that was her element."

"She does not deserve that final comfort," Jörð said. She stepped forward, reached out a finger, and tapped Cloithfinn on the forehead.

The former consort burst into flame and burned out in seconds, leaving nothing of herself behind, not even ash.

"She was not worthy," Jörð proclaimed. Vines grew up over the biers and covered them before blooming the same blood red flowers Jörð wore in her hair and on her belt. She snapped her fingers, and the world blinked out of existence.

CHAPTER SIX

The ground solidified beneath my feet and I looked around. I was in the castle great hall, surrounded by the trees that made up the living walls signifying the change of seasons.

Jörð stood in the center of the hall, and everyone who'd been at the funerals stood around her, comfortably spaced around the tables bearing food and drink, buffet style. There were hundreds more people than should've fit in the hall, but the divine apparently work in mysterious ways—either that, or Jörð was a fan of Doctor Who and could create a TARDIS whenever she pleased.

The goddess looked at me and gestured me forward. "You are the heir by appointment and by power?" she asked.

"I am."

"Dark power swirls in you, married to light. You are almost in balance, almost ready to restore my lands. You lack but one thing."

"What's that?" I asked. I knew I didn't sound gracious, but I was barely able to articulate anything, much less add the veneer of politeness to it. I hoped she knew.

"Maturity," replied.

"I'm almost forty!" I protested; good intent forgotten in the insult. I was tired of being too young.

"What is that age to a Fae?" Jörð said. "You are young, you are idealistic, you are rash. You are not ready to rule."

This was counter to everything I'd been preparing for the last couple years. So many people telling me I was ready...that it was time to take the Dark Throne, to free that land from Medb's tyranny.

But what if Jörð was right?

"Who else here could reign?" Jörð asked me.

I looked around. I didn't know most of the people in the larger crowd, but that didn't mean they weren't royalty material. "Connor for sure," I said. "He's definitely more mature, knows the politics of both Fae lands, and isn't idealistic at all. There are any number of folks who aren't in the court who likely could as well and would do a great job. There's got to be a lot of ideas out there on how to improve things for everyone. And of course, Tanwen, who was heir once upon a time."

Jörð turned and spoke to the crowd behind us. "Is there anyone here who would step forward to rule?"

No one moved, and I didn't know if I was relieved or disappointed. The entire future I'd been moving toward since a vampire had jumped out of Hedge and bitten me was tied up in the Dark Throne.

Jörð turned to Connor. "What about you?" she asked. You come from a line of rulers and could be either king or queen maker. Do you want the throne?"

"No. I'd rather be behind the scenes. I've no wish to rule," Connor said, inclining his head.

"And you?" Jörð asked Tanwen who was doing her best to disappear into the crowd at the edge of the grove. "You have the best claim."

Tanwen stepped forward. "I didn't want it then, and I don't now. I don't know the Heir Presumptive well, but from what I do know, I am content to let her lead. She may be young, but she is well-intentioned; idealism can be good if it leads to positive change."

Jörð turned her attention back to me. "Will you accept this crown and the responsibilities inherent in the job?"

"I will," I said. This hadn't been rehearsed, but the words came naturally and without hesitation.

"Will you end the abhorrent practices of slavery and kidnapping that should have ended three thousand years ago?"

"I will," I promised. "I would have anyway. I've made promises to others as well. I will end the slavery service of Earth-born witches and facilitate the payment of reparations."

A low murmur followed my pronouncement, and I bet there were a few people who wished they'd spoken up earlier to take my throne.

"Good," Jörð's voice rang with satisfaction.

A crown appeared in the air between the goddess and me. All the coronation plans that'd been made over the last couple days were being tossed out the window. Jörð was doing things her way.

"Will you make known my name throughout the land and restore the worship due to me? Even the dryads who were born of me no longer remember my name."

"I will not compel worship, but I will ensure that your name is known, that songs are sung about you, and that groves are dedicated to you."

"Good enough," the goddess said.

The crown, made of interwoven silver tree-like branches framing emeralds of various sizes, floated over to me. When it hovered in front of my eyes, I realized that some of the silver tree branches were, in fact, stylized birds with long flowing tails and tiny ruby eyes. The decoration was subtle enough that most wouldn't see it, but they were there. I looked at the goddess and she winked.

"Do you accept the crown, Eleanor?" she asked.

"I do."

Jörð leaned close to me and repeated the question in a voice so quiet only I could hear. "Do you accept this crown, Ciara?"

"I do," I repeated, and this time, I felt the weight of my promise. I was bound in chains that were tethered to the land. I could feel the land—like I had when reaching through Hedge—but now, there was so much more. Light and Dark. Joy and pain. Agony. Injustice. Grief.

I sank to my knees and clasped my hands over my ears. My fingertips brushed the bottom rim of the crown that had settled on my head. With tears streaming down my face as I absorbed all the pain and rage and hopelessness felt by the land and its people, I yanked at the crown to toss it away, to renounce the crown and the position. It wouldn't come off.

"Hold," Jörð said, her voice somehow soothing me through the agonizing fog that enveloped me. "Accept it into you and the hurt will fade. Open yourself to the land. To the people. Be a queen."

I gave up on trying to pull off my crown; I put my hands on the earth and tried to follow Jörð's advice. I slowed my breathing and tried for "open calm" instead of "panicked hyperventilation." The rush of energy continued, but once I stopped fighting it, it stopped hurting as much. It settled in me, accessible but not prominent. There was still agony, but it was pushed back enough that I'd be able to work around it most of the time. I relaxed further, breathing deeply. The incoming torment slowed to a trickle, then stopped. I pushed back onto my knees and braced myself to stand.

"Hold," Jörð said again.

I waited. A stream of energy hit me, hard enough to rock me back on my heels and nearly tipped me over. This was the balance. All the good and light and hope and kindness in the land. The green and growing things. The love. It filled me as completely as the suffering had and muted the pain.

When the incoming light had completely disappeared, I glanced briefly at Jörð before rising to my feet. Someone placed a cloak of shining green material at my shoulders and led me to the throne—a chair formed out of a single piece of wood, warm and welcoming, not to mention extremely comfortable.

"Here is your queen," Jörð announced to the gathered crowds. "All hail Eleanor the Unifier, Queen of the Fae!"

There was a much mightier cheer than I deserved. I smiled and waved like some dick in a suit had just named me Miss America.

Jörð held her hands up on either side of her tree crown that nearly brushed the high ceiling of the great hall and said, "Feast now, but do not forget me. I am awake, and I am your goddess."

The people cheered again, and Jörð smiled in satisfaction.

She turned back to me. "Rule this land wisely. I will be watching, and I will never be far away."

After that veiled threat, she walked over to the largest oak tree in the hall, stood on the mossy earth next to it, and melted into the ground, Wicked Witch of the West style.

My mouth was still frozen in an 'O' of surprise when Connor, Raj, Petrina, and Florence joined me on the dais.

"So, Your Majesty," Raj said. "In need of a Royal Bed Warmer?"

I smiled at him. His irreverence was exactly what I needed to jolt me out of my shocked stupor. I turned and pushed Connor in the arm. "There was a goddess! And I'm queen now! And you didn't warn me!"

"I didn't know!" he protested. "I knew people had once worshipped an earth goddess, but I assumed it was a primitive affectation."

"Primitive?" Petrina scoffed. "When there are people alive who remember it and it's at most two generations removed from you?"

"I'm not that old," he protested.

"Fine," Trina said. "Four generations."

Connor didn't protest.

"Y'all, I am exhausted. How long do you think I need to stay? I'm sure I'm supposed to mingle with my new subjects, which ew... Can we find a better word?"

"An hour at least," Connor said. "And if you're going to be the kind of queen I assume you want to be, you need to talk to every single person in the room for at least a couple minutes."

"It's not that I don't want that, it's just that...people are exhausting."

"Should've thought of that before you became queen," Florence said. Her voice was tight with stress. I turned towards her and threw my arms around her.

"I'm sorry, Florence. Everything's happened so quickly today. I'm handling it with my usual inappropriate humor, but I should've been checking on you. You and Petrina should head back to your rooms to rest and recuperate. I can't imagine this scene is what you want right now."

Petrina smiled at me and reached out for Florence's hand.

"No," Florence said. "I am a member of your household, and my place is by your side. I can cry later."

I looked at Connor and tried to raise one eyebrow to symbolize I was asking him if he needed to go. Instead, I raised both and widened my eyes uncomfortably.

"I'm not sure exactly what you're asking, Majesty," Connor said. "But I will also stay to help you through this. We are all in mourning. Coronations are often like that."

I turned to the crowd, pasted the brightest smile I could on my face, and prepared to walk out into the crowd in my blood-red mourning dress. As I descended the dais stairs, the dress changed color from red to a rich, verdant green ombre—the same colors of Jörð's hair, skin, and eyes.

Raj and I walked into our suite several hours later. I was drained—physically and emotionally—from the rigors of the day. There were so many things to do yet. So many decisions to make. This wasn't part of the plan. I'd always thought I'd take the Dark throne and make peace with the light, then Eo and I could co-rule in harmony while he found another, much more worthy, heir.

And now? I was a queen. A motherfucking queen. I had responsibilities and shit. Could I even go to the Dark to liberate the throne I'd already claimed in my head and leave this land untended?

"Eleanor, stop" Raj said, pushing me out of my doubt-spiral. "You won't solve anything going in circles like that. Today was a lot. You've dealt with so much in the last few years, but today is close to the top. You buried a man you'd come to regard as a friend, if not a father figure. You buried the woman who was the twin of your best friend and the great love of your other father figure."

"You make it sound like I have daddy issues," I said, poking him in the chest.

"Why else would you be dating a man over a thousand years older than you? Imagine the age-gap conversation this would inspire on Reddit."

I laughed a bit at the imagined responses to "I (F-late 30s maybe—not quite sure anymore) have been dating my bf (M1000+, dates were weird back then) for a while, but now that I'm a queen, should I worry about the age gap?"

"I love that you're familiar with Reddit," I said. "But I'm sad it's no more. Where else can we all judge the incels of the world?"

"Unfortunately, everywhere, my sweet," Raj said. He spun me around and started unlacing my dress. "But let's not talk about that now. You've had a stressful day and a too-long evening. You need a chance to relax and then go to bed."

He pulled my dress off over my head, and when he tossed it over the chaise in my dressing area, it turned back to the original red mourning color. Too bad, really—I liked the green. Raj ran his hands down my body from shoulder to hip and paused, staring at my nearly-nude body. Red flashes in his eyes signaled he was either feeling homicidal or horny.

"If your breasts ever drive me to murder, something has gone terribly wrong," Raj murmured in my ear as he hooked his thumbs under the flimsy and nearly transparent camisole-like creation I wore under my dress.

I didn't know if it was magic or engineering, but it somehow kept my breasts lifted enough to be comfortable and not sweaty, provided enough support that I didn't bounce too much if I took off at a jog, and never, ever showed straps that didn't complement or enhance whatever I was wearing. I was thinking of discreetly enquiring about the possibility of obtaining a sports-magic-cami. More support, less aesthetics...and a million percent more comfort. I'd make a fortune on the Earth plane if I could replicate it. All marketing campaign thoughts were pushed to the back of my mind when Raj's hands left my body—a torture worse than all the world's underwires.

Raj pressed a glass of wine into my hands and led me to one of the couches scattered throughout my suite.

"I don't even get a robe?" I asked as I leaned back and took a sip of my wine.

"I haven't had a chance to truly bask in your naked beauty in quite a few days," Raj said, looking completely unrepentant. "Of course, if you'd rather get dressed…"

"No. I'm comfortable now," I said. "I don't want to get up."

We drank our wine in silence for a while. It was nice not having to talk. I could share what I wanted through our link that was half vampire and his prey and half whatever love bond we'd formed. There were no known pairings between a vampire and a Fae in supernatural history, and thus no way to describe the connection we'd formed.

"Feeling better?" Raj asked, reaching across me to set down his glass of wine. His hand brushed across my breasts, lingering in a caress, as he settled back into a reclined posture.

I stretched my legs and draped them across his lap. "A little. Something's missing though…something that will really help me relax. Maybe some yoga or a meditation."

Raj's hand rested on my thigh and slid up to the junction of my legs. He rubbed his thumb on the thin material covering my clit until I gasped.

"If you still want to do yoga, I can leave," he said, pushing my panties aside and stroking the slick wetness of my center.

I writhed on his lap, pushing myself closer and harder against his talented fingers. When I couldn't take it any longer, I pushed his hand out of the way and straddled his lap. I pressed my breasts against his chest and lowered my mouth to his. When he opened his mouth to admit my tongue, I ran it along his teeth, pressing it against the sharpness of his fangs.

Raj growled at me and stood, cradling me in his arms. He walked across the room and dropped me on the bed. I scooted back, and he crawled after me. His eyes were glowing a steady red now, and the knowledge that I'd done this to him turned me on even more.

"I'm hungry," he said as I reached the head of the bed and couldn't go farther.

"Too bad there's nothing to eat here," I said, smirking at him.

"I'll have to make do with what I can find." Raj grabbed my panties, then pulled them down and tossed them aside. He returned to his place between my legs and breathed in deeply.

"Take your clothes off," I ordered.

"I guess I have to do what you say now, Your Majesty," he teased as he stripped.

"It's good to be the queen."

Raj was as naked as I was now, but instead of crawling up my body like I'd expected, he dove between my legs and licked the length of my slit. He settled in on my clit, licking and sucking until he drove me mad with it. Just when I thought I couldn't take anymore, Raj's fingers entered me and fucked me to the edge of the abyss and I soared over, screaming in ecstasy.

His fingers and mouth slowed and stilled while I lay basking in the afterglow of a phenomenal orgasm.

"Again?" he asked. "I've got the stamina, and I could go all night."

"No, no more," I said, laughing. "You'll kill me."

"You're immortal," Raj said moving up to lay beside me. He rested his head on my shoulder and his right hand cupped my left breast. "That was much shorter and sweeter than you're used to."

"You're an old man," I teased. "I can deal with a quickie every once in a while. But you're right—and you didn't even get a chance to get off."

"Sometimes, it's all about my queen's needs, and not mine. You needed a release after the tension of the day. You do not need to work for mine."

My eyelids were getting heavy, but I tried to argue. "It's never a chore, Raj."

"I know, my sweet. But tonight, you need this more than I need you. Go to sleep."

"Love you," I murmured.

"I love you, too," Raj replied. It was the last thing I heard before sleep took me.

I SAT in the ornate chair—one might even call it a throne, albeit a small one—that was at the head of the rounded triangle table in the king's—err...queen's—war room. I didn't know everyone in the room, but I did recognize most of the faces. In addition to my Earthly entourage, Connor was at the head table, as were Alanna and Tanwen. Cliodnah and Teagan. Wait a minute—hadn't Eo told me once he'd contemplated asking Cliodnah to serve as consort rather than Cloithfinn? I wondered how things would've played out if she'd been the consort. Speculation wouldn't do me any good, though; it was a waste of time and mental energy.

The rest of the table was made up of a healthy mix of the nobility who'd held the land and presumed they held all the power and the commoners who held at least as much power as the old guard. Everyone was chatting and there wasn't any apparent tension that needed diffusing. I smiled and hoped I looked beneficent. Two days into my rule, and already the land was at peace.

"Your Majesty!" someone shouted from the far end of the table. "I deserve to be closer to the head of the table! I'm ranked ninth in power now that King Eochid and Cloithfinn are gone."

A cacophony of demands rang out, and my first royal headache formed between my eyes. I closed my eyes and bowed my head briefly, then stood and looked out over the table. "Enough!" I said quietly.

Everyone shut up. The quiet voice always did it.

"We don't have definitive power rankings of everyone present," I said. "We have a lot of new faces at the table, and there's a good possibility that your rank could go down instead of up. For now, let us assume that until such time as we can finalize the new ranking system —" if I had my way, the new ranking system would be that no one was ranked at all, but I didn't want to spring too much on them at once "— that I am the most powerful, since I have the added power of the throne to back up the power many of you saw demonstrated. I will sit in the throne, and beyond that, there is no assigned seating and where you sit does not indicate your power or lack thereof."

There was a low grumble, but no one argued with me. I guess none of the nobility wanted it proven that the commonfolk were more powerful, and none of the so-called commoners felt the need to push it so early in their association.

I waited for the murmurs to completely die down and mentally composed and recomposed the mini-speech I thought I'd finalized last night. I'd spent the previous day holed up with my senior advisors—from both planes—trying to come up with a strategy for what I was about to do. Some of my plans had been in place before Eo'd died and I'd assumed the throne. Some of them had been initiated by Jörð during the coronation. And some of the things I was about to say would be a complete surprise to almost everyone in my inner circle. Raj reached out and squeezed my hand.

"You can do it," he said. *"No matter what, I've got your back."*

I straightened my spine and projected my voice with what I hoped resembled confidence—more for me than them. "Thank you for coming, everyone. As I'm sure you know, I was not intending to take the throne for a very, very long time, if at all. My coronation was certainly not a typical one, either, if my advisors are to be believed." I allowed myself a smile at my small "the Fae can't lie" joke that was likely trotted out by every emcee ever.

"My goal in returning was to help the former king shore up his kingdom and then take the Dark Throne for myself."

I paused to let that sink in and to give the collective gasps time to dissipate. So far no one had argued back, or fled the room, or pulled out a sat phone to give Medb a call to warn her. This was good. Or bad. If someone high up on the council had been working with Cloithfinn and Medb, and it'd be naïve to assume otherwise, they'd bide their time. I wished I could boot the nobility and keep the commoners, but I didn't want to start my reign with a civil war. The Light had seen enough bloodshed in recent years.

"Your Majesty," said the same man who'd tried to sit closer to me earlier. He bore watching.

"Yes, Erik?" I tried to smile again but came up short.

"Do you think it wise to challenge the Dark Queen now? Wouldn't it be better to wait a few years and get used to the burden of ruling before grabbing for another throne?"

I didn't like his tone, but that wasn't the issue right now. Cementing my role was. "I don't know if it is the wisest course, but it is the course I've been placed on. I have agents within the Dark Court, I have advisors familiar with the Queen and her depravities. And I have the word of one of her agents that she is responsible for meddling in our Realm. It is the Dark Queen who stirred Cloithfinn to rebellion, who funded her coup, and who supplied her fighters for the second attempt. Would you rather wait for her to make another attempt here, in your lands? Or shall I take our forces, use our knowledge, and claim my birthright to save two realms?"

Erik stood, "This is your birthright. Inheriting one throne doesn't allow you to lay claim to two. Are all humies so greedy?"

My face screwed up in confusion. "Humies?" I stared at him, trying to see through a glamour that didn't exist. He enhanced his looks, as did most Fae—slightly pointier ears, hair that was fuller and shinier, and features that were more interesting taking his face from interesting to generic.

"It's a term that some citizens of your realm have created to mean "raised by humans," Connor said with a wry smile. "It's supposed to be an insult."

"Made up specifically for me?" I asked.

"Yes, Your Majesty," Connor confirmed. "I heard it for the first time yesterday."

"Huh," I said, turning my attention back to Erik. He was flushed with either anger or embarrassment. I couldn't tell which.

"I am not going to waste time convincing you that my path is the right path," I said. "I will lead an army to the Dark Realm to claim that throne. It is mine by right of birth, as this one is by law of the land. When I have claimed it, the two lands will be united as they once were and Dark and Light Sidhe will be one people. My spies wait only for my word to start things moving there."

"How are you the heir to both Dark and Light?" Cliodnah challenged.

I'd been waiting for this question. I pushed back my throne chair to ensure I had plenty of room and smiled the first genuine smile of the afternoon.

"Like this."

I shifted into my dragon form, and I don't know if it was the raw power of the throne that was now mine fueling me, or my emotions pushing me too far, but the iridescent black and purple dragon that was my other form filled the space I'd made for myself and then some. I launched myself into the air, wishing I'd chosen to meet in the throne room instead of the council room, and flew three lazy circles around the ceiling before landing and shifting back into my human form. Wait—why was my form human? Shouldn't I look Fae as well? How had I never questioned my appearance?

Raj threw a robe around my shoulders and I drew it closed before returning to my seat.

"The Dragon Queen," someone breathed. "It is time."

"Grab that one," I said to Raj mind-to-mind. *"I have questions."*

"Now that I've proved my birthright, can we move on to the real items on the agenda?" I asked. Hearing no objections, I continued. "I will appoint a regent to hold the throne in my absence. I will appoint three people to serve as the commanders of my armies as we go to war. We will work together to plan the invasion using the new knowledge at my disposal, given to me at my coronation. And we will make a fucking plan to find, apprehend, and execute the traitor Finnegan Byrne. There will be no more deals. No more bargains. No more listening to his very good reasons to delay the execution. He is under a death sentence, and all members of my realm are deputized to carry it out. Any questions?"

The silence that followed my speech was so profound it echoed throughout the hall.

Then Florence raised her hand.

I nodded at her to speak.

"Who are your agents on the other side?" she asked.

"Isaac and Arduinna," I said. "And possibly Jack."

The room went cold. Frost patterns formed on the table and spiraled up the walls. As suddenly as they appeared, they were gone.

Florence stood up. "May I have your leave to go, Your Majesty?" She imbued so much disdain and sarcasm into her question I could almost feel it.

"Of course," I said. "We are adjourning now. Please be prepared to put forth your suggestions for regent by tomorrow afternoon when we reconvene." I stood, made eye contact with everyone in the room except my best friend, then left the room, leaving everyone else to follow in my wake.

CHAPTER SEVEN

I stomped—no strode forcefully, that sounded queenlier—into the pavilion in the center of the camp. I'd been in charge of this land for six full months now, and still had zero idea what I was doing. At least I was doing it with flare, though! Flare and military campaigning and long-distance relationshipping with my throne.

We'd been slowly meandering towards the Dark Realm for four of the last six months and didn't seem to be getting any closer. It was dreadfully unfair that the portal in Eochid's quarters had disappeared with his death. It was even more unfair that even with the map in my head that'd been planted there with my coronation, I couldn't lead my army across the border. We'd head out in one direction—I paused for a snippet of "Story of My Life" to play through my head—and run into an impenetrable wall. Sometimes literally.

I looked around the interior of my tent. Small cot shoved against one wall. Packs with my belongs against another. Soft, fluffy blanket rugs on the floor—the nod to my position. And one insanely hot vampire stretched out on the rugs watching me pace around the too-small space.

"Regretting not claiming the big tent?" Raj asked as I kicked a pillow out of the way.

"I thought they'd respect me more if I didn't act like a big shot," I confessed.

"They know you're queen," Raj pointed out. "Using the small tent doesn't do anything to make you more a Fae of the people. You'll earn their respect by treating everyone fairly and well and leading confidently. You'll also need to do a great job, but not too great. Be approachable, but not too approachable. And any other number of contradictory traits. I don't know if the contradictions are worse here because you're a woman, but they would be on Earth. You'd get away with more there because you're an attractive white woman, but only marginally."

Raj had been laying a lot of truth bombs on me lately, and they were starting to sound a little repetitive. He might be speaking truth, but it didn't improve my mood.

"This is the fifth time I've led people to a supposed passage to the Dark only to have it closed when we got here. I know that someone out there knows something and won't tell me. I feel like I'm being set up to fail and to fail in as humiliating a fashion as possible. It isn't fair!" I kicked the pillow again; it sailed through the air and landed on the cot.

Raj sat up and reached his hands up to me. I rolled my eyes. He didn't need help to stand. I clasped his hands in mine and braced myself to tug him up. Instead, he pulled me down next to him.

"It isn't fair," he said, grabbing my chin and making me look him in the eyes. "But it is reality. You can go out there and confess that you're stymied. They already know anyway, so it won't be a revelation of weakness. You can ask for help—tell them that you'd appreciate any insight. They know you're relatively young and very new to the Fae plane. Asking for help isn't weakness. You weren't raised to be queen, and it shows. Not being trained for this isn't weakness."

Raj kissed my forehead to lessen the blow of his words, but it didn't work. Tight anger curled in my chest. Maybe I wasn't raised to be queen, but I was born for it.

"My sweet, leadership is nurture not nature. You spent the first thirty-four years of your life living as an ordinary human. You spent the next few learning to lead a small group on proscribed quests. And now, you're queen of an entire realm. It makes no sense that you'd be brilliant at it right off the bat."

And that was the crux. I wasn't immediately brilliant. I wanted my so-called subjects to be awed by my queening. The magic had come to me easily. I'd learned to dragon with alacrity. I was a decent hand at sword combat. And I'd even learned to lie with the truth pretty quickly. I didn't have to work at things. I'd assumed ruling a small realm would be the same. Raj was right, but I wasn't ready to admit failure.

"It's not failure to admit you need help," Raj chided.

Fucking vampire, reading my thoughts all the time. It was the worst when he was right.

"What am I doing wrong, Raj?" I asked, crossing my legs.

"In your search or with your leadership?" he asked.

"Both, really," I admitted.

"I'm more qualified to advise you on leadership than magical Fae borders, and Connor is probably qualified to advise you on both. Have you asked him?"

"No," I said. I sounded sulky. Ugh. Some queen I was.

"Connor knows who you are and where you came from," Raj pointed out. "He'll help you. In fact, the only reason he's not helping you now is because you haven't asked."

"That never stopped him before," I groused. "I've received more than my share of unsolicited advice from Connor."

"You're the queen now, and he is following your lead and trying to respect your boundaries. It's early in your rule—if he just stepped in and advised you every time you were off course, he'd be trampling on your learning process and signaling that he didn't believe you were up to the job. But if you ask him for counsel, then you look wise enough to know when you don't know everything plus, you'll get some really good advice. It's a win-win."

I wanted to keep pouting about how difficult it was, but if I did, I knew I'd look foolish. I hated looking foolish. I climbed to my feet, adjusted the flowing green material draped around me that was half light-weight sweater and half royal robe, and walked towards the doorway.

"You don't have to ask him now," Raj said. "It could probably wait until morning."

"However will I occupy my time, though, if I don't take care of this immediately?" I asked, turning around and trying out my new and improved ingenue voice.

"We could find a way, I'm sure of it. We're both reasonably intelligent and highly innovative." Raj had stretched out on his side and was patting the rug in front of him.

"I need to let Connor know I expect to meet with him first thing in the morning, let the troops know that we'll have a later start tomorrow, see if anyone's grumbling so I can help mitigate their frustration, and reassure everyone that we will get there and soon!"

Raj sat back up. "You sound so responsible, Your Majesty."

"Would you have me any other way?" I teased.

He pursed his lips and pretended to think about it. "I guess not. Keep on queening. I'll be here when you get back." He stood and shed his clothing. "No guarantees I won't start without you, though."

My eyes followed his hand to his rapidly hardening cock, and I bit my lower lip. "I'll hurry."

I turned and dashed through the door to the tent and ran squarely into a man only a few inches taller than me. I looked up into an unlined face with amber eyes offset by light brown skin with golden olive undertones. White hair swept back from his face and brushed against his shoulders. He looked familiar.

I took a couple steps back into the doorway of my tent. Raj appeared behind me, pants on but unfastened and still shirtless, and I leaned into the comfort of his cool body. Then I really looked at this newcomer who'd been standing outside my tent flap, too close to be polite.

Red and orange flashed across my vision, and the short, unassuming man of indeterminate age disappeared as the phoenix charged to the forefront.

"Father Clement," I said. "To what do I owe this…" I'd meant to say pleasure, but I wasn't sure it was one yet.

"Thought you might need some help, Your Majesty," he said. "I am eager to see you fulfill the prophecies and bring unity to our people again."

He was talking too loudly and making me uncomfortable. "Would you like to come to the strategy tent?" I asked, trying to herd him away from my personal space.

"Not at all, dear girl," he boomed. "I have but one purpose here! To help guide you to the one, safe crossing and to keep your people safe when we get there." He backed away from me and into the mostly empty square in the center of our camp.

I was racking my brain, trying to figure out some way to diffuse the situation before things got out of hand. I liked control and didn't want to cede it to a showy firebird who appeared out of nowhere.

"Give me three days," he said, "And I'll be able to get you across the border."

I opened my mouth to request he again come talk with me and my advisors in the tent—just because I'd agreed to ask for help didn't mean I was bound to take it from anyone who showed up—when he burst into flames.

He danced around a bit in a grotesque modern dance, then stood, raised his arms to the sky, and collapsed in a pile of ashes.

"Fucking showboat," Connor said on my left. "Always has to make an entrance."

I WAS SO glad that Father Clement had decided to come along to guide us. I told myself that once an hour in an effort to keep it true. I beamed, hoping that everyone who could see me would assume I was delighted to be spending this much time carrying around a giant urn of phoenix ashes until such time he deemed it appropriate to regain his life and form and actually do the helping part of what he'd pledged.

It was the third day since he'd spontaneously combusted, and we weren't any closer to finding the gap in the wall than we'd been before. I was trying to be patient, although that wasn't really one of the strengths I'd list on my resume. Inaction was worse than fruitless action, especially since the results were the same. I glared at the sun where it hung at its zenith in the cerulean, cloudless sky.

"You should stop for the day, set up camp, and do some deep breathing exercises," Petrina said, riding up beside me. She was dressed in elvish riding leathers. "Florence chose a site a couple miles up the trail and Acantha—who was an excellent choice for Quartermaster—is overseeing the supplies for tonight."

"Florence was supposed to ride further than that," I said. Florence had been cold to me, both literally and figuratively, since I'd revealed that Isaac and Arduinna—and Jack, possibly—were my spies on the inside. Every time I tried to explain, she made excuses and rode away. Petrina was now our go-between, something she was obviously not enjoying. "We were going to go as far as the Bridge to Nowhere, mostly so I could see what that actually means, and we're at least three hours ride away, yet." I couldn't tell how far exactly—not without touching the earth, or at least concentrating enough to fall off my horse. I rubbed my backside as I winced from the memory.

"Florence got a feeling that we should stop and conveyed that feeling to Acantha," Petrina said.

"A feeling or a *feeling*?" I asked. Florence hadn't done much prophesying since the gates were open. I paused in my thought process— had she done any prophesying since I'd opened the final gate? I turned my attention back to Petrina and asked my question aloud.

"There's been plenty, just very little of it having to do with you directly," Petrina replied. "As for now, it's a *feeling* in the witchy sense of the word. Now, will you tell your army that we'll make camp in a couple miles so I can confirm with Florence that you're not being stubborn for the sake of artificial timetables? You have advisors for a reason. Let them advise you."

I sighed. I hated how often I needed that pointed out. Why couldn't I get it through my head that now that I was managing more than my own life, I needed a little external wisdom to get me through the day. I was so afraid of failing, of looking weak, that I was eschewing the help that could keep me strong and successful. This level of self-sabotage wasn't rational nor was it effective.

I leaned forward and caught Tanwen's attention. She and Alanna rode over to me and awaited my orders. By the expression on Tanwen's face, she already knew what I was going to say. Damn the supernatural and their enhanced hearing. Just once, I wanted to be surrounded by Fae who couldn't eavesdrop.

My gaze settled on Alanna, and guilt suffused me. I was an awful human being.

"What's got you all twisted?" Raj asked.

I ignored him. He knew where my brain was and stubbornly persisted loving me, regardless.

"What else would I do?"

The gentle humor in his voice prodded me out of my bad mood. *"I love you, too, Rajyapala,"* I said before straightening my spine. I might never know why I was prone to fits of self-doubt so severe they impacted me and everyone around me, but I needed to figure out how I could push my way through before I completely eroded the good opinions everyone around me had. I could do this. I might not be the Queen of—all—the Fae yet, but I was the undisputed queen of Fake it 'til You Make it, one of the more prosperous regions in DeNial.

"Alanna, we're going to camp a couple miles up the road. Florence is already preparing the site and has communicated with the Quarter-master." I hoped I sounded regal enough that no one would remember my argument with Petrina.

"Of course," Alanna's interpreter said. "I'll let the troops know. It's the third day, you know. Since the phoenix spontaneously combusted after promising to help us."

I hadn't forgotten, but I didn't want to talk about it. Father—or Phoenix, rather—Clement was a flaming pain in my ass. Like even less welcome hemorrhoids. "I look forward to any assistance he can lend us when and if he returns."

Tanwen opened her mouth, but before she could say anything,

Alanna laid her hand across the dryad's lips. I wasn't an expert at the interpreter/interpretee relationship, but I thought that might mean Tanwen was about to say something Alanna hadn't said first.

"Fine," Tanwen muttered. Her hand gestures were jerky and short. "I disagree, but in this situation, you're the boss."

Oooh, interesting. I loved watching relationship dynamics play out. Now that Florence and Petrina weren't sneaking around making out behind potted plants in hotel lobbies, I had to get my voyeuristic jollies somehow.

"I'm going to ride ahead," I said. "Once you get everyone else rallied, follow our trail." I had no doubt that they could. I was beginning to think that they would find me even if I snuck off into the forest under darkest night and hid in the darkest cave and buried myself up to my neck behind a shadowy outcropping. I looked around for Connor and Raj and motioned for them to join me.

I hadn't had a chance to talk to Connor about my search or garner his advice about my leadership. The arrival of the phoenix had thrown us all into an uproar, and in the hubbub, I kinda forgot. Or didn't let it come to the forefront of my remembering. Ugh. Honesty. Can't even lie to myself. It was definitely the worst part of being Fae. Well, that and the complete lack of coffee and beer. I was semi-seriously considering ducking out for a day to replenish my stash. Maybe find some marijuana seeds. I bet they'd propagate nicely and then we'd have something besides Fae wine at the end of the day.

"Your Majesty," Connor said, bowing deeply from the saddle. I'd given up on getting him to stop doing that. "How can I be of service?"

I filled him in on our Florence-chosen destination, then gritted my teeth for what I was going to say next. I pursed my lips, squinted at my Top Advisor, and opened my mouth to speak.

"Just spit it out, my Queen," Connor said. Then, in a much lower voice, he added, "You look like a constipated bugbear."

"Pretty sure I can have you beheaded for that," I replied under my breath.

"Might be a mercy at this point."

I smiled brightly and reminded myself that I liked Connor and usually enjoyed his sense of humor. "I am giving up," I admitted between gritted teeth. "When we make camp tonight, I'm going to have a private advisory session, and I'll need some advice."

HOURS LATER, the camp was set up, meals were served, and the nearby countryside was evaluated for its dangers—of which none were found —and its aid—which was the same as everywhere—abundant game flying out of the forest and in front of the archers in charge of hunting, more ripe fruits and berries than should be about this time of year, streams overflowing with fish ready to jump in the nets, and farms burgeoning with more harvest than the farmers knew what to do with. There were things that I definitely didn't enjoy about campaigning, and things I missed about living on Earth, but having Fae gifted enough to keep us supplied without wiping out the lands we were moving through was not one of them.

Only then did I convene my council. The jar of ashes that contained Father Clement sat on a trunk near the entrance to my personal tent, but so far, they hadn't offered up any advice at all. Raj, as always, was at my right hand. Connor sat across from me, stretched out on the pillows he'd commandeered, toying with the rim of a glass of wine. He had dark circles under his eyes and in this unguarded moment, sorrow shadowed his face. It was easy to forget that he still mourned the loss of Anoka. His jocularity fended off questions about his state of mind, and he was even more standoffish and private than Florence.

Speak of the devil...or rather, the witch. Florence walked through the entrance to my tent followed closely by Petrina, Tanwen, and Alanna. The latter was the reason that all the campaign tents had high ceilings and larger than average doorways. You can't make small tents when a good portion of your army are centaurs. Once everyone was settled with the beverage of their choice, I stood up.

"I appreciate your presence," I started. The servants cleared the room, and I flexed one of my little used powers and created an air shield around the tent to keep any eavesdroppers or inadvertent over-hearers out. "I don't know where I'm going. I have the maps of the Fae realms in my head, and I thought it'd be easy enough to find the gaps between lands. But we've been out here for months. Our people are grumbling, and we're no closer to crossing the border than we were when we started. At this point, I'll listen to any advice any of you have."

Connor cleared his throat but didn't sit up. "Your Majesty—"

"Please, call me Eleanor. No one will overhear you and suggest you're being too familiar. You called Eochid by his first name all the time."

Connor shrugged. "He was well established, and I had never been ranked more powerful than him. But, in this case, I will do as you ask. Eleanor, you know the gaps in the border move. That's why we took Eo's secret passage when he went to the Dark Realm to rescue…" his voice faltered. I saw him clench his fist for a moment before he continued. "…on our rescue mission. We needed something we could count on."

"If this was all one land, how come there are barriers between the Light and Dark anyway?" I asked. The whole idea of it had been making me peevish for days, but this was the first time I'd asked anyone about it.

"I don't know," Connor admitted. "They've been there for as long as I can remember."

"I know," Tanwen said. "Me, not Alanna." Her hands flew as she translated for the centaur. "I remember the end of the unified Sidhe. I hid in the forest during the civil war that split the lands. And when it was over, I was told that I was of the Light and that the land of the Dark was forbidden me.

"The most powerful Fae on both sides erected the barrier to keep each other out, but there was enough will—enough power—from those of us considered common to ensure it didn't seal completely."

"This all sounds very familiar," Florence pointed out.

"It is," Tanwen admitted. "In many ways, it was the test run for the barrier between Earth and this plane. It was at this time that our tradition of kidnapping human children and leaving changelings, which had been mostly folklore and exaggeration—the Fae do not birth so many children that they'd leave any behind—took on new life and led, in part, to our eventual banishment from Earth. The powerful Fae, in an effort to counteract the sabotage of the people, poured life into the barrier between Light and Dark, and later between Earth and Fae. The barriers themselves became near-living, although I don't believe they achieved sentience as some will claim. The number of gaps in the border remained stable, but their positions did not unless anchored by someone—or something—powerful."

"Well, fuck," I said. "I guess that's why every time I lead you all to a gap, it's already gone."

"They don't usually move that fast," Connor said. "A gap, unless used repeatedly, tends to stick around for a while."

"They're taunting me," I announced. "I know Tanwen said they weren't sentient, but that has to be the only answer. I can't believe no one told me this before when I was galloping up and down the border looking for passage." I held up my hand to forestall the inevitable arguments. "I know, I know, I didn't ask and I'm the queen and blah blah."

"You know now," Florence said. "So what are you going to do?"

I narrowed my eyes at the assembled advisors. "I have the beginnings of a plan, but not the expertise to carry it out nor the knowledge to fine-tune it. Will you help me?"

"Nothing would give me more pleasure than to break on through to the other side," Connor said.

I closed my eyes and massaged my temples. He was one step away from tormenting me with dad jokes. I grinned. It was kinda nice.

Hours later, I leaned back on my chair and looked around the room. It was nearly dawn, and we'd been up all night plotting. My plan itself was fairly simple. Walk to the border and create a gap large enough for my armies to walk through.

It was the how's and where's that were problematic. But mostly the how's.

I rolled my neck, wincing at the crackling noises, and turned my attention back to the map spread out before us. Connor and Tanwen were arguing over land features and practicalities trying to figure out that best place topographically and strategically to go across, since we were choosing our passage point. Raj joined them using his knowledge of the living map in my head to make suggestions about caves which I sincerely hoped the Fae in the room were quickly shutting down.

I was supposed to be working with Florence, Petrina, and Alanna on anchoring a gap. I refused to call them gates. I was not creating a new gate...although, every time the thought crossed my mind, the knowledge on how to do it floated behind like a helium balloon.

"Fine!" I yelled, grabbing the attention of everyone in the room. "I can make a fucking gate. I know how. I spent enough time suspended in them that they somehow became part of me. The destruction opened the doors to my knowledge of their creation. Is that what you all wanted to hear?"

"Umm..." Petrina said. "I don't think anyone here was expecting that."

A flash of light illuminated the tent, glowing brighter and brighter until it was too bright to see and all I could think of was old movies about nuclear war. I screwed my eyes closed, flung one arm over my face as warding, and leapt towards Raj to shield him with my body.

CHAPTER EIGHT

L aughter penetrated the pain stabbing through my eyeballs and burrowing into my brain. I sat up, keeping my eyes closed. "Is everyone okay?" I asked.

"Yes," Connor replied. I hadn't known before that a person could infuse a single word with that much irritation and sarcasm, but Connor managed to convey his disgust in a fraction of a second.

I blinked my eyes trying to remove the snow globe of brightly colored lights still floating in my vision. "What happened?"

"I'm afraid that I happened," someone said, their voice suffused with laughter. It sounded familiar… "Clement?"

"One and the same!" he announced.

My vision was clearing, and I stared towards the voice, willing him to come into focus. "What the hell?"

"I did tell you," he said. "After three days, I'd be able to help you."

"You didn't tell me you'd blind us all in the process," I said.

"I didn't expect to be reborn in a small tent. Most people keep me on an altar away from civilization."

"You might've left instructions," I muttered. "I've never midwifed a phoenix before."

He huffed. "My reputation clearly hasn't preceded me."

I waved his damaged ego away along with the last of the residual light flashes from Clement's fiery rebirth. "What's done is done. We have a plan—kind of—to cross the border, we're just working out the details. Why don't you join us? You can provide that assistance you so generously offered before spontaneously combusting with zero warning."

Clement walked outside, bounced against my barrier, then pushed through it. It broke and whiplashed back into me, knocking me off my chair.

"That was a real dick move, Clement," I yelled, squinting my eyes against the shiny new headache he'd given me.

"If I can break it, anyone can break it," he replied, coming back in and sinking gracefully into a cross-legged position on the floor.

"That wasn't the point," I muttered. "I wasn't creating an unbreakable barrier—it was a soundproof, invisible barrier. If I wanted to keep people out, I would've constructed it differently."

"Ooh, do you think you can build one I can't break?" He jumped up and clapped his hands together, eyes wide and looking altogether too gleeful for my liking.

"I don't know," I replied. "You seem pretty excited about the prospect, and I can't tell if that's confidence or assholishness. I do know that it's not recess, and we're not playing games right now. Ask me again sometime, and we'll find out."

"Fine," Clement said, returning to the floor and pouting altogether way too much for an ancient and immortal fire bird. "Where are we?"

Connor took over, and I made a mental note to send him a gift basket later. Not only did he know the land better, his temper wasn't as frayed. My confidence, already on the low side, had taken a huge hit when my shield had zipped back into me like an out-of-control tape measure. I hadn't constructed the shield to serve as a physical barrier, but it always had functioned that way before. Watching Clement walk through it so easily hurt my feelings. My ego was even more fragile than the bird's.

I exhaled slowly and leaned in to listen. Connor might be the better Fae to lead this discussion, but I had better learn. I didn't want to remain a figurehead—and since the second throne I was aiming to take might not welcome the inevitable rule with the same mild enthusiasm as the Light, I needed to be strong, and if I'd learned anything from my Earth education, Knowledge is Power!

"Here," Clement said, pointing at the Bridge to Nowhere. "It's close, it's mystical, and there's enough space for all the troops to get through quickly enough to avoid notice. Additionally, the bridge opens up into a series of caves, so we'll be able to spread out and hide until we can assess the situation on the other side.

I felt smug for a moment. That was exactly where I'd been headed. Not just because it had a cool, curiosity invoking name, but also because of strategy! But mostly curiosity. "Why's it called the Bridge to Nowhere?" I asked. "That sounds a bit ominous if we're talking about crossing it."

Clement smirked—his expression of choice, I was beginning to think—and winked. "You'll see, Your Majesty."

Petrina leaned forward. "We have the where. Let's talk about how. Eleanor can open sizable stable gates between and within planes. However, she's usually exhausted after the fact, and we don't know if she could hold this large of a gate open for long enough to get everyone through."

"She's right," I admitted. "I've never had to transport more than a half-dozen people. I think it's possible. I know how to build and stabilize them. I just haven't practiced and don't feel like my entire army should be my guinea pigs."

"Having a single person hold it isn't a great idea anyway," Clement said. Connor nodded in agreement.

"Why not?" I asked.

"It's unstable," Florence said. "And if the balance was disturbed at any time, it could drain you before you could stop it."

"Exactly," Clement agreed. "It also makes it more difficult to leave the structure in place behind us in case we need to beat a hasty retreat."

"So, what do you suggest?" I asked.

"We'll need an object of power to anchor it," Connor said.

"Three if we can manage," Clement agreed. "That'll give it a stable base."

"I can't believe I don't have 'objects of power' next to my twenty-sided dice in my Crown Royal bag," I said. Six pairs of eyes stared at me blankly. Raj gave me a thumbs up. Of all the people to have played Dungeons and Dragons, it had to be the guy who actually still had a dungeon.

"Are the objects in any danger?" Florence asked. "Is there a chance they'll be destroyed or lost?"

"There's always a chance," Clement said. "But if we build a solid gate held by three people strong in Fae magic, the chances are slim. Why? Do you have objects of power in your dice bag?"

"I don't, but I know where to find two," Florence replied. She stared at Raj and me, and it took me a minute to figure out why. I was slow on the uptake, lately.

"My sword would qualify," Raj admitted. He drew it and laid it on the table. Connor and Clement examined it, agreed that it would suffice, and returned it to Raj. I'd been worried that his sojourn in the ruby might've canceled out the power it held, but it looked like my fears were baseless. The Fae-made blade decorated with blood rubies was more resilient than I gave it credit for.

"What do you have, Your Majesty?" Clement asked.

I drew a blank for a moment until I noticed Florence staring at the scarlet bag tied at my waist. "Ohhh," I said. "I have the Orb of the Dark Realm."

"That thing's worthless," Connor said. "The Dark Queen had it made out of one of her enemy's children."

I gasped. "That's horrific! How could anyone let her rule after that?"

"When someone is willing to kill children and imbue them with magic to hold the throne, not a lot of people are eager to stand up to said personage," Connor pointed out. "How did you find the orb?"

"I don't think it's Medb's," I said. I was quickly shushed. I wasn't supposed to say her name. The powerful Fae can hear their names being spoken and find the speakers. That probably violates several laws in the former United States. It's hard to be worse than the NSA, but the NS-Fae are up for the challenge.

"This one doesn't have a dark energy, and it's pulling me home." I reached down into my bag that was always with me and pulled it out. It looked like an apple again—nothing I did. It seemed to be a natural camouflage that I had zero control over. Much like my magical eavesdropping. Either I didn't have the power or knowledge to listen for my name or no one was saying it. I wasn't sure which was worse.

"May I?" Clement held out his hand.

I hesitated. It felt wrong to hand it over. I didn't want to go Dark Bilbo on everyone, but it was mine. "How about you just look real close without touching?" I suggested in what I hoped was a casual voice.

"*Almost got there,*" Raj said. His mental voice was tinged with amusement.

Clement didn't push. He held his hand over it and stared as if he was trying to see into the heart of it. The apple orb vibrated in my hand. I could feel power rising from it. It reminded me of a less-intense gate power I'd encountered when opening the portals between this world and Earth. I drew it into me. It needed to be hidden away, private. The last thing we needed was to shoot up a beacon to announce our current location. Medb had to know we were coming. I wasn't so naïve as to think there were no spies among us. After all, I had my own in her court, as did likely everyone else.

"How much power are you absorbing?" Clement asked, not taking his eyes off the orb.

"Most of it," I admitted.

"Let it go, just for a second. I need to gauge its levels and how effective it'll be as an anchor."

I looked at Connor. That seemed practical but risky and I needed a second opinion. He nodded slightly. I hoped that was him signaling it'd be okay and not that he shared my concerns and we should delay. I stopped absorbing the power into the bottomless well of my reserves. Still more was rushing in even without my intervention. I reached out to block the flow, but the orb had marked me as a channel, and trying to stop the power now was like trying to dam the Columbia with Tinker Toys.

"It is enough," Clement said finally. "Put it away, if you can."

I looked at the orb that now looked less like a shiny red apple and more like an apple-sized faceted ruby, banded with gold and topped with a gold and emerald tree. "Time to go back in the bag," I said. Raj handed me the velvet bag I'd been keeping it in, and I squeezed the orb gently, silently promising that its day would come soon when it wouldn't have to be hidden away and popped it into the bag. As I drew the strings closed, I felt the power recede. I tucked it back into its pouch I had under my armor and smiled brightly. "So just one more thing?" I asked. "Let's go get that missing scepter, then."

I GROANED. "I think it'd be faster just to keep searching for an existing opening," I said, flopping on my bed. "I don't care what anyone says and how many legends there are...there are no scepters hidden near this stupid bridge."

Raj handed me a glass of wine. "Not with that attitude, there aren't. Although, I've been told that I'm pretty good at seeking out existing openings." He leered at me until I rolled my eyes and plowed through, ignoring his innuendo. For now.

"It's so weird that legends and the memories of my counselors are the same age. When this is all over, I need to hang out with some people my own age. I need to catch up with my fellow Xennial kids."

"I knew you were a social butterfly before the end of the world," Raj said. "Always the life of the party, flitting about from man to man and partaking of the delights on the edge of both digital and analog."

I pouted at him for a moment, then took a sip of my wine. "Fine. I wouldn't know where to find any fellow Xennials even if the world hadn't moved on. It's just..." I took another drink while I gathered my thoughts. "...everyone is so old. The youngest person besides me is Florence, and even she has a few decades on me. No one holds it over my head, but I don't have the knowledge or experience anyone else has. I'm the queen of a people who are centuries older than me, and I have no idea what I'm doing."

"The only thing you're doing wrong is trying too hard," Raj said. "Self-doubt is normal. In fact, I'd say it's preferable, to an extent. You have to balance over-confidence and the inability to see where you might be wrong with doubt and the inability to act. I'll help you fall on the right side—it's the digital versus analog argument all over again."

I eyed him skeptically. "I think you're taking my generation's defining feature too far in your metaphor."

Raj took my wine glass and set it down on the small table by the bed, then crawled up beside me and pushed me down. He propped himself on one elbow and leaned over me until his lips hovered just over mine. "You know what I'd rather take too far?" He slid his hand inside my shirt and traced the skin under my left breast.

I shivered as goosebumps erupted across the skin of my chest. "We are having a serious conversation about my inadequacies," I scolded. My breath hitched as Raj's fingers moved across my breast and teased my nipple into a stiff peak.

"We've had this discussion a hundred times in the past few months," Raj said, shoving my shirt up and sucking on my nipple until I squirmed beneath him. He sat up and grinned at me with a roguish glint in his eyes. The cool breeze that was omnipresent in my tent no matter how well I tried to insulate it caressed my breast; the chill against my wet skin sending a frisson of electricity through my body and igniting my core.

"But what if we missed something?" I asked as Raj pushed my shirt over my head before returning to my breasts, laving them with his tongue and leaving a trail of kisses between them. "What if we're close to finding the answer."

"It's forty-two," Raj said. "And now that we have the answer, why not get down to business?" His mouth trailed lower. I raised my hips to help him pull my breeches off and gasped when he blew on the brown curls marking the juncture of my legs. Raj tossed my pants on the floor and stripped off his own clothes before lying down beside me. He nipped at my neck, and the feel of his fangs against my carotid heightened my arousal. His fingers slipped up between my legs and teased me open, finding the quickly hardening nub of my clitoris. He stroked back and forth slowly at first, and then more quickly and with greater pressure. My hips rocked forward, and my ass left the bed as he teased an orgasm from me. I collapsed against the bed, but he didn't stop his ministrations.

"Let me know when you want me to stop," he whispered against my neck.

"Never," I gasped as he pinched my clit hard for a moment before continuing to stroke me. Just before I came again, his fangs slipped into my neck. He drank deeply and pulled out my orgasm by sliding two fingers inside me and fucking me with his fingers while continuing to stroke my clit with his thumb.

"Still never?" he asked.

"Shhh..." I said, placing one hand over his mouth. "I see entire universes. I'm looking for the Little Dipper and Pisces and Orion's Belt." I felt my eyes starting to close and shook my head to wake myself back up.

"Did you find the North Star?" Raj asked, pulling his hand back and resting his head on my chest. I felt his cock press against my thigh, and my arousal started to wake again.

I cupped his cheek and tilted his head so I could meet his gaze. "I don't need to look for the North Star. You're always right here with me." I rolled over so he was on his back, then climbed astride and lowered myself onto his cock. I closed my eyes in pleasure as he penetrated me, then squeezed him as I began to rock.

"I know you're exhausted," he said. "You don't have to..."

"This isn't about 'have to.' It's all about 'want.' And unless you don't want, let me give you what we both need."

"As my queen commands," Raj said. He took my hand and pulled it to his lips, kissing my palm and maintaining eye contact. The smolder was enough to light me on fire. Again.

I moved against him back and forth, leaning forward enough to tease my clit against the taut skin above the base of his penis. I quickened my pace, one arm across my chest to keep my breasts from bouncing too vigorously and watched Raj's face. I loved to watch him lost in the throes of ecstasy, and I loved knowing that it was me who brought him to that place again and again.

He opened his eyes and grinned at me. "Feeling a bit proud and possessive?" he asked, then gasped as I used my free hand to scrape my nails across his chest, catching a nipple. "Evil," he growled.

"You like it," I replied.

He didn't answer, but the expression on his face was answer enough. I picked up the pace again. I got myself to the peak just in time to meet Raj there, and together we plunged over the edge.

"I love you," I said once I had my breath back and had cleaned myself up. I laid down and curled my body around his.

"I love you, too, my sweet," Raj said. "Sleep now. I will keep you safe, and tomorrow we will find the scepter."

Thank you, I thought at him, too tired to verbalize. The gulf of obligation stretched between us, but for once, I didn't care. I could spend all of my very long lifetime devoted to this man and still not be able to repay him for what he'd done for me, what he meant to me.

I STOOD at the midpoint of the Bridge to Nowhere and steadfastly did not look down. I'd been assured that it wasn't a bottomless canyon, but there were actual fucking clouds below me blocking my view of the ground. The bridge, constructed of white granite that sparkled like an emo vampire in the sun, arched up ridiculously high and was devoid of any kind of safety railings. It was wide enough for five people or two centaurs to walk comfortably abreast, so one small Fae Queen in the middle of the middle wasn't in any danger, even with the unpredictable winds that swirled around me. I repeated this to myself trying to push down the unreasonable anxiety threatening to crush my lungs.

I sat down, knowing I looked ridiculous, and scooted closer to the edge. The Shadowglow Mountains marked the border between the two kingdoms and were mind-boggling high. The Dragon Tears River far, far below was—or at least had been when we'd camped beside it a few days ago at a much lower elevation—deep, swift, and cold. The person responsible for naming the natural features of the Fae Plane was creative and pedestrian at the same time, a feat not achievable by many.

One end of the bridge led back to my army's encampment. The other end led to a portal that, at least in theory, would spit us out in the Dark realm. In addition to it being a permanent but small door-way, not wide enough for more than a couple people to pass through side by side, there was the possibility that not everyone would end up in the same place. It was like a machine gun or fire hose—out of control and spraying everywhere.

The scepter was supposed to be here, and I was supposed to be able to sense it. But the gate energy overwhelmed my other senses, and I couldn't feel anything else. So I sat, alone, in the middle of the too high bridge with my head in my hands and tried not to despair.

A shuffling noise interrupted my not-at-all-sulky meditation. Petrina, warded against the wind in a fur cloak and wool cap, was about a third of the way across the bridge and headed my way. The vista behind Petrina was idyllic. The Light realm was spread out behind her. Rolling hills and valleys dotted with trees and streams and pastures of sheepish and cowish animals interspersed with fields of grapes and fruit trees and other things I couldn't identify. There were farmhouses and villages and the occasional, larger manor house, and roads wound between them. It reminded me of a child's drawing...

"Oh, shit!" I said, loud enough for Petrina to hear and emphatically enough for Raj to go on high alert.

Petrina was at my side and ready to fight in the blink of an eye, and Raj appeared on the other side of me moments later.

"What is it?" my pseudo daughter-in-law asked. "Is there a threat?"

"No," I said. "Not a threat. A realization. Look at the mountains behind me. What do you see?"

Petrina side-eyed me but did as I asked. "High, jagged peaks that look vaguely threatening poking out through the cloud banks. The peaks have snow scattered over them in dingy patches. There are no trees. No roads. No sign that they've ever been visited by anyone without wings. They're cold, unwelcoming, and dangerous."

"But do they look real?" I asked without turning around to take in the same view.

She cocked her head and looked back at me over her left shoulder. "Yes. Very real. Overwhelmingly real. They're not like the mountains I grew up with. Or even the Alps, which have some real jagged edges. These almost feel more real. This is more like the angry Lord of the Rings mountains. The ones that dropped snow on the hobbits for no reason."

I stared at her for a moment, trying to decide whether or not I was going to let that pass...or be a Gandalf about it. In the end, I decided to let it go. There was no reason to get into an LOTR argument now. That wasn't my point at all. "Right," I confirmed. "Like that. Now turn around. What do you see when you look at the Kingdom of Light?"

Petrina's view of my kingdom matched my own.

"It's like a fairytale illustration," she said. I watched her face as the realization dawned. "Oh, shit!"

Raj had beaten her there, but he had the benefit of dipping into my brain, which was cheating, but allowable. This time, anyway.

"Yeah," I said. "It's not as obvious as the weird-ass childhood nightmare apple tree, but that isn't reality. Or at least not real enough reality. It's not a glamour, or I'd be able to see through it. That means the magic is different. Deeper maybe? Tied to the earth and not a specific person. I don't know. I might need someone better versed in Fae magic to help me interpret this."

"Connor or the bird?" Raj asked. "I can get either of them here in moments."

Raj and Clement were not becoming fast friends. I don't know why they rubbed each other the wrong way. Even though Clement had given Raj and me the means to save ourselves when we basically sacrificed each other at the final gate, Raj avoided Clement as much as possible, and Clement wouldn't deign to speak to Raj at all. I'd thought initially that Raj's reticence might be due to Clement's ability to spontaneously combust, but since I was a living fire starter, that theory didn't make much sense. I shrugged. As long as they were professional and polite, it didn't matter. I'd get it out of Raj eventually. Or else they'd learn to rub each other the right way. I grimaced—not a picture I wanted in my head—then stood up, making sure to avoid looking down. Or to either side. I oriented myself back towards my camp, fixed my eyes on the bridge, and started shuffling forward.

"Something feels off," I said. "Maybe a storm coming in. I don't want to be up here anymore, but tomorrow I'll come back and bring Clement and Connor. Florence, too. Maybe Alanna if she wants. The more eyes on this, the better chance we have of solving it quickly." I halted and braced myself to look up and ensure that I was still headed in the right direction and not about to step off the bridge and plummet to my…well, fine. Not my death. I was a fucking dragon, and although I didn't advertise the fact, it was no longer a secret. I could shift in mid-air and swoop to safety. Probably. If I didn't panic and freeze up. And even then, Raj would likely catch me before I was dashed to pieces on the rocks below.

I raised my head with my eyes closed, inhaled deeply, and opened my eyes. I was headed the right direction. I looked up further and gasped.

"What this time?" Petrina asked. She was a couple feet behind me and to my right. Raj was similarly placed, but on my left.

"What do you see when you look out?" I asked.

"The same as before," Raj said. "Is your view different?" I felt him slip into my mind and look through my eyes. "Oh!" he said.

"Damnit!" Petrina said. "Someone tell me what's going on."

"It's all different," I said. "The landscape. The view. Everything. But the same, too, you know?"

"I most certainly do not know," Petrina said. "Since you haven't said anything helpful at all."

I tilted my head and tried to come up with the words to describe what I was seeing. "It's the same view. The rolling hills dotted with pastures of animals, fields of food, and streams and roads and houses. But now it looks…lived in. The fields aren't evenly spaced, and the wooded areas aren't all the same shade of green. The houses are different colors and sizes, and the roads aren't just curved or straight. They wind and detour and some end abruptly for no apparent reason. There's light and shadows. It looks real again."

"Turn around," Raj said.

I did as he requested, although even that slow spin was enough to ignite my vertigo. Once I'd done my one-eighty, I looked back towards the Shadowglows and gasped. They were no longer the harsh, unwelcoming peaks we'd seen from the middle. They were lower, capped with pristine fields of snow, and tinged with green that got lusher and more verdant in the lower elevations. A small cabin with light streaming through the window perched on gentle slope near an alpine lake. Five tall, straight pines stood in the clearing near the house, pointing up at the cheerful-looking puffy white clouds. Cheerful. Happy. Happy little trees.

"It's a fucking Bob Ross painting," I said. "It's as idyllic as the valley was before."

Petrina looked back at me. "I still see the hostile mountains."

Raj stood between us, looking back and forth between the two views and inching toward me. Finally, he stopped moving and held out his hand to me. "Come here," he said. "Petrina, you too."

I let him pull me in, and Petrina stepped forward to meet us.

"Now look," Raj commanded.

I looked first at the mountains. They shimmered, the Bob Ross illusion overlaying the harsher, jagged peaks. Then I turned carefully and looked back at the valley. A translucent idyllic countryside partially obscured the rolling hills and farmland below.

"How have we not noticed this before?" Petrina asked.

"The only person who's spent much time up here is Eleanor," Raj pointed out. "And she doesn't look around that much. Most of the people back in the camp are getting the Bob Ross view of the mountain, and if they look back toward the countryside they call home, it's real, exactly as it should be."

I looked down while Raj and Petrina speculated on the how and why of the illusions. My head was spinning a bit, and my breathing was a touch too fast. I needed to get myself together before I hyper-ventilated. Instead of the sparkly stone of the bridge, there was a large, round silver seal under my feet. It was about three feet in diameter, blended almost seamlessly into the material of the bridge, and was adorned with the images of tall, jagged peaks looming over rolling hills and valleys dotted with houses and small animals that looked like the unfortunate results of an experiment involving a sheep and an emu.

"Raj. Petrina. Look." I pointed at the seal, then squatted down to touch it. "It's warm," I said. "That's weird...this high—" The seal moved, spinning slowly clockwise and lowering, creating a perfectly round hole in the bridge.

"There are stairs," Petrina marveled, bending over and following the progress of the seal. "We should go down."

"Are you fucking kidding me right now?" I asked. "You want to walk down a mysterious spiral staircase that didn't exist a moment before? What if it dissolves under our feet and we set a world record for the high dive?"

"We'll be fine," Petrina assured me. "You and father can both fly, and I know you'd never leave me behind. Besides...we're all immortal. Don't you want to see where the non-existent stairs leading down from the Bridge to Nowhere go?"

Those were all excellent points. I didn't agree with any of them, but that didn't mean she was wrong.

"Fine," I said, not bothering to hide my discomfort or grumpiness. "I'll go." I held my breath and stepped onto the first stair, noting that at least these stairs had handrails. The stairs moved—a spiral escalator pulling me down to who-knows-where with no clear way to return. "Great. Another adventure."

CHAPTER NINE

After the first five minutes on the spiral escalator to hell, apparently, I closed my eyes and pretended none of this was happening. The bump at the bottom was enough to jolt me out of my happy place, and I stumbled forward, windmilling my arms in an attempt to stay upright and not plunge to my death. My feet stayed firmly attached to the ground, but my wings popped out anyway, fluttering lightly in an attempt to maintain my balance.

"We're here," Petrina announced, rather unnecessarily.

"Where's here?" I asked. My efforts to keep the snark to a minimum failed.

"Under the mountain," she intoned. "Speak friend and enter."

I gritted my teeth and plastered a smile on my face. There would be a time and place to work on her Moria knowledge. Now was neither.

"I hope there are dwarves," she said. "I love dwarves and haven't seen any since I was a little girl."

That caught my attention. I knew a fair bit doubt Petrina's last few human weeks and her transformation to a vampire, but she almost never mentioned anything before the witch trials.

"You've seen dwarves? In Sweden?"

"Oh yes. There was a great hall entrance near where I grew up. They'd come out occasionally to trade for fresh meat and fish. My grandmother said that when she was young, they came four times a year, and when *her* grandmother was young, they came eight times. But when I was alive, it was only once a year, and by the time I was an adult, they didn't come at all. So few people remained who'd seen them, that they were dismissed as children's stories. It doesn't take long for things to become myth, especially pre-social media."

While Petrina was talking, I'd walked around the cavern looking for anything that screamed "magical scepter" or "this way to the combo Taco Bell/microbrewery." So far nothing. There was only one passage leading away from the cavern. I was hesitant to leave the staircase that was our way out, but my hesitation was dismissed when the escalator spiraled back up, and the faint sliver of light disappeared, leaving us trapped.

"Fuck. I guess we should follow the path that's been laid out for us," I said. "I wish Florence was here. Where is she, anyway? I haven't seen much of her lately."

No one answered me, and I glanced over at Petrina. She was looking straight ahead, face impassive as always, except for the vein pulsing in her jaw. She'd either fed very deeply before our adventure or was so angry that her vampire-low blood pressure was spiking.

"Is everything okay, Trina?" I asked. "I'm no feelings wizard, but you look upset."

"Everything's fine with me," she snapped. "Of course, I'm not the one avoiding serious conversations about my mental, emotional, and physical state before running off to the woods to learn to control the new secret magic swelling in me and threatening to break my control. I certainly haven't exploded several trees by accidentally freezing them in frustration. And I am definitely not refusing to talk about it with the one person who I am supposed to trust and confide in. So fine."

"Um." I looked to Raj for guidance, and he smiled at me encouragingly. I was on my own. "Florence has new secret magic? How?"

"How the hell should I know? It's a 'secret.'" Her air quote gesture was so sharp I felt it to my core.

"When did you notice it first?" I asked.

"On the way to the palace right after we arrived. She's had a harder time keeping her temper since you opened the last gate, but after her sister died, the smallest thing will set her off, and whatever is in the way gets iced."

"Why didn't you say something?" I asked. I already knew the answer, but I couldn't help myself.

"It's not my story, not my place," Petrina said.

"She's my best friend," I pointed out. "She's always had my back when I've struggled with my power; I should be there when she struggles."

Petrina sighed. "She asked me not to."

"I have to talk to her," I said. "This isn't okay. It could be dangerous. The next few months are gonna be high stress and high stakes. I don't mean to make this all about me. I really don't. But she could end up killing all of if she can't manage her power and her temper. Ugh. Are there therapists here? She needs to talk to someone."

"That's a great idea, actually," Petrina said. "I'm embarrassed I didn't think of it myself."

"You've got a lot going on yourself," Raj said. "You can't take care of everyone."

I looked at Petrina expectantly, but she didn't elaborate. I rolled my eyes. "C'mon. You all know my issues. They're out there for everyone to see. I'm driven and competitive and have trouble asking for and accepting help. In addition, I have self-esteem issues, particularly in regard to my age, and am trying to harness the powers I didn't know I had until a few years ago while learning to be queen of one land and planning to usurp the throne in another. On top of that, I'm terrified of heights. So tell me, Petrina. What's going on with you?"

I rounded the bend of the tunnel and looked forward expectantly. Oooh—more tunnel. Hooray.

"I miss my clan," Petrina said.

I wrinkled my nose and looked at her? "You mean in Sweden? Isn't your family dead?" I mentally slapped myself. Could I be any more insensitive?

"No, dumbass," she snapped. "In Czechia."

"When you take on a vampire clan, you are bound to them, much like a wolf pack is bound to their Alpha," Raj explained. "You have a responsibility to make sure they are fed but not overmuch. You manage locations and feeding and shelter. And the ties are both physical and mental. You can feel each member of your clan, know if they are hungry or scared or if they've gone mad. And long periods of great distance are...uncomfortable. It's harder when you're new and the ties haven't settled yet, but you can always feel it."

"They feel like home," Petrina said. "And they need me. More than you do. More than *she* does."

I SAT on a bench in the middle of a vast cavern lit with a multitude of softly glowing smokeless torches that illuminated walls laced with gold and silver and studded with precious gems. Raj and Petrina sat on either side of me, and all of us pretended we were there by choice and not shackled to the ground with silver and iron chains.

I hadn't had a chance to follow-up on Petrina's bitter statement about Florence. We'd rounded a corner, all the lights had blinked on, and we'd been blinded long enough for the shackles, which grew out of the ground with no visible intervention from any living creature, to grasp our ankles and the stone bench to slide across the floor behind us and hit our knees hard enough to make us sit. Now, instead of quizzing Petrina on her personal life, I was on high alert, looking for enemies I couldn't see and knew nothing about.

Part of the cavern wall groaned and shifted. I stared at it sure that I was imagining things. A crack appeared. It gradually widened into a massive door that must have been at least fifteen feet wide and twice as tall. Framed in the center of the entrance were five diminutive figures, each heavily armed and more heavily bearded. They strode into the room, double-edged axes casually propped over a shoulder, and metal armor clanking as they moved.

"Who are you and what do you want?" The one in the middle demanded. His armor was a little shinier, his beard longer and more elaborately braided, and his helmet had emeralds encircling the base.

I used my incredible powers of deduction to determine that he was the leader, quite possibly their king.

"I am Eleanor, Queen of the Light Sidhe," I announced, trying not to wince or sound uncertain or do anything that would reveal my discomfort with my new title. "Who are you?"

"You come into my kingdom, my home, and you don't know whose hospitality you're encroaching on?" the dwarf scoffed.

I gestured vaguely upwards and explained. "We were on the Bridge to Nowhere and found a magic escalator, and here we are!"

One of the other dwarves laughed. "You found a magic escalator leading down from the Bridge Above the Clouds and you just...got on it? And you expect us to believe you have the wisdom and experience to be ruling the Light?"

Okay. Put that way, it did seem like terrible decision making. I smiled tightly. "We are on a quest. Something that belongs to me and my people is lost, and I need to find it and, return it to its rightful home. The search led me here."

The chains binding my ankles fell away, although Petrina and Raj were not similarly unbound.

"You said you were Queen of the Light," the leader said.

"I am," I replied. "Eochid was slain on the field of battle by the actions of the disgraced consort, Cloithfinn the Traitor." I'd been advised to start adding the epithet to her name if I had to speak of her at all. I was "influencing public opinion," or, as I liked to call it, "changing hearts and minds."

"I was Eochid's heir, and now I sit on the throne."

"She's Eleanor World-Breaker, the Catalyst," Petrina said.

The leader squinted at me, a sly smile dancing at the corners of his mouth and shaking his beard. "World-breaker, eh? We have a different name for her in the dark. Different stories. World-breaker, thrice-cursed, the Twilight Queen."

Twilight Queen didn't sound so bad, but thrice-cursed was not promising. I had a lot of questions, but before I could answer them, the clanking of chains announced that my companions had been freed as well. Petrina and Raj rose and stood to flank me, one on either side and a little bit behind me.

The leader of the dwarves turned his back on us for a moment and spoke into the darkness behind him. He turned back around, and I saw he'd traded his axe for a large goblet that looked as though it'd been carved out of solid gold and set with black stones whose hidden fire flashed when the torchlight caught them. He took a long drink, then stepped forward and handed me the glass.

"To friendship and alliance," he boomed. "The kingdoms of the Fae and the dark of the Dwarves will once more unite in fellowship.

I wished I had someone here to tell me if I was making the right choices, but I didn't. Raj was silent, although I caught the faintest hint of approval from our bond. I took a deep breath. Alliances were good, and no one had warned me not to ally with the dwarves. I smiled over the rim of the opal-studded goblet and took a long drink of the crispest, most refreshing beer I'd had in a very long time. I wanted to drain the glass—it was that good, and it had been that long since I'd had regular access to beer—but figured that would be an incredibly bad way to start a new formal relationship between two kingdoms. I handed the goblet back. "Thank you, both for your friendship and for the best beer I've had in…I don't even know how long."

A genuine smile split the leader's face. "I brewed that one myself. One of the benefits of being Mjödvitnir Dróttning, Skilled Mead Wolf, Wise King is I can stay out of the mines and spend my leisure time doing what I love most. And what I love most is good ale and feasting." He patted his ample belly, then passed the goblet to the Dwarf at his right. "This is Gloni, Valiant Queen, Shining One."

I bit back my instinctive reaction to finding out that the bearded beauty at his side was his queen and bowed my head to Gloni and Mjödvitnir. Gloni drank from the goblet and passed it to Petrina.

I really wanted to hit the right tone and really loved all the epithets. I took a deep breath, mixed a little Homer and Sturluson in my head, and said, "These are my companions. Rajyapala, Throneless King of Old, Bearer of the Ruby Sword, and my consort, and his daughter Petrina, golden-haired healer, shield maiden and defender."

Petrina and Raj drank from the goblet and passed it back. The other three dwarves were introduced as members of the royal household, each with epithets attesting to their wisdom and skill in battle. After the final dwarf drained the ale, he lowered the goblet and looked at Petrina. "I know you, little Petra, golden haired. You were at the market with your amma the last year we were able to make the journey to the surface. You gave me a flower and wished me safe travels."

Petrina laughed, and her face lit up the room. "You were smaller then, and your companions called you Bifurr, the Beaver. It is good that you've earned the name Brokkr, Blacksmith. It suits you, although you will always be Bifurr to me."

I wanted to make a beaver joke so bad. I bit my tongue and gave Petrina and Brokkr a minute to catch up, before recapturing the king's attention. "Your Majesty, I am so glad that our kingdoms have found alliance again. I look forward to receiving your guidance as I learn to rule a kingdom not nearly as magnificent as your own."

Mjödvitnir held out his hands. "You are welcome in my hall. Come, let us find food and drink, then you can tell me what you seek and why your quest brought you here. Will your vampires require food and drink as well?"

"No thank you, Your Majesty," Petrina said. "We fed well before embarking on this journey and would never impose so on your hospitality."

The king protested graciously, but I could see the relief on his face. He definitely didn't want to order any of his subjects to bare their necks for the undead. I followed Mjödvitnir through another tunnel, this one well-lit with the same smokeless torches that had ringed the great hall. The pathway was level and smooth, but the walls and ceiling were rough and dotted with more gemstones and veins of precious metals. "How do you make the smokeless torches?" I asked. "They look, smell, and feel like fire...they can be manipulated like fire." I grabbed flame with my mind and drew it into me until I held a fireball in the bowl of my hand. I snapped my fingers, and the flames flew back to the torch where they'd originated. "But they give off no smoke, and they don't burn the wood that fuels them."

"It is magic, of course," Gloni said. "We have artisans skilled in working with metal and gems and ale," she glanced fondly at her husband. "And we have those skilled at manipulating the elements, just as your people do. Those with the gift of earth build and shore up our tunnels, finding new gold and gems, building safe tunnels, and restoring the earth to its natural state when they're done. The air-weavers work with the earth-delvers to create ventilation shafts and to cleanse foul air. Water-singers make sure we have wells, deep and cold, that we have ice to store our food, and weave cold water and fresh air to cool the mines when they are too hot. And we have fire-dancers, although they are few in number, and seldom as powerful as they were in the days of old. They give us light and heat and warmth, without smoke or danger."

"Wow," I said. "That sounds amazing. We have so much to learn from you."

"Alas," Gloni said. "All we have is the knowledge of the past, and even that is not complete. There have been no discoveries, no innovations, no knowledge discovered in centuries. We are stagnant."

The dwarves made a sustained noise in the back of their throats halfway between a hum and a clearing throat. It was gritty and mournful, and their grief washed over me pulling tears to the corners of my eyes.

"Now is not the time for sorrow," Mjödvitnir exclaimed, clapping Gloni and me on our backs with his massive palms. The air rushed out of my lungs, which had the dual purpose of shocking the tears away and leaving me short of breath. "My table awaits." He swept open the huge double doors and led us into his great hall.

My jaw dropped. I'd seen Lord of the Rings more times than I could count, had read countless descriptions of mead halls, and still, nothing had prepared me for this. The great hall stretched forward before me bracketed between the doors behind me and the great, blazing fireplace at the end. The room was pleasantly warm and offset the chill of the stone walls. The walls themselves were decorated with tapestries depicting great battles and greater feasts. Dragons flew through the woven skies, chased from hordes of gold by dwarven armies. Three long tables made an enormous "U" in the center of the room. A fourth, placed nearest the fireplace in the open place at the end of the horseshoe, was raised above the rest. The tables groaned beneath the weight of food and drink. Mjödvitnir strode towards the raised table and took his place in the large chair in the center, Gloni at his side, her chair equally as ornate, but better suited to her slightly smaller stature.

"Friends, allies, fair folk, join me at my table. Tonight, we feast. Tomorrow, we trade." He clapped his hands and servers ran from the shadows bearing bowls of water. I followed the dwarf king and queen to the high table, found my seat between Gloni and Skirfir, metal-smith and bow master, and dipped my hands in the bowl of water handed to me by the servants. Someone else filled my stein with a frothy amber liquid.

The king raised his glass and roared for silence. His command echoed off the walls and ceilings and the murmurs of conversation faded away.

"Dwarves, today is a day to celebrate!"

A roar of approval washed over the room and mugs were tapped together in celebration. Once it was quiet again, Mjödvitnir continued his speech.

"Instead of invasion and a call to war, Gloni and I found a queen and a quest. New alliances have been forged and old enmities forgotten. Let us raise our cups to Eleanor, Queen of the Light Sidhe, World-Breaker, Thrice Cursed, Twilight Queen. Through her, the magic flows again, bringing new hope, new knowledge, new magic. To Eleanor!"

"To Eleanor!" the hall of dwarves roared. I raised my glass in return and drank deeply, hoping they weren't going to demand a speech. Fortunately for everyone, speeches were not required—at least not before dinner. Servants brought out trays of meat and fresh bread and roasted root vegetables, the aromas permeating the air and making my stomach growl loud enough to be heard over the clanking of cutlery against plates and tables. I dug into the food laid out before me and tried really hard not to think about three words Mjödvitnir had said in his speech.

Old enmities forgotten. I hoped they could be forgotten on all sides, or I was in trouble.

WHEN I WOKE UP, the first thing I heard was jackhammers. I guess my bedroom cave must be pretty close to the mining tunnels. I opened my eyes, and the light from the torches near the door nearly blinded me causing a sharp pain to shoot through my head and lodge behind my eyeballs. My mouth was tacky from dehydration and my stomach was roiling. Was I hungover?

I rolled to one side and pushed myself into a sitting position. My head spun and my stomach went from agitating to full-on armed insurrection.

I was definitely hungover. I was alone in the room, although it looked like Raj had spent the night with me. There was no note letting me know where he'd gone and nothing that indicated what time it was.

I found my clothes which had been laundered and pressed and a large tub full of steaming water behind the divider on the far side of the room. Next to the tub was a pitcher of cold, clear water and a covered tray next to some fruit and dry toast.

I chugged a glass of water and slipped into the tub, moaning in satisfaction as the heat relaxed muscles I hadn't known were tense. I sipped on some more water and nibbled on the toast, careful not to drop any crumbs into my bath.

When I felt almost human again—or almost Fae, I guess—I dried off and dressed, then lifted the lid off the tray. There, still warm, was a plate with more toast, this time with butter and jam, a short stack, two eggs, and several sausage links. There was also coffee. Honest to god coffee with a small pitcher of cream next to it. I looked around suspiciously. First beer and then coffee? Had I died? Had the escalator been an illusion causing me to plummet to my death? How had I ended up in heaven?

I decided that it was more important to get through the coffee and breakfast than think about the afterlife. If I was dead, I'd still be dead after breakfast and could figure things out then.

I'd just finished wiping the last bits of egg and syrup off my plate when someone knocked at the door. I swallowed. "Come in!"

The stone door slid open noiselessly, and Gloni walked in, her beard braids tied with a variety of shiny ribbons today. "How are you feeling, Your Majesty?" she asked.

"Fantastic now," I said. "Thank you so much, Your Majesty."

She laughed. "Call me Gloni, and I will call you Eleanor if you don't mind."

"Please do," I said. "It's a bit silly otherwise." I grinned at her. It was kinda nice talking to another queen. I wrinkled my nose. That was still weird as fuck to think. Another queen. Because I was a queen. Gah. Queen. What a weird word when you started to think about it.

"Are you okay, Eleanor?" Gloni asked.

"Yes. Just thinking about the absurdity of me being a queen. I grew up on the other side, you know. Earth. I was thirty-four, which in earth years is more than one-third of the average lifespan, when I found out I was Fae, and not only Fae, but royalty. It's only been a few years—time is funny when you hop back and forth so much—since then, and now I'm Queen of the Light Sidhe. I still feel human half the time, but I'm immortal, more or less. And queen. And having small talk about my existential crisis with another queen."

Gloni reached out and grabbed my hands in hers. "Breathe, Eleanor. It'll be okay. It's an enormous adjustment for anyone not born to it to take the throne." She let go of one hand and pulled me along by the other, leading me down the vast hallway. "We dwarves don't have much of a hierarchy system, at least compared to some other folks. When Mjödvitnir and I die, new rulers will be chosen by popular vote. It's usually a great fighter or a skilled artisan and someone who has shown they can excel in battle and in diplomacy. Dwarves are hard-headed and short-tempered, and it takes a steady hand to manage this many people. I'd never imagined myself queen, but after the previous king, a widower, died during the last great battle when we drove back the alliance of giants and rock trolls, there was little doubt that I would be elevated to this position. I was the only one in the king's regiment to survive the ambush. I not only saved the rest of my people, I led them to victory. It was inevitable that I'd be chosen to rule. Mjödvitnir had been the sweetheart I left behind. He often takes the front seat because he's louder and more jocular than me, but we rule as equals, and we rule because I was chosen."

"Wow." I didn't know what to say. "It's so great to meet another queen who's also a war leader. It's not as common on Earth—it's hard to find anyone who believes a woman can lead anything, much less countries or armies."

"That's because men struggle with it so much, and they want to believe that they're superior. Anything that's difficult for them is impossible for anyone else," Gloni said. "It can be the same here with the young ones, although that attitude doesn't last very long. Not if they want to see their mothers and sisters and find wives, if they want them."

I had a lot of questions about the structures of dwarven society, the nature of rule, interpersonal relationships, beards, and how to start a trade agreement to import ale and coffee into my kingdom, but before I could ask, Gloni stopped in front of a wall. It didn't look any different than any of the other walls. At least not until Gloni said, "Open up."

Cracks appeared in the wall in the shape of a door. It opened silently inward. We waited until it'd opened all the way then walked through. Mjödvitnir was standing in the middle of the nearly empty room. Only the three of us were present, and the only thing in the room was a...tree. A tree with green leaves and ruby red apples grew in the center of the windowless room that was far below the surface of the earth. It grew out of the solid rock floor and stretched up towards the solid rock ceiling.

"I don't know if this is what you're looking for," Mjödvitnir said. "But I'm guessing it is. What else could this be but an enchanted fairy item trying to hide itself?"

CHAPTER TEN

Several hours later, I walked out of the hidden door Mjödvitnir and Gloni promised would drop us a couple miles upriver of the camp. In addition to the orb of the Dark Throne, I was now the proud new owner of a scepter that liked to pretend it was an apple tree trunk. I couldn't wait to find out what part of the tree the crown was. My money was on canopy, but I was keeping my bet private for now.

I paused on the outcropping that overlooked the river and the valley below. For a minute, I thought the dwarves had played a trick on us and sent us to an inescapable ledge then slammed the door behind us. I checked over my shoulder. The door was definitely closed now. Maybe if I knocked real loud, they'd let me back in, but I had a sinking suspicion that the guard and artisan cheese maker who'd escorted us out was already hightailing it back to the main hall and away from the "creepy outer tunnels," as he put it, inspiring confidence in everyone. Or at least in me.

I looked around, but all I saw was the edge leading to a long, long drop onto the jagged rocks below. After all this time, I couldn't believe that this was the way I was going to die.

"I found a path!" Petrina said, pointing straight down.

I inched over to where she was pointing and looked down. My head swam and my stomach threatened to rebel. My back was against the cliff wall almost before I registered my feet were moving. When I opened my eyes again after the vertigo dissipated, Petrina was trying unsuccessfully to hide her laughter behind a hand. Raj was wearing an expressionless enigmatic smile, but I could see the corners of his mouth twitching.

"What?" I demanded. "You know I hate heights. It's not nice to laugh at someone's phobia."

"I'm sorry, my sweet," Raj said. "It is unkind of us. But you seem to have forgotten one thing in your overwhelming fear."

"And what's that?" I snapped.

"I can fly. You can fly. We don't have to walk down that ridiculous trail of a thousand switchbacks," he said. "Shift. Fly. Do a few loop-the-loops and land on the ground below. Petrina and I will meet you there. You know the height doesn't bother you when you have wings."

I took a deep breath. He was right. I looked around. There wasn't nearly enough room on this ledge to shift into my full dragon form, but I didn't want to do this half-assed. Or half-bodied, if you will. "You go first," I said. "I need as much room as I can get."

"As you wish," Raj said. He bowed, took my hand and kissed the back of it, then turned it over and planted a soft kiss in my palm. His fangs nicked the soft skin of my hand and the heat and thrill zinged through my body igniting the banked fire in my core. I watched while he licked up a drop of blood.

I met his eyes and remembered our first dinner together and his illicit sip of blood. I'd been his from that moment. From before—since the first time I'd seen him when I'd been negotiating the release of the hostage I'd taken in his ill-advised scheme to kidnap me and lock me up to prevent the apocalypse.

Good times. Who knew you could go from a failed kidnapping plot, travel through half a year of double entendres and sexual tension, and end up here? On a ledge with the love of my life and his gorgeous undead daughter, ready to fly. My smile grew. "I love you, old man," I said.

"I know," he replied, then held his hand out to Petrina and jumped. Nerd.

I looked around the ledge and tried to determine the best position to shift into my dragon self without losing my balance and plummeting over the edge before I was ready. I finally settled in the center, stripped down and bundled my clothing into a bag—should've done that before and handed my clothes off to Raj—then inhaled, closed my eyes, and pictured my dragon form. Long and lithe with four solid legs tipped with shining claws. A long serpentine neck, tiny horns adorning my reptilian face, and two nostrils, one long tongue, and sharp, piercing fangs. A long tail balanced the neck, and my huge, batlike wings that stretched out as wide as I was long. My iridescent purple scales caught the light and swallowed it. I was light and darkness at the same time.

My body changed and reformed itself. The cold wind caught me, and I shivered as I shifted. I couldn't delay long—the cold of the mountain range would slow my blood and send me into torpor. Heat built in my belly, trying to counteract the chill in the air. I exhaled explosively and watched as twin columns of smoke rose from my snout. My mouth gaped open in a toothy grin and I roared. The sound shook the trees, causing snow to fall from the greater heights, and a stream of fire belched forth, melting everything in its path. I wanted to bellow again but causing an avalanche might not be the best decision.

I shifted slightly and stretched my wings out. I grabbed my bundle of clothes in one claw, lumbered forward two steps, leaned forward, and waited to feel the wind catch my wings. As soon as I felt the updraft, I launched myself into the air.

Bliss.

Flying was better than anything I could've imagined. The stress of leading, the anxiety about leading a conquering army, the guilt over everything that had happened over the last few years... It all fell away. Up here, it was just me and the sky. I did a couple barrel rolls to warm up, then went into a twenty-minute session of fancy flying. I chased my tail through the air, dive bombed a cloud, scared a flock of geese, and tried to pirouette on my tail. The last didn't work, but a free fall is only scary if you don't have wings.

Once the chill of the high elevation air started to outweigh the warmth I'd built through the airy dancing, I looked around for the place I was supposed to meet Raj and Petrina.

"Where are you?" I asked. The sun was nearly down, and the landscape was fading into a monochromatic palette of purples and blacks.

"Almost right below you," Raj said. *"Do you see the lake?"*

I did a lazy circle, flying lower than I'd dared when the sun had been high in the sky. A smooth dark area took shape; there were trees lining the sides closest to the mountain range and a vast valley spilled out the other direction.

"Found it," I said.

"Land on the valley side. We're waiting for you."

I circled in for a landing and dropped on the beach. I was shivering by the time I shifted and pulled my clothes back on. They were a little worse for wear—my acrobatics had caused me to forget I was holding them, and I'd pierced holes in everything.

"Nice crotchless panties," Raj said, taking form as he stepped out of the trees at the edge of the lake.

"I just wanted to be sexy for you," I told him, flinging the useless underpants at him. "How far to the camp?"

"Less than an hour if we walk. About ten minutes if you want to take the vampire express," Raj said.

"I am always ready to get my ticket punched on the vampire express," I said, wiggling my eyebrows suggestively.

"Ugh," Petrina said. "Can you carry us both at the same time? It's the only way to make sure you two make it there with clothing intact." She gave me a once-over with pursed lips, then added, "Mostly intact. Eleanor, you are the queen. Have a little dignity."

I grinned at her. "They didn't hire me for my dignity. They hired me for my kick-ass fashion sense, or, more accurately, I inherited the throne from the man who passed me off as his daughter for reasons I still don't understand, but probably include securing the succession and sticking it to Cloithfinn. Possibly as a way into the Dark Realm. I don't know."

"Still working on that subterfuge and sarcasm?" Petrina asked.

"Every day," I sighed.

Raj picked us both up and shot into the air. A few minutes later, he landed in the middle of the makeshift square in our camp. Three guards moved towards us, weapons at the ready. I stood up straight and mentally ran through all the ways I could convince them I belonged there, and was, in fact queen. The first guard skidded to a halt about ten feet away, dropped his sword down to his side, and knelt, bowing his head.

"Your Majesty," he said.

The other two guards followed suit.

I guess I didn't need my bona fides after all.

"Please stand," I said. "There's no need to kneel in my presence." They stood and shifted nervously from foot to foot.

I either needed to give them a job or dismiss them, I realized. "Can one of you send word that I need a hot bath prepared and food and wine in my tent?" One of the guards sped off into the night. "And please, find Connor, Clement, Florence, Acantha, and Alanna and let them know that I need to speak to them in the main pavilion in one hour." The other two guards disappeared into the darkness.

My stomach growled. I'd eaten well with the dwarves but shifting and flying always took a lot out of me. I looked back at Raj and Petrina. "Do you need something? Someone?"

"Yes," Petrina said. "I need to eat and bathe. And find fresh clothes. I'll be in the pavilion in an hour for your big reveal."

Raj dropped a kiss on my head. "I'll be back in our tent in time to scrub your back."

The vampires disappeared in the opposite direction of the guards, and I trudged slowly back towards my tent. A whirring noise caught my attention, and I whirled around to figure out what it was. A crossbow bolt lodged itself in my shoulder where seconds before my throat had been. Pain exploded through me—it was worse than being shot with bullets. The bolt was iron—I could feel the poison spreading through my bloodstream with every beat of my heart. I fell to my knees. I wanted to call out but couldn't open my mouth. My vision grayed around me, and the last thing I heard were footsteps and someone yelling, "The queen's been shot!"

The world went dark.

I'D BEEN CONFINED to my tent for a week since being shot by a poison-enhanced iron bolt. I'd been close to death the first time I was poisoned, and I'd been shot in Savannah—I did not enjoy the experience of mixing the two.

Raj, Florence, Connor, and Petrina were taking turns guarding me and serving my food. Technically, we still didn't know who'd shot me, but I don't think it was any great mystery. Who else had tried to kill me more times than I could remember?

My only hope was that he hadn't stuck around long enough to learn that he'd failed, and somewhere, somehow, I'd take him by surprise and, after pinning him to the ground with some fast-growing bamboo, I'd disembowel him, taunt him a little, then leave him to the tender mercies of Hedge Antilles, Jr. and whatever wildlife happened by.

I'd missed the big reveal—Raj and Petrina had told the others what we'd done and where. I gathered I was in a bit of trouble for opening relations with the dwarves, but the chagrin seemed half-hearted at best. No one would let Clement see the scepter, and he was irritated. He paced outside my tent at all hours and would occasionally stick his head in to glower about overprotective "Earthers" who didn't know how to let a Fae heal in peace.

Today was the first day I'd felt well enough to take a short walk outside. I was flanked by too many guards, many of whom were suffering from a guilt complex due to their not being psychic enough to prevent an assassination attempt by a slippery snake that I'd failed to capture and kill too many times already. I'd spoken to Alanna about it, and she promised to do what she could to assuage their guilt, but I wasn't seeing the effects of it yet.

I straightened my shoulders, winced, and headed off towards the pavilion for a strategy meeting. Now that we had our three objects of power, we were ready to test my gate opening abilities. As we approached the tent, I heard rustling in the bushes to my left and spun around, senses on high alert. It turns out that surviving an assassination attempt is hell on a person's startle reflex. Every small noise or movement out of the corner of my eye sent a surge of adrenaline though my body as my fight or flight kicked in.

There were people in the shrubbery. I waved my guards back and signaled them to be quiet, then drew my sword, redoubled my air shields to deflect anything Finn could throw at me, and crept forward.

I was about to leap into the undergrowth and stab first. I was still a little uncertain if I would bother asking any questions afterwards. Every time I paused, he escaped. Before I could decapitate anyone, a voice halted me in my tracks.

"Did you leave me behind on purpose?" Florence asked.

"No. Of course not," Petrina said. "Raj and I went to check on Eleanor, and on our way back discovered the secret entrance to the dwarven kingdom."

"Will you tell me before you do leave me behind?" Florence's voice cracked, and the raw emotion in her voice brought tears to my eyes. I'd never heard her sound so vulnerable.

"Yes," Petrina said. "I will tell you. And I will invite you to come with me."

"And I'll invite you to stay," Florence replied.

"I love you," Trina said. "Always."

"I'm sorry," Florence said. "I thought this would be better. I thought we'd be better. I just can't."

There was a rustling of cloth. "It's okay," Petrina said. "You're young and raw from loss and just learning what your power means. I love you enough to let you go if that's what you need. Maybe in a hundred years we can find our way back to each other."

"No," Florence said. My heart broke in tandem with hers. "You will have moved on by then. You'll be tied in blood and heart to someone else."

"Are you ending things now because you've seen someone else in my future?" Petrina asked, her voice tight with fury. "You do not get to decide for me. The future is mutable. You know that. Perhaps the only reason I do end up with someone else is because of this. Now. This moment when you push me away for the last time. Are you sure this is what you want? Or are you doing this because you think I deserve what you saw in your vision?"

"I saw two futures," Florence said. "And I know which one ends better."

"If you loved me as you've professed, you'd talk to me. Tell me what you've seen. Allow me to be an active participant in decisions about my future. I'm old, Florence. I've loved and lost before. I know what risks there are in any relationship, but I prefer to take those risks with my eyes open. Have you learned nothing from your fuck-ups with Eleanor?"

My eyes widened. Petrina almost never cursed. She was pissed. And I was eavesdropping. I had a penchant for being present for their relationship milestones, and there was a shrubbery involved last time, too. That one was a potted palm in a hotel lobby, but I was starting a trend. A deeply uncomfortable and completely unethical trend.

I pivoted and took a wide detour around them and walked the rest of the way to the pavilion. Raj, Connor, Alanna, Tanwen, and Clement were waiting for me. Florence arrived a few minutes later. A frosty wind announced her presence before she walked through the doorway. Petrina was several more minutes behind Florence, and her eyes were rimmed in red. She looked at me, and I knew she knew I'd heard part of their conversation.

I didn't know what to do or say. Florence was my best friend—had been for ages. And Petrina was a good friend and my kind of daughter-in-law. I didn't want to pick sides, and I knew they'd never make me. And this wasn't really about me anyway. Florence was making a mistake and hurting two of my favorite people in the process. She was letting her grief and her worries about her control talk her into bad decision making, and all I could do was support her as much as she'd let me and let Petrina know that I loved her too.

"Can we get started?" Clement said. "It's been a week since these fools returned from their palaver with the dwarves, and we're not any closer to a solution than we were before."

"I must have heard you wrong," Connor said. "Did you just refer to the queen and her consort as fools?"

Clement shifted in his seat, then grabbed the wineskin and poured himself a glass of wine. He drank deeply and took several breaths before looking at me and nodding his head. "I am sorry, Your Majesty. I spoke without thinking and let my emotions rule my tongue. It will not happen again."

I smiled as graciously as I could. He'd actually apologized, which is something most Fae avoided doing as it opened a debt. "I accept your apology," I said. "Now, let's get on with it."

Raj handed me a glass of wine, and I leaned back into the cushions of the chair I was sitting in. I was still very sore and easily tired, which Clement knew. Everyone was on edge tonight, and I didn't know how to relax them. So I didn't try. I grabbed the velvet bag I kept on my belt at all times and placed it in on the table.

"As you know, we were successful in finding the scepter. The dwarves were guarding it and relinquished it to me freely. Also, they have beer *and* coffee, and we're trade partners now. Someone figure out how that works. Anyway. I have the orb. I have the scepter. We have Raj's sword. Between the three objects of power and my own innate abilities as the Gate Opener/World Breaker/Catalyst/Thrice-Cursed/The Twilight Queen. So many names for just one person."

"With any luck, you'll end up with as many epithets as years," Connor said. "That is the mark of a ruler."

"I'd love to know more about the thrice-cursed and twilight queen monikers," I said. "But dwarves are remarkably close-mouthed when they want to be, even when you pour a barrel of ale into them. But, that's neither here nor there. What's important is that I can feel gate energy, I can see the entire Fae Realm mapped out before me, and we have the objects of power. It's time for next steps."

"What do you propose?" Alanna asked through Tanwen.

"I propose a test," I said. "I am still healing, and don't want to rely on my strength or stamina for the full army as yet. However, I believe that I can hold a gate long enough to send a few scouts through to let us know where we'll come out, what the conditions are there for hiding and housing the army, and to see if they can pick up news of the queen and castle."

"If you can't hold open the gate, how are you going to get word back from the scouts?" Clement scoffed.

"I have my ways," I said. "I'd rather not be too explicit, but there are those here who can vouch for the reliability of the information I will receive."

"Who then will you send?" Connor asked.

This was the hard part. Raj reached for my hand under the table and squeezed it gently. I took a deep breath. "Raj, as my trusted consort, will lead the scouts. He has, with Alanna's help, selected four others to accompany him. They are all Fae with strong elemental abilities, experience in the forests, and skill with the bow. Two are of Dark Fae origin, and will be able to easily blend in with the locals, should it be necessary. The others, and Raj, are all skilled at glamourie."

"Is that your total party, then?" Connor asked Raj. "Five is a good number for a stealthy operation."

"Six," Petrina said. "I will go. My magic differs from Fae magic and will escape detection. I also have healing magic, which might come in handy on such a mission. There are other healers here, so my presence is not needed."

The last statement sounded like a barb to me, and I winced in sympathy. I wanted to look to Florence for her opinion about Petrina's volunteerism but didn't.

"Very well," I said. "Six. I will open the gate tomorrow as the sun sinks behind the mountains. But now, I need to rest." I stood, nodded to my council, and walked out of the pavilion.

I POURED a glass of wine and stared moodily at the entrance to the tent I shared with Raj. It was our last night together for a while. Other than when I went with Connor to the Dark Realm to rescue Anoka, we hadn't spent much time apart in the last few years—not since New Orleans and our reconciliation in Santa Fe. Except when I was unconscious and he was trapped in a ruby, but we were technically together then, so I wasn't sure it counted.

Raj was tying up loose ends with Alanna for the scouting mission, and then had walked Petrina back to the tent she shared with Florence. My friend was nowhere to be found, so Raj stayed to comfort Trina. I was getting bits and pieces from him through our link. I couldn't begrudge Petrina her sire. She'd had a shit night for sure. But I needed him. If it was to be our last night together for the foreseeable future, I needed to be held. To be kissed. To be fucked into exhaustion so I could sleep without worrying.

"I can do all of those things," Raj said from the doorway.

"How's Petrina?" I asked. "I didn't mean to summon you with my angst. I know she needs you more than I do right now."

Raj poured his own glass of wine. "She will be okay. Not today, and maybe not for a while, but she is strong. And she needs rest and sustenance now. Not me. She'll have me all to herself for a father/daughter bonding vacation soon enough. Tonight, you need me. And even more importantly, I need you." He threw back the wine and stared at me. His eyes flashed red, matching the rubies on the hilt of his sword.

A shiver of anticipation raised goosebumps on my arms. "Where do you want to start?" I asked. "I needed three things, so are we starting with the holding, the kissing, or the fucking?"

"I believe you requested to be fucked into exhaustion?" Raj said. He unbelted his sword with one hand and let it fall to the floor.

I set down my wine and undressed, tossing my clothes in a heap against the side of the tent.

Raj moved towards me, stalking me until I fell backwards onto the bed. He crawled up between my legs, glass of wine still in his hand, and looked down at me. "I think I'll start with the kissing," he declared. He tilted the wine glass and splashed wine across my abdomen, then chased the alcohol with his tongue, lapping it up. Kisses and nips followed his tongue until all the wine was gone. Then he repeated the process on my breasts. Wine pooled between them, and Raj drank from me. He took the wine from my skin, then pierced my breast with his fangs.

Over and over, he spilled wine, then kissed it away. I was burning for him within minutes. My hips left the bed and tipped towards him, asking—no demanding—what I couldn't articulate.

"Do you want something more?" Raj asked. He dipped his fingers in the glass he'd set down by the bed and traced wine-soaked designs over my skin, then erased them with his tongue.

"Please," I begged. "Please."

He dipped his fingers in the wine once more and dipped his hand into my wet folds, then rubbed them over my clit. His mouth followed, and he sucked the hard, velvety nub into his mouth and swirled his tongue around it. "Is this what you want?" he asked against my skin, vibrating the delicate skin at my core. His fingers sought out my slit, and moved in and out, spreading my wetness around while I bucked and moaned my pleasure.

"More," I gasped.

Raj slid up the bed to lay beside me, then rolled over and quickly stripped, then he rolled me onto my hands and knees and moved behind me, entering me in one smooth motion. He held there for a moment, then began to thrust into me. He grabbed my long braid with one hand and pulled back, sending tingles of pleasure across my scalp. Those nerve endings connected with every other erogenous zone in my body and elicited a scream of pleasure. I took a brief moment to congratulate myself on my habit of always setting up sound-proof shields around my personal dwelling, before Raj's cock pushed away all rational thoughts.

I rode a wave of ecstasy, never quite cresting it, until I was sure I'd lose my mind for the pleasure and frustration it was causing. Then Raj changed his rhythm slightly and pulled my hips up and back. His right hand reached around and found my clit, and he rubbed it in time with his thrusts. Seconds later, I found my release and my mind shattered with my orgasm. Raj followed me into the abyss.

After cleaning up, I crawled back into bed and into his arms. "That was magnificent," I said.

"It's a dirty job, but someone's got to do it," he said.

I punched him lightly on the arm, then snuggled against him. "Just one more thing I needed," I said.

"I will hold you as long as I can," he said.

Our lips met in the darkness. I could feel my eyes drooping with exhaustion. "Forever," I answered.

CHAPTER ELEVEN

I stood at the highest crest of the Bridge to Nowhere and tried really hard not to think about it. I held the scepter in my right hand and the orb in my left. Raj's sword was at my waist. Raj and Petrina, along with the others chosen for this mission, were at the far side of the bridge facing the solid mountain. It was time.

"It will be okay." Raj's mental voice wrapped me in a caress. *"We'll stay in touch. I love you."*

I raised the scepter and the orb above my head, wished I had a third hand for the sword, and closed my eyes. I could see the gate energy in the side of the mountain ahead of me—it was alive, but lacked anchors, structure, and will. It was raw, pulsing energy without a set destination. There was too much energy to simply direct—it was alive. Greedy. It wanted more and wasn't picky about where it came from.

I felt it reaching out to me and slapped it back. The tendrils then went looking for other power sources. I watched, eyes still closed, curious to see who it would seek out first. Curling tentacles of pure gate power twisted around, darting through the ether like a bloodhound looking for a scent. And like a hunting dog, they came to attention and pointed. I followed the direction of their attention. It was no surprise that Florence, Alanna, Connor, and Clement were targeted. I noted the others who'd become targets; they'd be important additions to my council. As I watched, the tendril targeted on Florence started swirling and twisting around her, but she blinked out of existence and the gate energy closed on nothing.

I gasped, and my eyes flew open. Florence was standing in the same place she'd been a moment ago, looking as unperturbed as always. I kept my eyes open and let the gate sight wash over me again. This time, with the gate-world vision overlaying the real-world, I could watch as Florence dropped out of sight. She'd completely disappeared on the magical plane. I added that to my list of questions for Florence when I cornered her later.

But for now, it was probably best if I gathered the gate energy and used it for its true purpose.

I closed my eyes again and called the energy to me. Once more, I raised the symbols of my throne and of my power over my head and spread my arms out to create a perfect triangle between orb, scepter, and the sword at my waist. Lines of energy connected the objects of power and flowed through me. Across the bridge, the energy was inversely mirrored. I drew the gate energy to me, filtered it through my power objects, and sent it back into the gate itself, creating a six-pointed, three-dimensional portal. I couldn't tell what power anchored this gate—there must be something to have created such a long-lived and stable gate, and right now it didn't matter. I concentrated on keeping the energy stream flowing smoothly—first through me, then through the gate, then spun through the void and back to me.

I opened my eyes to watch. The gate spiraled open like a camera lens, or like that old sci-fi movie with James Spader, and beyond it I could see forest, dark and tangled and twisted.

"Go!" I said to Raj. "It's stable and safe."

He stepped forward, leading his small company through the opening. I waited until I got the signal that they were all through and out of range of the gate, then slowed the flow of energy, siphoning it back into the gate without taking more, until it closed and disappeared.

My shoulders ached—I hadn't noticed how much effort it was taking until it was over, but my arms were trembling when I lowered them. I dropped the orb into the pouch at my waist, then slipped the scepter in after it. And then I collapsed in a heap in the middle of the impossibly high, OSHA violating bridge.

"I'm tired," I said to anyone who was in earshot. I could feel myself falling asleep as the exhaustion and cold threatened to overtake me. Right before I passed out, I remembered something.

Raj and I couldn't communicate between realms.

Fuck.

I can't believe I hadn't remembered—that no one had remembered. I marched up to the mountain, determined to pull him back until we could figure out a way around this weakness. I pulled his stupid ruby blade so I could pull on its power, and a piece of paper fluttered out and fell at my feet.

"Don't worry. I'll find my way back. Love always. Rajyapala."

"Fucking vampire!" I yelled at the mountain, although his confidence bolstered mine.

In response, the mountain dropped a boulder on me.

Something shoved me out of the way, and I skidded to a halt at the edge of the bridge against a daring pine tree trying to make a life for itself. I watched as the boulder that had been falling towards my head a moment before bounced off the glacier that had suddenly appeared where I'd been standing and angled off to dive into the river below.

It seemed like forever before I heard the splash that announced it'd reached its final destination, and I hugged the pine tree as a new wave of vertigo dizzied me.

"Stay back!" Florence yelled. "Don't let them see you!"

"Who?" I screamed.

"Giants!" she said. "There are giants attacking!"

"Actually, those are rock trolls," Connor said. "And only a few. Giants are much, much bigger."

I looked up, straining my eyes to try to see the creatures big enough to make Florence think giant. There was nothing there. Then a peak moved and separated, and I realized that the mountain at the end of the bridge wasn't nearly as tall or jagged as I'd thought. The peaks were alive. And not with the sound of music. Nope. Nothing so fun and anti-Nazi as that. This was the sound of unintelligible grunts and falling boulders.

"How do we get rid of them?" I yelled at Connor.

"We don't," he replied, sounding altogether way too calm for someone dodging boulders as big as a house. "We need to get out of here and let them get this out of their system. They're very territorial, but also lazy. They won't chase us; they'll go back to sleep."

"I'll hold them off," Florence said, voice filled with grim determination. "Take Eleanor and the others and get out of here."

"You're coming, too," Connor said. "If we run for it, we'll be out of range before they've noticed we've moved. You're not going to stand here and make a desperate last stand."

"He's right, Flo," I said, hoping the hated nickname would get her moving. "Either we all go, or none of us go."

"Fine," she growled. "But I am bringing up the rear."

I crept past her and grabbed Connor's hand.

"You can do this," he said to me, squeezing my hand comfortingly. "I've got you."

"Let's go!" I said.

We sprinted past Florence. I heard her start running as soon as we were by but couldn't concentrate on anything but the end of the bridge. Boulders hurled by us, but by the time we were at the high middle point, they were crashing well behind us. We slowed our run, then stopped. I leaned over, put my palms on my knees, and tried to catch my breath. Florence ran by me seconds later and skidded to a halt. The three of us turned and looked back towards the mountain side. It'd returned to stillness, but the jagged peaks no longer had patches of snow, and they were not an exact match to the formations that'd been there before.

"Rock trolls?" I screeched. "Why are they here? Why are they at all?

And why has no one given me a primer on what to expect wandering around this land?"

"I thought they were extinct in the west," Connor said.

"Is this the west?" I asked. "This is the first I've heard of "here" having a direction. Just admit that you've no intention of giving me any useful information and be done with it."

"We're west of a lot of places," he shrugged. "And this is the first time I've seen a rock troll since I was young."

I took a deep breath, closed my eyes, and counted to ten. When I opened them, he was still there, serene and smug. "I have never wanted to punch someone in the face as much I want to hit you right now." I channeled my inner peace and smiled. "In addition to rock trolls, are there any other creatures we may or may not encounter that might be hostile?"

"It's hard to say," Connor hedged. "Hostile is such a subjective term. From a certain point of view, the rock trolls weren't hostile, just territorial."

"Can the 'certain point of view' bullshit, Obi Wan. What else is out there? Rock trolls, check. Giants? Manticores? Ogres? Motherfucking orcs?"

"There are giants, but they're usually don't leave the northern wastes. I've never seen a manticore—" he saw me giving him my hard stare and revised mid-statement "—nor have I ever heard of one in the realm. I think those might be an earth creation. Ogres are misunderstood—they just want to be left alone to hide in their caves and disembowel the odd farm animal from time to time. And orcs are a definite no. Maybe Tolkien took a lot of his inspiration from the Fae Plane, but not all of it."

"Wait, what?" I asked.

"When this is all over, I can take you to Rivendell," Connor promised. "But I can't take you to Mordor or the Lonely Mountain, and I can't introduce you to an orc."

I digested this new information as we walked back toward our encampment. It wasn't until Connor left me to go find a hot bath and fresh clothes that I realized that once again, Connor had said a lot of words with very little substance. I turned to Florence to invite her to share my evening meal and a bottle of wine, but she'd already disappeared. She was avoiding me. I knew the signs—she'd been writing them on every wall we passed since we'd opened the final gate—and these were unmistakable.

I'd give her one more day while I worked with my advisors to prepare the troops to move through the gate, and then I'd confront her. Not only was she violating the best friend's code by keeping secrets, she was violating the safety of our mission by hiding her new abilities. It hurt that she hadn't come to me, but I couldn't let that consume me now. I needed to be there for her, whether she wanted it or not.

PETRINA
INTERLUDE

Petrina whipped around as the gate crashed closed behind her. She hadn't expected the noise—the other gates she'd walked through had closed unobtrusively. The others. Plural. Gate hopping was becoming a habit. She shook her head and looked around, trying to get her bearings and trying not to think about what she was leaving behind.

If you'd told her three years ago that she'd be on a mad quest punctuated with strolls through portals created by the Fae who'd seduced her father, Petrina would've laughed. And if you'd added that she'd be nursing a cracked heart because the witch she'd fallen in love with was slipping away, she would've gently suggested that whoever was willing to make such outrageous claims needed to seek medical assistance.

She knew she was spinning thoughts to distract herself. She'd been brave and given a good speech, but inside she was dying. Whoever invented that stupid saying about setting free the ones you love should die. Preferably at the end of a dirty blade. The thought of being the one to slide a rusty sword into the offender's guts and wiggle it around for a bit made her feel a little better. A smiled spread across her face.

"I don't know what you're thinking, but whenever you smile like that, I know someone is marked for death," Raj said, walking up beside her and leading two horses.

"No one in specific," she answered. "Just the people who invent trite clichés."

"They deserve to die slowly," Raj agreed. "Do you need help with your horse?"

Petrina flipped him off and mounted in one graceful motion. He smiled and did the same.

"You got all your best traits from me," Raj said. "It makes a father proud."

"At least I didn't get your looks," Petrina retorted. "I'm gorgeous."

Raj scoffed. "I'm the jewel of Kanauj. People of every gender fought to grace my bed."

"You didn't make them compete," Petrina said. "You let them all in."

Raj shrugged. "I made them fight a little. I was a terrible person when I was young."

"You were terrible when?" Petrina teased.

"I'm much better now. A thousand years did wonders for my ego."

"I can't even imagine how immense it must have been then, if this is humility."

"You're an unruly brat," Raj said. "You're grounded. No phone. No television. And definitely no boys."

"I promise, Father. I'll be good."

Raj nudged his horse closer to her and reached out to touch her hand. "I know I'm making light right now, but I can feel the hurt pouring from you. If you need anything at all—a shoulder to cry on, an ear to listen, or a poisoned dagger in the dark for the one who hurt you—let me know."

"Thank you." Tears stung the corners of her eyes and she blinked furiously to hold them back. "I'll be okay. It's not my first time."

"A person doesn't get used to heartache," Raj said. "Whether it's the first time or the tenth. It all hurts. I've been through it enough times that I'm qualified to give a TED talk."

Petrina laughed, as Raj had wanted her to. She glanced over his shoulder to the others who'd come with them. She knew they would prove useful—having Fae with them was vital for this mission to the Dark Realm—but she was nostalgic for the days when she and Raj rode alone because no one else could keep up. "We should go," she said, pointing her chin at the patient Fae waiting.

"There will be time to talk later," Raj agreed. "But it's later than it should be, and we need to find a secure place to camp for the night and get our bearings."

Petrina glanced at the sky. She hadn't walked in daylight since the morning Raj had saved her from burning, and she still had trouble remembering that the sun could be used to mark the passage of time. A couple centuries away from the light—and a couple decades before that when everything was too light or too dark—and the sun's passage in a strange new plane became meaningless. She shrugged to herself, leaned forward to encourage her horse to get going, and followed the Fae into the forest.

A COUPLE HOURS LATER, they were housed in an abandoned barn set in a valley with a stream rushing through it. The Fae built a small fire, and through either magic or woodscraft—likely a combination of both—they kept the smoke from rising and betraying their location. While the Fae cooked their evening meal, Raj and Petrina made comfortable nests in the hayloft, ostensibly to keep a better watch, but also to separate themselves from the Fae they didn't know well enough to trust.

Raj leaned against the window frame, scanning the valley in front of them. The light was nearly gone, which would make it easier to spot a casual approacher with a lantern or torch, and hard to see someone of ill intent. "Do you want to talk?" he asked softly enough that even the Fae wouldn't hear.

Petrina glanced down at the others anyway. None of them glanced up, although they were professionals and wouldn't let on if they were eavesdropping. They looked like they were intent on their meal and not paying attention to the vampires lurking above. "Not really," she replied.

"If you did not want to talk, you wouldn't have first made sure no one was listening," Raj pointed out with his impeccably annoying logic. He pulled out a wineskin and two glasses from the satchel he'd retrieved from his horse and held one toward her.

Petrina hesitated for a second, then accepted the wine. She took a small sip, then another. "This isn't Fae wine!" she said.

"I've been saving it for a special occasion," Raj said. He pulled another skin from his bag and called out to the Fae below. "Wine?" When one of the Fae—she couldn't remember her name—looked up, Raj tossed it down. A chorus of appreciation came from below, and Raj turned his attention back out the window. There was nothing visible now but shades and shapes illuminated by the weak starlight. No moon tonight. It would've been a good night to be on the move, if they'd known where they were going.

"It won't do you any good to keep it all inside. Drink deep and talk, daughter."

Petrina sighed and took a long drink of her wine—a Cabernet Franc from the Loire Valley if she was any judge of wine. She couldn't pinpoint the year and didn't want to ask. It didn't matter anyway. Fixating was another way to delay.

"Florence and I have been...involved since Santa Fé," Petrina said, looking down at her glass. "But the attraction started much earlier. Almost immediately."

"I'm not sure what to say here," Raj confessed. "Am I to pretend this is new information, or are you giving me unnecessary exposition to gird your loins for what's coming next?"

"The latter, of course," Petrina said. "After Eleanor caught us making out while lurking behind a hotel lobby potted palm, I knew our secret was out. I fell hard, Father. I did not expect her. I've been alone for a very long time and had gotten used to it. There's not been anyone serious since Magdalene."

"That was well over three hundred years ago!" Raj said. He was so outraged that Petrina cracked a smile.

"There's not been anyone for any length of time," she clarified. "I haven't been celibate, if that's what you're worried about."

"I am relieved," Raj said. "I was beginning to think I hadn't raised you right."

Petrina leaned against the barn wall and looked through her lashes at her sire—the man she'd called father since he'd saved her and countless others from burning. He was witty and often irreverent. He hid his heart behind jokes and self-deprecation, but she knew he felt as deeply—maybe more deeply—than anyone else she'd met. He was incredibly good at reading people, vampire or not. She credited this ability to his long life combined with his ability to read the thoughts of most folks he encountered. He always knew when she needed a humorous jab or two to relax her so she could let her guard down, when she needed an unconditional shoulder, and when she needed to be prodded into action.

"She was everything I thought I'd been looking for these long years. Strong, beautiful, passionate, and powerful. Ice to my fire. Youth to my age."

"And is she?" Raj asked, tipping more wine into her glass.

"Yes and no. She is all the things I said, but she doesn't bring balance. At first, I was sympathetic. She was young and bereft. Losing someone is hard, not knowing what happened to them is harder, and having it be a twin, the other half of your soul, is hardest still. I told myself that when we found Anoka—or word of what had happened— things would be different. She'd find the balance she so desperately needed." Petrina took a long swig of wine and lapsed into silence.

She watched her father watch the dark and finished her wine before speaking again.

"We found her sister, and then she agonized about repairing their relationship. Again, unsurprising and absolutely necessary. And then, we traveled to save Isaac, and I started to notice little things. She started having nightmares that rearranged our sleeping quarters. Her temper grew shorter as she struggled to hide how much more power she had. I don't know when it happened, but I suspect it started when the last gate opened, intensified when we visited the

Fae Plane for the first time, and exploded when Anoka died, shoving all her power from decades on this plane into Florence with no warning."

"How powerful do you think she is?" Raj asked. He'd turned away from the window to stare at Petrina. "Is she a danger?"

"She is the most powerful witch I've ever met," Petrina said. "More powerful than me. More powerful than the Queen of New Orleans. Her power differs from that which Eleanor and the Fae wield, but if she and Eleanor went head to head, I don't know who'd win."

Petrina saw Raj's jaw clench as he turned back to his watch. She knew he was upset. It's one of the reasons she hadn't wanted to tell him.

"I wish you'd said something before. I would've liked to warn Eleanor."

"She will be okay. They are friends—best friends, yes? They will not fight to the death before we return," Petrina said. "And not only can Eleanor handle herself, if Florence were to be so stupid as to attack, she would be alone, while Eleanor has some of the most powerful Fae in the Light at her back. Florence could challenge Eleanor, but she couldn't handle Eleanor with Connor, Clement, and Alanna. The troops there are loyal to the queen, not the Chief Advisor to the Throne."

"I know you're right, but I still fear."

"So do I," Petrina sighed. "I am not what she needs anymore. Maybe I never was. But I told her I wouldn't stand by and watch her hurt herself by trying to hide who she was and what she could do. I said if she wouldn't tell Eleanor, I would. And I told her that I wouldn't stay on this plane when this is over and we've won—or lost. I miss my clan too much to leave them behind. It's been too long already. And she told me she wouldn't come with me to live with a "bunch of feral bloodsuckers in the backwoods of Eastern Europe." And so, here we are. I love her, so I'm setting her free."

Raj held out his arm, and she slipped under it.

"I'm sorry, daughter. I don't see a way to make it work, but I've been wrong before. Often, in fact. Don't give up yet."

"I won't," Petrina lied, leaning her head against his shoulder. "Everything will be just fine."

RAJ SAT UPRIGHT, jerking Petrina off his shoulder.

"What is it?" she asked.

"Torchlight," he said, pitching his voice loud enough to alert the Fae below. They'd put out the small fire, spread their bedrolls on the floor, and fallen into silence sometime after she'd finished her story. But with Raj's word, they were on their feet and alert

"Orders?" one asked.

"Capture with kindness, and bring here," Raj said. "We don't want to alienate the local populace on behalf of the queen who intends to rule them."

"Very good, Consort," the Fae said. The Fae filed out of the barn and melted into darkness.

Petrina turned her attention back to the area outside the window. The torch was bobbing through the darkness. Either the bearer had no fear of them or had no idea they were there. She saw the Fae surround the intruder and creep forward, but without the enhanced night vision a vamp had, they'd be invisible.

"It's okay," Raj breathed. "It is one against many, and the one doesn't know he's surrounded."

"Of course I know, bloodsucker," the figure called. "I just didn't want anyone to feel bad about their stealth."

"Dog," Raj called back. "I should've known it was you by your stench."

"Are you going to call the hunters off, or do we fight?" Isaac asked.

"He's a friend, or at least an ally. Let him pass," Raj commanded.

Petrina smiled. She didn't know Isaac well—they'd only met briefly in the Czech Republic, but she liked the werewolf. He wasn't as mad as people, including himself, believed, and he had a sense of honor that wasn't often found in this day and age. She jumped from the hayloft to the floor below to await his entrance.

"You're just trying to get out of sharing more," Raj said, floating down beside her. "He's a bad sort anyway. You want to avoid him as much as possible."

Isaac strode through the door. His dark skin gleamed over muscles larger than she remembered him having. His hair was loc'd and pulled back from his face, framing velvety brown eyes. The biggest difference, though, was the baby he wore in a carrier on his chest.

"You have a baby?" Raj asked, confusion lacing his voice.

Isaac looked down at the child as if seeing them for the first time. "She's not mine," he said.

"That's worse," Raj said.

Petrina stepped forward and held out her arms. "May I?" she asked.

Isaac cradled the infant for a moment, holding the child closer to his chest, before pulling her out of the carrier and handing her over.

"Whose is she?" Petrina asked, cooing at the baby and pressing butterfly kisses over the infant's forehead and surreptitiously sniffing her head. She'd long ago—even before Raj had sired her into vampirism—given up any hope of having a child, but this one wakened long latent maternal desire like no other child she'd seen in the last nearly four hundred years of her life.

"Medb's," Isaac said.

Petrina jumped back, and Isaac lunged for the baby.

"She's safe with me, wolf," Petrina said. "She's a child. I don't blame her for the numerous hurts her mother delivered to my friends. To you. My question is only where you stand."

"The queen gave her over to Diane—Arduinna—as a charge mere days after her birth. Diane stated she wasn't maternal. Medb pointed out that she wasn't either, and it didn't matter. I took over the care of the child so that someone would love her."

He leaned in and grinned at the baby who smiled back and raised her tiny fists in the air, gurgling cheerfully.

"How is it the queen trusts you with the babe?" Petrina asked. "After all, you were her prisoner, prisoner of the mad vampire, and you escaped with Diane. How does she trust either of you?"

Isaac shifted uncomfortably. "Diane told her only that I escaped, and she went after me to recapture me. When I refused to return and turned into a wild beast, she was forced to take drastic action to save herself. She triggered the rock trolls and let them have their way."

"But, she cannot lie," Petrina stated.

"She didn't. I escaped, she followed after me. I refused to return and went mad. She led me through territory that belonged to rock trolls, and they threw boulders and body parts at me. She was grievously injured, fell through a door, and was eventually saved by a witch. And she never would've returned unless either she had me in tow or she had seen my corpse with her own two eyes. As for my identity, I'm glamoured to look like a lady's maid."

Isaac pulled a necklace out of his pocket and dropped it over his head. The tall, Black shifter shrunk into the form of a satyr, complete with hairy goat legs, cloven hooves, bare ample breasts, and long, brown hair plaited in two braids and trailing down his back.

"Oh wow," Petrina said. "That is...something."

"Because the charm is in a necklace rather than cast on me directly, it's harder to detect. Diane is the only one in the Dark who knows who I am."

"Why are you here?" Raj asked bluntly.

Petrina cradled the child closer and took a step back to a position behind her father's right shoulder. She wasn't trying to challenge Isaac, but she couldn't risk him taking back this baby, this battery of power and energy, and making a run for it. She liked and respected the werewolf, but she didn't necessarily trust him.

"I knew you'd be here. Diane told me to come and lend my assistance. We made a vow to Eleanor, and we intend to honor it."

"Are you truly on Eleanor's side?" Petrina asked. "Is Diane?"

"I am," Isaac confirmed. "Diane is...well, Diane is on Diane's side. She is on the side of whoever is winning. I believe she wants to fight for the Light, realm of her power, but Medb offered more power, more prestige. It's why she became an advisor for the President of the United States and why she remained to advise her during the apocalypse. Her first loyalty is to herself, and her second to power. But she gave her oath and will not be foresworn."

"I thought you were in love with her?" Raj asked.

"I was. I *am*. I just recognize her limitations in both interpersonal relationships and consistent loyalty," Isaac said. "I don't need more right now."

The baby cried out. Isaac reached for her, but Petrina pulled back. "What's her name?"

"Inge," Isaac said.

"Hero's daughter?" Petrina asked. "That's bold."

"Who, though?" Raj asked, tapping his fingers on his chin.

"It isn't me," Isaac said.

"Petrina clearly said hero," Raj said. "Of course it isn't you. No need to deny her a third time." The arm he slung around the were-wolf's shoulder softened the insult.

"She was not chaste, and she used whoever was willing," Isaac said. "I don't know what kind of hero would allow himself to be trapped in her web, but clearly..."

"The queen likely means herself," Petrina said. "Men are so predictable." She curled her arms around the infant until the babe was hardly visible. "She must be protected."

"She is," Isaac said. "I am her protector. Please return her to me."

For a moment, Petrina didn't know how she'd respond. Letting go of this child felt almost impossible—she was everything Petrina had forgotten she wanted. But Inge wasn't hers. She loosed her grip and handed Inge over to the wolf. "Don't make me regret this," she warned.

"Do your part, then," he replied. "I'll feed misinformation to Mebd, I'll pass on false reports, but if you don't show up, it'll be my head on the line. I have a boy, loyal only to Arduinna, who can pass on any messages. He will know nothing more than we tell him, and we will tell him that you're betraying your queen, not that I'm betraying mine."

"And what of Diane?" Raj asked. "Is she still dividing her efforts between advising the president of the former United States, her role as Diane, head torturer for the Dark Queen, and the werewolf-nanny's long-suffering girlfriend?"

"She keeps her promises," Isaac said. "To everyone."

"That must be exhausting," Petrina said. "To serve so many. It must be taking a toll on her health, both physical and mental."

Isaac grinned tightly over the top of Inge's head. "She keeps her promises," he said again. "See that you and Eleanor keep yours."

"It's not Eleanor you'll need to worry about, Dog," Raj said. "She would walk to the ends of the earth to save you. She has. Her first loyalty will always be for her friends."

"He's right," Petrina said. "Eleanor is not perfect. But she is loyal to those she considers friends. You only have to see how many times she's walked back from killing Finn to know how much it would take to make her turn her back on you. You know this. You know that she is worthy of your trust…don't let your hurt take the reins here. If you're feeling betrayed, look elsewhere."

Isaac put his charmed necklace back over his head, and in the form of a small satyr, he walked out, carrying the child, and disappeared into the dark.

ISAAC
INTERLUDE

I saac stood over Inge's cradle, watching her sleep. From the moment he'd held her in his arms, everything had clarified. Returning to the Dark Realm, to Medb's Castle, had nearly broken him again. He'd endured so much in the Raven Queen's—as she was now asking to be called—dungeon. Michelle, the vampire who'd tortured him on and off for nearly a century was still a member of the court, albeit a disgraced one, and every time he saw her, he couldn't decide if he should run or risk everything to take her out. His amygdala was about the only part of his brain still working.

But then Medb had visited the suite he shared with Diane and deposited Medb's baby in the forest Fae's arms. Diane had recoiled and tried to hand her back, citing her distinct lack of maternal desire or instinct. Medb smiled and offered Diane a choice. Take over care of the infant until such time as she could be trained to be a useful member of Medb's court or spend the rest of her very long life in the very cages Diane had helped build.

Diane smiled, took the babe, and as soon as Medb was out of view, deposited the squalling child in Isaac's arms. "Take her," Diane said. "Find someone to feed and water her, or whatever small children need. Keep her clean. Keep her quiet. And keep her out of my way."

Isaac had frozen, but when he looked down and met Inge's eyes, a connection formed, and the clouds parted. Every glimpse he'd had of sanity with Diane paled in comparison to the clarity he felt when he held this baby. She was unpolished magic—more powerful than anything he'd seen. And she lit up the world around her. An instinct welled up—one he hadn't felt since watching his baby sister play in the dust outside their home so many centuries away.

Inge became the center of his life. His anchor, his touchstone. *His* child. With a clear mind, he knew better than to show how much he cared for her... The members of Medb's court, even Diane who still professed to love him, were suspicious of unconditional love. Everything here had conditions and strings. And if they looked too closely at his affection for the child, they'd look more closely at her. Isaac couldn't risk Medb seeing Inge's power grow by leaps and bounds. The queen, as pleased as she was to have an heir to mold, wouldn't tolerate a threat to her throne.

So Isaac stayed quiet, wore the glamour Diane had given him any time he left their suite, and took care of the baby. And when no one else was around, he cradled her in his arms and whispered to her, telling her to hide her power, hide her glow.

He thought it was working until he'd let Petrina hold the baby. She'd felt it, too. His only consolation was that the blonde vampire was unlikely to betray them to Medb.

Footsteps sounded in the hallway, followed by the low groan of a door. Diane had returned.

"Isaac!" she called. "Where are you?"

Isaac walked out of the area recently designated as both nursery and his quarters. He'd moved into the nursery and out of Diane's rooms to be close to the baby at her suggestion. It was easier to keep an eye on the child, to shush her at night when hunger or wetness or nightmares woke her.

"What did you learn?" Diane asked. "Did you make contact?"

Isaac contemplated how much to tell her. She'd been honest about her commitment to Eleanor. But she'd been honest about her commitment to Medb. She was the one who'd told Eleanor at the beginning of it all, that in order to be the perfect Fae double agent, you had to be equally committed to all sides so you could always speak the truth without the meanderings the Fae relied upon to mislead and misdirect. The truth had to be unimpeachable. Isaac had two things Diane didn't when it came to playing more than one side—the knowledge that his mind wasn't as fractured as it'd been before, and the ability to lie.

"I met Raj and Petrina at the abandoned farm on the border just as you'd said. They had a few other Fae with them. It is obviously a scouting mission. We arranged to pass information through our designated go between that you selected."

Diane nodded. "Did you show them the child?"

"As instructed," Isaac said. "They showed little interest in her other than brief inquiries as to her parentage."

"What did you say?" Diane demanded.

"That her mother was the Dark Queen, and that I didn't know the man who was her father."

Diane smiled. "Perfect. I will prepare a detailed description of our primary troop movements to relay."

"Primary?" Isaac asked.

"That means the main body of the Queen's army," Diane said. "The others will be needed elsewhere. We wouldn't want the peasants revolting while all our attention is elsewhere, would we?"

Isaac noted the full stop between the beginning of her statement and the end. He doubted Medb was worried enough about an uprising to commit all her forces in one place. He let it go, though. "Of course not," he said. "But if you think they'll be a danger to Eleanor, I need to warn her."

"They pose no threat to the Queen," Diane said. "Now, tell me Eleanor's news quickly. I missed you and want to repay you for your service to me by servicing you." Diane undid the clasps holding her tunic on and dropped the top on the floor. Her high, brown breasts jutted towards him. She lifted them in her hands and used her fingers to tease her nipples into stiff peaks.

Isaac's breeches stirred in response. He knew what she was doing

—using sex to keep him from questioning her too closely. Despite that knowledge, he had no intention of turning her down. Diane was an enthusiastic and creative lover, and he would let her use him for as long as he could. He walked towards her unfastening his pants.

"She is poised to send her troops through the gate that emerges from the base of the Dragontooth Mountains, although they call them something different on the Light side."

"I know which gate you mean. It's clever but dangerous. How could she hope to move that many Fae through the Dragon's Gate? It's notoriously unstable."

Isaac shrugged as he palmed her hips and pulled her close, sucking one of her nipples into his mouth and biting down gently. He released her long enough to say, "I don't know, but Raj seemed confident." He dropped to his knees and unfastened the ties that held up her leather pants.

"He puts too much faith in his lover," Diane gasped.

"They called him consort," Isaac murmured against the velvety skin of her low stomach. He pushed her pants over her curved ass and lightly flared hips, past her muscular thighs that could crush a man's head if he wasn't careful, and down to her feet. She stepped out of them and backwards until she hit a wall.

"Consort or lover," Diane said. "One should never trust them..."

"I trust you," Isaac said, pulling first one of her legs and then the other over his shoulders so she straddled him. He inhaled deeply, his nose teasing her depths, then shot his tongue out to taste.

"You shouldn't," she said, then moaned.

"I know," Isaac said, tongue tracing patterns on her clit. "But I've always been a sucker for love."

Several days later, Isaac was finishing the note to Raj that would accompany Diane's assessment of Medb's troops and their likely movements. He knew it'd be reviewed by Diane's messenger and the contents reported back to Diane, so trying to come up with the right words to tell Raj the things he was leaving out without alerting Diane was trickier than he'd thought.

For the first time since his bond with Eleanor had been broken, he wished for it back just so Raj could visit him in his dreams again.

Inge cried out from the bassinet next to him, and he threw his pen aside, grateful for the interruption.

"What's wrong little bird?" Isaac crooned, scooping her into his arms. "Are you hungry?"

"Bird?" a voice said behind him.

Isaac whirled around, holding Inge tightly against him. He was overwhelmingly conscious of his lack of glamour. He wore it everywhere, but Diane had issued an order that no one was to violate her inner sanctum and had posted guards outside the rooms to enforce her command. No one had dared to defy her. Until now.

A woman stood in the doorway. She had the luminescent beauty of the Light fae, rare in the Dark Realm that boasted a less showy beauty. Her skin was the reddish brown of the Sahara at sunset, her eyes were honey brown, and her long dark-brown curly hair shone in the lamp light. Pointed ears peeking through the riotous curls indicated she was an elf.

Isaac stammered a greeting while desperately searching for a cover story. "Little bird is a term of affection," he said, finally answering her initial question.

"I know whose daughter she is," the Fae said, walking in and closing the door behind her. "I came to see her at the queen's suggestion. But it was your presence that made me volunteer for the job."

"My presence? I'm only the nanny."

"Funny, you don't look like the nanny who appears in public when the child is shown off to the court."

"She's on vacation. I'm the substitute."

The woman laughed, her voice like silver bells. Isaac shivered. "I admire your ability to lie as much as I delight in your inability to do it well. But I have been rude. Allow me to introduce myself. My name is Inneacht. I was once Heir to the Light Throne with my twin, but my father offered me a different choice. Hold the throne with my twin or marry a prince of the Dark and give birth to the Catalyst, the child destined to free us all and unite the realms under one rule."

Isaac felt his jaw drop. He turned and put Inge back into the cradle, then sat down. *"You're* Eleanor's mother?"

"I am. I arrived many centuries ago to wed Mata. He was the eldest child of Donall, the Crown Prince, and grandson of Ciannait, Dragon King of the Dark. Mata was an...interesting husband. He truly embodied the hot-blooded dragon stereotype. His temper leveled mountains—or at least medium sized hills. Our union was one of mutual benefit, not mutual affection. And it was not fruitful. For centuries I stayed in the court and did my duty."

"Can I get you something to drink?" Isaac asked. He was overwhelmed with the information spilling out and needed a respite while his mind caught up. He poured her a glass of wine without waiting for an answer, and after pouring one for himself, he picked up Inge and sat down again. The feel of the child in his arms slowed his racing thoughts and helped him focus. The wine relaxed the tension in his shoulders and let him speak smoothly again. "I have been a terrible host," he said. "I was not expecting a visitor at all, much less the mother of my very dear friend. Please, continue your tale."

Inneacht nodded graciously and took a sip of wine. "There came a day when a newcomer arrived in court. He was tall with flashing dark eyes that saw into my soul and made me feel things Mata never had. He was Ciannait's son from the wrong side of the sheets and had grown up in the northern Keep, one of the guardians of the border held against giants and the horned ones. He was beautiful. His skilled tongue talked me out of my clothes and into his bed within hours of our meeting where he showed me how skilled his tongue truly was." Inenacht sighed.

Isaac looked down at the baby in his arms. She was almost asleep, and besides—she wouldn't understand Inneacht's words, much less her innuendo.

"Did I make you blush?" Inneacht asked delightedly.

"Almost, Your Highness," he replied.

"This is fun," she said. "The Fae are so hard to shock. Anyway, as I was saying, I took a lover. You must know that is not an unusual thing to do. The Fae live long lives, we often marry for power instead of love, and we are not fertile. Taking a lover or ten throughout one's life is expected—nay, encouraged. Any child borne of such a union will be claimed by the bearer's spouse and not the lover and the parentage will be an open secret. I tell you this so you understand that my affair with Connor should not have excited undue attention, nor should it have been upsetting to anyone at court as long as I was discreet. After all, Connor himself was the product of the King and an unwed daughter of the Raven Court. When the mother didn't want him and he proved the dragon blood bred true again, Connor was sent to live with his father's family."

Connor...that name sounded familiar, but Isaac couldn't place it. He set down his empty glass and turned his attention outward again. "I wonder if I can guess where this is going?" Isaac asked.

Inneacht clapped her hands together, splashing wine over the edge of her glass. "Yes! Please guess!"

"You and Connor were caught together, and defying tradition, your husband did not turn a blind eye?"

"You are correct, of course. Instead of ignoring my affair as I had ignored so many of his over the centuries, he threw me in prison. It was a lovely prison with all the comforts I was used to, but a prison nonetheless. Impenetrable. Or so he thought." She smirked. "Connor continued to visit me. He'd bring me news of the outside world, treats to sustain me during his long absences, and his body to help me forget Mata's quarterly visits. Mata hadn't yet given up on fathering the Catalyst, and since that's what I'd pledged myself to do, I continued to welcome him."

In spite of the thoughts swirling around his head as he tried to make sense of everything and connect the dots of what he already knew, Isaac was hanging on Inneacht's every word. "How did you get free? You obviously are."

"Am I?" She asked, tilting her head and regarding him. "I suppose I am. As free as you, anyway. But that's a ponder for another time. One day, Connor brought me word of the Dragon King's death. Ciannait had been old—one of the first kings after the Fae Realm sundered, so it was not a surprise that he'd finally let go of this world to return to the next. Donall took the throne, as was expected, but he was immediately challenged, which was unexpected. There was no one with power that compared to that of Donall, or so the Court thought. It came out later that Ciannait had been augmenting Donall's power so the throne wouldn't pass out of his direct line. He'd reasoned that once Donall took the throne, the residual power that fueled the throne would be enough to keep up appearances and eventually everyone would be enough used to Donall's rule that no one would question him.

"But he made one mistake. He confessed his line's weakness to his lover, a woman who'd captured his heart when she seduced him into her bed. Eithne, Raven Jarl and ruler of the southern Keep. Connor's mother kept a secret from the Dragon King. She'd had twins."

Inneacht paused dramatically and looked at Isaac wide-eyed, waiting for him to catch up.

"Wait. So Medb was the daughter of the High King and Connor's twin sister? She comes from both the dragon and raven lines?"

"Not quite," Inneacht said. "Medb is Connor's sister, daughter of Ciannait and Eithne. But she is a Raven as Connor is a Dragon."

Isaac shook his head. "I'm not sure that's how genealogy works," he said.

"I don't know genealogy," Inneacht said. "I only know the truth. Medb attacked the throne, killed Donall, and spared Mata when he pledged his loyalty to her." Inneacht's lip curled in disdain. "He groveled. He promised her control of the Catalyst. He all but handed her his balls in a satin-lined sack. His visits increased, as did Connor's until he was called into his sister's service. On his last visit, he kissed me passionately, promised me he'd find a way to get us to the Light, and said goodbye. I only saw him one more time."

She paused so long, Isaac wasn't sure she would continue. Finally, she cleared her throat. "May I?" she asked, holding her arms out to the babe asleep in Isaac's arms.

Isaac handed Inge over. Inneacht stroked the baby's brow. "She's so soft. I barely got to hold my baby, born after a thousand years of waiting. Ciara was born early. Her arrival timed with Mata's last visit but not Connor's. They both believed the story I didn't dispute, that Ciara was Mata's, the Catalyst promised of a union of Dragon and Phoenix, darkness and light." Her voice broke. "Medb had promised to raise the child if it was born with the mark of the Raven, but Ciara bore the Dragon's kiss."

"What mark?" Isaac asked. "I didn't see anything."

"And you've seen all of her there is to see?" Inneacht asked, brow arched.

"Yes," he said.

"And you never saw the living dragon?"

"Only her tattoo," Isaac said. "She didn't have any birthmarks."

"What happened after the ink drew the shape of her spirit to the surface?"

"She...oh."

Inneacht nodded. "So you see. All I knew then, though, was that my daughter had been taken from me. Mata told me with no little glee that Connor had taken the babe to the woods to destroy it and returned with blood on his hands carrying the heart of a child. I refused to see Connor again, and later heard that he'd fallen in love with one of Medb's witches, only to be cast into exile." She lapsed into silence.

"How did you find out Eleanor's true identity?" Isaac asked.

"A careless tongue after so many years. When my servants thought me asleep, they gossiped about what they'd heard about the new threat to the throne. A woman, raised in the human world, had opened the gates. We felt the plane shift when the final gate opened, and I knew my child was destined to fulfill the prophecies. I don't know the name Eleanor, although it is a very pretty name. But her true name, Ciara, will be written on her heart."

"She calls herself Ciara nic Mata when she dares to speak her true name," Isaac said.

"I hope she will someday learn the rest of the truth, but for now, what she doesn't know will protect her. I would visit you again, to learn more of my child, to hold this babe again, daughter of the queen who ordered my child killed. Now, I am tired. Thank you for your time, your wine, and for letting me take comfort in the touch of an infant." She placed the sleeping baby back in her cradle and left as silently as she'd entered.

ISAAC WAS FEEDING Inge her afternoon bottle when someone knocked on the door. He knew who it was. No one ever knocked. Diane lived here, so she came and went as she pleased—although it felt like she was always leaving, never staying—and no one else was allowed in. Inneacht, on the other hand, had visited every day for the last four days, usually around this time.

"Come in, Inneacht," he called. "There's wine on the sideboard, or I can make you some tea."

He heard the door open and close and the tinkling sound that told him she'd opted for wine. When he walked into the main sitting area with the baby, she was stretched out on the chaise swirling the wine in her glass.

"It's lovely to see you again," he lied. He'd secretly hoped today would be the day she wouldn't return.

"You're the first person I've talked to in forty years besides the women who bring me food. You know the daughter I'd mourned for the better part of those four decades. And you've spent time in the outside world. I want news—of the war, of my child, of the Earth Plane I never visited. All of it. I've told you my story, and then some. Now tell me hers."

"I don't know much," Isaac said, handing Inge into Inneacht's waiting arms. "I met Eleanor shortly after she learned who she was and traveled with her while she opened the first four gates. I can tell you who she was then—powerful, impetuous, stubborn, passionate, and soft-hearted, although she'd punch me if she heard me say that last part. Once she accepted her fate as the catalyst, she did everything she could to mitigate the effects on the world. I left her after the fourth gate, but even though I'd hurt her terribly, she kept the promise she made and came after me when she could to ensure I was okay."

"You love her," Inneacht said.

"Yes," he replied. "Very much. At first, I thought it was the kind of love that would transcend lifetimes. Later, I was glad of the memory of the love we'd shared. But now I know that we will always be connected, even though we're no longer tied together. More than anyone I've met—" he glanced at the child in Inneacht's arms, and amended his statement "—almost anyone, she changed me for the better." When he looked back up, it wasn't Inneacht's face who looked back. It was Diane's.

"What?" He set down the wine he'd been drinking and stared at her in confusion.

"Did you think you could get away with this?" she asked.

"With what?" he asked. "I haven't done anything!"

"You betrayed my trust like you've betrayed everyone who's ever had the misfortune and bad judgment to put their faith in you."

Isaac wrinkled his brow. He'd selectively mislead Diane, but even if she'd interpreted his coded message for Raj, it wouldn't have read as a betrayal...just Isaac being more thorough with his warnings and preventing a messenger from reading the full text. It didn't make sense. But maybe... He looked at the wine swirling in his glass. He was getting confused again. He needed the child. On cue, she started crying. Diane looked at the baby with disgust.

"I'll take her," Isaac said. The moment she was back in his arms, she cooed at him and fell asleep. His mind calmed again. He wasn't going mad. Not this time. It was a trick or a test, and one he finally felt qualified to pass.

"Who are you?" he asked.

Rebecca, Alpha of the Black Hills pack, dear friend and former lover, and someone he'd only seen once in the last hundred years shifted on the chaise across from him. "You came into my territory, challenged my mate, forcing me to kill him, and left me to clean up the mess. A mess made worse by the havoc your little Fae princess left behind. I gave you shelter. I gave you aid. And you betrayed me."

"No," Isaac said. "I didn't. You were strong, strong enough to lead. I gave you the opening you wanted, and you walked into it with eyes wide open. The Rebecca I know is strong and never blames others for the challenges she encounters, and certainly not for the ones she sought out. Try again, whoever you are." He watched as Rebecca's face slid away and was replaced by the blond hair, blue eyes and pale skin of Emma.

"Is this better?" she purred. The woman who wasn't quite Emma stood up and sashayed over to him. When he wouldn't move the baby so she could settle in his lap, she sat next to him and ran a hand up his thigh. She squeezed hard. "Ohhh, can't get it up for me anymore? What's wrong, puppy getting old?"

Isaac rolled his eyes. "Emma was never like that," he said. "I don't know where you get your information, but you should demand a refund."

The change this time was instantaneous, and it cut to the quick.

She stood, all six feet of ebony goddess, and stared down at him. "Because of you, I am dead. Because of you, we all died. You were weak. You could not protect us. You are a disappointment. No woman has ever had such a disappointing son. I may have died that day, but it was a mercy. I would rather be dead than live with the memory of your weakness. You are not worthy to be my son."

Isaac closed his eyes. He knew it wasn't his mother. She'd screamed at him to run, to save himself. But the face, and the voice... It was too much.

"Big wolf, why'd you let me die?"

He opened his eyes. His baby sister stood in front of him in her dusty dress and tear-streaked face, a rivulet of blood trickling down from the gaping wound in her chest. Isaac reached out his hand, then pulled it back.

"Little bird, I'm sorry," he said. "I tried."

"Why didn't you take me with you?" she asked. His baby sister started sobbing, her body heaving with tears and grief and pain.

"I'm so sorry," Isaac said again. Tears streamed down his face as he watched his sister fade away and swirl into the dust of the desert where he'd watched her die.

"Always sorry," Eleanor said, rolling her eyes. "But never able to change your ways. You keep fucking up. You can't protect the people you care about. You left me when I needed you most. I opened myself to you, I *bound* myself to you, and still you left me for the faintest possibility that you'd be able to save someone else you'd betrayed half a century ago. Is that your life now? Betraying new people to try to mitigate the betrayals of the past? You're going to be very busy. There are a lot of people in there." Eleanor stood and tapped his forehead.

Isaac felt the madness swirling up again, threatening to engulf him. Inge reached up and brushed her tiny, perfect fingers across his chin. His mind cleared again.

"Michelle," he spat. "Why are you doing this? Stop fucking around."

Eleanor laughed, stood back, and let the glamour fall. Isaac put Inge in her cradle and pushed it behind the couch

"You needn't worry about the brat," Michelle said, baring her fangs. "I'm not going to risk my welcome mat and kill the queen's spawn."

"What do you want?" Isaac asked, exhaustion lacing his voice. "I won't come back. You have nothing more to offer."

She cycled through the bodies she'd tried on. "I can offer you all sorts of things. Which do you like best?"

"You can't tempt me with my past. I have moved on. Just because hurt and guilt remain doesn't mean I am unable to live my life forward. You've lost. Go away and tell whoever is pulling your strings that you failed."

"I wonder why every important person I pulled out of your head was a woman?" Michelle asked, settling back into her own body again. For a minute, her usual glamour failed, and Isaac saw her for who she really was. Pale skin, gaunt with hunger and pulled too tight across her bones, blond hair brittle with age and lack of care, and sunken blood-shot eyes that had once been blue, but now were filmy with age and malnourishment. "Have you never met a strong man to keep in your head? Where was your father? *Who* was your father? Was it because you didn't have a father, because your mother was the town bicycle, that you've spent your long, long life submitting to every strong woman who walked by instead of learning how to be strong yourself?"

"I was raised by strong women, I've chosen to be with strong women, and I will never regret taking the backseat to the women I've known. Except for you. Your strength is derived from making others weak."

"I've always had a weakness for weak men—my sire is cut from the same cloth as you. He's spent a millennium chasing love and fleeing war and what does he have to show for it? Nothing. Every vampire he brought into this life has wasted it on appeasing humans or squandered it on madness."

"You've definitely taken the latter path to extremes," Isaac noted.

"You think so?" Michelle sneered. "You know he's taken your place now. In her bed and in her heart."

"Raj? Raj is your sire?" Isaac was genuinely taken aback. How had he missed this? Did Eleanor know? Did anyone?

"He didn't tell you? That's how he was able to find me in Portland. A real shame. I'd finally found a great setup, some fun friends, and a bunch of local doggies to play with, and he had to come ruin everything. But still, he couldn't bring himself to kill me. He has such a soft spot for his creations. Weak. Weak like you."

Isaac had been slowly backing towards the end table near the door to Diane's chambers. There was a sword leaning against the table. He thought that'd be easier than changing into a wolf and attempting to take her out. He was vulnerable during the change, and it wasn't instantaneous. Finally, his questing fingers landed on the sword's hilt. Michelle wasn't even paying attention to him anymore. She was ranting about Raj and how he'd always preferred his other children to her, even that dead asshole Mehmed.

Isaac stepped forward while she castigated the sofa where he was no longer sitting. Just before the sword penetrated her back, she whipped around and deflected it with her arm. The blade sliced through her skin and stuck in her humerus. She pulled back, yanking the sword out of his hand. "You can't take me, puppy," she said. "I've been in your head. I know all your hopes. All your fears. And all your tricks." Michelle pulled the sword out of her arm and held it up. "But I can take you." She thrust forward as she finished speaking.

The door burst open and Raj and Petrina stepped into the room.

"I have never been so happy to see you, bloodsucker," Isaac said as the sword slid though his abdomen and he slid onto the floor.

RAJ
INTERLUDE

R aj watched Isaac fall, the sword almost all the way through, and turned his attention to Michelle. He sensed Petrina moving to Isaac's side and pulling him out the way. He wasn't worried. Not much, anyway. Between Petrina's healing gifts and Isaac's natural werewolf resilience, he'd be fine. Probably.

"So good to see you, Papa," Michelle simpered at him.

Raj stared at her until she backed up, legs hitting the chaise behind her. She swayed but kept her balance. "I'm surprised you could tear yourself away from your little princess," she said.

"Do you believe that after a thousand years of existence, you of all people can find barbs that will wound me? If I cared so deeply about what others thought of me, I wouldn't have ascended the throne in Kanauj. I wouldn't have attracted Sam's attention on the battlefield and been born into this life. And I wouldn't have had nearly as much fun."

"What about me?" Michelle challenged. "You turned me and abandoned me. You left me on my own to die."

"He didn't," Petrina said. "You were a favor. A favor to me. To you. And when things didn't turn out as you wanted, you ran. You ran away from the man who sired you at your request. You ran away from the woman who'd loved you for decades. You chose to be alone. You chose to be bitter. This life is on you."

Raj held up his hand, and Petrina fell silent.

"I have changed people for love," Raj said. "I changed Mehmed because I'd once loved him and wanted him to love me. I helped him change Radu for the same reason. And I changed you because I love Petrina more than any child I could've born myself. I thought the prison I created in Portland to hold you forever would protect the world from your madness. You escaped me then, but you won't do it a second time. You, more than Mehmed, were my biggest mistake, and I'm ashamed it took me this long to correct it."

Michelle hissed. "Bring it, old man. You're much too soft hearted to kill me, even if you—"

Her head sailed across the room and bounced against the far wall. Isaac stood behind her, sword in hand and a look of grim satisfaction on his face.

"Well done, dog," Raj said, offering a handkerchief to Isaac.

Isaac took it and cleaned the blade. "Thanks for distracting her, bloodsucker."

Raj turned to find Petrina. She was holding Michelle's head in her lap while pink-tinged tears streamed down her face. "I loved her once."

"I know," Raj said, dropping to his knees next to his daughter. "I am sorry it ended this way. I would've done anything to spare you this pain."

"You do too much to spare me pain," she sniffed. "I'll be okay. I mourned her so long ago."

Raj pulled her into his arms and looked over Petrina's head at Isaac. Isaac took the hint, picked up Inge, and left the room, leaving Raj with his grieving daughter.

He let her cry while Michelle's head and body slowly disintegrated. When Petrina held nothing but dust, Raj pulled her to her feet. "We have to go. We're not even supposed to be here."

"Take me with you," a woman said from the doorway. Raj turned to look at her. She was dressed in nondescript breeches and a tunic, and her hair had been braided and tucked back out of the way.

"Who are you?" Raj asked. "And why would I take you anywhere?"

Isaac came back into the room. Raj shifted his attention to the werewolf. "Are you okay? I don't know everything that happened, but you look...not alright. Do you want to come with?"

Isaac shook his head. "I can't leave the baby, and I don't think where you're headed is the best place for an infant."

"You'd take him and not me?" Inneacht asked indignantly.

"I still don't know who you are," Raj said. "I know Isaac."

"Is this any way to treat your mother-in-law?" the woman demanded.

Raj was seldom surprised anymore—a thousand years of life can do that to a man—but this was a jaw dropping moment. "My what?"

"This is the vampire you told me about, correct?" she asked Isaac.

"He is," Isaac confirmed. "The Light Queen's consort. Raj, may I introduce you to Inneacht, Queen Mother apparently. Inneacht, Rajyapala and his daughter Petrina."

"Consort? Queen Mother? But that means..." Inneacht trailed off then sat down abruptly. "Are you sure?"

"Yes," Raj said. "Didn't you know? Eleanor has been on the throne for more than half a year, now."

"And the former occupant? Deposed?"

"Dead," Raj said.

Inneacht crumpled in on herself, and for the second time that afternoon, Raj found himself comforting someone through their loss.

"How did you know Eochid?" Raj asked.

"He was her brother," Isaac said. "Her twin."

"You knew this but didn't tell her he was dead?" Raj asked.

"I didn't connect the dots. I'm still rusty in that area. She'd said she, along with her twin brother, were heirs to the Light throne, but she came here to unite Light and Dark. It was centuries ago—I didn't think..."

"Nor should you have," Raj said. "Of course not. You've never even met Eo and his death isn't at the forefront of your mind other than a fact that it happened to someone else." Raj looked at Inneacht, whose sobs were beginning to fade into hiccups. "Of course, you must come with me, then. I'm not sure how Eleanor will react when she meets you, but she'd never forgive me if I didn't give her the chance."

Raj laid his head in his hands and winced as Inneacht exclaimed—for at least the tenth time that day—how everything had changed since last time she'd left the palace grounds. He was sympathetic—of course he was—but he was also tired, trying to evade the spies Medb had lurking in the woods, and searching for an out-of-the-way place to hole up for the night with the more silent than usual Petrina and the "I haven't talked to anyone new in centuries so I will share all the thoughts I've had in the last hundred years" Inneacht.

He wasn't supposed to have gone into the capital at all, much less the palace. But when Isaac's messenger had trotted into his camp two days after Isaac left to deliver messages about troop movements, Isaac's encoded suspicions about what *wasn't* being said, and a warning to be wary of the messenger Diane had procured. Once again, his plans were turned upside down. The messenger had shimmered and straightened until Arduinna stood in the middle of the small camp, smiling like the cat with the canary.

He wondered who she was at the end of the day when she was alone with the silence of her thoughts. Was she Arduinna, the goddess of the old forest, woods queen, antlered hind, presumably the oldest of her personas? Was she Diane, dark Fae and huntress? Seth, tailored advisor to the United States president? Or this errand boy who reminded Raj of an unfortunate mixture of satyr and centaur. A sattaur maybe? The boy ran on four goat legs and had a child's torso, humanoid face, and goat horns curving out from above his floppy ears.

It didn't matter. What had mattered was Arduinna's promise—and her warning. Isaac was in danger and needed a savior. Again. She was harder than she'd been as Diane—less sympathetic. What affection she'd shown for Isaac in Czechia wasn't apparent here. And sure, not everyone wore their hearts on their sleeves—even Raj had found discretion to be important from time to time, but when he'd asked why she couldn't save him, she said she was fresh out of savior complex, but if he wanted Isaac to survive Michelle again, he should shake his sexy ass and get a move on.

So Raj had agreed to go back with her, convinced Petrina to come as well, and sent the rest of the Fae under his command to scout along the eastern border to find places to bivouac the troops while they regrouped and readied for war.

She'd disappeared as soon as she'd led him to the door of her suite, and he'd not seen her again. He'd had to rely on his memory of their way in, Inneacht's imperfect and wildly out of date knowledge of the castle grounds and secret passages, and the thoughts he was able to glean from the palace staff as they made their way out as unobtrusively as possible.

And now, they were almost back to the rendezvous point he'd arranged, and he was exhausted. It'd been a long, long time since he'd spent this much time being tired, but ever since his Ruby nap after Eleanor had opened the final gate, he was spending a lot more time looking forward to his next nap.

Eleanor suspected, but they didn't really talk about it. She was busy learning how to be Fae, how to be queen, and how to be an open and caring partner had taken a backseat. He didn't begrudge her this time; they had the rest of their lives together—and that would be a very long time. But he felt different and could speak to no one else about it. Petrina would listen, would feel sympathetic, but she was suffering the loss of two lovers, one old, one new, and didn't need to be burdened more.

He would do his best to not show his exhaustion, to do what was required of him now so his love could take her throne, and later, he would reserve a solid week with her away from the demands of the crown for wine, whinging, and...he searched his mental thesaurus for a fucking synonym that started with the letter 'w,' to keep up the alliteration, but was left wanting. Wine, whinge, and womanizing?

He just wasn't up to his old standards.

Finally, he caught sight of the overgrown path that led back into the woods towards the farmhouse they'd agreed to meet at—although not the same one where he'd entertained Isaac and Arduinna. He could already imagine the feel of his bedroll beneath him.

He increased their pace, reached out his senses to ensure they weren't being watched, something he did several times an hour, then led Inneacht and Petrina off the main road and into the woods.

The farmhouse came into view. He pushed himself forward as a visual announcement they'd returned. No one rode forth to challenge him. He looked around the clearing—it was empty. No horses. No trickle of smoke from the small cook fire. No smell of food or unwashed Fae. And no thoughts drifting through the aether.

They were gone. Or had never arrived. No, there was a fresh scuff in the dirt, a used midden in the trees opposite Raj, and the water pump bore signs of fresh use. They'd arrived, but they hadn't stayed.

"Trina—stay out of sight with Inneacht. There's no one here. I'm going to sweep the barn and house."

She didn't answer, but he felt her affirmation.

He checked out the barns first. They, too, showed signs of recent use, but there was nothing here. He walked toward the house, apprehension settling over him. Something was wrong—there was something, or someone, inside. The energy felt familiar but strange. He couldn't place it. He drew his sword—a poor substitute for his ruby blade, but he'd carried it after Vlad had traded the family heirloom for a crash course in zombie-manufacturing from Marie Laveau —and pushed open the door with the tip. Nothing shot out at him, so he proceeded cautiously.

The door slammed behind him taking with it the shields that'd prevented him from sensing the person within.

She sat at the table in the small dining room with a glass of deep red wine in front of her. She had long, wavy hair, shiny and black like a raven's wing, brown skin a few shades lighter than Raj's, and features that were achingly familiar. She looked like a darker version of Eleanor. If they were side by side in sepia, they'd look like twins.

Until Medb smiled. No one would ever mistake the cruelty on Medb's face for Eleanor.

"I've been wanting to meet you," she growled. "You're the vampire who helped the so-called Queen of New Orleans double-cross me, aren't you?' The one warming the pretender's sheets?"

"One and the same," Raj said. He sat down opposite her, poured himself a glass of wine, and crossed his legs. He held up his glass, "To old memories."

"Marie still owes me the head of your playmate," Medb said.

"She has no intention of reneging," Raj said. "She's a vamp of her word. I wouldn't worry about it."

"Who said I'm worried?" the Dark Queen snapped.

"You're here, in my secret meeting place, asking me about my friends and lovers. Odd move for a confident queen."

Medb stood. "I have a warning and offer for Eleanor. If she ceases this ridiculous foray into my land, I'll not challenge her right to sit on the Light Throne and will sign a non-aggression treaty."

"Isn't her claim to the throne at least as valid as yours?" Raj asked. "She's the granddaughter of the king you deposed."

"I deposed my half-brother" Medb growled. "I had as much right to the throne as he did, and I was stronger. I deserved it."

"I will carry your message to Eleanor," Raj said, closing his eyes and draining his wine. "And I sincerely hope you get everything you deserve." When he looked back across the table, she was gone.

Raj scoured the woods after he'd cleared the house and ushered Petrina and Inneacht in. He wasn't sure why he felt so protective of the elf he'd just met—she was probably powerful enough to take care of herself against anyone but Medb. But she was also Eleanor's mother, and now that he had her and knew who she was, there was no way he was going to let anything happen to her before he delivered her to Eleanor.

The woods were empty—he'd suspected they would be. He didn't feel anything else alive in the vicinity, but the scent of blood and death drew him to a hastily dug pit a mile or so away from the house. Inside were the Fae who'd accompanied him and Petrina to the Dark Realm. Each had been eviscerated and beheaded. One more thing for the Medb to answer for. Raj covered the pit with dirt and rocks and made a simple marker. He hoped Jörð would find them and welcome them back into the earth.

Burial complete and secure in the knowledge that no one was watching, he shot up into the air and spiraled outward, looking for the place he'd crossed over into the Dark Realm as well as confirming what Arduinna and Isaac had told him about Medb's troop movements.

The main troops were exactly where the map Arduinna had annotated specified they would be, but based on Isaac's warning, Raj looked further afield. It was hard to travel swiftly when he was in unfamiliar territory, so it took a day to get to the northern border. At first glance, it looked like either a tournament or a banquet or a minor war between dragons and giants was taking place, but after a few days with Inneacht, he knew better than to assume the dragons wouldn't fight on Medb's side. After all, Mata was theoretically the Dragon Jarl as well as Eleanor's purported father. She had a lot of people vying for that title, actually. It'd be a fun Maury show if such things still existed.

Raj flew in closer and drew the shadows around himself. If the giants and the dragons were truly fighting, he'd count them out for the big war, but if they were feasting an alliance, that would put a significant wrench in their plans.

"It's impossible to keep the giants fed," a brownie groused. "I thought serving dragons was bad enough, but this is ridiculous."

"I heard they'll be heading out in about ten days," the second Fae said. Between them they carried a large, cast iron cauldron filled to the brim with a rancid-smelling bubbling stew on a pole the size of a middle-aged tree. "Break, Ern?"

"Yes," Ern replied. They set down their burden and leaned back, holding their backs as they shrugged and stretched. Raj crept close enough to listen in without being seen.

"Are they heading home at last?" Ern asked.

"There's to be a war," the second said. "And the queen—" both spat their disgust; brownie number one's didn't clear the stew and landed with a sickly plop.

"I've never been so glad not to have a gag reflex," Raj muttered.

"—is calling the dragons in. I served the Jarl and the giant's Ardar-lida last night. I wouldn't say they're planning on double-crossing anyone, but they were mighty conspiratorial about the events after crushing the Light's armies. Got a few good laughs in about turning her tricks against her."

"They're stupid if they think the Light will fall so easily," Ern said. "They've been biding their time for centuries and now they have the World-Breaker on their side. If they didn't think they had a chance, they wouldn't be on their way."

"You don't have to tell me," number two said. "But no one asks us for advice. They'd learn a lot more if they did. Who else goes every-where and hears everything? If the Jarl wants to know who's plotting against him, who's sneaking into whose bed in the middle of the night, and what the reality of any situation is, they'd have to go no further than you or me."

"You speak the truth, Hugh," Ern said. "Short-sighted, the lot of them. 'Course, nobility often is, whether they're dragons or ravens or elves. The Light ones will be no better."

They picked up their burden again and shuffled towards the feast. Raj noted their position on his map and crept out of the stronghold to head south. He needed to see if the Ravens were massing as well. If they were, the Dragon and giant alliance would march towards the Ravens and flank Eleanor's troops, closing the Light in a deadly vice.

FLORENCE
INTERLUDE

Florence stood at the edge of camp and stared at the mountain on the far side of the bridge. She'd been standing there every day for the last three days. She didn't know what she was looking for. She couldn't open the gate. She couldn't even sense its presence.

She could bring down the mountain, though. She could turn the river below to ice. She could create a blizzard and a hailstorm and destroy the stupid bridge. She could kill everyone in this camp with less effort that it would take to trudge back to her well-appointed tent and have a glass of wine. Her well-appointed but empty tent.

She pushed the rage back down and resumed staring at the place where Petrina had disappeared three days ago.

They'd argued. People did. When she and Savannah had been together for what Florence had assumed was the rest of their preternaturally long lives, they'd fought like cats. It didn't take much for one of them to come out, claws extended and hissing. And just as quickly, it'd be over and they'd ask for forgiveness in each other's bodies.

This...this was different. The rise in power hadn't started with the final gate as she'd led Petrina to believe. It'd started with the second—the first she'd been present at. When she'd helped Eleanor channel the magic out of the gate in a controlled flood so it wouldn't destroy everything in its path, she'd channeled it through herself. Partly because she didn't know how else to do it, and partly because she wanted to feel the foreign magic.

The power filtered through Eleanor, flowed into the magical weir they'd woven, then, once it was out of Eleanor's immediate grasp, through Florence before flowing into the world. When the gate closed, the power reversed it course, traveling more gently at the mouth of the river and wildly at the source. Florence got a second bump of power and the main force whipped through Eleanor like a supernatural game of crack-the-whip.

Once she learned that she could, she did. She took more and more into herself each time. And with the rise in power came more volatile emotions. She knew the others had noticed—Eleanor had mentioned it more than once. She was the elder, the calm in the storm, and she couldn't even keep from giving people frostbite when her temper flared.

She'd rationalized it by telling herself that every filter lessened the negative effects it had on the world around her. That it lessened the effects on Eleanor. And it was true. She delayed the destruction of the modern world enough that more would live and mitigated the effects on Eleanor allowing her to recover more quickly each time. But that was a lie as well. Even if it'd had no positive effect, even if it'd sped along the destruction of technology or harmed Eleanor, she wouldn't have done anything differently.

The power took root in her. It was foreign—she was human and controlled human magic. This was wild magic, Fae magic. What made Eleanor stronger and confident undermined Florence's control.

But she had it in check. She was wielding the power; it wasn't wielding her.

At the final gate, she'd followed the pattern she and Eleanor had established at the previous gates. But when Finn staked Raj and Raj stabbed Eleanor and the magic had broken loose, igniting every volcano in the Cascade range and permanently changing the geography of the Columbia River Gorge, it'd broken something loose in her, too.

She had abilities she'd never dreamed of—never heard of occurring in any Earth witch. She tried to play it off as a natural effect of the magic returning to Earth, but she hadn't fooled Petrina.

She'd never fooled Petrina. And instead of turning to the woman she loved for help, she'd pushed her away. Lied to her. And when Petrina said that Florence was young and out of control, Florence snapped.

She'd found every sore spot Petrina had revealed in the time they were together and pushed at it. She dug up every regret, every insecurity, and every iota of guilt. And she'd capped it all by bringing up the death of Petrina's first love, the woman who'd followed her into the cave, willing to sacrifice herself to slake the new vampire's thirst, and who'd taken her out into the world...and she'd accused Petrina of murder, or being unfeeling for not turning her love, for not still mourning her, and for letting the woman take the risks inherent in being the human companion of a new vampire.

What she'd said was unforgivable, and now that her temper was back in control, she desperately needed to be forgiven.

And the only way to ask is if she could get control over the magic she'd stolen and learn to truly wield it instead of being as out of control as she'd accused Eleanor of being.

And the only way she could do that is if she stopped lying to herself.

"It's a start."

Florence whirled around to see Clement standing a few yards behind her. She raised her hand, a glowing orb of jagged ice appearing there, and cocked her arm back to throw it. Then she took a deep breath, lowered her arm, blinking the icy projectile out of existence, and nodded at him.

"Tell me what I need to do," she said, then took a deep breath and added, "Please."

FLORENCE STOOD in the entrance of Eleanor's tent watching her friend —the queen, Florence reminded herself—study maps of the Dark Realm Connor had recreated from memory, the relics they'd found in the palace library, and the maps that lived in Eleanor's head.

Eleanor was young, tempestuous, and often too stubborn for her own good, but she was going to be a good queen. She'd grown so much in the last few years. She asked for help when she needed it and accepted aid when offered, even when unsolicited. She'd grown, if not comfortable with constructive criticism, at least open to it. For a woman who'd spent her whole life never considering strategy beyond the occasional games of Settlers of Catan she was roped into playing in college, she was almost there. Almost ready.

Soon, she wouldn't need Florence anymore. If she ever did.

Eleanor looked up and caught sight of Florence in the doorway. A wide smile spread across her face.

"I'm so glad you're here!" she said. "I've been thinking about you all day but couldn't find you."

"I was at the Bridge," Florence said, not moving from the doorway.

Eleanor's eyes pinched together at the corners for a moment, then widened again. She'd shut her grief and worry away to present that brave face everyone had drummed into her that royalty needed to have.

"Come in," Eleanor said. "Don't stand there. It's cold outside."

One of the ubiquitous servants brought a chair forward and set it next to Eleanor, bowing to their queen. Eleanor looked up at him, nodded her thanks, and said, "I won't need anything else for the evening if you want to take off, Dafyd. If you see Sera, have her bring some of that ale the Dwarf Queen sent with me. Don't go out of your way, though."

Florence looked at the man who'd brought her chair, then really looked at him for the first time. He was of middling height, if he'd been a human. But for a river sprite, he was tall. Florence looked around the room again—this time taking in the servants who stood in the background, waiting to be needed, waiting to protect their queen if necessary. Eleanor hadn't been able to shoo out everyone since the attempt on her life. But rather than outwardly chafe under the restrictions, she'd given in gracefully.

"Do you need anything else, Your Majesty?" Connor asked, rolling up the maps.

"Nothing more tonight," Eleanor said. "You're welcome to stay and have some beer with us, though."

"Maybe some other time. Right now, my bed is calling to me."

He exited, and after a glance, the tent emptied of all but one guard, although several others ringed the tent. A brownie appeared carrying a small wooden cask and two mugs. She was followed by a minotaur —renowned for their ability to taste even the smallest traces of poison and all but extinct now, according to Connor. The brownie set everything down and poured two beers. The minotaur picked up one of the mugs, inhaled deeply through her nose, then took a small sip, swished it around her mouth, and swallowed.

Eleanor watched her expectantly. After a few moments, she shrugged and handed Eleanor the mug. "It is safe, Majesty," she said.

"Your service, as always, is appreciated, Tinafa."

"If you really appreciated me, Your Majesty, you'd find someone to gift you barrels of Bourbon instead of beer," she said.

"I'll be on the lookout."

Tinafa turned and left the tent, closing the flaps behind her.

Eleanor sighed, took off the silver crown Connor insisted she wear, and rubbed her forehead. She unclasped her cloak and let it fall behind her. "Everything is so heavy," she complained. "But you're not here to listen to me bitch about the literal weight of the crown. Have some beer—it's really good. It rivals anything I could've found in Portland. Rose, are you sure I can't tempt you with a glass?"

"I'm afraid that would be terribly irresponsible of me," the guard in the corner said. "I am, after all, supposed to be keeping you safe. It's best I don't compromise myself."

"Suit yourself," Eleanor said. "But someday, I'll catch you when you're not working and then we'll tie one on."

Florence watched the exchange between the queen and her guard and marveled at the easy flow between them. Eleanor, by virtue of not having been raised as royalty didn't hold herself above those who now served her. But she also didn't try too hard to be their friends. She was...herself. And she was doing a great job.

The witch picked up her beer and held it out towards Eleanor. "To friendship," she said.

"To my bff, Flo the Ho," Eleanor replied, then grimaced. "Never mind. I was just workshopping our girl squad nicknames, but that one is not working for me. Let me go again." She held up her mug and clinked it against Florence's. "To my bff, Florence, the most bad-ass practitioner on two planes."

Both women drank before setting down the mugs and taking a deep breath.

"I am glad you're here," Eleanor said. "I miss you. I know you've been avoiding me, I know it has something to do with your magic, or your relationship, or our friendship, or all three. But I can't fix things or be a shoulder if you won't talk to me. So talk. Say what you need to say, and if you want my help, tell me what you need. You're my best friend, my teacher, my first adviser, and one of the few people I'd do anything for. Don't try to hide from me the way you hid yourself from the gate's magic. I saw you disappear, and I know that means you have gate magic within yourself. I just want to know how and why you didn't tell me before."

Florence glanced over her shoulder at Rose before she could stop herself.

"Rose won't say anything," Eleanor assured Florence. "She's pledged to the throne, and since she's lucky enough to be one of the few people allowed to guard my body at all times, she has sworn some pretty restrictive oaths about what she can reveal and to whom about what she hears or sees."

Rose waved reassuringly. "I have seen some things," she said in a conspiratorial whisper. "After what I've had to live through, there is nothing you could say that would shock me."

Florence felt a grin creeping across her face. "Still shocking people with your inappropriate libido and absence of all shame and propriety?"

"I wouldn't be me if I wasn't," Eleanor replied. "Now. Spill."

FLORENCE LAID on her sleeping pallet and stared at the ceiling of her tent. Overall, Eleanor had taken everything well. Almost too well. She shook her head. *"No,"* she told herself. *"Don't slip into paranoia. She is your friend."*

Florence rolled over and regarded the empty space beside her. It still smelled like the vampire who'd shared her blankets until three days ago—copper and berries and vanilla. Florence moved over into Petrina's customary place and buried her face in the pillow. She'd been so certain Petrina would elect to stay here, in the Fae Plane, so she could enjoy the sunlight and sleeping again. So she could dream again. Maybe if she worked harder at being a partner, Petrina wouldn't leave.

She was lying to herself. Petrina was tied to Eastern Europe. She'd have to sever her ties to her clan to be free, and that would leave a bunch of baby vampires leaderless. Petrina was never going to stay here. She'd told Florence more than once that this plane could never be home, but somehow the witch had been certain she'd change her mind.

The eastern sky was beginning to lighten by the time Florence's eyes drifted shut.

She woke to the sound of shouting and distant screams. They were under attack!

Florence leaped out of bed, dressed as quickly as possible, grabbed her sword, and ran out of the tent. The camp was in chaos. The supply tents were burning, as were the makeshift stables. A centaur—not one she recognized—ran by her, a spear lodged in his side. She looked around, trying to find Eleanor in the crowd, but the queen wasn't visible. She was either going to be in the middle of the violence or spirited away and hidden by her determined guards. Either way, she was probably well protected and didn't need Florence's help.

The smell of smoke and blood and the screams of children drew her to the edge of the encampment just past the tree line that shielded the tents from the icy winds coming down from the mountain and across the river. A half dozen tall Fae with pale skin and silver hair were stuffing brown-skinned children—no more than five or six years old—into burlap bags, tying up the openings, and tossing them into a bonfire, laughing maniacally as they did so.

Something tried to penetrate her brain—why were there children in the camp? She'd not noticed any before now. But the screams of agony, quickly silenced, coming from the fires drove the thoughts away. She had to do something! She reached out with her magic and froze the flames, froze the Fae.

"Think!" she yelled at herself.

Florence looked around frantically. Her gaze fell on the mountains. They were heavy with snow—there must have been a late-night blizzard. She could use this. Ice and snow were her weapons of choice, the ones she'd been born with. And she would use them now to save the children. So many lost children. So many never seen again. She stretched up her power and felt the snow and ice. It was waiting for her. Eager to be used. Ready to answer her call.

"Florence!"

Someone was calling her. She shook her head. She'd find them later. Now she had to save the rest of the children before it was too late. There wasn't time to delay. She reached again, grabbed hold, and pulled—oh-so-gently—until the largest drift dislodged.

It slid down the mountain, slowly at first, but then faster, picking up speed and volume as it careened towards the camp and the white-skinned Fae who were taking the children.

"Florence, stop!"

No time to stop. No time.

She grabbed a boulder and pushed it into the path of the coming avalanche. These Fae would never hurt anyone again. She pushed more boulders into the torrent of snow racing down the mountain until it was a deadly tsunami of rock and snow.

Someone grabbed her shoulders and shook her.

"Florence!" Eleanor screamed. "You have to wake up. You're going to kill us all!"

Florence shook herself awake and looked back towards the Fae who were murdering the children. There was no one there—only a stand of birch trees ringed round a flame-red bush. No Fae. No fire. No children.

A roar caught her attention, and she looked up—the avalanche she'd called was rushing towards the camp. That was real.

The last of her dream fell away, and she shook the haze away from her eyes. The scene in front of her didn't change—they had only a few minutes before they'd be overtaken. She reached out to stop it, to return things to how they'd been before her nightmare took hold. It was too late. She was drained of power. She'd put everything she had into freezing the Fae who didn't exist and creating the avalanche that did.

"I can't," she confessed. "I can't stop it." She watched, tears freezing against her cheeks. Her pride and folly would do what all the assassins who'd come against them had failed to do. Kill the queen.

"I'll start melting the snow," Clement said, dashing in front of her. "Connor—can you and Alanna divert the boulders?"

"I can raise a wall to help divert the flood you're going to create," Connor said. "Does anyone know if there are any villages in the flood-plain downstream?"

Tanwen's voice rose over the rest. "Alanna and I will reroute the larger boulders away from the camp."

"What do you need me to do?" Eleanor asked. "I don't want to wade in and create more problems than I solve."

Clement grunted. "Can you fly downriver and warn anyone near the banks that they could get hit with a flash flood?"

"What of Florence?" Eleanor asked.

"I've got her," an unfamiliar voice said. "She's safe with me, and we'll be safe from her. At the first hint of shenanigans, I'll knock her out."

Florence watched as Eleanor shifted into her half form and

launched herself into the sky. Connor, Alanna, and Tanwen stepped forward to join Clement.

Heat swirled around him, then spun off towards the avalanche. Large boulders flew up and out of the snow, hovering for moment, then hurled off in various directions and out of the path of the avalanche.

A rock and earth wall rose out of the riverbank, curving toward the river. It looked like a limestone bobsled course, curling over the river and snaking its way downstream.

The snow, dotted with fallen trees and dirt, kept rushing towards them, but Florence saw the moment it hit the heat Clement was generating. The snow flew up and piled against the fiery barrier. Ice crested the barrier and froze, creating a solid crystalline wave that hung in midair. The trough of the wave started dripping, a gentle shower that refroze as more and more snow crashed into it. Soon, the icy swell of the wave was weighted down too much to hold, and it broke, crashing down into the river below.

The river spilled its banks as the water was displaced by massive chunks of ice. The freezing water shot up like a fountain and drenched everything around it, including the people at the banks desperately trying to save the camp.

The largest rocks had all been diverted so Alanna moved to Clement's side while Tanwen joined Conor in creating an Olympics-worthy slalom course to slow the rush of water.

Florence watched while Clement continued to heat the snow until it melted and refroze into the icy waves overhanging the river and Alanna directed the melting water into the earth and rockslides of the world's largest water park. The frozen waves kept crashing into each other, building up faster than they were melting, until the air above the river looked like an ocean storm.

A figure dropped out of the sky onto the highest wave and skated towards the camp, wings held out to either side like a sail. When she reached the edge of the ice, she soared into the sky and drifted to the ground next to the others. "No one in danger downstream," she announced.

"We're sorted here," Clement said, voice thin with strain. "If we have any nymphs or water sprites in camp, they can take over. A frost imp would be welcome, too, to keep the ice from melting faster than the diverters can handle it."

"I'll see to it," Eleanor said.

"What do you want me to do with the witch?" Rose asked.

"Take her to my tent and ask her to wait there. For now, let's make sure no one's been injured. Send word to have hot food and drink prepared for Clement, Connor, Alanna, and Tanwen."

"I'm sorry," Florence said—her first words since she'd woken up. "I didn't mean…"

Eleanor looked at her, and the disappointment and weariness in her face cut Florence to the core more than any amount of anger could have. She shivered, cold for the first time in her life.

"We'll talk later," Eleanor said. "Wait for me in my tent."

The queen turned her back on Florence and walked away, talking to the Fae who trailed her in tones too low for Florence to hear.

Florence's shoulders slumped in defeat. Everything she'd ever warned Eleanor of, every reason she'd hammered in the need for control, every lesson she'd ever taught…Florence had failed.

She followed Rose to Eleanor's tent and took the chair Rose indicated with a jut of her chin. Guards took up a post outside the tent flap, and Florence felt a binding to prevent anyone from leaving fall into place around her.

CHAPTER TWELVE

I stood in the center of the highest point on the Bridge to Nowhere and took in the scene. My army was lined up to cross through. Standing five abreast, they spanned the entire bridge and spilled into the valley behind me. Connor and Clement estimated it would take two hours to march everyone through if we made haste slowly.

Arduinna had popped in the day before to let me know Raj was ready for us. She didn't stick around to answer any of my questions and didn't give me any details. Just, "It's time. He knows you're coming and has a place identified. Later."

So, I'd called in my counselors, and they'd rallied the troops. Butterflies the size of harpy eagles fluttered in my stomach. So much was riding on today—on the next few days and weeks. I wasn't sure if the nervous stomach was excitement about seeing Raj again after three weeks apart, nerves about standing on an impossibly high bridge while hundreds of Fae streamed around me like a rock in a river, keeping the gate open and strong long enough for everyone to go through, or the impending war. Or maybe it was Florence ramping up my anxiety. We'd not spoken much since she'd nearly brought the mountain down on us. I'd tried to reach out to her once I was through being pissed off that she'd hidden her instability from me for so long, but she rebuffed all my advances like the stubborn witch she was. I was confident we could repair our friendship—if she'd let me.

I shook my head. Time enough to think about my erstwhile best friend later. Now, it was time. As I'd done before, I looked for my connection to the earth through the bridge, then identified the corresponding place in myself. I raised the scepter and the orb above my head and closed my eyes. The gate energy in the side of the mountain was ready for me this time. It reached out toward me, flowing into me and out through my objects of power. It fell more easily into the form I'd held almost a month ago, and this time, the tendrils of energy that reached towards me were more inquisitive than greedy. It recognized me and was content—or at least patient.

The energy swirled through me, the symbols of my authority in each hand and the ruby blade at my waist connecting me to my land and my love and forming a triangle of power that was reversed and hundreds of times larger as the anchors I held found the anchors in the mountain. This time, I was aware enough to identify the points holding the portal in the mountain—the hearts of the mountain. The apex was a ruby larger than my head, connecting with the ruby on my sword. The dragon gem representing fire and recognizing the dragon queen's right to use the gate and pass through the mountain.

In the lower left corner, corresponding with the orb I held in my right hand was a jade teardrop wrapped in a ribbon of gold. Earth and metal connected to fire above and reached out to me, stable in my power and control over the earth. The final anchor was chunk of lapis lazuli, pure blue and surrounded by silver threads in the rock. It shot a line to the scepter in my hand, air to air. Three elements in the rock reached out to three elements in my hands. All that was missing was water—the only element I couldn't control.

And then it hit me. Opal and diamonds in the center of the mountain's triangle shot forward and knocked me back. I couldn't breathe through the pressure in my chest as the water in the mountain looked for the water in me. For too many moments, I thought I'd failed in the most spectacular way, and then the opal searching for the corresponding point in me moved from my heart to my head. I don't know what it found, but the light and power and energy stopped pushing through me and surrounded me. I opened my eyes in time to see the gate open like an enormous aperture. Unlike the first time I'd opened the gate for Raj and Petrina and the rest of the scouts, this time it was almost effortless. I knew I wouldn't be able to hold it forever, but right now it was effortless.

I gave the signal to Connor who stood next to me to ensure I didn't get accidentally bumped over by any of the troops as they streamed by. Connor signaled to Alanna who was heading up the army at the front, and moments later, vibrations under my feet signaled movement. It was a long time before the people near me started moving forward, and longer still before all the troops were in front of me.

I closed my eyes. I knew I could hold the gate open longer if needed, but I was getting tired.

"The last ones are through," Connor said, touching my arm. "It's time for us to go." He helped me up onto the back of one of the three centaur guards who'd lagged back with us to carry us to the gate with as much speed as possible in case we needed to rush.

"Thank you, Ger," I said to the one who was carrying me. He was one of a set of triplets who'd known Alanna since she was young. She had complete trust in them, which meant I did, too.

His sister Genny grinned at me as Connor vaulted onto her back. "It's such an honor to bear you through the gate and closer to your destiny," she said. "We'll tell our grandkids about this."

Their last sib, Gin, snorted and struck the ground with their front hoof. "If we make it that far." They stood still and waited for Florence to climb astride. I hadn't realized the witch had hung back with us until she and Genny moved abreast of me and Ger. Connor and Gin flanked me on the other side and the six of us rode forward.

When we got to the gate, I touched Ger on the neck. "Can you stop for a moment, please?" I closed my eyes and reached up and out, finding the anchors in the mountain again. They were still shining brightly. I nodded. They'd hold, and I'd be able to find them again, even from the other side.

"Okay," I said. "I'm ready to go."

"Wait up!" called a voice behind me. I dropped the scepter and orb into the velvet bag and my waist and drew my sword as Ger spun around ready to fight. Running towards us was an entire company of dwarves led by Gloni.

"Hold!" I commanded the centaurs and Florence. Connor was as relaxed as ever. "These are allies."

"Dwarves haven't been allies for centuries," Genny spat.

"Well, they are now," I said.

Gin slapped Genny's bare arm, and I pretended not to notice the silent castigation.

"Of course, Your Majesty," Genny said.

Gloni reached me and nodded her head.

I matched her motion and then grinned. "What are you doing here?"

"We thought you might need some help, and we'd love to have a free land again. More market for Mjödvitnir beer, more buyers for our other creations, and fewer incursions by the rock trolls."

"You're more than welcome," I said. "But I'd appreciate if you'd all get through as fast as you can while remaining unobtrusive. Florence, can you and Genny ride through with Gloni so no one on the other side gets the wrong idea and attacks? Tell Clement I want the dwarves housed as far away from the main camp as possible. They need to be the last thing any spy sees."

I sensed more than saw the grimace on one of Gloni's captain's faces and turned towards him. "No offense meant, Master Dwarf. You all are an unexpected ally—and will serve that role better if we have the element of surprise. If we weren't at war, I'd walk proudly by your side through the main street of both the Dark and Light cities—and share a tankard with you anywhere. In fact, tell me the name you go by so I can seek you out after. I'll stand you as many beers as you can drink."

A broad grin broke out under his bushy beard. "You're on, queenie!"

I grinned at the informal address and glanced at Connor to make sure he knew everything was okay and that no one should take offense. He rolled his eyes and winked.

"Find me after the war is won. Ask for Reginn, son of Hreidmarr, metalsmith, deft of hand...and drinker of fine ale!" he finished with a roar.

I laughed, "Reginn, queen-friend, I cannot wait to drink a beer with you. I imagine the stories you have will warm me even more than the beer!"

Reginn saluted me with the battle axe he was carrying and looked to his queen. She nodded, and he led the rest of the dwarves through the gate.

I was starting to fade by the time we were once again alone on the bridge.

"Majesty, are you ready?" Connor asked, rousing me from my exhausted reverie.

"Yes," I slurred.

Connor looked at Ger. "Get her through now. We're right behind you."

My centaur galloped through; I felt like a sack of potatoes. I couldn't find my seat and every movement jolted my bones. Ger skidded to a halt, and I slid off his back. Someone caught me and held me upright.

"We're here, your Majesty," a voice familiar yet unidentifiable said. "You need to close the gate and you need to do it with control."

I shook my head. I was too tired. I felt my eyelids start to slide closed.

"Majesty!" Connor yelled. "You need to stay awake a bit longer!"

"Let me," a quiet, familiar voice said. I liked it. I felt safe and loved. I smiled. "I've got her," the woman continued. "Get everyone going where they need to be going and send for her vampire."

I slumped into the woman's arms. "I'm tired," I said. "Wanna sleep."

"Soon, Eleanor," she said. "Just one more thing first. Stand up straight."

"Can't," I said. I knew I needed to, but I didn't want to...posture was too hard. "I need a nap. And a beer."

"I'll help you. Draw on my strength."

I pried my eyes open and looked at the woman holding me up. "You were bad, Florence," I said. "You lied."

"Not exactly," she said.

I laughed around my exhaustion. "You're Fae now, then. Lies of omission."

"Just hold on to me, pull my strength if you need to. But before you recite my failings, close the fucking gate."

I stared at her. Florence almost never swore. She was right, though. Gate first. I straightened and held up my sword, grasping the bag with orb and scepter in my other. I found the anchor points both within and without, and slumped. It was too much. I could feel the gate energy eating away at me and knew I wouldn't be able to stop it before it overwhelmed me and used me like a grenade to explode my army.

"Run," I said.

"Shush," Florence retorted. "I've got you. Pull my strength."

I felt it then—earth magic, different than what swirled through my body and too strong to be denied. My spine straightened and my mind cleared. I closed my eyes, pooled the magic Florence was funneling towards me, and disengaged the anchors. First the ones in the mountain, then the ones in me. The gate slowly collapsed in on itself, pulling its magic back out of me and into itself. I collapsed quietly and dramatically on the floor.

"Eleanor!" Raj called from far away.

"She's fine, just tired," Florence said. "The gates are down. Take her to her tent and let her sleep. She did it."

I couldn't keep my eyes open any longer, not even to greet Raj. I felt him pick me up and thought I heard him say he loved me. And then, I slept.

I stood in the middle of my war tent and inhaled sharply. If our spies were to be believed—and since Raj was in charge of them, I didn't see why they shouldn't be—Medb's main force was less than a three hours' march away and the dragons and their giant allies—something no one really believed were too far away to be a problem. At least for today. It was dark, and the lanterns were lit. My forces were, for the most part, asleep.

The first battle was about to be met. I was sick with it. Everything I'd done in the last few years had led me here, and I was having second, third, and forty-fifth thoughts. I was leading a force to war. They wouldn't all survive. I looked around the command tent. They wouldn't all survive.

I wanted to call it off. Reopen the gate to the Light and rule that realm. Take everything back. Why did I need two thrones anyway?

The orb and scepter at my belt vibrated as if they could hear my innermost thoughts. Every time I considered going back, they vibrated. The one time I'd made it all the way to Connor's tent to tell him to retreat, the scepter had smacked me in the kidney—impossible based on physics, but totally possible based on the sharp pain in my low back.

I took a deep breath. "We are almost at war," I said. "We've all made the choice to be here, for better or worse. We must move forward. You all know what to do—Alanna, hold the centaurs on the left flank to move in once Medb's committed her main force. Clement, the right flank is yours. Bring in your battalion on Raj's signal. Connor, Florence, Raj, Petrina—you're with me. We'll wait for the main force and attack, first with magic waves designed to disorient. Medb's witches will be on the offensive, and we need to take them out. Confuse them, disarm them."

"Kill them?" Florence asked. We still weren't one hundred percent okay, but we were close enough to forgiveness to warrant a grin. "If that's what disarmament means to you, cold war operative," I said.

She rolled her eyes. "I was no one's *operative*. We'll get it done."

Connor stepped forward. "And what of the dwarves?"

I grinned. "Oh, I have a role for them. We all know this is only the beginning, right? Let's not get cocky. Get out there. Do your best. We have the superior force, we know where her ambush troops are, and we are going to win!"

A small but heartening cheer rose up in my tent, and I smiled. Raj reached out and squeezed my hand, and I turned my smile to him. The last twenty-four hours had been a whirlwind. All I wanted was ten minutes to catch up before the battle, but Medb's troops had shown up before I'd woken up from my magically induced coma. He was hiding something from me, but when I tried to tease it out, he deflected, sometimes physically, and there was always something else to keep my attention. I shrugged. It'd keep. There wasn't anything that wouldn't keep.

I walked out into the masses of people starting to gather as they woke, breakfasted, and armed themselves. I offered as many encouraging words as I could. There were too many for me to remember everyone's names, but I did my best to acknowledge everyone I did recognize. I looked in the eyes of the people who'd followed me to this point. Some of them would die. Die for me. Die for the idea that we deserved to be one united realm. Died to remove Medb from the throne. Died because their parents and grandparents remembered a better world. I wasn't sure it was enough, and I knew I couldn't dwell on it if I wanted to get through this.

As soon as most of my troops slated for this battle were milling around, gathering into companies and preparing for the day's battle, I climbed onto a makeshift stage Alanna had raised out of the ground for me and looked around. I'd given speeches. I'd talked to everyone. But today was like no other day. Today had to be special. More. I took a breath, caught Raj's eyes for a moment, and spoke.

"I am honored to be among you today!" I called. "Never before have I seen such an impressive group of Fae. Every one of you is here because you believe in me, in our mission. And I am grateful for your presence." So far, so generic. Nothing to inspire and ignite. I needed more. "For too long, magic has pooled here and not flowed freely between worlds. Too long have Dark and Light been separated. I woke the sleeping magic and restarted its flow, and I can unite our realms again. Once Dark and Light are one, two halves of a whole, we will have the balance promised by the opening of the final gate.

"I am Eleanor, twilight queen, catalyst and world breaker. I have the blood of dark and light in my veins, I have the knowledge of human and Fae to guide me, and I have the best fucking army of Fae in all the realms at my back!"

A steady roar rose from the ranks, swelling over me and pushing a smile onto my face. Battle speechifying wasn't too hard. Talk up the cause, throw out your credentials, and hype the warriors. Instant standing O.

I sobered.

"It's not going to be an easy road," I said as the applause died away. "Medb will hit us with the main force, will flank us with her secret armies, and hit us when she thinks we're down. But it's not an ambush if we know it's coming. And we have something she can't anticipate. Stand strong today, look to the north and south, and fight for my honor, for the honor of the Light, and for the future of all Fae!"

Swords and spears and bows were thrust into the air. The warriors filed into formations within their individual companies and moved into position. I turned around and Alanna called to the earth to raise my dais so I could see the field in front of me before taking command of the centaur cavalry on the left flank. Clement was already in place with the large beast cavalry on the right. Florence, Petrina, and Connor were with the center companies. And Raj was by my side to help direct the troop movements psychically.

As dawn broke, a thick fog settled over the battle in front of us.

"Hold steady," I said as we stood at attention for longer than we'd expected. The fog, although it felt natural, whispered sinister things to the wind. "She's baiting us."

We stood, frozen in time, until the sun started to burn away the fog. As the battlefield in front of us darkened into visibility, I gulped. Thousands of warriors stood in front of us. Our troops, which we'd anticipated outnumbering Medb's by fifty percent, were, in fact, outnumbered by almost ten to one.

I drew in a sharp breath. *"There are so many,"* I said to Raj. *"We should run."*

"No," he replied. *"We will prevail. Don't let your fear take over. We are better prepared, more cohesive, and we have one other thing on our side."*

"What?" I asked. My throat was so tight with anxiety I could barely breathe.

"You, my queen," he said.

The battle began. It was hard to see who was winning from here. My army wore scarlet and gold, but Medb's was gray and gold. Figures fell on the field and were still.

"Is this how it always is?" I asked Florence, the only one of my advisors who remained at my side.

She sighed. "It's my first war. But yes. Fear, hate, anger, death. This is the way of war."

I looked at her. "I don't care what you did or why. You're my best friend. But next time, talk to me or I will kick your ass." I turned my attention back to the scene in front of me.

Her hand reached out and grabbed mine. "I do not deserve forgiveness," she said.

"None of us do," I agreed. "But I forgive you, nonetheless. Don't let it go to your head."

She squeezed once, then let go of my hand. "We will win. I will make sure."

Florence sprinted into the fray, and I screamed wordlessly. I didn't want a sacrifice. I just wanted a fucking friend.

THE SUN WAS SETTING behind me, illuminating the battlefield in front of me in an eerie, macabre red. We were at a stalemate for the day, but if I was honest with myself, the Light had lost the field. Over a quarter of my troops had fallen in battle, and another large percent were too injured to fight again any time soon.

Medb had briefly appeared on the field riding an enormous scarlet dragon, who, if I was any judge of dragon expressions, and I thought I was, was singularly unimpressed with his royal passenger. She'd smote a couple foot soldiers, sought out my gaze, and tipped her ostentatious ribbon-bedecked top hat I was sure she'd had made for this specific occasion. I hoped it was special for this occasion. If it turned out Medb had a secret steampunk side, that needed to remain between her, whoever curated her wardrobe, and her god.

Raj and Florence were standing beside me; Connor, Alanna, and Clement were getting the official reports from the captains so we could regroup and restrategize for the next day's fighting. Raj took my hand.

"It is not hopeless," he said. "I've won the first battle and lost the war—this doesn't have to mean anything."

I knew he was right. I could feel his sincerity through our link and had read enough of history to know that one battle doesn't predict the outcome of the war. But I'd never lost before. I'd had to work hard for a win once or twice, but looking back on the last three decades, it was pretty obvious that my life had been easy as fuck. Even when things had gotten harder, it'd been an adjustment and not a real struggle. I wanted to suck it up. To roll with the punches that had come fast and hard today. But I'd lost. I'd lost and been taunted. By a usurping motherfucker riding a dragon.

"Eleanor?" Raj asked. "I know this is hard. I know you're struggling with how to handle this loss—both personally and strategically—but we need to regroup and figure out our next move. Medb outnumbers us by so much it's almost unbelievable. Especially since we had what I thought was decent intelligence form behind enemy lines. I have two suggestions if you'd be willing to hear them."

I closed my eyes for a minute to hold back the tears of anger and frustration that were threatening to spill forth. It had never occurred to me that I wouldn't win. The throne was mine. I could feel it calling to me. I'd found the orb and scepter that'd been lost for forty years. I was the catalyst. World breaker. The goddess had recognized me. How could I not win?

I took a deep breath and opened my eyes. "Let's talk strategy. I wish Isaac was here instead of relying on his weird missives. Does he need to be extricated? Extracted? Or whatever they do with spies?"

"I think he's okay for now," Raj said. "He's pretty busy with his many duties, and I don't think we could tear him away from Inge even if we tried."

I shook my head. Finding out that Isaac was nanny to the queen was oddly not the most surprising thing I'd learned recently.

"Well, let's not lose sight of his precarious position. I don't want him to be compromised. But I do want to know where Medb got all these extra troops."

"I'll call in the generals," Raj said. "In the meantime, you should change. Get out of the bloody clothes and into something comfortable. There's wine on the sideboard."

I smiled at him. "Wait a minute." He paused in the doorway. "I don't tell you often enough, Raj, but I love you. Without you—without everyone, of course, but you especially—I don't know where I'd be. You keep me centered and grounded even when it seems impossible. I know I'm not always the easiest to be around, but you don't make me feel bad about it."

Raj paused with one hand on the tent flap and looked back at me. Then he dropped the flap and walked towards me in three long steps. He grabbed my chin with one hand and tipped my face up until our eyes met. "I don't know who told you that you weren't easy to be around, but if I ever encounter that person, I will drink them dry. You are not difficult. You are not high maintenance. You are not "a lot." You are you. Eleanor. My twilight queen and queen of my heart. You are exactly the right amount, and anyone who says otherwise is not fit to lick the mud off your shoes."

I wasn't sure that I was supposed to be swooning and contemplating dragging him off to bed after that small speech, but I was. Fuck yeah, I was enough. The exact right amount. My chest swelled, and I reached up to brush my lips across Raj's. "Thank you for always knowing the exact right thing to say. I'm gonna nominate you for a Nobel Prize."

"Don't think they have a Nobel Prize for best lover or most attractive person, but I appreciate you recognizing my attributes," Raj said. He kissed me back, lightly but seriously. "Change. Have that drink. I'll be back with the council and someone else I want you to meet. Someone who's recently been behind enemy lines."

I caught the tension this introduction was causing but couldn't pick it apart. I guess I'd find out soon enough what he hadn't been able to tell me in the almost zero time we'd had alone together since being reunited.

I did as he suggested and changed out of my blood and muck-stained clothing into a pair of yoga pants and over-sized sweatshirt. I didn't often wear my Earth clothes when I'd be seen, but tonight called for maximum comfort. I poured a glass of wine, hesitated for a moment, then reassured myself that Raj wouldn't have encouraged me to drink it if it wasn't safe. I drank deeply—blackberry cobbler, tobacco, and forest loam floating over my tongue while the alcohol warmed my chest, and the wine dried my mouth. Fucking perfect. If I ever had time for hobbies, I was going to become a wine connoisseur.

I was curled on a low settee with my second glass of wine when the first of my councilors arrived. Alanna and Tanwen walked in. Alanna had a large bandage wrapped around one shoulder and a nasty looking bruise rising on the left side of her face.

"Are you okay?" I asked, rising to my feet and looking around for a first aid kit or some morphine or anything to help out.

"I'm fine," Tanwen interpreted. "Just annoyed and sore. I'd take a glass of wine, though, if you have one."

I poured two glasses and handed them over, trying to meet Tanwen's eyes to get a more complete report, but she avoided me adeptly.

Next to enter was Clement. His clothing was pristine—red and gold leathers—but his face told a different story. He had a cut across his left cheek that disappeared into his hairline. Connor followed with Florence. They were both grimy but uninjured. Gloni, followed with my new dwarf friend Reginn. Raj was the last to return, and he was accompanied by a woman I didn't know. She was tall, bright, and almost blinding. I couldn't place her, and didn't think I'd met her before, but something about her was familiar.

"Inneacht?" Connor said, staring at her in disbelief and what looked like a little awe. "Inneacht? You're... "

"Connor," the stranger said, striding forward and placing her hands on his shoulders. "It's been a lifetime, hasn't it?"

I watched their exchange which had more things unsaid than said, and tossed significant looks at Raj, hoping he'd introduce his beautiful Fae guest.

Once Connor and the newcomer had finished staring and subtexting, Raj looked at me and said, "Everyone, this is Inneacht. She's lived as a 'guest' of the Dark Court for centuries but is originally of the Light. This is Inneacht, Phoenix Jarl, former heir to the Light Throne, twin to Eochid, lately gone from this plane, and Queen Mother."

Raj was staring right at me when he pronounced her last epithet. Queen Mother. That was the mother of the installed ruler, right? Twin to Eo, mother of the queen. I was queen. That meant that...

"Mother?" I croaked.

CHAPTER THIRTEEN

I paced the perimeter of my tent resolutely refusing to look at the woman sitting in the middle of the room sipping a glass of wine. After I'd rebuffed the hug she'd offered, she hadn't spoken to me directly. I couldn't tell if she was hurt by my rejection—which was more shock than actual rejection—or giving me space to get used to the idea of having a living parent after all this time.

Inneacht had answered all the questions she could about Medb and her plans. We didn't learn too much from her, which wasn't surprising. Her sole interaction with Medb in the last forty years was when the faux queen requested she check on Isaac and Inge. I was a lot more suspicious of that request than anyone else seemed to be. Why would Medb ask the mother of the Catalyst—the catalyst who was supposed to be dead—to check in on her own kid? Nothing any of the Fae did made sense to me.

I drained my glass. I wasn't making sense either.

I stopped pacing long enough to pour myself another glass of wine. Thanks be to whoever made me that the Fae can metabolize alcohol like no one's business. The last thing I needed tomorrow was a hangover. I had so many questions, comments, accusations brewing in my head that I didn't know where to start. Logically, I knew that my whole life wasn't her fault. Well, it *was* in that she gave birth to me. But she hadn't arranged it to play out the way it did. Probably.

When I finished my second glass of wine, I wasn't any closer to finding the right words as I'd been before. Fuck it. Since when had finding the right words ever mattered to me before?

"Inneacht," I said, whirling around to face the luminous Fae seated on my couch.

"Mother," she corrected.

I rolled my eyes. "Inneacht. I'm gonna need a family tree. I was passed off as Eochid's kid for so long that it might take people a minute to adjust their thinking and assign my parentage to his sister instead. The sister I never heard mentioned." I narrowed my eyes at her. After all, we had only her word that she was Eo's twin.

"Do you often hear the Fae speak of the dead?" she asked.

I thought back. I couldn't remember anyone talking of who'd come before. Even with Eo being gone less than a year, no one said his name. Or Cloithfinn's name. "Nooo," I said slowly, drawing out the "o" as I wracked my brain.

"Gone isn't exactly forgotten, but it's considered unwise to talk too much of those who've gone before. You know that the powerful Fae can hear their names spoken and find the speaker, right?"

I nodded. "I've been told, although I've seen no evidence of that myself. I've never heard anyone gossiping about me, and I'm one of the most powerful Fae in the last several millennia."

"And is Eleanor your name?" she asked. "Or is it—" her voice trailed off into a barely audible whisper, and I leaned forward to catch every word. "—Ciara?" The last word was so quiet even a vampire couldn't have heard her unless they were close.

I straightened up. Not even Eo had known my name—or if he had, he'd never mentioned it. No one had.

"How?" I started. "How did I know?"

"I whispered it to you when you were born. The midwife allowed me to hold you before they took you from me, and I named you. They showed me the heart, you know."

"What heart?" I asked. There was too much going on to follow any of the threads being cast out.

"They took you from me to kill you," Inneacht said. "Connor came for you. He looked me in the eye, said he was sorry, and carried you away to kill you. He returned to the castle with your heart—or at least what he said was your heart—as proof that he'd carried out the task the queen had given him. They made me stand in the throne room and watch him present it to the Raven Bitch. And then, she gave it to me as a memento. For years, I've kept the box with your heart in it in my quarters. But then the rumors started—the Catalyst was moving. Something I hadn't experienced in decades—centuries maybe—woke in me. Hope."

"Connor did what?" I needed a nap. And a clearly spelled out timeline with all major characters defined. Maybe a family tree. Definitely another drink. I poured more wine and filled Inneacht's glass as well. "He brought a baby heart to the queen and passed it off as mine? And everyone believed him? How? What did he say exactly?"

"I don't remember his exact words," Inneacht said. "I was exhausted and in pain—yours was not an easy birth. And I was griev-ing. I'd wanted you for so long and didn't even get a chance to do more than hold you for a couple minutes before you were ripped from my arms to be killed. But whatever he said satisfied the queen, and that devastated me."

"I told the queen and her court that I had fulfilled the wishes of the true queen and seen to the destruction of the one who threatened the throne."

"And she fell for that?" I asked. "And then fell for it again when Marie said something similar?"

Connor shrugged. "I had a tiny heart in a box, I was covered in blood, and I had been elevated when I helped her take the throne from Donall."

"Why would've you helped her?" Inneacht demanded.

"Why do you think?" Connor demanded. "She's my sister."

"Wait a motherfucking minute," I said. If I thought I was having trouble processing before, this was too much. "No wonder she believed you. How long did you stay in her court after that?"

"One more night. Long enough to see Anoka again, to pledge my undying love, and to assure her that I'd find a way to get us both out."

I sat down on the ground and stared at the floor.

"It didn't take you long to replace me," Inneacht said, the edge in her voice bordering on accusation.

"You were pregnant with another man's child," Connor said. "My nephew's child. What was I supposed to do?"

"You idiot," Inneacht raged. "What made you think she was Mata's?"

THE TENT SPUN around me and my vision blurred. It was a good thing I was already sitting down, because this was...a lot.

"Are you saying?" I asked at the same time Connor said, "Why didn't you tell me?"

I looked at Connor and Inneacht. Holy fuckballs, Batman. I'd been orphaned for almost twenty years, and even when I found out they were my adoptive parents, I still didn't have anyone. I'd gotten used to not having a family after my parents died in a car accident on the way home from my college graduation, and even though Eo had been my presumptive father—a fact that he, Connor, and I all knew to be false —I'd still known I was alone in the world.

And now, all of a sudden, I had two living parents.

"I would've told you," Inneacht said to Connor. "But the only time I saw you after I found out I was pregnant was the day you took her from me."

Connor winced.

"Where'd you get the heart?" I asked. It was probably the least important detail of all of this, but I couldn't stop thinking about it.

"Baby pig," Connor said.

Another thought hit me. "Raj! Did he know" —I gestured wildly around me— "all this?"

"He knew I was your mother, obviously. That's why he agreed to sneak me out of the palace and bring me here. The only other person before now who knew the true identity of your father was the wolf nanny. I believe you dallied with him once upon a time?"

I really hadn't had enough time to catch up with Raj once we were reunited, and either he was keeping things from me, or I was too... everything...to hear his surface thoughts.

"*A bit of both,*" he said in my mind. "*I knew Connor was your father as soon as Inneacht showed up demanding I take her with me. The thought rose unbidden in Isaac's mind, but I didn't reveal my knowledge to anyone. I try not to preempt people's big reveals unless necessary. And besides, you have been busy.*"

"*Wanna join the family reunion?*" I asked him through our mental link. "*Guess it's time for you to get to know your in-laws.*"

"*If you want me there, I will come immediately.*"

The mental picture he sent me made me want to kick Inneacht and Connor out and deal with them tomorrow. I missed Raj's touch and falling into bed with him was infinitely preferable than dealing with new family times.

"*Please.*" I then turned my attention outwards again. "Raj is on his way here. We can be one big, happy family. I should probably get Petrina, too. She's kinda like your grandkid now, right?"

"And what of the witch?" Inneacht asked. "Is she not the sister of the one Connor left me for?"

Connor huffed. "I didn't leave you. You were married to the crown prince and pregnant with his child. I was helping my sister depose your father-in-law. It was a very complicated situation."

"I need to know more about your sister," I said. "How come you've never said anything about this before? Don't you think it might've been nice to share your inside knowledge of the woman we're up against? And also, is overthrowing the Dark Throne a hobby? A calling? How long will I sit on the throne, should we win, before you decide to get rid of me in favor of the next generation?"

Connor was spared from answering for the moment by Raj's arrival.

"Forces are gathering on the hills to the north," he said by way of greeting. "We're going to have to table the family reunion for now. Connor, if you have any information that will help us drive back Medb's dragons, now's the time."

I did a mental calculation. "Connor, if you're my father and Mata's uncle and Medb's brother and the old king's son, are you..."

"A dragon?" he finished. "I am. Although my sister is not—she takes after her mother's family. That gift usually runs true in the women of the line."

"This seems like it could've been relevant information when you & Eo were training me. You both knew what I was. I'm flying blind here. Half literally."

There were too many fucking secrets. Too much information conveniently forgotten or held back until later. And it didn't seem malicious, or even purposeful. It was just a bunch of assholes who were used to never sharing information, a thousand plus years old, and very full of their own importance. I huffed.

"We knew the dragons would attack from the North," Raj reminded me. "We know they have a tentative alliance with the giants. We are prepared for this. Gloni and her army are ready for this. Now that we know Connor is more familiar with those fighting, perhaps he can help inform the strategy, but we are as ready as we can be for this."

"I'll join Gloni," Connor said. He bowed to me, nodded to Raj, and then turned to Inneacht. "I was wrong," he said. "I don't know how I can make this up to you, how I can atone for the hurt I caused. Even if she was truly Mata's daughter, what I did was cruel. I'd like to believe that if I'd stayed, I would've found a way to tell you the truth, but if I'm being honest, I don't know. I haven't thought about you and how you might be feeling in years. Decades. Too long."

Inneacht smiled tightly. "One of your greatest faults has always been your compulsion to tell the whole truth at the most inopportune times. I have not forgotten nor forgiven, and I don't know if I ever will. Now go. Mata leads the dragons now. Perhaps he can be reasoned with."

"Does he know who I am?" I asked. "Does he know his supposed child leads this force?"

"I don't know, but it'd be worth telling him who your mother is in case he is unaware of your identity," Raj said.

Connor rolled his eyes. "I'll fly out to meet them under the flag of parlay. I'll greet him as family, make sure he knows who your mother is, and see if I can convince him to back down. After all, it should be their dream to have a Dragon return to the throne, even if Mata will never sit on it himself."

"He's power mad and not bright," Inneacht said with a curled lip. "The usurper probably promised him something. I think she said she'd marry him after I died."

"Aren't they related?" I asked. "Isn't Mata her nephew?"

Inneacht nodded. "Yes. But it's more complicated than that. The Raven and Dragon families are regarded as totally separate, no matter where they come from. There are few that would bat an eye if Connor and Medb were to wed, though they are twins."

"Um. No," I said. "I'm not down with twincest. I'm gonna make some laws about this immediately. Maybe right now. It's my first executive order."

Inneacht patted my arm. "It's uncommon for siblings to wed, no need to worry. I was just trying to explain why Mata might believe he has a chance at the throne."

"I'll talk to Gloni on my way out," Connor said.

"Come back," I said. I might not have fully accepted that he was my biological father, but I'd known him for a while now, and he was one of my favorite Fae.

"You can't get rid of me so easily," he said. "I'll be back by midday, although I expect you'll know whether or not I was successful before that."

I watched him walk out with a sinking feeling that this was the last time I'd see him.

GLONI AND I stood on a raised dais facing north. The dragons hadn't made their first move yet, but neither had they retreated. There weren't any giants in sight, and I was crossing my fingers the uneasy alliance had fallen apart before it started. Nerves churned my stomach, and I was positive that any sudden movement would cause me to lose my breakfast on Gloni's shoes. She patted my arm. "Do not despair. The dwarves have never lost to the dragons. All will be well."

Florence approached on my other side and grabbed my hand. Raj and Petrina were keeping an eye on Medb's main troops and the south where the ravens were purportedly gathering. "It'll be okay," she said.

"Are you saying that to make me feel better, or do you *know*?"

She didn't reply, which was answer enough. I turned back to my watch, scanning the horizon for any movement.

"Something's coming!" someone yelled from the dwarf forces in front of us.

I squinted, and for a moment thought the dwarf might've been mistaken, but then I saw it. A smudge of darkness growing larger by the second sped towards us. A dragon—larger than the one Medb had ridden into battle the day before—was flying toward our camp faster than I would've thought possible.

"Ready!" Gloni yelled.

The dwarf ranged company raised their crossbows while the rest of the troops dropped to their knees and out of the way.

"Hold steady!" she yelled.

None of us knew what Connor looked like in his dragon form, and it'd been a real shame if we brought him down with friendly fire. The dragon dropped from the sky several yards in front of my dwarves' army and changed shape. It was Connor—his clothing shredded. He sprinted through the ranks.

Once he was within easy earshot, he yelled, "They're coming! Be ready!" The dwarves turned back toward the north waiting for the signal, and I jogged down to where Connor had collapsed. He was bruised and bloodied, and his hair had been singed. I helped him up and into the arms of a nearby medic. He tried to wave away the medical attention.

"I'm fine. Tired and sore, but fine. There will be plenty of others to care for soon."

"What happened?" I asked, splitting my attention between him and the northern horizon.

"Mata was not excited to see me, and he declined my suggestion that he either back Inneacht's child or at the least, stand down."

"Did he offer an explanation as to why he didn't want to take his place in my court as the supposed father of the queen? Is the Queen Father a thing? I've never heard anyone in England call it that."

"He's not interested in a cushy court life unless there's a throne to go with it," Connor said. He took the wet rag someone offered him and started dabbing the blood off his forehead, wincing as he hit a particularly sensitive spot. "He's convinced himself that he's on the cusp of greatness and will finally regain his throne."

"Why does he think he'll get it now when it's been withheld from him for half a century and more?" I asked. A dark smudge had appeared on the horizon, and with each passing second it grew larger and larger until it filled my view.

"He is under the impression that Inneacht is dead. Her life was the barrier for all these years."

"That's ridiculous," I said trying to keep my voice steady through the increasing fear as I watched the dragons approach. "He could've divorced her at any time. Or had her killed, if that's what was standing in the way."

"He didn't explain the minutiae of his arrangement with Medb while his goons were kicking my ass," Connor said testily. "But I imagine some of it was Medb using Inneacht as an excuse and keeping her protected and alive to hold Mata at arm's length."

"Did you see the giants?" Gloni asked.

"I did not, Your Majesty," Connor said. "That's not to say they were gone…they are excellent at camouflaging themselves, despite their immense size."

I stood and drew my sword. I couldn't leave the dwarves to fight this swarm alone.

Connor reached out and grabbed my arm. "Your Majesty, you

cannot walk into this battle. You are the commander of these forces, and there are more fronts than this to pay attention to. The main army will attack again today, and we must keep watch on the ambushing force to the South. The dwarves know what they're doing. Watch."

I did as he said and saw the crossbows rise again. When their queen gave the signal, they fired, and a rain of bolts filled the air. Most found their marks in the soft underbellies of the oncoming horde, but only one dragon fell. A continent of dwarves I hadn't seen before swarmed the fallen beast, and within seconds, the thrashing stopped and the smoke rising from their nostrils trickled to a stop.

Another wave of bolts filled the air as the queen commanded a second volley. This time, three dragons fell and were summarily dispatched by the teams waiting in the rocks. Being the defending army had its advantages—all the best hiding spots were staked out.

The crossbow contingent dropped their bows and drew axes and fastened on their shields. I wasn't sure how an army of land-bound dwarves was going to counter a sky full of dragons, even if the dragons were outnumbered three to one. The first wave of flames swept over the company. As one, they raised their shields and created a seamless triangle. The dragon flames not only didn't penetrate the defenses, they were reflected back, singing eyes and wings. Another dragon fell.

But still, they came, belching fire and smoke. Some smaller, speedy dragons were darting in and out dropping boulders and trees they'd ripped from the nearby hills. The distinctive sound of a trebuchet caught my attention. A hail of rocks, burning pitch, and iron filings flew through the air. When the dragons recoiled from the attack, they breathed in the iron and filled their lungs with poison.

I started to feel hopeful—maybe this was the turn in the tide we needed. I turned to smile at Connor but stopped when I saw the wide-eyed horror on his face.

"Giants," he said. "The bloody giants are here."

CHAPTER FOURTEEN

It'd been another rout. Once the giants joined the dragons, we couldn't keep ahead of the onslaught. Medb's regular forces attacked shortly after the giants arrived, and we were kept busy defending our position and trying to stay alive. I pulled back all the forces behind our small perimeter and commanded everyone to stay back. We would not go on the offensive today.

I was sick with the idea that so many had died. Were dying. Again. I'd done this.

All I did was rain down death and destruction. First, I destroyed Earth and now I was doing the same to the Fae Plane.

"Eleanor. Stop."

Florence's voice pulled me from my spiral of despair and guilt.

"Do you remember what you told me when first we met about the events that had taken place around Portland when you opened the first gate? About why you needed to continue?"

I closed my mind and called up that memory.

"I said that I don't half-ass things. I either commit or I don't. In retrospect, that sounds like a terrible way to go through life."

"Nothing wrong with putting your whole self into something. I think whole-assing it is almost always appropriate. But beyond saying you were committed to opening the gates because that's what you decided, you also told me that if you and I couldn't find a way to mitigate the damage, to stop the loss of human life, that you'd stop. You'd give up your life to save the lives of hundreds of thousands of humans who might be killed by the uncontrolled magical bursts."

I dropped my head into my hands. "I didn't do very well there, did I? People still died."

"And if you hadn't opened the gates, people would've died anyway. Once the first gate opened, nothing would've stopped that tide. You and I did the best we could. That's all we can do at any moment. The best we can. Commit to a path and stay on it unless better information comes along."

I squinted at her and tilted my head to one side. "I'm not sure I'm following. Am I supposed to keep on with this war even though we're taking heavy losses, or am I supposed to gather my people and go?"

"Your counselors, those who've had exponentially more experience in war than you, haven't advised you to stop. You have the kind of relationships with each of them that allows them to be honest with you. Keep those lines of communication open—really listen to what they're telling you. If they say it's time to pack it in, you do it. But if they're advising you to stay the course, believe them. They might be ancient assholes, most of them, but they are strategic. None of them wants to be bogged down in a losing war. Don't get wrapped up in guilt. Don't get stuck in your own head."

I closed my eyes and took a deep breath. I remembered what I'd said what seemed like a lifetime ago when Florence and I first met in a video lottery business in Rapid City, South Dakota. "I'm with Spiderman on this—with great power comes great responsibility and all that. I brought everyone here, not just for the throne that calls to me, but for the land that wants to be healed. For the families separated by an invisible divide. For the Dark Fae suffering under a despotic rule. Walking away because I'm scared of failing isn't leadership, and I will lead." I straightened my spine and looked up and over the crowds of people milling around seeking medical care and food and comfort and sleep at the end of a second hard day of fighting.

Power rushed through me and I felt my wings break through the back of my shirt.

"Raj—can you confirm my airspace is clear?"

"Give me a minute, my sweet," he said.

I fidgeted waiting for the all-clear, but a great, inspirational speech in the face of defeat wouldn't be very effective if I was assassinated mid-sentence.

Raj appeared beside me, and I jumped. He laughed, and I threw an elbow. *"Jerk."*

"You're all clear, Your Majesty," he said aloud. *"You still haven't gotten me a bell. I have to take advantage of it sometimes. I have your back. No one will hurt you under my watch."*

I stretched my wings and launched myself into the sky.

"Armies of the Light!" I called. My voice carried farther than I'd expected; nearly everyone in the camp was turning to stare at me. It was dark other than cooking fires and the few torches that marked the paths to the privies, medical tents, and other important destinations. A purple glow surrounded me and lit me up for the crowds.

"The last couple days have sucked major ass," I started, because as queen, I was nothing if not dignified.

Fuck that shit. They'd heard me be dignified. I'd been following protocols and speaking correctly and bringing the ceremony. It was time they got to know their queen for real.

"We have lost two major battles. We've lost too many of our compatriots. And it feels like we're up against an inexorable tide. When I first thought about this war to retake the Dark Throne, it was for me and not you. And for many of you, you probably don't see it any differently.

"But I'm doing this for all of us. Those who grew up noble with the big houses and household witches to enhance their power might not feel it the way you will but imagine a realm united. A realm where you don't have to be rich to wield power. A realm where there are no slaves. No hereditary houses that everyone pretends don't exist. That's what I'm fighting for. The Light and Dark to come back together in balance. They call me World Breaker, because that's how we heal. The dwarves call me the Twilight Queen because I am the balance between light and dark. I will be your Dragon Queen by virtue of my father, but I am your Phoenix Queen, born of Inneacht, sister to Eochid, daughter of Belenus, the Fae god of sun, fire, and healing."

Clement walked forward, hands clasped in front of his waist and gazed up at me. He didn't say anything, but a smile played around his lips.

"So, tonight, we will mourn the dead and care for the injured. Tomorrow we will fight again. And when the so-called-queen falls before us and the Dark Fae are freed at last, we will raise a glass to victory!"

A low roar started off to my left—I suspected the dwarves were behind it—and spread across the field until all my people were cheering my commitment to getting them killed on the regular. I plastered a smile to my face and lowered back to the ground. The glow around me dissipated, and I was once again in the dark.

RAJ WAS WAITING when I returned to my tent. I didn't know how I'd get through each day if it wasn't for him. He was at my side every minute of the day, lifting me up when I needed a boost, running my errands when I needed extra hands, and always waiting for me at the end of my day with a glass of wine, a neck massage, and little else.

"I hope you know how much I appreciate you," I groaned as he dug into the knots that had formed in my shoulders.

"I know," he said. "You invite me into your dreams."

I tilted my head to the left to give him better access to the tight muscles at the base of my neck. "What dreams?" I asked. The warmth of the tent, the alcohol, and his talented fingers were sedating me.

"You have very explicit dreams sometimes," he said. "And if I'm asleep, you pull me into them."

I jerked my head back up and smashed the back of it into his nose. There was a muffled grunt behind me, and the massage stopped. I thought I was beyond being embarrassed, particularly when it came to

Raj. He'd already seen every part of me—both physically and mentally. Or so I'd thought. A slow, hot flush crept up my cheeks as I remembered the dream I'd had the night before about Spock, a briefcase full of carrots, some alien experiments, and ultimately sexual frustration.

"Oh my god," I said. "Sorry about your nose, but I'm afraid we have to break up now and I am just going to lay down under my bed and let the earth take me. Give my apologies to the troops and send them home. Just don't tell them about the carrots."

"You have a lot of sex dreams about carrots," Raj said, resuming the massage. "My favorite was the one where you saw the French carrots wearing berets and riding tandem bicycles and followed them home for a very strange threesome."

I hadn't realized that a person could literally die from dream shame, but here we were, about to test that theory for the first time.

"Stop," I begged. "Please, no more." If he got to the one where I'd married a lobster and moved to Maine, I wasn't sure I could take it. At least there weren't carrots in that one, though.

Raj laughed against the side of my neck. His breath raised goosebumps on my skin, and I shivered. "If it were up to me, all your dreams would end with you satisfied. More than satisfied. Limp, exhausted, sated, but utterly sure you'll never get enough of me."

I set down my wine and twisted around to twine my arms around his neck. "All my best dreams do end that way," I said, pulling him close for a kiss. "I wouldn't trade you for all the carrots on the USS Enterprise."

"I am much more skilled with a carrot than Spock could ever be," Raj murmured, sliding his hands up and under the shift I was wearing.

"I don't know," I teased, twining my fingers in his hair. "He had an entire suitcase full of carrots of various sizes and shapes...what do you have that he doesn't?"

Raj bared his teeth at me and the fangs that were usually virtually unnoticeable glimmered in the lamplight.

"Oooh, big scary vampire!" I said in my best little-girl voice as I opened my eyes as wide as I could. "Are you going to bite me?" I clasped my hands in front of my chest and fluttered my eyelashes.

"I vant to suck your blood," he intoned.

"Is that a wooden stake in your pocket or are you just happy to see me?"

He laughed, and his fangs no longer looked prominent anymore. I knew they were there. Knew that if I reached out and ran my tongue along his teeth, I'd feel them, that I could puncture my lip against them. But somehow, I never saw them unless he wanted me to.

"Vampire magic," he reminded me. "I don't want to scare the pretty ladies away."

"Or the pretty men?" I asked. I grabbed my glass of wine again and took a sip.

"Nothing scares the pretty men away," he said. "Turn around and take off your shirt. Let me finish your massage and then I'll show you what I can do that Spock can't."

I did as I was commanded and stretched out on the bed. Raj's wonderful hands drifted over my skin from waist to shoulder before settling in on the muscles at the base of my neck and slowly traveling downwards, following the trail of knots. The tension drained out and was replaced by heat pooling low in my core. The things this man could do to my body. He was about to get extremely rewarded for this. My eyes closed in bliss.

"WAKE UP," Raj said.

I sat up, blinking groggily. "What time is it? What's happening?"

"All three sides are closing in. The Ravens moved in in the night and are poised to attack from the south. The dragons and giants are harrying the northern lines, and Medb's main force has already started their attack. They're catapulting rocks and balls of flaming pitch at us through the dark. It's pretty easy to avoid and extinguish now, but the sun will be up in about an hour, and I'm assuming their aim will get even better then."

I jumped up and started digging through the chest at the foot of my bed. Raj handed me the clothes I was desperately trying to find.

"Wear these. And slow down. This is urgent, but you don't need to rush out of here half asleep and fully panicked. Take a moment. Breathe. Get dressed. There's time to pee and get a glass of water and brush your teeth. Connor, Gloni, Alanna and the others will be waiting for you in the war room. Most of your counselors were asleep, too."

I inhaled deeply, held it for the count of five, then exhaled forcefully, pushing the air back out of my lungs. I took a beat, then repeated the process several times until my heart rate returned to normal and the adrenaline surge of being woken from a sound sleep after a night of...

"Damnit," I said. "Did I fall asleep again before..."

Raj kissed my head and offered his hand to hold me steady while I dressed. "You did. It's okay. You need the rest and the relaxation more than either of us needed release."

I pursed my lips and zipped up the soft, black hoodie I was wearing over my more traditional Fae clothes. I couldn't fault the comfort and style of the tailored tunics, breeches, and leather boots, but sometimes, a woman just wanted the comfort of an oversized hoodie with the local PBS logo on the back. "I'll make it up to you," I said. "It's been happening too much lately."

Raj kissed my cheek and handed me a glass of water. "I know you will. After this war is won and we have oodles of freetime, like royalty does."

I punched his arm. "Sarcasm is not always required."

"It's always required," he answered. "But I'll let it go for now. You've got this. We planned for this moment. We are prepared."

"Like we were prepared for the giants?" I asked. My spine straightened as I prepared to exit my tent and walk through the makeshift streets of my encampment.

He shrugged. "There are always surprises in war," he said pragmatically.

"For once, I'd like to be the surpriser and not the surprisee," I said sourly. "I need some good news for once."

"I think I have some, Your Majesty," a voice said from the shadows.

I shrieked and jumped sideways away from the voice and into a tentpole. My people were so lucky to have such a graceful monarch.

"Do you not remember me?" the voice asked.

I peered into the darkness but didn't see anyone. Obviously, someone was there—unless I was hearing voices—but they were apparently invisible.

"Not invisible," Raj said. "Just one with the shadows."

"Oh. I forgot. I so seldom manifest anymore." A figure stepped forward, giving the impression of darkness detaching from the shadows. They were about three feet tall with black skin, black feather-like hair, and wings instead of arms. Their face had two large orb-like dark eyes that lacked a pupil. A long, sharp beak with two nostril holes took the place of a mouth. Their humanoid legs ended in talons, black of course, and if you stared too hard or too long at Branna, they...moved. The feathers would shift, and faces would peek out between gaps in the wings. Branna's chest had two breast-like protrusions that were too low and too lacking in nipples to look quite right, and hanging down their backside was a wide, notched tail. They, for there were many creatures in there, looked like large humanoid crow.

"Branna!" I said, rushing forward, although whether to hug them or give them a good smack for their seeming betrayal and abandonment, I didn't know.

They stepped back and out of the way, neatly sidestepping me.

"What are you doing?" they asked.

"Hugging you?" I replied. "Then maybe kicking you in the shins."

"No."

I shrugged. I wasn't usually much of a hugger anyway, and completely understood Branna's reticence towards the embrace and the kick. I shifted gears. "What are you doing here? And now? Shouldn't you be out killing those who threaten the queen?"

"I felt you cross the border. You have two of the three objects of power that tie you to the throne," they said. "I've been waiting for an opportunity to come see you without being obvious. Today is such an opportunity. And those monks were coming to kill you with magic and exploding powder weapons. I took care of them and their weapons."

"Walk with me," I said. "I need to meet with my war council. We have another battle soon."

"I know," they said, their voice vibrating in several tones simultaneously.

I looked at them sharply. Branna was a sluagh—a manifestation of the spirits of the dead. They—and the host at their command—comprised much of the wild hunt and relished the battlefield where there were many souls to gather as they departed their mortal coil. I remembered the last time I'd seen them—in the battle between the evil monks, vampires, and shifters in the Czech countryside—they'd delivered a pile of dead, evil monks to Medb. They'd never hidden the fact that they cared more for the throne than the person occupying it, but I thought we'd been friends. Maybe friendship with the embodiment of battlefield death was more difficult than I'd thought.

"Why this one and not the previous battles?" I asked. "We've been losing terribly and there have been many dead on both sides."

Branna looked at me but didn't answer.

Dread built up in my chest until I could barely breathe. They were here now because this battle would be a feast and not an appetizer. "Will we win?" I asked, not sure I wanted to know the answer.

"I don't know," they replied. "I cannot see the outcome, and all the dead look the same to me."

I bowed my head. I had to stop it. Even if we were the victors, that still meant too many dead—too many who were only fighting because a queen called them forth. I took a resolute breath and strode towards the command tent. Hopefully, I wouldn't be too late to put an end to this madness before any more people died.

"The ravens are attacking!" someone yelled. I looked to the southern sky. Dawn was beginning to lighten the southeastern horizon, but the swarm of darkness like an evil fog was still barely visible. I blinked and rubbed my eyes.

People had talked about the ravens, and I had foolishly imagined a host of bird-sized creatures. What I hadn't considered is that on the

Fae plane, Branna was a bird-sized creature. Each raven was between three and seven feet long with wingspans to match. Several were harnessed together in groups of four and six and pulling chariots full of armed warriors through the sky.

"The dragons are coming!" A voice yelled from behind me.

CHAPTER FIFTEEN

I stood in the middle of the command tent. There was activity all around me as the various commanders of my forces conferred with each other and with the runners who'd go out to relay orders to the troops. I knew Alanna and Tanwen were anxious to join the rest of their forces in their efforts to repel the southern incursion, and Gloni was equally motivated to join the dwarves to beat back the combined armies of dragons and giants.

It was a lot. We'd known going in that we'd have to fight the ravens, and we'd prepared for the dragons, but the giants had been unexpected. As were the sheer numbers Medb had in her main force —we needed to know more about them. I needed to pull back from the main front and divert my forces to the other two fronts. We were penned in and losing. I opened my mouth to give the order to pull back the centaur cavalry to help defeat the ravens when Raj interrupted me before I could speak.

"I have an idea," he said sounding more tentative than I'd ever known him to be. The vampire was nothing if not bold. But something about this, about what he was about to say, was playing against insecurities I hadn't even known he had. I wanted to dive into his mind, to figure out what had damaged his confidence and fix it, but I held back.

Not only was he my love—someone I needed to trust to fight his own battles—he was my named consort, and someone who needed to be trusted by my people to lead them in my stead.

I took a step back and let him have the floor.

When he spoke again, his voice was strong, steady, confident. "I've studied warfare and battles almost my entire life," he said. "I have participated in more than I can count. And I have seen the smaller, outnumbered, and outclassed forces take the day and win the war. I know how we can take the Ravens and the main force, regardless of their number. I need assistance in determining how to delay the Dragons and giants." He walked to the table where we had everything laid out, Risk style, and started rearranging our troops.

Connor and Alanna watched closely, and I watched them. The tension that had kept their shoulders raised up around their ears melted away, and for the first time since we'd found out about the giants, they lost their twin looks of grim determination.

"This is doable," Connor said. "Clement and Petrina should take control over the southern forces, as we'd originally planned. Alanna and Tanwen can command the main forces if you'll be willing to join them as their eyes and ears and coordinate the timing."

"Of course," Raj said. "But that leaves the dragons to you and Gloni. Do you have an idea on how to delay them?"

"Harry them and keep them from advancing as long as possible," Connor shrugged.

"My army has been busy building mini siege engines," Gloni said. "With a little pitch and someone to help us light some fires, we'll be able to hold them back. Dragons can't fly with holes in their wings, and once they're grounded and human-shaped, they're a lot easier to defeat."

"What of the giants?" Alanna asked. "Won't they make things more difficult?"

Florence stepped out of the shadows in the back of the tent. Ever since she'd nearly destroyed the entire army, she'd stayed quiet during council meetings—if she even showed up for them. She was convinced—and she was probably not wrong—that the others were not interested in what she had to say.

"I have an idea," she said softly.

I looked around the table. Gloni was listening with no judgment, as were Inneacht, Raj, and Connor. Clement was cleaning his nails, Alanna and Tanwen had matching hard expressions on their faces, and Petrina was knotting her hands and not looking at anyone.

Florence looked at everyone but Petrina. I hadn't seen them talk since she'd returned with Raj and Inneacht. I tried to stay out of my friends' personal lives—for the most part—but if they didn't at least talk to each other soon, I was going to have to intervene. As soon as we'd won the war, at least. If they truly didn't want to be together anymore, I obviously couldn't force it just because I knew they were right together. But if it was a stupid misunderstanding because Florence was spiraling out of control and refused to trust either her girlfriend or her BFF, that was an issue I could push forward.

"What's your idea, Florence?" I prompted when her pause went on longer than I'd expected.

She collected herself and started speaking, first to her hands, and then to the group once her confidence grew. It was weird seeing my bestie and my boyfriend, too of the most self-assured people I knew, hesitate.

"If I understand what I've heard, the giants are not necessarily the brightest of our opponents—big, clever, mean, and kinda stupid. Am I right?"

A murmur of agreement made its way around the circle.

"The dragons are smart for the most part, so it'll be harder to fool them, but if we can startle the giants, maybe they'll panic and scamper, and with any luck, take a few dragons out with them. It'd be a bonus if we can make the dragons hesitate as well. So, if we can figure out what will spook the giants, we can create it. I'm not a great illusionist, but I know we have people here who are. Let's take out the giants. They might be the scariest, but they're also the weakest link."

"Goodbye," I said in a clipped British-esque accent.

PLANS SET AND FINGERS CROSSED, we all went out to our various command posts. As the queen and commander in chief, or whatever I was, I was supposed to stay as far away from the front as possible, but as an actual fucking person who cared about the lives of my troops, I couldn't hide in my tent. I accompanied Connor, Gloni, and Florence to the Northern front and trusted the rest to do their parts.

A company of Fae came with us—Fae whose gifts hadn't been deemed powerful enough to put them on the front lines, but too powerful to leave behind. Each of them was skilled in glamourie—they'd come along to hide our numbers and aid in springing the traps that the Dark Fae had set for us. After their services were no longer needed, they'd been reassigned to the medical and mess tents.

A brief but intense brainstorming session had yielded few ideas regarding what the giants might fear enough to flee back through the ranks, but once we pushed the question back to all our troops, we had a lot more ideas. Our giants were frost giants—reminiscent of the toned down for mass consumption Jotunheim in the MCU. That they were cooperating with the dragons was unusual—they typically avoided fire at all costs.

Knowing they were frosty and fire intolerant narrowed things down for us, but not enough. Until one young dwarf came up with the winning idea. They glanced around nervously and bit their lips before speaking. "While it is accepted that fire and ice are opposites and have the power to repel each other, there is something that my people fear more than fire. We live under the mountain, we hunt for our meat and game in the mountains, and we are comfortable in the harsh and cold. But what we fear more than anything is avalanche. Enjoying snow and ice makes you cautious. I imagine that those who live on the great eastern shore fear the killing wave, and those who live on the plane fear the earth shakes. We fear the element we resonate with most when it turns deadly."

"That's a start," I said. "Any other ideas?"

There were none. I didn't know if everyone agreed this was the best way to use illusion, or if no one had anything better so they just kept quiet.

"Avalanche it is," I confirmed. "Gloni, will your people continue to harry the dragons, taking down as many as you can? If Mata flies into battle, he's the priority."

"Agreed," Connor said. "Mata leads them, but I don't think they'd stay if he fell. Enough resent my sister for taking the throne from the dragon line, even if her father was the last great Dragon King. Cut off the head, and the body will fall."

"How certain of this are you?" I asked. If we could eliminate the dragon threat with the loss of one life, I was willing to do a lot to make that loss happen.

"Not enough to bet on it," he said.

"Let's do this then," I said. Florence joined the group of illusionists and had a quick whispered conversation. I wanted to believe she'd be okay, that she could do this, but the last time she'd let her magic fly free, she'd nearly brought a mountain down on us. I walked forward to join their conversation.

"Once you've held the snow back long enough for the pressure to be almost inescapable, step it back. Let go of any supports you're still shoring up and let gravity and winter do their work."

"What of the illusions the rest of us are to create?" a young woman who looked old enough to be barely out of middle school asked.

"Enhance it," Florence said. "An avalanche isn't always dramatic— at least not at first. Make it louder, roll some giant snowballs down the mountain. If you can create tactile illusions as well as visual, add some chill and ice pellets to the mix."

"And the dragons?" someone else asked. "Won't they try to melt the avalanche and the snow to save their allies?"

"I'd be surprised," Connor said. "This alliance is likely uneasy at best. I don't know how Mata got the rest of the dragons to agree to this, nor do I understand what could have lured the giants in unless it was the promise of greater autonomy in the borderlands. Obviously, we should keep an eye on the dragons to see if they go out of their way to help the giants, but my guess is they won't do anything to help unless they're threatened."

"What if we take a few of these magnificent glamourers and have them create a force coming from behind the dragons?" I suggested. "We'll have the avalanche in the front threatening the ground troops— the giants—and another enemy army with crossbows sneaking up behind? If nothing else, it'll divide their attention and delay their attack."

"That's a great idea," Connor said. "Let me shift and I can carry three of you behind enemy lines to better create your illusions."

"That sounds dangerous," I protested. "Especially since we'll be stampeding the giants back that way."

"We will be fine." Connor waved my worries away. "Four powerful Fae ought to be able to keep themselves safe."

I didn't like it, but I didn't argue.

"I will walk with you to the northern perimeter," Clement said to the group assembled to harry the giants and dragons. "I have some ideas of magic that might be effective against fire."

Clement pulled Gloni, Connor, and Florence aside for a hurried strategy session, then Connor took three of the illusionists and flew north, hidden from sight by the powers of one of the Fae he carried.

Florence and her company worked on loosening the snow enough to be ready to fall with the smallest provocation. And I stood with Gloni and the dwarves waiting for the sun to rise and the battle to begin.

I'D STAYED with the northern forces until the avalanche had brought the mountain down on the giants. As predicted, they fled, trampling their compatriots under foot. The dragons who'd been brought down by the dwarves' excellent aim were stomped to a pulp as the giants fled the torrent of snow, rock, and ice. No one else came, and I hoped it was because they'd turned to fight Connor's imaginary forces.

I headed to the southern front to see how Raj's plans were shaping up. The Ravens were the weakest link—or at least that's what we believed. Crafty and dangerous in one-on-one situations, they had trouble fighting as a unit. I was told I wouldn't want to fight one in a dual, and should never agree to a game of wits, iocane powder or no, but in war, they fell apart at the slightest provocation.

That prediction had also proven true. Our southern forces consisted mostly of archers and spear bearers, with just enough swords people to clean up any messes that hit the ground. Watching the ravens flounder in the face of my light infantry buoyed my spirits and my confidence. If we could beat back this front, we had a chance. Not an enormous chance, but a chance.

By the time the sun set, the ravens had been routed, and a temporary nighttime truce was called. I couldn't tell if they'd quit the field entirely or if they were recouping to attack again the next day, but at last, we'd had a win, no matter how small it might turn out to be. Two wins, if things had continued to go well on the northern front.

I walked back into camp with a straighter spine than when I'd left that morning. Maybe the tides were finally starting to turn.

I sought out Raj. We'd not been in touch during the day other than cursory progress updates that didn't tell the whole story. I was looking forward to hearing how his fight had gone. All he needed to do was hold the day—our real offensive wouldn't start until the Ravens were scattered—and the last update I'd had sounded like they were achieving their aim.

I grabbed a bowl of stew from the mess tent and headed into the command tent. Raj, Petrina, Inneacht, Clement, Alanna, and Tanwen were there already. Florence, Gloni, and Connor—the northern command—were still missing.

"Has anyone checked in with the dwarves and other northern forces?" I asked around mouthfuls of stew.

"Not since this morning," Raj said. "I'll head over there now and see what's up. I thought all was going well."

"It was when I left just after midday," I confirmed.

Raj disappeared from the tent, and I dug in while Alanna reported on the main front.

"It will be easy to get Medb to commit," she said. "They were aggressive and overconfident. They may outnumber us by ten to one, but they're only fielding about a quarter of their troops—the rest stand around and look intimidating."

"That's weird," I said. "Why wouldn't she use everyone she's got if she's going to bother to throw them on the field at all?"

Before we could pursue that question, Raj interrupted. *"Ready the medics,"* he commanded mentally. *"Send as many as you can to the northern front. I'll bring Florence and Gloni myself."*

I relayed his command to the rest, and the cautious optimism we'd been enjoying shattered as runners went to fetch medics. Raj appeared moments later with Gloni in his arms. She was barely recognizable—she'd been very badly burned. Her hair was all but gone, and what was left was brittle and smoking. The skin of her left arm was blackened and flaking away, and her face was a mass of contusions and puckered burns. Raj laid her on the lambskin rug someone had thrown on a nearby cot and disappeared.

I wanted to help—to do anything—but I knew that I'd be in the way, so I pressed myself back against the tent wall and watched in horror. Petrina knelt by Gloni's side and held her hands over the still, charred body of the queen. Petrina's eyes were closed, but pink-tinged tears streamed down her face as she evaluated her patient.

"She lives, and her heart beats," Petrina said. "But without immediate healing magic, stronger than I can supply, I don't know if she will survive. Even if she does, she will likely be permanently scarred and will lose the use of her left arm as well as an eye. I will do what I can to stop further tissue damage and dampen the fires that still burn under her skin, but she needs more than me, and she needs it soon."

"There are dryads on the way," someone said. "Their healing magic is second to none."

"They can place an injured person in a healing box of living wood made from healing plants and slow their life functions to give them time to heal," Inneacht said from my right side. I jumped; I hadn't heard her approach.

"Like hibernation?" I asked.

Clement joined us. It was the first time I'd seen him acknowledge Inneacht in my presence since I'd outed him as a god. If we all lived through this, I was going to hire a court historian to put together my family tree and write the history of Fae. Too many of the old gods running around making messes, meddling where they ought not meddle, and running away when they should hang around and fix the problems they helped create.

"It's more like a suspended animation," he said conversationally. "But hibernation is close enough."

"Can you do something?" I asked. "Give her a fancy feather or something like you gave me and Raj before the final gate?"

"They don't grow on trees, you know," he said testily. "Not to mention, they don't work the way you imagine. I pluck three feathers before I am consumed and reborn. Since I recently experienced a rebirth, I will not have any more for quite some time, and those I do have are already spoken for. Would you be the one to choose who will cheat death? How will you decide who is worthy? Is it these two? Your lover? Or the unnamed archer on the front lines of your army, risking life and limb for a queen who will never know his name?"

His words cut through me—was it up to me to decide who got the get out of death free cards? Would I ask him to hold back from Gloni to possibly save Raj? And would I choose my friends over anyone else? I shook my head. I couldn't. "I shouldn't have asked," I said.

His tone softened. "I understand. You are young, and these are your first battle losses. It will get easier—or at least you'll be more numb to the pain. Your forces won a battle today, and you have not lost the war. Take heart, get some sleep, and trust in the medical magic of your dryads."

I closed my eyes. I was dead on my feet, and although I wanted to stay by Gloni's side until I knew whether she'd live or die, I knew I needed to sleep. As soon as Raj returned with Florence, I'd get some rest. What was taking him so long?

I reached out to him and got a terse, *"On my way."* Something was very wrong. I found Petrina's eyes across the crowded room and crossed to her side, grabbing her hand tightly. I knew I wasn't strong enough to hold her back, but I hoped I could serve as a grounding force.

Raj ducked into the tent with a mass of charred blankets in his arms. Only when I heard Petrina gasp and start to sob next to me did I realize I was looking at what was left of Florence. Two of the illusionists who'd gone out with the company trailed after Raj. They were both charred as well, although not as badly as either Florence or Gloni.

"She saved us," one said. "When the dragons came to stop the avalanche, she and Gloni shielded us with their bodies and their magic. Wave after wave of dragon fire, and they held them all back for ages. I don't know what happened. I didn't see. But they fell, one after the other, as if they'd gone to sleep. And when they fell, so did their shields."

The other Fae illusionist took up the story. "Whatever the cause, the dragon nearest us must have sensed the change. He sprayed us with dragon-fire. The field went up in flames. Kira and I were behind Florence and Gloni, pushed down under the piles of snow Florence had called to protect us and guard the retreat of the others. The snow and ice melted, but it was enough to keep us alive. But they took the full force."

I stepped forward and looked at the figure in Raj's arms. He held her gingerly as if a sudden movement would cause her to disintegrate. No wonder it'd taken him so long to return with her. She looked as if she could crumble to ash and blow away with the slightest breeze.

"Father?" Petrina said, her voice breaking. "Can you?"

"No," he said. "She's too weak, too injured. I would kill her trying to drain her, and she doesn't have the strength to drink from me. All we can do is wait and hope. She lives yet. Her heart beats. But she is hanging on by a thread."

"Let us take her," Inneacht said, walking forward with Clement. Raj looked as though he might refuse for a moment, but then something passed between him and Inneacht, and he handed her over.

Clement walked by me and I felt the brush of feathers against my face. He dropped his glamour—one of the few that I couldn't see through unless I tried—and a flash of golden red washed through the tent leaving sunbursts in my vision for several minutes after he disappeared with my mother and my best friend.

It was only after my vision cleared that I had another question. "Where's Connor?"

CHAPTER SIXTEEN

P etrina was pacing in the middle of my tent while Raj and I
watched from the bed. She'd shown up not long after I'd
finally gotten to sleep, so not only was it the middle of the
night, I was also running on my eighth straight day of minimal sleep
and my millionth day, give or take, without coffee as a regular guest
star in my life.

I'd been up too late the night before as we tried to get word on
Connor and the two illusionists he'd taken with him, but everything
came up empty. I was trying not to think about it but couldn't stop all
the horrible possibilities from running through my mind. Not only
was he a trusted advisor, he'd become my dear friend—and apparently
my dad. And we hadn't even had a chance to explore that side of our
relationship.

I was down three friends in one incursion that should've carried
minimal risk compared to the other things we'd done. Logically, I
knew it wasn't my fault. I just couldn't convince my heart to step
back.

Raj was trying to talk her down—or at least get her to stop pacing
—long enough for us to hop out of bed and get dressed. There's being
comfortable with nudity and then there's not wanting to run around

naked in front of your boyfriend's kid. Ugh. I was so tired that even my internal monologue was getting ridiculous.

"Trina," Raj said. "I know you're upset. And I know Clement and Inneacht won't let you in, but stop and think about what's going on. You've been a healer most of your life. You've had your medical knowledge progress with the ages, and you know that infection is a very real danger for burn victims. What we don't know is the effects that dragon fire has on a person. Right now, Florence is under the best care that we can give her, and it'll be a lot easier on her healers if they aren't having to rebuff a scared and angry vampire every few minutes."

I slid out of the bed while Trina was focused on Raj and put on the spring green robe laying in the nearby chair. I made tea while Petrina resumed her pacing then sat down and tried to pull my thoughts together.

"I've known Florence for only a little longer than you, and my relationship with her is obviously very different. But I'm worried, too. More than worried. Terrified. And if I'm this sick and scared, I can't even imagine how you feel."

"I told her I was leaving her," Trina said, tears thick in her voice. "She didn't trust me enough to talk about how she was struggling with the influx of power. She refused to talk about our future after this is over. And when I suggested she return with me to the clan I left behind, she told me a prophecy told her I'd be happier without her. My last words were words of anger. If she dies, I will have that weighing on me forever. And after Magdalene, I swore I'd never leave things like that again." She broke down, sobbing into her hands.

I put my tea down and went to her, pulling the tall, blonde, Nordic beauty into my arms and patting her hair soothingly.

"She's not dead," I reminded her. "She's healing. There's a chance."

"Did you see her?" Petrina yelled through her tears.

"I did. She looks terrible. It's hard to believe she was still alive after all that. But she was. And she is. Even if I wasn't first on the notification list, you would know. So take a step back and breathe." I winced. Telling a vampire to breathe was always a little awkward. Some of them were sensitive about that.

Petrina sniffled but didn't answer.

A fully clothed Raj joined us and handed Petrina a handkerchief.

"There shouldn't be so much snot," she said, blowing her nose. "Why do vampires have mucus?"

I didn't have an answer for that and was pretty sure she didn't really want one. I returned to my tea and gave her the time she needed to pull herself together.

Once she'd dried her eyes and the stream of tears had slowed to an intermittent trickle, she took the cup I handed her and sat down on a small stool facing me.

"I shouldn't have woken you and had hysterics in your tent," she said by way of apology.

"Of course you should've," I said. "That's what friends and step-mothers are for. Once we've finished our tea and after I get dressed, we'll head over the medical tent to check on Florence and Gloni and all the others who are there. Then you can decide if you want the distraction of the battlefield today—and if you can focus enough to be of use there."

"Fine. Good. Okay." Petrina set down her cup without having taken a single sip. She stood up and walked outside. I could hear her pacing out there and dressed hurriedly. It was almost time to get up anyway. There's no sleeping in when you're fighting a three-front war. I was crossing my fingers that today we'd be down to two fronts. I needed the southern forces to join the main force if we were going to execute Raj's plan. Hopefully what was left of the Raven armies had either fled or joined the main company.

I'd leave a few people in the south to keep an eye on things, harry any hostile raven stragglers, and offer quarter to any who wanted to surrender and declare their allegiance to me, but now that that battle was mostly won, I didn't want to decimate their remaining forces. After all, when I won, I'd be their queen, too.

The second I left the tent, Petrina was at my side. It was still dark —not even a hint of light in the east—and the torches that led the way through the camp were guttering. There were a half dozen large tents and two small ones set up as our medical center. I'd been spending time there every afternoon, meeting with the injured, getting status reports from the healers—mostly dryads—and trying to boost morale as best as I could. It was not my favorite part of queening, and not one I'd thought of before agreeing to the gig.

We didn't start with any of the large tents, though. Petrina dragged me to one of the small ones. A guard was stationed outside both small tents to prevent anyone from going in or out. Not only for the security of a foreign queen and one of my chief counselors, but also to keep well-meaning loved ones from disrupting the healing process.

"Your Majesty," the guard said, bowing.

"Linia," I replied. "No need to stand on ceremony this early in the morning. Are Clement and Inneacht still in there?"

"The Queen Mother left a short while ago. I believe she was going to her tent to sleep. The Phoenix is still in there with two of the dryad healers. He left instruction that he was not to be disturbed and that no one should be allowed in." Linia smiled apologetically. "Not even you. But…"

I held up my hand. It was a confusing time for my subjects. I was their queen because Eo had claimed me as his daughter and heir. But now Eo's twin sister had returned after centuries and said I was hers and not Eo's. Which meant she had a greater claim to the throne than I did. And then Clement, aka Belenus, who'd been the consort of Eo and Inneacht's mother but also was the god of fire and rebirth, was here.

"If he said he was not to be disturbed at all and specified that meant me as well, we will respect his wishes. In the medical tents, the healers are in charge. If he does step out for any reason, can you let him know I'd like to see him."

"Of course, Your Majesty," Linia said, bowing again.

Petrina hadn't said anything during my exchange with Florence's guard, but I'd felt her tense when I didn't push my way in. I slipped my arm through hers and pulled her towards Gloni's tent. "If he doesn't want anyone in there, it is because they're in a precarious position with her healing, not because they want to hide her condition from you. Let's go check on our other friends. Clement will emerge eventually, and then we will have word."

"Fine."

We walked the few feet to the other tent, but before I could greet that guard, Petrina spun me to face her. "I am being discourteous and rude," she said. "You're doing everything you can to ensure Florence is well cared for and to help assuage my worry and guilt. I should not be taking my fear out on you. You deserve better."

I slipped my arm around her waist and gave her a half-hug. "I understand your fear and would never judge you for it."

I glanced to the east where the barest hint of dawn was starting to take hold. "For now, though, I must regroup with the others as we prepare for today. Will you join me?"

She considered for a moment then shook her head. "No. I will offer my services in the medical tents so I can stay preoccupied but will be close in case..." Petrina's voice broke and she broke away from me, dashing the tears from her eyes.

"Take care," I said. It wasn't enough, but it was all I had at the moment. I went in search of breakfast and my much-reduced war council.

TWO COMPANIES of centaurs assembled on either side of the battlefield in long columns, while the main body of our forces were spread out between them in a shallower line. Raj assured me this formation had proven effective and defeating superior numbers before, and Connor and Clement had agreed with the assessment. These three men had the most education and experience in warfare of all of us—Petrina had been a skirmisher but tended to stay away from wars because they were, in her words, "a stupid way for a bunch of men to waggle their penises at each other," and she wanted no part of that.

Florence, for all her secret government experience she wouldn't tell me about, admitted she knew little about large-scale warfare, particularly when it came to pitched battles in a pre-gun powder era. Alanna wasn't any older than me and had never gone to war. Tanwen, although the oldest of us all, had spent more time in the forest than on the battlefield. And that's how I found myself taking the advice of three old men, something I tried hard never to do on general principle.

I sighed and watched as my troops got into formation. Soon, it'd be light enough to see Medb's forces. No matter how many times they'd come into view, it was always shocking how many she had. My guts twisted in a turmoil of nerves, and I had to talk myself down from losing my breakfast. The sky gradually lightened behind the hill that separated Medb's camp from mine. I gasped in new horror as the line of figures took focus, and I saw her ground troops.

There were siege engines flanking her main forces with piles of incendiary projectiles in nearby wagons. Perhaps we could preemptively destroy those?

I turned to Raj to suggest it, and he nodded. "Great idea. On it." He issued a command to one of the runners standing nearby. Presumably, that message would get to the proper commander who would make it so without devolving into a wartime game of telephone. It was out of my hands now.

The sun rose higher into the cloudless blue sky, shining beams of light directly into our eyes. It'd been overcast every day, and I'd subconsciously been anticipating clouds again. It was going to suck if we couldn't see the enemy coming at us. Maybe, if I asked real nicely, Medb would agree to hold back until midday.

"Relax," Raj said. He was the only one of my original counselors still standing with me. Connor was still missing. Florence and Gloni were gravely injured. Clement and Petrina were in the houses of healing. And Alanna was again leading the southern centaur contingent herself. Tanwen obviously rode with Alanna. And so, Raj and I were all that were left to direct this strategically tricky and decidedly iffy battle.

A horn sounded from Medb's troops, and they began to move forward.

I tensed and watched Raj. He watched impassively. And waited. When the first line of the enemy was almost two-thirds of the way across the field, he signaled to one of the three horn blowing people nearby. The trumpeter blew one, long blast, and before the echoes had fades, the sky was blackened with flaming arrows. Most fell on the approaching army, but some were aimed towards the siege engines and their ammunition stockpiles.

I let out a small cheer when one of the piles went up in flames, quickly catching the wooden catapults on fire as well. I hoped they wouldn't pull themselves together quickly enough to lob the flaming balls of whatever at us before they burned up.

A second volley of arrows joined the first, and the front rank of Medb's army moved inexorably closer, albeit with many fewer soldiers. Once the opposing army was too close to be effective arrow fodder, the archers fell back through the gaps between the front ranks of my troops.

The next lines of light infantry held steady and waited for the battle to come to them. I surveyed the field—the infantry was mostly elves, river and tree Fae, and fauns. Behind the elves and other light infantry were three-quarters of the dwarf companies. The remaining dwarves were guarding the northern border in case the giants and dragons returned prematurely.

Once Medb's forces had committed, ours began falling back, bowing towards me. The main line softened into a "U" shape with the centaur cavalry making up the vertical arms of the letter. Even though I knew this was part of the plan, my stomach still twisted watching the controlled retreat.

Instead of watching my people fall back before the lines of satyrs that made up Medb's front ranks, I turned my attention to the rest of the field. As I noticed yesterday, not only was she holding back most of the troops, even now when it looked like we were being defeated and their aid could make the rout legendary instead of merely complete, they were...wrong.

"Raj," I said, pulling his attention from the tableau unfolding in front of us. "Look at the rest of Medb's soldiers. There's something not quite right with them. They're not moving."

He followed my gaze, and I watched his eyes narrow. "You're right. Not only are they just hanging around in disorganized clumps, they're... I can't quite tell what they're doing. Hold on." Raj called over one of the messengers. "Brand, find me one of the airborne scouts and have them come here immediately."

The small chameleon Fae scampered off. His ability to blend in anywhere and his natural speed gave him a natural advantage when it came to navigating the battlefield without coming to any harm.

Our fallback was nearly complete. The opposing forces didn't seem to notice that the arms of our troop formation hadn't fallen back with the main body of our army. As Raj was about to give the signal to execute the next part of the plan, Brand returned with Bex, a Fae with the body of an elf and the head and wings of an eagle. I didn't know if there was a word for her on the Earth Plane, but here, I just called her badass.

"Hey, Badass Bex," I greeted her. "We need an eye in the sky."

"Your Majesty, Consort," she said, bowing. "What do you want me to look at?"

I explained my confusion about Medb's reserve troops and their actions—or lack thereof. Bex nodded and took off. The undersides of her wings were a shimmery light blue, and she dressed in similar colors, making her all but invisible against the blue sky.

I held off on that thought and returned my attention to the battle. Raj was appearing increasingly nervous as he watched things unfold.

"Hey, what's up?" I asked, hoping his nerves weren't because we were about to be obliterated.

"It's been a long time since I've been in charge of any army," he said. "And my track record isn't stellar. I don't want to be the reason you're not victorious."

"You won't be," I said. "And you know it's true if I can say it. I believe in you and in your plan. If you think it's time, pull the trigger."

He reached out and squeezed my hand, then gave the order. One of the trumpeters blew his horn in four long, loud blasts. The light infantry melted out of the way, falling behind the dwarves, and the centaurs who'd been surreptitiously angling inward turned and flanked Medb's army from behind, closing in behind them and trapping the larger force in a circle of my soldiers.

Great swaths of satyrs were falling to the dwarves' axes, and I held out hope that Medb would surrender soon so we could let them retreat with dignity. Unfortunately, I greatly overestimated Medb's empathy for her ground soldiers. I looked towards the hill where the bulk of her forces stood waiting.

Was it my imagination, or were there significantly fewer than there'd been before? *Shit!* Had they found a way around us? I was frantically scanning the field ahead of us, chosen by us because with the mountain at our backs it'd be next to impossible to sneak up behind us. In addition, there was no cover between us and them that would allow a significant force to move without notice.

The front line of dwarves swung their axes as if they were one body, perfectly synchronized, and I watched as three dozen satyrs fell. A movement on the hill caught my eye, and I looked up in time to see a large group of the reserve soldiers flicker and disappear.

My jaw dropped as realization dawned over me. Bex landed beside me. "Your Majesty, I don't think the other soldiers are real. I watched several of them flicker in and out of reality and then disappear."

"I just saw the same," I agreed. "And it was when a large group of satyrs were downed."

"I will return to the air to continue scouting," Bex said. "But it is my professional opinion that the remaining forces are not a danger to us."

"I appreciate your efforts and agree with your assessment."

She bowed and took off into the sky again.

For the first time since we'd lost the initial battle, I started to have real hope. We'd forced back the ravens. We were winning this battle and the visible reserves were illusions or echoes or something that tied their existence to the lives of the soldiers dying at the hands of my troops.

The slaughter was nearly complete, and still Medb didn't signal for her forces to retreat. The sky darkened over the battle as Branna loosed the hunt. I'd seen it before in Czechia, but this was at a scale almost unimaginable. By the time Branna left, their company was double what it'd been before, and the dead on the battlefield were greatly diminished in number.

I watched, sickened by what I was seeing, but unable to determine a different path forward. What would happen if I halted things without a clear concession from Medb? I wished I knew more. Wished that Connor was by my side to tell me how it was on the Fae Plane.

"The sun is setting," Raj said. "We can either place torches and continue to fight until there is no resistance, or we can call a halt until tomorrow, letting those who still live return to their camp and allow them to retrieve their dead after we've cleared the field of our dead and wounded."

"What do you recommend?" I asked, knowing what I wanted to do already.

"I recommend breaking for the night. Our soldiers are exhausted. Many have minor wounds that need to be tended to. They're hungry and it's getting cold."

"Then let's do that," I said. "Tomorrow we can finish this."

I walked back to tents as the signal calling a halt for the evening sounded across the bloody field.

I WATCHED the funeral pyre that I'd lit to burn the bodies of the dead who hadn't joined Branna's hunt and tried to hold back my sobs. I couldn't keep the tears from trailing down my face, but I wasn't going to break down. Not now. Not here.

Raj stood behind me and a little to my right. I could feel his presence but didn't want his comfort right now. We'd won, but right now it felt like a Pyrrhic victory—the emotional toll was so high I wasn't sure how to go on.

When the flames had burned low the mourners had mostly dissipated in search of food and rest and comfort, I turned and walked back to camp. I needed food and rest, too, but before I could seek those out, I needed to visit the med tents.

Tanwen had joined the ranks of our casualties when she'd taken an arrow to the shoulder. What should've been a simple fix had turned complicated when the arrow was revealed to be carrying a poison that was especially deadly to dryads. We'd lost dozens—nearly sixty—to the unknown poison, and although our healers were able to draw it out in a slow and agonizing process, only those healers who weren't also dryads could do so safely.

Tanwen would live. Many others would not. And we still had no word on Florence or Gloni. And Connor was still missing, although the bodies of the illusionists he'd taken with him behind the dragon lines had been recovered in the river at the edge of our camp. They'd been burned and broken, stripped naked, and returned.

It felt disrespectful to add them to the pyre—they'd been burned enough—but we had few choices. The dwarves took up their own dead, fortunately few in number, and wrapped them in cloth they'd pulled from the packs of the fallen. I'd learned then that each dwarf carried their own funereal wrappings that would preserve their bodies until they could be returned to the mountain.

I walked up beside Petrina who was staring at the med tent Florence was in and took her hand. She looked exhausted. She'd been pulling poison from injured dryads all day. But I knew she wouldn't sleep until she could see Florence again, no matter how that turned out.

"Any news?" I asked, knowing there was none.

She squeezed my hand but didn't answer.

I turned towards Petrina to offer comfort and to say goodbye; I needed to find food and clean clothes and my bed. We may have won a decisive victory, but we still had the dragons to contend with and whatever forces Medb managed to scrape up to throw at us tomorrow. Before I could open my mouth, the flap of Florence's tent was pushed aside and Clement emerged.

Even on the day he'd spontaneously combusted in the middle of my camp on the other side of the mountain, he hadn't looked this exhausted. He caught sight of us and walked over. His shoulders were bent, and he shuffled like a man feeling every one of his several millennia.

Petrina froze beside me in a way that only a vampire can.

"Tell me," I commanded, trying not to think about how I was commanding the man who was not only my grandfather, but also a god.

"She will live."

CHAPTER SEVENTEEN

I watched the sunrise over the eastern hills, and for the first time in days, there was no activity brewing. I wasn't sure what to think of that—we hadn't gotten any official confirmation that Medb was giving up, and based on what little I knew of her, it didn't seem likely. My understanding of war was that it ended when the losers either sent someone in with a white flag to negotiate terms, the enemy queen was vanquished on the field of battle either in the middle of some kind of melee fight or in a duel to settle things once and for all, or when a ring gets thrown into a volcano.

I didn't want to pin my hopes on Frodo. I hadn't seen anyone with a flag of any color approach, and we couldn't solve things on the field of battle if the other queen didn't show up to fight.

Holding patterns sucked. I wanted to rejoice in my victory and turn all my attention to worrying about my friends and finding ways to heal them faster.

Footsteps sounded behind me and I whirled, sword in hand, to confront the interloper on my thoughts. It was one of the battlefield messengers—Elmin, I think his name was.

"They're asking for you at the medical tent, Your Majesty."

"Thank you, Elmin." I sheathed my sword and turned to follow him back into the camp.

There was a small crowd gathered at the edge of the med tents. I was pleased to see Tanwen up and about, leaning against Alanna who looked like she would gut and then trample anyone who looked at Tanwen the wrong way. Petrina was standing next to Raj, her hand in his, and a look of start terror on her face.

Reginn and two other dwarf captains whose names escaped me were also in attendance. I took my place on Raj's other side and looked expectantly at the two people who were the center of everyone's attention.

Inneacht, my mother, looked exhausted, although her beauty shone through anyway. She stepped back and gave Clement the floor.

"Something about the story we heard from the two who survived intact the attack that felled Gloni and Florence struck me. We heard that they stood against the dragons, shielding themselves and their illusionists, and then suddenly they each fell over with what seemed like zero provocation, dropping their shields. This led me to believe that there was more to the story than being overwhelmed by dragon fire. So I searched both the Queen and the Witch, and I found these." He held out his hand. I leaned forward and peered closely, along with everyone else present.

"Needles?" I ventured since he seemed to be waiting for a response.

"Dart tips," Clement confirmed. "I tested the substance found within the hollow points of the darts, but it was not a match for the poison administered to the dryads through arrows. I wracked my brains trying to figure out what this substance could be. And then I had an idea. I popped back to a veterinary clinic a few years ago and compared the substance to a strong tranquilizer they use to knock out large animals. It was a match. Florence and Gloni were hit by tranquilizer darts. The main body of the dart melted underneath the onslaught of dragon fire, and all that was left were the metal tips embedded in their necks."

I couldn't believe what I was hearing. "They were knocked out and left to the dragons? And taken out from behind the shields, which leaves me to believe that it was one of ours?"

"I believe your suppositions are correct, Eleanor," Clement said. "And now for the piece of information I was withholding before. You asked me when Gloni returned if I could hand her one of my feathers to save her from death the way I'd saved you and Raj at the final gate. I intimated that things were much more complicated than that and informed you that I had already allocated the three available feathers, correct?"

"Yes." I didn't know where he was going with this, but I needed him to stop drawing things out and just tell us what was going on already.

"What I didn't tell you was that I'd already handed them out before your commanders took on the dragons, assuming—correctly, as it unfortunately turned out—that they'd need them more than anyone else. If they'd returned unscathed, they were to return the feathers for me to hold onto until someone else needed them."

"So they're okay then?" Petrina asked, sounding as confused as I felt. If they were okay, I honestly believed he could've led with that.

"In order to be resurrected from ashes—or any old death, really— you must first die. A resurrection really isn't, otherwise. Both women were alive when they were brought to me, although barely so. I've kept vigil the last couple days trying to decide what to do. I can't very well finish them off just so they can be reborn. That wasn't the deal. But nor can I leave them to suffer with such horrific burns. Finally, I decided I should let you decide how to proceed—those who love them best, or at least in the case of our Dwarven Queen, in their stead. Connor has obviously not returned to us, but as he was in possession of one of the feathers, I have high hopes he's alive. The two here in my care, however, are on the edge of life and death. As it is impossible to lose one once it's been freely given, I hadn't even thought to look to ensure they still possessed the keys to their rebirth."

If the situation had been any less fraught, I would've rolled my eyes. Clement was such a pompous ass. However, he was a pompous ass who may have just saved my best friend's life, so I was going to let it go for now. Raj squeezed my hand, and we waited for Clement to continue.

"Florence's was easy to find—it was between her skin and her clothing, and had melted onto her, almost like a tattoo. The feathers do interesting things when exposed to flame. And the skin around the feather is no longer charred. She has passed through the veil between life and death and is slowly coming back to us. When I saw the healing last night, only the skin on the left side of her torso looked new. Now, the burns have disappeared from much of her chest and abdomen as well. It is my educated guess that once the entire torso is healed, including all those vital organs you mortals keep in there, the process will accelerate."

"She's going to be okay?" Petrina asked. She sounded more numb than excited, but after Clement's long lecture, I didn't blame her. He might be a god, but he was a shitty people person.

"She's going to be okay," Clement confirmed. "I do believe that all chances of infection are over, and that by this time tomorrow, she'll be awake and within the week, ready to get up and get on with her life."

"I don't believe it," Petrina said. "Can I see her?"

"Yes, yes, of course," Clement said. "But let me deliver the other half of my news."

He turned towards the dwarves who were beginning to look cautiously optimistic. "Unfortunately, when I performed the same search on your queen, I was unable to find the feather. The only sign she'd ever had it was a faint glow on her low back, unburned, that marked where she'd carried it. I don't know now if she gave it away or if it was taken from her, but the sad news is it doesn't matter. Gloni does not have the means to resurrection, and I cannot help her anymore."

As the weight of Clement's words drifted over the dwarves, there was a low, collective moan. "What do we do?" Reginn asked.

"The choices are the same as they were before. We can hold on, make her comfortable, and wait for her to pass the veil on her own. Or there are certain substances that can accelerate the process without pain or suffering. I will leave it to you and your beliefs.

Either way, I will do my best to shield her from the pain of her burns."

"Let me gather our people and we will sing her back to the mountains, as she deserves," Reginn said.

"It shall be as you say."

The crowd scattered, and Petrina disappeared into Florence's tent. I was elated and devastated at the same time. I'd looked forward to trips between our thrones, to cementing our royal alliance as well as our burgeoning friendship. But to have Florence live—I would've traded about anything for that.

"Walk with me?" I said to Raj. "I need to clear my head. Someone will find me if anything changes anywhere, right?"

"Of course," he said.

We turned to walk towards the river, but someone was blocking my path.

"Princess," Isaac said, nodding to me.

"It's Queen, now," I responded. As I did, movement from inside his cloak caught my eyes. I refocused my attention only to find myself making eye contact with the biggest, brownest eyes with dark, long eyelashes and the sweetest little face I'd ever seen.

"You have a baby," I said.

BACK IN MY TENT, head-clearing walk with Raj aborted, I sat stiffly on the edge of the bed holding Inge. I'd know about her—Raj had given me a full report—but seeing Isaac carrying her was something different again.

"Why are you here with Medb's baby?" I asked. I'd never actually held a baby before and wasn't entirely sure how I'd ended up holding this one.

"Diane disappeared a couple days ago with instructions to stay put and not try to find her or communicate with anyone on your side. Medb's been gone for a while now, but that's pretty typical. I don't think she's seen Inge more than two or three times since she was born. Since there was no one left to keep an eye on me who knew I was not just a nanny Diane hired to keep an eye on the baby, I thought it was an excellent opportunity to leave."

"But you brought the baby?" I asked.

"What was I supposed to do? Leave her behind?"

"She's excellent leverage," Raj said.

"She's not leverage," Isaac replied, a growl starting low in his chest. His eyes flashed from their typical deep, soulful brown to the amber color of his wolf's.

"Of course not," I said, glaring at Raj. "I don't even like babies, and I know that."

Raj shrugged and grinned at me. I narrowed my eyes. He wasn't serious about the leverage jab, but I didn't know where he was going with it. Didn't matter. What mattered was what we were going to do with an infant now that she was here.

"Do we have to give her back if Medb asks? Are we kidnapping otherwise?"

"Big questions with big answers, none of which need to be answered now," Raj said.

The sound of pounding feet outside the tent drew my attention, and I thrust the baby back at Isaac as someone ran into my tent.

"Dragons," they gasped.

"Stay here," I commanded Isaac, then ran outside and followed the crowd to the battlefield we'd cleared yesterday. An entire host of dragons—at least two hundred, it seemed—filled the sky. In front was the same dragon I'd seen Medb ride on the only day she'd shown her face. She was riding it again, and the dragon looked just as pleased this time. He was holding something in his claws—something white.

He darted forward, and my archers raised their bows.

"Hold!" I called out, and the silence that followed was near deafening.

The dragon dropped his bundle in front of the first line of my soldiers, then retreated back to join the rest of his compatriots, although he did remain enough in front of the lines so as to leave little doubt that he was the most important one there.

I walked forward, the crowd parting before me. I felt a presence at my side and looked over. Inneacht had joined me. Her jaw was tight, and a vein pulsed in her temple. I didn't know her well enough to interpret all her facial expressions, but I'd put money on suppressed rage.

I knelt by the bundle that'd been dropped from thirty feet in the air. A piece of paper was nailed to the white cloth. I ripped it off and turned it over.

"I do not surrender, human sow. Prepare to die."

Short and to the point. At least this eliminated any doubt as to her immediate future plans.

I pulled back the cloth on the bundle with my sword, prepared to deflect any booby-traps that might spring forth. What I saw instead turned my stomach in horror and disgust.

"Move!" I yelled thickly. I turned to the right and vomited on the ground where someone's feet had been moments before. "Someone get Clement," I said when I'd purged myself of everything I'd eaten over the last few days.

Inneacht crouched beside me and placed a cool hand on my knee. "You need to stand tall and be strong now," she said. "They are watching you, seeing how you react to this man's corpse being discarded at your feet. They cannot know that you are anything but disgusted by the smell and appearance. Let the medics take him away. Clement will see to him. In the meantime, you have a challenge to answer."

As much as I hated to admit it, she was right. I rose to my full height, which in a sea of elves wasn't very tall, and I strode out onto the field in front of my army. They had dropped Connor's charred corpse at my feet with a note driven into his body, and they wanted to watch me fall apart. I would not give them the satisfaction.

"I guess the so-called Dark Queen likes losing so much that she's come back to do it again!" I called out. My troops took the cue from me and laughed raucously. "Got any more fake soldiers you wanna parade in front of us because you couldn't find enough actual soldiers to join your army? Or are you just gonna ride your pet dragon around like a little girl on her holiday pony?"

I didn't have a lot of experience with battlefield taunting, but from the stream of fire that erupted from her dragon-mounts nostrils, I knew I was at least hitting one of them where it hurt. I was trying to buy enough time for the dwarves to get in to position—provided they were planning on sticking with us now that their queen had been taken out in a war that they'd joined out of friendship.

It hadn't occurred to me that more than abandoning me to my own devices on the battlefield, they'd want revenge over the dragons who'd killed their beloved queen. The laughter behind me was replaced by a low, steady chant that vibrated my internal organs, but not in a totally unpleasant way. I risked a glance behind me, both to make sure that Connor had been moved, and to see where the noise was coming from.

The dwarves were marching forward, chanting in low, harmonic tones, brandishing double axes in each hand. I turned back to the dragons.

"We've decimated your main forces. We routed the Ravens—your own people. And now you bring the dragons back? They've made two attempts at us and were rebuffed twice. Why not quit the field? Surrender. Your armies can live as free folk. And the dragons can go back to their stronghold in the north, secure in the knowledge that a dragon queen once more sits on the throne and rules both Dark and Light."

Medb's dragon swooped forward, and she sneered at me. "You only think you've won, little girl. But the time for playing dress up with your crown and throne has passed. Turn around and go home. And maybe I'll let you keep your Light Throne. For now. Or stay and suffer the consequences."

I laughed. "You've been playacting since you killed Donall and usurped the throne. If you'd really been strong enough to hold it through your own power, Ciannait would've named you his successor before he died. You draw power from everyone in your kingdom, making them weak. If you were ever forced to stand on your own merits, I could strike you down without blinking twice."

I gritted my teeth and hoped that I was having the desired effect. I didn't want the dragons to attack.

"The lead dragon is Mata," Inneacht whispered in my ear. "You'll need to take him out."

That had been our original plan, and what Connor was hoping to accomplish on his journey north. I took a few more steps forward, threw down my sword, and stripped out of my battle gear. Most of my people hadn't seen this transformation—hadn't seen more than my half form—but it was time they did.

It was time they saw their Dragon Queen in all her glory. I called to the magic deep within my soul, poured all of my fear and hope and anger and sense of justice into it, and let it spill through me, bursting forth faster than it had ever done before. In less than a minute I'd gone from rather diminutive queen to big-ass dragon. I roared my displeasure across the field, careful not to scorch the earth. I launched myself into the air and shot a second plume of fire in front of me, barely missing Mata and Medb as he twisted away. I noticed the other dragons draw back, giving us space within the center of the field, and I shot towards Mata, stopping a few yards away to again roar my challenge.

"Put me down, you incompetent idiot," Medb spat.

Mata executed a perfect barrel roll and dropped her on the ground. I saw her transform into a large raven and wing away towards her camp; I didn't attempt to follow.

CHAPTER EIGHTEEN

Once he'd disposed of his demanding passenger, Mata quickly righted himself and flew at me faster than I'd expected. I hadn't ever fought in my dragon form—at least not another dragon. I wasn't quite sure what to do or how to do it. But I knew how to fight, and I knew I was larger, more powerful, and had greater access to magic. So I guess I'd just wing it.

I grinned. You know it's gonna be okay when you can still make *and* appreciate terrible puns.

I dove under him, then straight up, turning at the last second to jam my shoulder into the soft area in his upper chest. I heard the breath leave his lungs in a whoosh of air and followed it up with a stinging thwap of my tail across his face. I sped out of reach, then turned in time to see him belch a huge cloud of smoke and flame at me.

Was this all he had? I grinned a dopey reptilian grin and decided to show off a little. I wanted the rest of the dragons to see what they were up against and decide to let me settle this on my own. I was banking on the assessments of Connor and Inneacht, as well as my own uninformed observations, that the rest of the dragons weren't happy following Mata and wouldn't come to his aid to save him from being trounced.

I'd just finished congratulating myself for the battle I hadn't won yet when a glancing blow struck across my shoulders. I rolled with the blow but still lost several dozen feet before I regained my balance and got my wings positioned correctly to catch the current and soar back up again. I pulled my wings back alongside my body and dove towards Mata, jaw open and claws outstretched.

He bellowed forth a plume of fire, and I closed my eyes against the heat, striking out with one claw in an attempt to throw him off his balance while I was still blinded. I hit something with my left front foot and added an extra kick hoping it'd be enough to give myself time to regain my sight. I pushed myself back against Mata's body to get some distance from him and heard him bellow with either rage or pain. I was fine with both, actually.

The force of the wind cleared my vision, and I wheeled around. I didn't see him, but a whistle of wind made me look up. He was dive bombing me, wings outstretched and forelegs reaching forward with claws extended.

I brought my wings forward then pushed back through the air to move backwards and out of range of his wicked looking talons. One razor-sharp claw scared against my soft belly, and I felt the skin split, but it was a minor injury. I shot upwards, then immediately forward, making Mata roll onto his back to defend.

I looked down at him. His wings were spread out to either side and slightly behind his head, and all four legs were pointed straight up. The ground below him was a variegated green that enhanced the dark green of his scales. I reached down with my back legs and took a moment to admire the contrast between my purplish black and his green scales. Then I grabbed at him with my claws, trying to dig into the skin of his belly.

He moved at the last minute, and I missed, but my almost-strike was more damaging that his had been. I'd sliced open his belly; he was bleeding freely as he wheeled away from me. It wasn't life-threatening, at least not if he landed and got patched up immediately.

Mata roared again, fire streaming forth from his mouth. I was ready this time and spun out of the way. He tore after me faster than I'd expected, and I again had to be on the defensive and move so I wouldn't be bowled over. Over and over, Mata dove at me with more speed than finesse, and repeatedly I rolled out of the way and let him speed by me.

Initially I was irritated—I wasn't doing anything but dodging his attacks. This wasn't a fight; it was a dance. Or rather, two very different dances to different pieces of music that the other couldn't hear. But soon, I realized that each of his rage-filled dives was a little slower than the last. He was losing blood with every pump of his wings and was tiring quickly. I was getting the feel for the air, learning to anticipate his movements based on the air currents, and expending almost zero energy.

I risked a glance up towards the dragons hovering in the background. It didn't look like any of them were prepared to make a move to defend their leader. Mata dove at me again, announcing his attack with another spurt of smoke and flame. This time, instead of diving out of the way of the fire, I attempted a shield to deflect the fire. I'd never done active magic while flying before and wasn't entirely sure it'd work.

It did, and I chuffed in satisfaction when the flames split and went around me like a river going around a rock. I increased the vibrations of my wings and rose up in the air just far enough to avoid Mata's attack. We did a few more exchanges like that—him breathing fire at me as a precursor to a speeding attack, me finding a new way to divert it and then moving just enough to be out of the way—but I was getting bored. Also, it seemed prudent to conserve my energy in case I had to take on any more of the dragons. I couldn't count on them to all be this easy to defeat.

The next time Mata rushed at me, I diverted the flames again, dropped below him, and rolled onto my back, thrusting my claws upwards and gouging his belly. The rate of blood loss accelerated, and he lost what little control he had left. The next time he attacked, he didn't even bother determining where I was—just dove at the last place he'd seen me. I dropped on him from above, pushing him towards the ground, and rode him like a circus pony until we were close enough to the ground that I could make out the individual leaves on the shrubs lining the river. I flew up and off him, but he hit the ground.

He roared like a bull and scratched at the dirt, raising a cloud of dust, and launched himself back into the air. I flew backwards, doing my best to dance through the air. I was taunting him with the ease with which I was moving. Mata dove at me again, and this time when I moved out of the way, I thrust my right foreleg out and caught his left wing, rending a large hole in it.

He managed to stay aloft and dove at me again. This time, I tore his right wing. He lost it then and plummeted towards the ground.

"You'll have to finish it," Raj said.

He was right. I knew he was, but I wasn't looking forward to this.

I flew down and hovered over Mata trying to decide if I should use my jaws or the sword of air I wielded when steel was unavailable. Would I kill him as a dragon or as a woman?

He shifted shaped as I landed, making the decision for me. I wouldn't tear apart his Fae form with dragon claws. I shifted to my half form—it made me feel less naked—and drew the sword of tempered air and light I'd created when I was first learning to control my elemental magic. As I approached him, I took a good long look at the man who thought he was my father and apparently didn't care enough to not try to kill me. If I hadn't been raised by a wonderful human couple and if I didn't know who my actual father was, I'd probably be in therapy for the rest of my life. As it stood, I probably should book a therapist for the next couple centuries. At least.

Mata was bleeding from several wounds and swaying on his feet.

"Surrender," I said. "Surrender, and I will let you live."

"You will?" he gasped.

"I will let you live in the same way that you let my mother live. Captive for centuries."

"I'd rather die," he declared.

"Okay," I shrugged. I reached out with my sword and pushed at him with the tip of it. He lost his balance and fell to his knees. I leaned over and whispered, "You are not my father. Connor is." Then I lifted my sword and brought it down, severing his head from his body.

I turned and faced the horizon where I knew the rest of the dragons were waiting.

"If you want to fight, now's the time. But if you want a chance at independence and an alliance when I take the throne, I suggest you leave now."

The dragons rose into the air one at a time and flew north. One remained and flew towards me. I tensed and prepared to shift again to fight. She landed, a shimmer surrounding her. When it dissipated, a woman stood in front of me wearing what looked like scaled chainmail.

"Skin of the man who thought he owned me," she said when she saw me noticing.

Holy shit.

"How do you..." I trailed off, not sure I wanted to ask a question that would highlight my inexperience.

"Keep my clothes on?" she asked, a smile playing at the corners of her mouth.

I nodded.

"It is something we learn as children," she said. "But it is not instinctive. Have you had a teacher?"

I shook my head. "No," I managed to say. She was seriously intimidating, and I was painfully aware of my nudity.

"Then you are doing remarkably well," she said. "Find me when you take the throne, and I will be your teacher. And kick Connor when next you see him. He should've taught you more."

"He's dead," I said.

"Is he?" she asked, then shimmered back into her dragon self, red gold scales reflecting the late afternoon sunlight back at me and nearly blinding me. When I could see again, she was gone. The field was empty. I knew it wasn't over—Medb still hadn't admitted defeat—but for the moment, there was a respite.

I TRUDGED BACK TO CAMP, a lot more exhausted than I'd thought I was now that the adrenaline had worn off. It was a good thing the dragons decided not to challenge me. My shoulders ached with the effort of keeping myself aloft for so long. If I could move the next day, it'd be a miracle.

Alanna met me halfway between where I'd landed and the camp and handed me some clothes. After I was dressed, she knelt, offering to carry me back. I smiled gratefully and carefully signed my appreciation. I'd been trying to learn as much sign language as I could during the last few months but was embarrassed to admit I hadn't gotten very far.

She smiled at me, and we headed back to camp in silence. It was only when we crossed the stream that created the natural border on the eastern edge of our encampment that I noticed the blood drying on her skin and the hair of the horse part of her. When she halted, I slid off her back, wobbled a moment on my unsteady legs, and then stepped back until we could see each other's faces.

I pointed at her back and clumsily signed, "What happened?"

She grimaced and looked away, refusing to meet my gaze. I narrowed my eyes and gave her my sternest, most queenly look. "What did you do?"

She signed something back at me, but it was too fast for me to follow, especially with my limited vocabulary.

"I wish I understood," I said. "When this is over, learning your language will be the first order of business for me and the rest of the court. But for now, is Tanwen up to interpreting for me?"

Alanna smiled and nodded. Tanwen must be much better if Alanna looked this happy about it.

We walked towards the med tents. The makeshift streets were almost empty, which was weird considering the sun was still up, we weren't in the middle of a battle, and their queen had just won a spectacular battle against the dragons. It's not that I needed cheers and accolades, but it would be nice if someone noticed I'd returned victorious.

"Where are you? Where is everyone?" I thought at Raj.

"There was an unexpected skirmish," he said. *"Bring Alanna to the war tent. Tanwen is here."*

I touched Alanna's arm to get her attention. Once I was sure she was looking at me, I said, "Raj told me Tanwen is at the war tent and has suggested we go directly there to talk about the unexpected skirmish."

"The Unexpected Skirmish" was going to be volume three of my memoirs. I hadn't decided on titles for volumes one and two yet, but they were going to cover my dos and don'ts for dating and one-night stands and how to grow a sentient hedge without even trying.

We took a sharp turn to the war tent. The inside was cozy and warm, and there was spiced wine waiting for me.

"There are clean clothes waiting for you behind the curtain," Raj said.

I took my wine and headed to the back of the tent. I was shivering by now, and hastily stripped out of what was left of what I'd worn to the battle. After bundling up and sipping more of the wine, I was ready to face the news. I was guessing things weren't great if we had to have a meeting about it, and Raj hadn't told me already.

I returned to the main part of the tent and took my seat at the head of the table. There were so many empty chairs. Tears threatened to overwhelm me for a moment, and I closed my eyes to ward them off. Now was not the time. Instead, I smiled at Tanwen. "It's so good to see you up and about again. How are you?"

She smiled at me, nodded her head in that half-bow so many people did when they saw me, and replied, "Much better, Your Majesty. I feel almost back to myself again."

"I'm so glad to hear it," I replied. "And the others? Florence and Connor?"

"Florence is healing," Clement said. "She's not awake yet, but I'd be surprised if she didn't wake for a bit this evening."

"And Connor?" I prompted.

"He's dead, Your Majesty," Tanwen said.

"Are you sure?" I asked.

"He was a charred husk when the dragons dropped him," Raj said. "I didn't hear a heartbeat or sense any blood circulation."

Vampires were amazing EMTs. Always there with the vital signs and blood transfusions.

"Where is he?" I asked.

"In his tent," Clement said. "We didn't want to do anything with his body until you'd had a chance to say goodbye."

"Where's his feather?" I asked. "Did you look for it?"

Clement met my eyes without blinking. "I did not."

"Why not?" I pressed. "You looked when Florence and Gloni were brought back, and they were in nearly as bad a shape as Connor."

"It's been too long," Clement said. "If he hasn't started healing by the third day, he won't."

"How do you know it's been three days?" I knew I was being pushy, but I couldn't let go of what the dragon had told me before she flew away.

"You're right," Inneacht said before Clement could answer. "We don't know. Everyone assumed based on when Florence and Gloni were found. Father, please."

Clement glowered but didn't argue. I had a feeling that the phoenix god was not often challenged and was even less often wrong. He got up and stalked out of the tent. I waited a moment, then went after him.

I MADE a detour through the kitchen area of camp to grab something to eat. My stomach was attempting to wrap itself around my backbone, reminding me I hadn't had anything since breakfast and I'd thrown that

247

up before engaging in some high-energy taunting and a dragon battle that, while not as vigorous on my part as it could've been, had still burned through my reserves and then some. I was going to need new clothes soon. Again. My weight loss routine would be a big hit with all the women's magazines more concerned with appearance than health. "Burn calories by burning magic faster than your body can handle! Eat all you want and still lose fat! And muscle!" I was going to make a fortune in the diet industry as soon as I figured out how to replicate my routine.

I shook my head, trying to clear it. I wasn't going to get more sleep any time soon, so I needed to, at the very least, keep my body fueled. I detoured back towards Connor's tent. By this point, Clement would've had enough time to determine if Connor still had his phoenix feather and if it was doing its job. He should've had enough time to get over any displays of temper at either being wrong or listening to his hard-headed granddaughter regarding his even harder headed son-in-law. Or whatever. My family tree was fucked up, even when I didn't think about the fact that my maternal grandfather was a god.

I stopped dead in the middle of the makeshift street, closed my eyes tightly, and said to myself, "Get it together, Eleanor." My thoughts kept wandering down side streets and into dark alleys, mugging my focus and memory of where I was going and what I was doing. When this war was over—and hopefully that'd be soon—I was going to sleep for at least a month. I wondered if dragons hibernated. They were up in the north which, while not as cold and snowy as the north of North America, was still mountainous, glaciated, and chilly in the winter. Perhaps I'd do a sabbatical to get to know my people. In winter. In a warm cave with a soft bed.

My eyelids relaxed, and I swayed on my feet. I snapped my eyes open and shook my head again. I had to stay awake, at least a little longer. Besides Connor, I still needed to find out about the skirmish. I forced myself forward again and sent a wave of reassurance towards Raj who was leaking worry at me.

Connor's tent was brightly lit from within, and the warm lamp-light spilled out from under the doorway and cast shadows against the canvas walls between the interior blankets hung for insulation and warmth.

I pushed into the tent and looked down at the man I'd recently learned was my father. He was a crispy critter, and I thought that with all respect. Clement knelt beside him, passing his hand over the blackened and burned form of the dark elf. Raj stood against the back wall next to Inneacht.

"I can't sense anything," Clement said, voice laced with frustration.

"His heart is beating," Raj said. "It is slow—too slow—but it's moving, and blood is moving through his veins, slowly and sluggishly, but surely. He is alive."

"Impossible," Clement said.

"Damn. I was hoping I'd left enough time to avoid arguments and growly tantrums."

Three pairs of eyes turned to look at me. Oops. I hadn't remembered to keep the inside stuff inside. I smiled brightly and took a bite of the meat and potato hand pie I'd snagged from the mess tent.

Inneacht covered her mouth with her hand, and I hoped it was to hide a smile. The Fae were weird. She'd just escaped centuries of relative imprisonment, the seeming betrayal by the man she'd loved—and who'd impregnated her—reunions with a father she hadn't seen in a millennium and the daughter she thought was dead, the news that her twin brother had recently been assassinated, and to cap it off, the afternoon had witnessed the death of her husband at the hand of her daughter. And yet, instead of the blubbering mess I would've been, she was hanging out in a tent with three of the aforementioned people potentially laughing at my rudeness. To a god. Who was her dad.

I took another bite of my food and groaned in delight. I really needed to sit down before I passed out mid-chew.

Raj brought me a chair and held my elbow as I sat. I finished my food and the water someone had placed beside me. During the rest of my repast, Clement hadn't moved once. I hadn't seen him blink or twitch or breathe. He looked meditative. Or dead. I tried to stay as still as I could so as not to interrupt whatever he was doing—and it wasn't difficult. My blinks got longer and longer, and soon I was jerking awake every few moments instead of fighting off sleep.

Arms encircled me and someone lifted me up.

"No. Need to stay," I said.

"You're asleep," Raj replied. "The news will keep, and Connor will be here in the morning."

"Will he? Promise?" I asked, my eyes already drifting closed again.

"I promise, granddaughter," Clement said. "He will be here."

CHAPTER NINETEEN

I was awake and dressed and almost all the way through the breakfast that had been waiting for me when I woke. No one had disturbed my rest, and I hoped that it was because nothing dramatic had happened in the night—no new attacks, no status changes for Connor or Florence, and no fallout from the skirmish I still hadn't learned the details of—and not because someone was forcing me to rest out of a misguided effort to force care where none was wanted.

I wrapped myself in a fur cloak and ventured into the pre-dawn chill. I debated briefly whether to visit Florence and Petrina first to check on Florence's progress or to head directly to Connor's tent. Clement had promised Connor would be there in the morning. Although the Fae did not easily promise anything, I still harbored doubts. Even though the dragon I'd spoken to the day before had implied he yet lived, and even though Raj had heard a heartbeat and sensed blood moving through his veins, and even though Clement had made me a promise, I couldn't shake the feeling I was about to bury someone else who was close to me.

I steeled myself, reminded myself that Petrina and Florence wouldn't welcome early morning visitors whether or not Florence was awake, and headed toward Connor's tent. While I walked, I scrolled mentally through the day's to do list. I needed to check in with Reginn and the rest of the dwarves to determine their plans now that their queen was dead and the dragons no longer a threat. I needed to check the troops at the southern border to see if there'd been further incursions by the Ravens or if they'd either gone home or joined Medb's main army.

I needed reports on casualties and supplies and strategies. I needed to a plan to defeat Medb once and for all. I needed word on our spies on the other side—it was time to pull everyone in, which meant getting in touch with Arduinna and having her pull the plug. I needed to send an emissary to the dragons to request a peacetime meeting, although that could probably wait a couple days.

So many things and I knew I wasn't hitting all of them yet. I needed Connor to be okay. He was, first and foremost, my chief advisor. He'd been attached to the Light Throne for around forty years and knew the ins and outs of ruling. He also had lived in the Dark Court for a long time before that and would know the first steps I needed to take to solidify my reign there as well.

And, he had a few things to answer for.

I was three quarters of the way through mentally drafting a law that would make it a capital crime to withhold pertinent information from me when I reached Connor's tent. Fucking Fae and their fucking secrets. They were worse than the vampires, werewolves, and witches of the world combined. How hard would've it been to say, "Oh hey, Eleanor? Beeteedubs, the Dark Queen we're always going on about? The one you're planning on overthrowing? Yeah. We're kinda twins. You know how it is. Our dad was the old Dragon King. Mom was a Raven. Anywhosits, I'm a dragon, too and could totes teach you some reptilian tricks. Also, you'll never guess who your mom is! Lol. Anyways, Eo's your uncle, as they say in Merrie Olde Faeland."

I was in a thoroughly dark mood when I stomped into the tent. If Connor was among the living, I was seriously considering changing his status immediately. I mean, for fuck's sake.

I pushed my shoulders down my back, straightened my stance, and took a deep breath, held it, then exhaled. I was as calm as I was ever going to be.

I LOOKED DOWN at the body lying in the middle of the room. Clement was in the same position he'd been in when Raj had carried me to bed the night before and Inneacht still stood in her position against the back wall of the tent.

Isaac stood next to her, baby still wrapped up and attached to his chest.

"Where's Raj?" I asked. He'd not been in our bed when I'd woken up, and I hadn't heard from him while walking around grumping in my head.

"Procuring you coffee," Isaac said. "He said something about the dwarves having a secret stash and headed out to find it about twenty minutes ago."

I tried to let that go, too. The dwarves were welcome to all the secret stashes they wanted. I had no rights to their coffee, and they were already generously sharing their beer with me. I smiled beatifically and did three deep breathing cycles. I was a peaceful butterfly. So fucking peaceful. Copasetic even.

This queening thing was taking a toll. But ultimately, it didn't matter. I couldn't appear anything less than calm and collected if I wanted to keep morale up and confidence high. I was going to have to develop a meditation practice and find a yoga teacher. I needed something to help me center myself physically, emotionally, mentally, and spiritually.

There would be coffee. And I would be grateful.

"How is he?" I asked Clement.

"Alive," was the terse response.

"He's angry at himself for missing it before," Inneacht offered.

"I've never seen anyone that far gone come back," Clement growled. "Except you."

I tilted my head and squinted. "What do you mean, except me?"

253

"Do you think I left you to recover alone?" Clement sounded offended. "You tore open the fabric between realities, ignited the Cascade volcanoes, caused a major earthquake with the resulting tsunami, and burned like a torch for hours. I wasn't sure one measly phoenix feather would be enough to bring you back without intervention. Of course, you erected an impenetrable barrier around yourself, preventing anyone from intervening, but I watched and I waited. It would be better, of course, if you could be reborn in your own ashes the way I can, but you have too much dragon in you. The dragon and the phoenix are opposites but yet the same. Fire and ash and rebirth in a perfect circle. To use one of the many Earth symbologies, you are both yin and yang. But this man, your father, is not so well balanced. He is dragon and raven. There is no light, no balance. To see him come back from beyond death is…unprecedented."

"If Florence and Connor had their feathers, where was Gloni's?" Inneacht asked. "Would she have given it away?"

"I didn't know her as well as I'd planned to in the future, but I don't believe she would've, except maybe to one of the others on the mission with them."

"No one who returned carried the mark of the phoenix," Clement confirmed.

"And you said it cannot be lost inadvertently?" I asked.

"Only freely given or stolen." Clement nodded and went back to staring at Connor.

Raj interrupted my train of thought with a large cup of coffee. It didn't smell quite like the coffee I'd consumed vast quantities of on Earth, but it smelled like coffee. Black, rich, dark. I inhaled deeply. Now I was copasetic. I wondered how hard it would be to start a coffee farm here. The dwarves might have the corner on the import business, but there was no reason I couldn't grow my own.

"Shall we convene here?" Raj asked. "We have plans to make yet, and the more minds the better."

I looked around. "Is there room enough for Alanna?"

"If we shift some of this furniture over, yes."

I stuck my head out of the tent, looking for my guards. I knew they'd be there, and only the presence of Clement kept them out of the tent. "Please let Petrina and Alanna know that we'll be meeting here as soon as they're able."

"Can someone tell me about the unfortunate skirmish?" I asked, watching the reactions of everyone in the tent, trying to figure out what was going on. Raj looked down, and his knuckled whitened on the hilt of his sword. Inneacht's serene expression as she gazed at baby Inge didn't change. Clement didn't react either—just kept his staring vigil focused on Connor.

Isaac, however, was a different story. His jaw clenched, and he closed his eyes. A vein pulsed in his temple. I peered more closely. Was that? Yes it was. A tear had formed in the corner of one eye and was about to let go to course its way down his chiseled jawline. What would make him...

Inneacht reached her arms towards Isaac; he scooped the baby out of the carrier and handed her over. Inneacht smiled and cooed at the baby, then looked up at the rest of us.

Oh. Oh! "Arduinna?"

"She was leading a small contingent of forest spirits across our southern border. Our scouts gave them the benefit of the doubt and watched without engaging. Alanna and three other centaurs were called to investigate. When they approached Arduinna's group, Arduinna attacked."

"Attacked us?" I asked. It didn't make sense. She was on our side— we'd had a deal. "We had a deal," I said. "She passed us intelligence, was our person on the inside. Because of the information she sent, we knew about the sneaky secret armies of ravens and dragons. Why would she attack? Are we sure?"

"We're sure," Isaac said. He hadn't said much since showing up at the camp with Medb's baby. I glared at the infant. Sure, it might be irrational to be angry at an infant because her mom was a pain in my ass, but until I could glare at Medb herself, the baby would have to stand proxy.

"But..." I trailed off, putting the pieces together in my head. "Arduinna has never been on anyone's side but her own. She must

255

have thought she was throwing in with the winner. She didn't think we'd survive the day. Or the war. Why? What are we missing?" I stood up and paced with the coffee in my hands. I paused every fifteen steps to take a sip of the delicious nectar Raj had delivered to me. "Ugh. Why am I asking you all? Or myself? Where is she? I'll go get it straight from the horse's mouth. Or the deer's mouth. Whatever."

I looked around the room and almost missed the look of anguish that flashed on Isaac's face before he reschooled his expression into stoicism.

"Oh fuck." The loss hit me like a ton of bricks on my sternum. She and I hadn't been close—but other than Finn, she was the Fae I'd known the longest. We'd shared a lot—most of it misdirection and lies of omission—but she'd almost always been there when I'd needed her. And now...I looked at Isaac again. This wasn't about me. I'd lost a part-time friend, a full-time spy, and the most duplicitous Fae I'd met —which was saying something. Isaac had lost another woman he loved.

I didn't know how to comfort him—it probably wasn't even my place anymore. And I didn't know how to absorb it. Arduinna's death was almost anticlimactic after everything else. I hadn't been there. It was nothing grand. It was...a mistake? A miscommunication?

"What of the others who were with her?" I asked, trying to stay professional and hold back the tears I had no right to cry.

"All but one were killed as well," Isaac said in a monotone so devoid of emotion that it made my heart ache for him. "The one who survived confirmed they were not coming to join us. They were supposed to penetrate our lines and take you out."

"Why'd they attack then?" I asked, putting away the assassination plan for the moment. "Arduinna could've just said who she was—I would've welcomed her and everyone with her."

Alanna and Tanwen walked in. "We can answer that," Tanwen said. "One of the folks in her company was also on the front lines shooting the poison arrows at us. Alanna recognized him, and he apparently recognized her as well and knew the gig was up."

I pursed my lips. "It still doesn't make sense. There are so many ways around that. I'd like to talk to the prisoner."

"We thought you might," Tanwen said. "He's being brought here now. Petrina is dragging him."

"He'll be intact and able to answer questions," Raj assured me. "Petrina is very good at dragging without doing any lasting harm."

"Good?" A useful skill to have, maybe, but I've never been happier that Petrina was on my side.

THE TENT FLAPS parted and Petrina tossed the prisoner in. He narrowly avoided Connor's bed, hit the ground, and skidded to my feet. I jumped back. My dragon wings popped out of my back before I could stop them. No one else looked alarmed enough at what was laying at my feet.

"How does this man appear?" I asked. I wanted to know what glamour he was using before I stripped it from him.

"He's shorter than you, stout, aged, and has big buckteeth," Raj said. "He's wearing iron-studded boots, which is why Petrina was carrying him around. They seem to be permanently attached to his feet."

"Does he have a hat?" I asked, looking down at the man bound at my feet. I noticed he was chained with iron manacles—useful for Fae prisoners, but probably ineffective on any Fae who could wear boots with enough iron in them to make my skin crawl from five feet away. He was here because he wanted to be.

"Yes. A red stocking cap," Raj said. He could tell something was off, but I was holding this close to my chest and he wasn't getting specifics from me.

"*Draw your sword,*" I told him through our mental link.

Raj slowly and silently pulled the ruby blade from its sheath at his waist.

I couldn't believe that after all this time, I hadn't seen through the double layer of glamour. Hadn't realized who this man truly was.

Even in my dreams, he'd appeared as I knew him. I couldn't remember the last time I'd seen him when I wasn't distracted by a hundred other things—preventing me from looking deeper. But now I was the fucking queen, and he was my subject. I could strip him bare and show everyone his true face. Without ever uttering a single untruth, he'd lied to me so many times and so creatively that I had missed every obvious sign.

"Raj, can you remove his bonds?"

My request caused a visible reaction from the others in the tent. Even Clement looked up from his vigil over Connor's still form.

Raj didn't hesitate. He held out a hand, Petrina tossed him a key, and Raj unlocked the manacles from around our prisoner's wrists and ankles, gathered up the chains, and tossed everything outside. Every Fae in the tent relaxed infinitesimally when the iron levels dropped—Inneacht's shoulders dropped, and she took a deep breath. There was still tension—I'd just freed a prisoner who'd nearly killed Tanwen—but the air was clearer now.

He was still wearing his iron-studded boots, but I could work around those. I looked down at him and when he met my eyes, I saw fear in them for the first time. I was used to lust, possession, jealousy, cunning, hate…but even when he should've feared me in the past, he'd always mocked me with his gaze. Not this time, motherfucker.

I unfocused my eyes and concentrated until I could see what the others were seeing, then I grabbed at the illusion with two mental hands and pulled it off like I was skinning a rabbit.

Finn lay on the ground in front of me wearing his customary smirk. His shock of bright red hair spilled around his head, contrasting against his pale skin and the dark floor of the tent.

"How are you going to facilitate my escape this time, Ellie?" he asked. "Everyone knows you won't ever finish it—you can't."

I took my eyes off him for a second and glanced around the room. Petrina was holding Isaac back, and from the tension in her arms, it wasn't easy. Raj was unmoving, but I knew him well enough to know that the statue-still stance masked his readiness. He was waiting for my signal, and the moment I nodded, Finn would be minus a head.

The most surprising reaction in the room, though, was Inneacht's. I was pretty sure the only thing holding her back from clawing Finn's eyes out was the baby still in her arms. If looks could kill, Finn would be dead twice over.

"For those who don't know, this Fae I knew as Finnegan Byrne is Bricriu Ó Fionnagáin son of Cloithfinn." I spat out his true name that he'd been so foolish to give me. "He befriended me, bedded me, and served as the agent of both thrones. He was responsible for—or at least complicit in—the deaths of Eochid, Anoka, Emma, and countless others. He's made several attempts on my life. Was responsible for the deaths of our dryads, and nearly for Tanwen's life. And his attack on our centaurs indirectly resulted in Arduinna's death, robbing us of the opportunity to question her. He has centuries of sins to answer for, but only one life with which he can pay. I do not want to play the role of judge, jury, and executioner...but I will make an exception in this case. But before he dies, I want you all to see the true face of this man."

I reached down again, found the edge of the glamour more tightly wrapped around his being than the face of the Irishish half-elf I'd known for over a quarter of my life and yanked. This glamour was so much a part of him that I knew it hurt to have it torn from his psyche the way I was doing it, and a small, dark, petty part of me was glad.

Once the illusion was removed, the Fae in the room gasped.

"A red cap?" Inneacht said looking at Finn with revulsion.

He looked similar to how he'd first appeared, but now he was gnarled. His fingers were long, crooked, and ended in talon-like nails encrusted with dirt and blood. His teeth were even more prominent than they'd been before and were edged in black and green. But the cherry on the murderous Fae sundae was his hat—no longer a red stocking cap or a shock of red hair, now it was a Phrygian cap. The crown dripped slowly, and the scent of blood rose in the tent.

My gorge rose, but I swallowed it down.

"This is what's been tormenting me for a decade. This is who is responsible for the deaths of so many. Raj, if you would?"

Raj grinned, fangs fully extended and eyes glowing red. "I'd be delighted, Your Majesty." He raised the sword high.

"Bricriu Ó Fionnagáin, red cap, traitor, assassin, and murderer. I sentence you to death," I said.

"Am I allowed last words?" Finn asked, baring his nauseating teeth at me, showcasing the stringy leftovers of his last meal.

"No," I said.

Raj brought down the blade and severed Finn's head from his body. The head rolled away and touched the edge of the tent.

Clement leapt up and stared at the body. He laughed, but there was no humor in it. I shivered at the mockingly cruel delight. "Bring me the head," Clement demanded.

I nudged it towards the phoenix god with my foot. No fucking way was I picking that up.

"I'm not really a head person," I said. "I got my fill with Rasputin. Once you've carried a super undead undead's head around in a bowling ball bag—heh—you kinda lose your taste for it."

No one else laughed at the ball bag, and I made a mental note to get new friends with better senses of humor.

Clement placed Finn's head near the oozing stump of the red cap's neck.

"Watch," Clement said, staring down at the body.

We watched. Nothing happened.

I opened my mouth to ask a question.

"Watch!" Clement commanded again.

I saw it then. Finn's head was wiggling towards the stump, which was reaching out with veins and arteries and sinew and muscle towards the severed head. After nearly a half hour of this, Clement growled, shoved the head down onto the stump of neck, and then stood back up.

Seconds later a grin spread across Finn's face.

Isaac growled. I looked at him. His eyes were glowing amber, and he was about twenty seconds from wolfing out. I backed up and motioned for everyone else to do the same.

Finn's eyes opened and looked around the room as best they could without cooperation from the rest of the head.

I waved my fingers at him when he saw me.

"Oh shi—"

Isaac shifted and tore into him, ripping him to shreds. It was brutal and gory, but none of us moved until Isaac was satisfied. Clement bent over and picked something out of the scraps of body that used to be Finn. He held up a red-gold feather.

Anger roiled through me. Finn was responsible for so much—and now one more death was added to the list.

"Gloni's feather," I guessed.

Clement nodded.

"We'll never know how much damage he truly did," Petrina said.

I stared down at Finn's remains. "We don't need to know. It was too much." I waited for the sadness, regret, and guilt to hit me, but I felt nothing but relief. And release. Something broke in me. A tangible snap in my brain caused galaxies to appear in my field of vision and brought me to my knees. I sensed more than saw the glow that surrounded me—reds and oranges enclosing me in a tear-drop shield. The shield cracked around me, following Finn's spirit as it spiraled out of this world, leaving me exposed.

When I opened my eyes again, the glow as gone, but the heat was not.

"Guess you'll have to learn to glamour after all," Petrina said.

I cocked my head to one side in confusion, then looked down at my hands. Instead of the light tan skin I was used to seeing, my hands and arms had a purple sheen—almost iridescent. I reached up and felt my face. My features felt different. Elongated. I fingered the tips of my ears—the mild point that'd always been there was now pronounced.

"Does anyone have a mirror?" I asked.

CHAPTER TWENTY

W e'd taken two days to rest, recuperate, and reconnoiter. I was painfully aware we were letting Medb do the same, but we needed it. The dwarves, led by Reginn, decided to stay to help us finish it, but I had a feeling my dreams of a beer- and coffee-rich alliance were a lot more tenuous than they'd been before. I hoped that whoever was chosen to lead the dwarves next would be willing to continue the friendship—not just for beer and coffee—but we were *all* going to need each other in the future.

Tanwen was fully recovered, and she and Alanna, along with some of the bird Fae, were scouting the lines to ensure we wouldn't be subject to any more sneak attacks on either or north or south flanks. Medb was doing something on the other side of the hill—the number of people in her camp was growing but was nowhere near her former numbers.

There was nothing to be done now. When the sun rose tomorrow, I would lead the attack to end this war and reclaim my throne.

Air stirred at my side, and I looked to the left. Florence stood beside me. The lines that had begun to appear on her face marking her age had disappeared giving her the appearance of a very young woman. Her hair though, was no longer dark streaked with gray; it was the white-gray of the ash left after everything burns.

"How are you?" I asked.

"Tired," she replied. "But not as tired as yesterday." Her voice was lower, rougher. Clement said it might never return to its former range.

I turned and pulled her into a fierce hug. "Don't you ever do anything like that again," I said. "You scared the shit out of me. Out of all of us."

"I promise to never try to trick a dragon again," she said. "As long as you never ask it of me."

I released her and turned back towards the eastern horizon. "What will you do after?"

"I don't know. I am torn in two directions by the two people I love most in this world. I promised you I'd stay, that I'd always be by your side. And I have promises to keep to the practitioners who've lost so much to this realm. But..."

"Petrina," I finished for her.

She nodded, and we stood in silence until I couldn't stand it any longer. "Don't be stupid. You have to go with her. How often does love jump your bones like this?"

I wasn't looking at her face, but I knew she was rolling her eyes at me. "You're crude."

"You love me."

Her hand slipped into mine and squeezed. "Thank you."

For the first time since I understood what was happening, the weight of someone's gratitude didn't open a gulf of indebtedness, and I knew it was because I owed her so much more that the balance would never tip towards me.

"You know I'd do about anything for you, Witch," I said. "But in this instance, there is no debt between us."

"You stood by me when few others would've. When no one else did."

"Friendship and love aren't only for the good times. Besides, what kind of a PSM would I be if I abandoned you when the going got tough?"

"PSM?" Florence asked.

I grinned at her. "Platonic soul mate. Do you like it? I think it encapsulates what we are so much better than besties."

"I love you, you ridiculous dragon."

"I love you, too, you stodgy old witch."

"Not sure about the new look, though."

I gasped, pretending to be offended. "How very dare you. I am beautiful."

"I preferred you shorter than me, and the hair/skin combination reminds me of a very weird week in 1969." She shuddered.

"Are you calling me a bad acid trip?"

Florence didn't answer, but I heard her snort of laughter.

"Someday, I'll get the rest of your story if I have to pry it out of you with prying torture devices that I'm sure exist in the soon-to-be-mine dungeon."

"There's nothing you could invent that I haven't trained to withstand."

"Fuck you very much, Florence. You know it drives me crazy when you drop tantalizing tidbits like that."

"Why do you think I do it?" She wasn't even bothering to hide her laughter now.

"Ugh. Totally rethinking our PSM status." A feeling of peace stole over me.

"Is there room for two more earthlings on this hill?" Raj asked.

"There's no one else I'd rather spend the rest of the afternoon with than the people who were with me almost from the beginning."

Isaac put his arm around Florence's shoulders but didn't say anything. He hadn't—at least not in my presence—since he'd ripped Finn to shreds. Raj stood next to me, almost but not quite touching. I reached out one pinky finger, found his, and twined them together.

"Will you be okay?" I asked Isaac. "Is there anything—"

"No," he growled.

I looked down at the ground in front of my feet and tried not to take it personally.

"Sorry," he muttered.

"Think nothing of it," I said. "Shit's hard, and you've gotten the short end of the stick for a hundred years and more."

"Did I ever tell you how I became a wolf?" he asked.

"No." He'd never talked about his past.

"Raiders came to my village and killed my mother and sister in front of me. I ran. My mother told me to, and I listened instead of staying to fight. I ran and ran until I was nearly dead from exhaustion and dehydration. And that's when they found me—a pack of desert wolves. They changed me to save me. When I was strong again, I went back and found the raiders who'd killed my family, who'd killed everyone in my village. And I tore them to pieces and scattered their flesh in the wind."

I didn't know what to say, so for once I listened to my gut and said nothing.

"I hate so much. I am nearly consumed with it. And for what? My mother and sister are still gone. Emma is gone. Diane is gone. You are lost to me. I have nothing."

"Don't be an ass," Florence said. "You have friends. You have us. Eleanor is not lost to you—she followed you across two planes, two continents, and three countries just to make sure you were okay. Don't devalue her friendship—that's worth more than any mate bond."

"I'll be your friend, too," Raj said. "I'll be nice and only objectify you some of the time. And if you ever need a shoulder to cry on—or nibble on—I'm your guy."

Isaac laughed, hesitantly at first, but then great, knee-slapping guffaws overtook him.

I took a step back and stared. "You broke him."

"Many are so overcome when they realize they have a chance to warm my bed," Raj said.

"If I roll my eyes any harder, I'm going to give myself a migraine," Florence said.

"For once, I'm with you," I agreed.

Isaac finally got a hold of himself.

"There's one more thing," I said. "One more connection you have that's gonna make this all worthwhile."

"What's that?" he asked, no longer looking grim. The edge of anger was gone from his voice, and he sounded almost like the man I'd danced with so long ago. Intense but open.

Petrina walked towards us with Inge. The baby cooed and held her arms out towards Isaac. He took her, ran a finger down her cheek, and leaned over to nuzzle her nose with his.

"Who else is gonna take the baby?" I asked. "I sure as shit don't want her, and no matter what happens to Medb, I don't think she'll be in a position to raise a child. She's been yours since she was a few days old. There's no one else more equipped to be her dad."

"I've never had a child," he said.

"You love kids, though," I said. "You were a pediatrician for fuck's sake. And as weird as it is for me to give you someone else's kid without their permission, I'm telling you—as queen, this child will become a ward of the state, and the state is giving her into your care until it's her turn to sit on the throne."

"Thank you," he breathed. "This is...this is everything."

I looked back to the east. The sky was purpling with dusk and the first stars were beginning to appear. "Guess we'd better make it official then. I'm gonna grab some food, a nap, then kick some ass."

I watched my friends walk away, Isaac with Inge and Florence and Petrina holding hands but with a gulf of space between them.

"We're alone," I said. "I don't even think there are any guards around at the moment.

"What are you suggesting?" Raj asked, hand on his chest and eyes wide.

"I have a blanket, and it'd be nice to watch the stars come out."

"Hmm... I do have a bottle of wine and two glasses with me, just by chance."

"Perfect."

I LOOKED around me making sure everyone was in position. The sun wouldn't rise for another hour, but I wanted to get the jump on Medb —if that was even possible. My guards, not to mention Raj, Inneacht, Florence, and well…almost everyone…had argued strenuously against me leading the armies into the last battle, but if I wasn't willing to risk myself, how could I ask anyone else to put their lives on the line? Clement had my back, which actually wasn't that comforting. He could always self-immolate if he was injured and return in three days —just like Jesus! Holy shit! I had some questions when I got back— after the battle was over.

Raj had taken my place overseeing the battle. He could communicate with everyone, relay orders, and keep an eye out for surprises with the help of our eyes in the sky. Connor stood—or sat, rather— with him. He wasn't walking yet—and wouldn't be for a while, but he was awake, aware, and in full possession of his faculties. He was also in full possession of his crankiness. I was holding off on my planned berating until he'd been cleared for jumping jacks at the very least.

"*Everyone in place?*" I asked Raj.

"*All units have checked in and are waiting for your orders. Be careful.*"

"*Always. I love you.*"

"*I know,*" he replied, amusement and affection tinging his voice.

The eastern horizon was slowly lightening with the coming dawn. I raised my arm. "*Now,*" I told Raj. I started forward; a thousand Fae at my back. We took our time—minimizing the noise as much as we could—until we got to the base of the hill that separated our camp from Medb's. I held my arm up again, and this time everyone stopped. I crested the hill alone and looked out over Medb's assembling army.

She had more troops than I did, but they didn't give an overall impression of cohesion the way mine did.

Light streaked over the horizon, turning the puffy clouds behind Medb's camp pink and coral and peach. They weren't set yet. If we waited much longer, they'd be in place and we'd lose the biggest benefit of our morning offensive.

I crept back to the line and gave the signal to Raj and my unit. The first ranks marched up the hill and stood at the top, the rest of my army spilling back behind me like a bridal train. I raised my sword into the sky and shook it. My armies roared at the top of their lungs. Medb's lines had begun to scramble when we'd come into view, but with our challenge, their organization fell into disarray.

"What are you doing, you fools!" someone screamed. "Get in line!"

Fae of all sizes and shapes scrambled into place while I dropped low and let my archers take the first shot at the enemy. Although not every arrow found its mark, enough did. Bodies littered the edge of Medb's camp. The archers took one more volley, adding to the enemy fallen, then fell back through our ranks and out to either side to watch for incursions from other directions and guard both our flanks and our retreat, should it be necessary.

I stepped forward. "If you wish to surrender, set down your weapons where you are and move to the large oak tree in the clearing to the south. You will not be harmed either now or after I have won."

A few Fae dropped their weapons and moved towards the tree, but they were met with scorn, then sword points, and the ground under the tree remained clear. I shook my head. I'd been afraid that would happen if anyone took me up on my offer, but I still had to try.

"If your so-called-queen wishes to surrender to me, now would be an excellent time for her to do so, before any more lives are lost."

Silence was my only response. Where was Medb? I hoped she was hiding in her pavilion but was afraid she had some new treachery up her sleeve. There was nothing more to be said and taunting the ground troops wasn't as much fun as picking on Medb or Mata.

I ran forward, sword raised, and felt my armies follow. We fell on them before most had a chance to arm themselves.

It was a slaughter. At first. It wasn't long before I felt the surge from Medb's troops that signaled enough had been able to pull themselves together and coordinate a defense. This is what I'd been waiting for. I sheathed my sword, crouched, and shifted. Once the change was complete, I took to the sky. The armies were sprawled out over the field, meeting in a hundred clashes along the front line. In the center of the enemy troops was a large black tent. I circled it, trying to determine if Medb was in residence. No one went in or out, and the tent shimmered in the sunlight in a way canvas usually doesn't. To test a theory, I inhaled deeply, then let out a burst of smoke and fire.

Nothing happened. The smoke and flame disappeared on contact with the tent, dissipating like it'd never existed. I growled. I needed Medb to come out if I was ever going to win this. I wheeled around and roared again, directing a stream of fire across the field. Fae fell before me.

My army pulled back, out of the line of literal fire. I let loose one more blast of fire, scorching the ground below me. It cried out in pain. I'd gone too far. I landed in the middle of the panicking army, raising a cloud of soot and dust around me. When I spread my wings, more Fae fell. I lashed my tail, bowling over still more. When all semblance of order had disappeared, I looked up at the sky. It wasn't even mid-morning yet. The entire battle had taken less than two hours.

I shifted into my half form—which was closer to my true form than I'd ever suspected—and looked around me. "Who now, will surrender? Drop your weapons." I didn't even have a chance to issue the direction to head to the large oak tree in the southern clearing. Weapons clattered to the ground and so many people rushed to the tree that Fae were trampled by the mob. I stalked around the large tent until I found the opening, conveniently facing east and out of the line of sight of my army.

"Hey, Medb," I called. "It's just you and me and my army. Wanna come out and play?"

NOBODY CAME out to fight me. I stood, arms akimbo, and tilted my head.

"Medb," I called in a sing-song voice, extending her name into two syllables. "Do you wanna build a snowman?"

No response. This was nothing short of insulting. Not to mention ridiculous.

"Is this really how you think family should act with each other, Auntie?"

The entrance to the tent was ripped open. "I am not your aunt, you insolent, petulant, troublesome child."

Medb stood in the doorway, her feathered hair—real feathers, not fashionably feathered hair from the 80s—streaming down around her shoulders.

I did some mental calculations, then crouched, held up my left index finger, and sketched in the dirt. "This family tree looks a lot more scandalous than it really is," I said, straightening up and dusting off my hands against the iridescent purple skin of my thighs. "Okay, so here's you—" I pointed. Medb didn't take her eyes off my face. I sighed. "Fine, you don't have to look. But you're my aunt. Even if the truth you thought you knew was correct, you'd still be something like my great-aunt twice removed. I never really understood that part. But, your brother is my dad. Your dad was the last true Dragon King. Donall didn't have the scales to rule."

"Donall was not your father," she retorted. It was the first time I'd heard her speak directly to me.

"Donall was not your only brother," I pointed out. I really wanted to pull some Yoda shit right then and there but was pretty sure she wouldn't get it. Fuck it. "There is another," I intoned. It seemed appropriate. Medb was staring at me like I'd lost my mind. I smiled. As a wise man once said, it's vital to throw your opponent off their rhythm.

"I do not follow your convoluted sentences and incomprehensible thought patterns."

"You and Donall shared a dad, sure. But you have a brother with whom you shared both parents, don't you?"

"Connor was not your father," she said decisively. "And whoever told you that was either a liar or a fool."

"Inneacht told me."

Medb deflated. Just for a moment, but I noticed.

"We have equal claim," she declared. "I have as much right to the throne as you. More. My father was the king. Donall was not fit to rule. Connor made no claim. You need to wait in line."

"If your right is unassailable, why then did you need to craft a new scepter, a new crown, a new orb? Why did the dragon throne not accept you? Tell me, *Queen Medb*, if you are the true queen, why are you so afraid of a prophecy? Of me?"

Her jaw clenched and her grip on the hilt of her still-sheathed sword tightened, but she didn't respond.

"You know, every time someone promised to bring the head of the *pretender* to the queen, they were promising to decapitate you? You've been a laughingstock for years. And now, here you are. Let's count out your supporters, shall we? Mata is dead, and with him any hope of a dragon alliance. Diane is dead, and with her any hope of help from Earth. Cloithfinn, dead. Even those who claimed to support you once upon a time are gone. Anoka is dead. Connor was burned to a crisp by the dragons. Finn was ripped to shreds in front of my eyes and will never take another order from you. Is there anyone else? Anyone loyal to you? The vampire you kept as a plaything and pet torturer is dead. Inneacht has escaped your clutches. And have you checked on your baby and her nanny lately? Last I heard they were making a run for the border...and you know that nanny was one of Diane's Earth creatures, right? They're probably halfway to Uruguay by now."

I'd finally hit a nerve. "You dare take my daughter?" she roared. This was perfect. It was so much easier to win when my opponent was losing control.

"Do you even remember her name? Or has that detail faded away just like the identity of her father?" A low blow, but one I could feel ashamed of later.

Medb erupted. There was no other way to describe it. One minute, a woman with feathers instead of hair—odd, but attractive in its way —stood in front of me. The next, a six-foot-tall humanoid with wings and the head of a raven. Her half form wasn't as cool as mine. Or at least, that's what I was going to tell myself.

She opened her beak and squawked, then spoke. Her speech was rough, a bit mangled, and difficult to understand, but still intelligible.

"You think your stupid taunts will be enough to win? I have powers you can't even imagine."

I shrugged and lifted my hands to study my nails. "If you thought you could beat me in single combat, you wouldn't have thrown away thousands of Fae lives while you hid in a tent. I will never disparage the ravens—my own grandmother is one, and if she yet lives, I hope to meet her someday—but we all know that it's not your raven heritage keeping you from truly claiming the throne. It's you. You're no more fit to rule than Donall was. The only difference is he knew it. If you think you can beat me, why don't you step out of your pavilion and show me how it's done."

She glared at me but didn't move.

I backed up a half dozen steps and beckoned her forward. "Bring it." In my head, I answered myself with, "Oh, it's already been broughten." I couldn't help it. I laughed. At Medb's look of outrage, I waved dismissively. "So sorry! I'm not laughing at you. Just remembering a movie I used to love."

"You will regret your mockery," Medb said.

"The only thing I'm regretting right now is not remembering to put on sunscreen. Do you know if dragons can burn in the sun? I wasn't expecting to stand here quite this long."

That did it. Medb burst forward, through the barrier of the tent, and launched herself into the air. "Try to keep up, child," she screeched. "I'll make it quick for you."

CHAPTER TWENTY-ONE

Medb was faster than I'd expected, bursting forward and exploding into a shower of black feathers. I scrambled backwards, stumbling a bit in my haste to escape her beak and talons. I pulled at the dragon within and shifted while still backpedaling. That was a mistake and a half. Tripping over two feet had nothing on tripping over four and a tail.

I didn't fall—something I was more than proud of—but it was a near thing. I flung a wing up to protect my eyes from Medb's claws, and when I dropped it again after I'd regained my balance, she was no longer in front of me. I looked around cautiously but didn't see her. I launched myself in the air and immediately felt a hundred and ten percent more graceful. Dragons were not natural sprinters.

I scanned the immediate area for Medb but didn't see her. She wouldn't have run away again, would've she? If my taunts weren't going to be answered, why wouldn't she just stay in the tent and ignore me until I got bored? Unless she didn't want to wait for me to get bored and just needed to make a break for it.

I flew even higher. I could see my army. They'd retreated back behind the river and were ready to march forth again if I needed them. The members of Medb's forces who'd surrendered had been rounded up as well—I assumed they were enjoying my hospitality under moderate guard and with more than adequate food. The rest of Medb's troops who hadn't surrendered but found themselves leader-less and at loose ends were either skulking back into the forest where they'd presumably either emerge later surprised that a whole war had taken place and pledge their loyalty to me or find other like-minded Medb loyalists and foment rebellion against my future rule.

But no Medb.

No dragons in the north nor flocks of too-large birds in the south. And...wait. I flew even higher and peered towards the eastern hori-zon. It was dark, but not the dark of imminent dusk—which was several hours away anyway. The dark was moving. Writhing. Flying towards me.

Oh. Fuck. This was not a mano a mano situation. Medb still had the Raven clan on her side, and they were legion. Shit. Fuck. How was I going to survive an attack from a treachery of ravens? Was that better or worse than an assault from a murder of crows?

"You can do this," I said to myself. I wished I was anywhere else. Anywhen else. But specifically sitting on my front porch, looking at Hedge, eating pizza and drinking a microbrew. I missed beer. And fast food. Fast food...

A plan started to take shape. I had maybe three minutes before the ravens were upon me. I wasn't sure where Medb would be in relation to the rest of the flock but based on how she'd behaved for the rest of the war, I assumed she'd be in the back. She was definitely a lead from behind kinda monarch. It was too bad; I'd love to take her out early and try to reason with the rest, but there was nothing I could do to change the situation now.

I spread my wings and let the air currents lift me higher, so I was looking down on the incoming raven horde. When they were a couple hundred yards away, they moved into an arrow shape. The lead raven didn't look like Medb, but I wasn't particularly familiar with any of them, so it was hard to tell.

I let them get close. Their eyes sparkled in the sunlight, and it might be my imagination, but they looked cruel and self-satisfied. I took a deep breath, exhaled, then inhaled again and held my breath. When they were less than forty yards away, beaks open and magic crackling around them, I opened my mouth and roared.

Flame belched forth in a mighty stream. I pulled the heat from the air around them to feed the fire, making it hotter and hotter until the front ranks were Oregon Fried Corvid.

Dark bodies rained from the sky. I didn't take the time to determine if they were dead or alive—there'd be opportunity enough for that later. I dove down and flew towards my camp, then did a quick loop and flew back towards the birds. They'd reformed into the arrowhead shape, smaller than the last, but still sizable. The formation protected the birds on the inside, and from the feel of the line, allowed them to weave their magic without facing immediate danger.

The air between us crackled with electricity. I ignored it—lightning was akin to fire, after all. How much damage could it do?

I sent another stream of fire towards their line. This time they were prepared for me, and only the front few birds got crispy. When I inhaled again in preparation for changing position, they hit me with the first lightning bolt. It was even more awful than Luke had made it look on the Death Star (2.0). Every nerve ended fired at once and it felt like my blood was boiling in my veins. Stars danced in my field of vision, and in my brain, and in the air around me.

I hit the ground hard enough to jolt me back to my senses and to rattle my teeth in my mouth.

Holy shit. I'd never been struck by lightning before, but that had to have been at least ten times worse. If I'd had any hair, it'd be singed and standing on end. I could feel my bones and internal organ sizzling and vibrating, but whether it was from the fall or the strike, I didn't know. My vision grayed out and my eyes drifted closed.

"Eleanor?" Raj asked, his voice urgent in my mind.

"Fine." I amended my almost-lie. *"Fried a bit, but fine."* I shook my head to clear my thoughts, then looked up. The ravens were above me,

hovering eerily in a way that was definitely not natural. When they saw me look, they started croaking. They were definitely laughing at me. I stood and prepared to launch myself at them.

As one, they released their bowels and whitewashed me and the ground around me. I'd been looking up, gauging the distance between me and them, when they'd let loose. Fortunately, my mouth had been closed, even if my eyes hadn't. Gross. I pushed off the ground and into the sky, determined to use their stinking, stupid feathery bodies to wipe the shit off my face.

I felt the air ionize almost immediately, but this time I was ready for them. I sent a stream of fire at the leaders in the arrow formation then dove beneath them, pushing back up and through their ranks, scattering the birds and disrupting their attack.

They regrouped more quickly than I'd anticipated, and I got another bolt of electricity, this time hitting me right in the ass and spreading through my body. I dropped again but recovered before I hit the ground this time. I wheeled around. There were still too many of them, and I couldn't take more than one or two more strikes. No way would I be able to clear their ranks before they took me out. I needed a new strategy.

This was a different fight than the one I'd had with Mata. He'd been rash and aggressive. All I'd needed to do was tease and let him wear himself out.

The ravens were trying to do the same to me. Get me riled up, attack, take me down, repeat. I needed to calm the fuck down, back up a bit, and let them come to me. I wouldn't win by picking off a half dozen at a time. Not when there were more ravens than I could count. They wove in and out, confusing my eyes and hiding their numbers.

I needed something else. Air frying them had been a good initial attack, but unless I could find another way, I was gonna be a one hit wonder.

I circled them, staying far enough away to avoid the lightning strikes, but close enough to keep an eye on them. Like migrating geese, they rotated the leader position. All except a few ravens in the center of their triangular formation. That must be Medb and the Jarl

—the top birds. I flew a few more lazy circles, trying to recover from the electrocution, and strategized. Or tried to, anyway.

My eyes scanned the area, looking for anything that would help beyond asking my army to sneak in and start picking the birds out of the sky...actually, why couldn't I do that? Sure, it wasn't exactly sporting to ask your backup to step up when you were having a duel, but I hadn't started this mess. I was about to tell Raj to send in the archers and raptors when another smudge on the horizon caught my eyes.

The thought of the ravens being reinforced sent a pulse of despair through my body. This shouldn't be happening. We'd all but won. This was a formality. A way to humiliate—and hopefully permanently dispose of—the usurper. As the smudge got closer, it didn't separate into individual ravens. It was one big fucking crow.

Branna.

I wasn't sure why they were here now—the hunt had been getting their fill, but they'd stayed away—and I hoped they were still loyal to the throne and not the person occupying it. And then I saw it. A stand of dead oak trees in the clearing away from the larger forest. They were brown and leafless and dry. Any nymphs who'd resided in them long since fled. Perfect tinder.

I circled faster now, causing the birds to wheel around with me. I moved a little further north and a little more closely in with each successive circle, slowly enough that if they noticed what was happening, it didn't raise any alarm bells.

Branna had stopped at the edge of the forest and perched on a huge snag to watch the proceedings. I tried to ignore them and concentrate on the task at hand.

As I flew, I wove light and air around me, over and under, until I'd created a large invisible sphere around me and the corvids. Also enclosed in my shields was the stand of dead oak trees. When I was close enough to feel the crackle of their electricity against my skin again, I let loose a roar that reverberated against my shields and spewed fire past the birds and into the waiting tinder beneath them.

The trees caught immediately, and tendrils of smoke and flame quickly became an inferno. The build-up of pressure announced an imminent strike, and I dove into the trees, shielding myself against their electricity with my fire. The bolt followed me in but hit the tree I wove around.

The tree exploded outwards, flinging shrapnel through the air. I landed gently, hunkered down, and wrapped my wings around me.

Bodies hit the ground, and the odor of burning feathers surrounded me. I stood, burst back up through the trees and smoke, and looked around. My dome was full of smoke like the world's worst snow globe, and if there were any ravens left, there weren't enough to stay in formation and offer any kind of threat.

I landed again, this time outside the stand of still burning trees, and thanked whoever thought up dragons that they'd enabled us to breathe through smoke. I pulled the heat back into me, putting the fires out. Then I opened the smallest vent I could manage without losing control of the entire shield and pushed the smoke out. It needed little encouragement—smoke loves it some hot chimney action.

When the smoke cleared, I could finally see who was left. I shifted to my unglamoured form—purplish bat wings, fiery red hair, tail and all.

Medb stood opposite me. She was wearing her humanoid head but had kept her wings. A couple dozen other ravens were in various states of mobility behind her, with two in their human forms. Twenty-five was still too many to fight, but most of these birds didn't look particularly interested in throwing down.

"Finally ready to take me on yourself?" I asked. My voice was thick and hoarse from smoke inhalation. I might be able to breathe through the smoke, but it sure as soot wasn't doing my throat any favors. "Or do you need to bring in more people to hide behind?"

She coughed, then spat a thick, ashy wad of phlegm towards my feet. Birds were gross. "I have many loyal to me who are willing to fight for me. It's a shame you cannot muster the same support."

I laughed. "I don't need other people to fight my battles for me. I'd be a shitty queen if I always hid behind my supporters, and I'm not sure how loyal my friends would be if I always sent them to die in my stead."

The still-mobile ravens behind her were slinking off into the distance, and I lifted the shield on that side to give them passage if they chose to go. They did.

"It's not a queen's job to die for her people—it's the people's job to die for their queen."

"Yikes. That's a lot of not okay," I said. "How can you lead if you regard your people as nothing more than cannon fodder? Why do you want to lead?"

Medb looked totally taken aback. She actually reared back, tilted her head, and pushed her wings back to maintain her balance. "Power. Of course, power. And fear. No one dares look down on the queen on pain of death."

"And yet, you are still alone in the end," I said, gesturing around me. "No one here to fear you. Tell me how you want to end this because I'm tired of talking. You have my throne, and I want it back."

"It was never yours to begin with," Medb shrieked, drawing a sword almost as long as she was tall. How was that even possible?

"Thanks for keeping it warm for me, Auntie M," I said. I drew my sword from its hidden air sheath. It was a good three feet shorter than hers. I stepped forward, thrust and braced for the impact of her ridiculous weapon, but it didn't come.

Instead of either defending or attacking, she was staring at something over my left shoulder. I wasn't sure if I should look—what if it was a ruse?—but after a solid minute of watching her face take on a rictus of fear, I side stepped and turned.

Branna walked through my shield and smiled. "It's time," they said, and I heard every one of the dead's voices come through the slough's mouth.

"You promised!" Medb said, shrinking back.

"I delivered. I am loyal to the throne. To the crown. To the queen. Just not the queen you hoped. You can die honorably at the end of Eleanor's sword, or I can call forth the hunt and let your soul be ripped from your body, shredded, and scattered in the wind. You'll be gone, and soon forgotten. No one will sing of you. It will be almost as if you never existed."

Medb looked back and forth between me and Branna, eyes wild and afraid. She dropped her sword, turned, and bolted.

Branna laughed, and the macabre timbre of thousands of souls cackling together raised goosebumps on my arms. "I was hoping she'd run." They leapt into the air and spread their wings. Dark shapes broke from the feathers spread wide and reformed as crows. They flew forward like a dark cape, and harried Medb across the field.

When she'd nearly reached the tree line at the far end of the field, Branna dove, and behind them dove the corvid souls representing the wandering dead of thousands of years and countless battles. When they rose up again, Medb was gone, and soon even her screams were carried away by the winds.

I'd won. Holy fuck. I won.

I WALKED BACK towards my camp. I was exhausted beyond anything I'd felt yet. I wanted to curl up on the ground and take a wee little nap before returning, but Raj's voice in my head urged me on. I had to keep walking—keep moving. The war was over. I was queen of dark and light. And a nap was not on my royal agenda.

When I reached the place where Medb had fallen, I saw her body. It was untouched and lifeless. Soul-rending was a much more delicate operation than I would've thought.

"*We need to burn the body,*" I said to Raj. "*Can you send someone over to collect it and anyone else who needs funeral rites? These are all my people now, and I would treat their fallen with respect.*"

"*Of course,*" he said. "*Do you want to wait there?*"

"*Very much,*" I replied. Fatigue rolled over me in waves, and it took every ounce of willpower to stay upright and awake until the cadaver crew and Raj appeared.

"I'll escort the queen back to camp," he said. "Bring the fallen queen and her supporters back. We will burn them with our own."

Raj hooked his arm through mine. "They will want to fete you," he said. "You've won. You vanquished the bad guy. And you've united two realms that have been separated for too long."

"Can't we party tomorrow?" I asked, wincing at the whine in my voice.

"You will, but tonight you have to make an appearance at the impromptu celebration. But first," he leaned away from me and wrinkled his nose, "a bath. You're covered in bird shit and reek of smoke."

I laughed, lightly at first, and then heartily enough that I had to stop walking and put my hands on my knees. When the note of hysteria wound its way through my laughter, I tamped it down and stood up. "It was a crappy fight," I said. A giggle escaped before I could stop it.

Raj shook his head. "The Fae have no idea what they're in for," he said. "It's gonna be all dad jokes, juvenile humor, and bad fast food from here on out."

"They said I was gonna change the world. Why not use my power for good? Do you think I could get a Taco Bell franchise here?"

"You're the queen—anything's possible."

CHAPTER TWENTY-TWO

I stood in the shadows near the large celebratory fire on the outskirts of the camp. The warmth danced around me and pushed away the chill of the night air. Stars lit up the sky in a way I'd never seen before the world started ending. The constellations were unfamiliar here, but I no longer looked for comfort in the stars. This was my sky now—these were my people. And surely someone would be able to point out which myths went with which cluster of stars.

My army of Fae were passing around casks of wine supplemented by beer and mead supplied by the dwarves. They weren't celebrating as loudly as the Fae, but they were here in number to add their voices to the songs of victories past and some of victories present that sounded like they were being composed on the spot.

After I'd smiled and waved—which had been after I'd bathed and eaten—enough, I'd slowly pulled away from the crowd. My mug of beer was never empty, but no one sought me out for congratulations either. Raj was out circulating through the crowd pretending to be spreading cheer on my behalf, but in reality, making sure angry stragglers from Medb's forces weren't sneaking in to start trouble.

Groups of Dark Fae had been showing up. First in twos and threes, but once they were welcomed with open arms after a few pointed questions, more and more started showing up. I looked for the Ewoks but didn't see any. Nor did I see Eo or Gloni or Emma force ghost their way into the celebration.

Someone brought me a chair, and it was all I could do not to thank them effusively. I sank into it and groaned. Everything hurt. I was sore in places I didn't realize could be sore.

Another chair was deposited beside me, and moments later, Inneacht helped Connor into it.

"What are you doing here?" I demanded. "And how are you mobile?"

"Strong genes, I guess."

I punched him lightly in the shoulder and he winced.

"Oops," I said. "But you deserve it. You owe me so many explanations. How could you leave so much out?"

"I didn't know I was your father."

"That's not what I'm talking about, and you know it. You didn't mention your family at all. And even if Mata had been my father, you still were related to me somehow. Great uncle? Second cousin? I don't know, but you're a dragon, and not only did you pretend to be a dark elf masquerading as a light elf, you knew who I was—what I was—and you didn't say anything."

"I didn't want to unduly influence you. You needed to rule on your own, learn the rules on your own... The power had to be yours."

"Right. Like everyone else who's taken the throne? No one ever trained them showed them the ropes, gave them pointers on air combat? Did you figure it out on your own, *Dad*?"

Connor inhaled loudly, and I knew he was counting to ten and summoning up all his patience to deal with his willfully obtuse daughter. "Obviously not. But you were always going to have a hard sell of it. You still will. People will be coming out of the woodwork for years thinking they can challenge you—because you didn't grow up here or because you're too human, for all your Fae blood or because you used your connections to con your way to the throne. But now I—and everyone else who's met you can attest that you did all this on your own with a handful of ragtag supernaturals from another realm."

It almost made sense. "Yeah, but if I was lightyears ahead of where I'm at now because you'd cared enough to give me a few pointers or at least fucking tell me we shared dragon DNA I'd be that much scarier and less likely to be challenged. I don't need my reputation to be unassailable if my power is."

"Would've you trusted me if you'd know Medb was my twin? Even if you knew the rest of my story, felt the truth of what I told you?"

I wanted to say yes, but he was right. "No. I would've always been hesitant, would've looked for what you weren't saying. It was hard enough to trust you as it was."

"Precisely. It's a lot easier to take the long view of everything when you have a couple hundred years behind you. Tell me something, though—now that you know who I am, who you are, and who Medb was to you... Will you rule like Medb?"

"No. I don't think I can. The throne called to me almost from the moment the dragon came to me, but I would like to believe I wouldn't have challenged Medb for it if she'd been a good ruler. But she took the worst of the Fae customs and went ten steps further. Did you see her soldiers? They were underfed, underclothed, and exploited. I don't expect to be hailed as a savior, but I do hope that eventually the Dark Fae will grow to respect me. I've got some big changes coming. I'll piss off a lot of people—mostly the nobility—but I hope that I'll make more people happy than not."

"Now, imagine you'd been raised here—that Inneacht and I had snuck off with you and raised you in the woods until you were old enough to challenge Medb—maybe in a couple hundred years. You'd have access to the training, education, and power that comes with being raised by two incredibly powerful Fae, but you wouldn't have the compassion and empathy you got from being raised by your human parents. Would you want it any other way?"

"Ben and Ida," I said. It was the first time I'd spoken their names out loud in almost twenty years. The first time I'd even thought about them without the pain of loss breaking my heart all over again. It had always felt wrong to speak their names aloud, and now, knowing what I know about Fae attitudes about death, I wondered if that was a nature versus nurture thing. But they had sacrificed so much and deserved to be remembered.

"What?"

"Those were my parents. Ben and Ida Morgan. I don't talk about them. Their deaths wrecked me, and I tucked it away for a long time. And now, it's hard to remember the details from before the power took me, but I don't want to forget them. You and Inneacht may have made me, but they made me who I am."

"And that, my dear child, is why I let you believe as you did."

"Your logic is missing something, but I'm too tired to untangle it right now."

"Just as well. I'm too tired to defend it. I'm going back to bed now. You should do the same soon. Find that vampire of yours and make him take care of you."

"I'm glad it was you," I said. I leaned over and kissed his cheek. "Out of all the possibilities, you really are the best."

"I'm glad, too." He put an arm around me and pulled me close, planting a kiss on top of my head. "But no sweet talk is gonna get you the keys to the car."

"Awww, dad! Not fair," I whined.

He laughed against my hair and leaned back. "I think I love you, Eleanor."

"Ciara nic Connor," I corrected. "Goodnight, Father."

IT HAD TAKEN five days to pack up our war camp, send off the dead, and make our way to the Dark City, but here we were. "Why don't the cities have names?" I muttered to Connor as we prepared for our grand entrance.

"They do, of course," he said. "Some call this city Tinnu, whilst the capital of the Light is Anarórë.

"Oh. But…"

"We have two cities across two realms and most people live somewhere else. It's simple enough to say, 'I'm going to the city.'"

"Ah, like pretentious San Franciscans?" I asked.

"Like suburbans everywhere, San Francisco not excluded. Are you ready?"

I absolutely wasn't. Everything that'd happened leading up to my first coronation had seemed like a blur and was now so far back in my memory—the way eight months can be when you've lived a lifetime in the intervening time—that this felt unreal. Connor was at my left side, and because neither he nor Florence were up to a miles-long trek into the city through the crowds everyone was sure would show up to cheer me on, I had agreed to come in on what was more parade float than carriage.

Raj was on my right. I don't know where they'd found tailors and seamstresses and fabric in the middle of a war zone, but we were all kitted out in some of the most amazing finery. Connor had dropped any pretense of glamour while he healed—not that it was necessary to hide that he was Dark Fae here and now, anyway. His dark skin that shimmered when the light hit it just right, high pointed ears, and black hair flowing down his back marked him not only as Dark Sidhe, but also pointed to his Dragon roots. He was wearing lavender pants that gathered into suede boots and a long blousy tunic the same color as his pants, belted at the waist and hitting the top of his thighs.

Raj had definitely had input into his own costume—he was dressed in loose yellow silk pants and a long, russet-colored jacket that fastened up into a high collar. The bright colors set off his dark skin perfectly, and he looked really comfortable.

I couldn't argue with how I'd been dressed, either. My dress was variegated green fabrics that cinched at my shoulders with silver rings, leaving my arms bare and showcasing my dragon tattoo. The silk fabric gathered over my breasts, leaving rather more of my cleavage exposed than I was used to, was belted at my waist with a circle of silver branches with emerald leaves, then draped out into a soft, flowing skirt that ended just above my ankles. My hair had been washed and styled until it flowed down my back in waves. Threads of silver wove through the tresses. I was fancy. Even fancier than I'd been for my first coronation—which was appropriate, I guess, since this was a bigger deal.

I inhaled, looked behind me to ensure that Inneacht, Isaac, Florence, Tanwen, and Reginn were still on this ridiculous float with me, Alanna and an honor guard of centaurs spread out on either side.

"Am I ready?" I asked, echoing Connor's question. "I kinda have to be. Turning and running away isn't much of an option."

Raj put his hand on my thigh, and the cool pressure calmed the butterflies that threatened to erupt in my stomach.

Connor nodded at the driver, and we started forward. The gates to the city—Tinnu—opened wide and cheers erupted from the other side. We wound our way through the streets to the castle. The crowds were packed three and four deep all throughout our circuitous route, and enterprising vendors were hawking flags with what I could only assume was my portrait on it. By the time we were near the castle gates, the number of Eleanor faces waving in the breeze was overwhelming and I fought the urge to vomit from sheer nerves.

"Almost there," Connor whispered. "Once we cross onto the castle grounds, it'll be a little more sedate."

We crossed the threshold, and the crowds dropped off as Connor had promised. The carriage stopped in front of the huge doors that led into the castle itself. I allowed myself to be helped down, then paused while my retinue gathered behind me. We walked slowly up the stairs and into a huge entry hall. Fae lined the walls—castle staff, I assumed. Most of them looked terrified, and I noticed that most of them had on the same kind of collar Anoka had worn when Connor and I had rescued her. My list of things to do immediately kept getting longer.

"It'll be taken care of," Connor said. "Before your coronation, they will all be free."

"I appreciate your attention to detail," I said smoothly. I placed my left hand on his arm and my right on Raj's arm then paused. Florence and Inneacht followed immediately behind me, then Isaac and Inge, followed by Tanwen, Alanna, and Petrina. A contingent of dwarves marched behind them.

At the end of the entrance hall were two more large doors—guess you weren't anyone in Tinnu unless you had a big door, but immediately before the door was a corridor leading off to the right. When we passed the corridor, two women stepped out in front of us—one in a purple gown and the other in black and white—and curtseyed.

I didn't know who they were but based on the reactions from the Dark Fae escorting me, this was a big deal. I nodded deeply back at them and held out my hands, hoping I was doing everything right. The women stood and took my hands. "Welcome home, Eleanor," the one in purple said. I recognized her then, and a genuine grin split my face. This was the dragon who'd told me Connor lived—and advised me to kick him a little when he got better.

"Your greeting is both gracious and welcome," I said. "I am happy to be here, and I look forward to knowing you better."

"Call me Aeldress, Jarl of the North. I have many names, but that will do for now, Niece. My brother was your grandfather, and I have ruled the north since he rose to the Dragon Throne."

"But Mata..." I started, then clamped my mouth shut. Here and now were not the places to ask questions about power and family disputes.

Aeldress smiled tightly. "I swore an oath I could not wiggle out of in a moment of weakness—my brother was a charmer—but you rendered that oath moot, something I appreciate more than you could know. But we have time to catch up later in private. You should meet Eithne, Raven Jarl and Defender of the South."

"And your grandmother," the Jarl said, squeezing my hand rather harder than was necessary. Her black eyes glittered as she stared at me, and I knew this wasn't the first time we'd met. She'd been one of the ravens who'd escaped through the shield I'd lifted during my final confrontation with Medb.

"Hi," I said. I didn't know what else to say. Too many new relatives, some of whom didn't seem that excited to meet me.

"The Ravens stand ready to pledge themselves to the Dragon throne as we have always done," she intoned with zero sincerity.

Connor elbowed me and it hit me with a start that this was his actual mother. She hadn't even spared a glance for him, instead her eyes were searching the people behind me and I moved into her line of sight before she could lay eyes on Inge. "The Dragon Throne is more than happy to receive the Ravens and once more cement our long alliance," I said. "Shall we now proceed into the throne room? I would be honored if the Jarls of North and South would escort me the final steps."

Since there was no way to get out of that without looking rude, Eithne turned and took the hand that Raj released while Aeldress took the other. The three of us walked abreast into the throne room.

I'D SEEN IT BEFORE, of course, when Connor and I had been here in disguise, but now the windows were thrust open and light streamed in, illuminating the darkly gleaming obsidian walls and furnishes. The Jarls walked me to the base of the dais, then let go of my hands and stepped aside.

On the dark wooden throne were an orb and scepter, both made from shining wood.

"These aren't right," I said. "None of this is right."

I stepped forward, ignoring the gasps of my inherited courtiers when I breached the etiquette of my private coronation. I placed my hands on the throne and nearly cried out in pain. "This is not the Dark Throne; this is an abomination. A spirit trapped forever and forced into this unnatural shape." I touched the scepter and orb. I'd been forewarned what I would find, but the reality was even worse. "The children's souls are trapped?" I whispered in horror. I'd assumed it was bad, but not "kids trapped for decades by the woman who'd killed their whole family" bad.

I had to free them. I just didn't know how. I looked around the throne room, hoping the answer would come to me, but the solution didn't step forward and introduce itself to me.

I looked back at the throne and the twisted symbols of power Medb had wielded, then looked around again. This time, a large tree, burned and scarred but still standing on the far side of the room caught my eyes. It reminded me of the greenery in the Light throne room—the trees that marked the seasons and were danced and feted to mark and encourage the passage of the seasons. But this tree would never again bud in spring.

There was something here, a connection I wasn't making. I shook my head, conscious of everyone's eyes on me. I reached down again and placed my hands on the scepter and orb. This time, I felt the children's spirits more clearly.

"Florence, do you have the true orb and scepter?" I asked.

"Of course, Your Majesty," she said.

"Bring them and walk with me."

We approached the burned-out tree. Inside the scarred trunk was a hollowed-out place where I imagined his heart would be. I placed the grotesque and twisted items inside the hollow, took the true symbols of power, and touched the orb to the scar in the trunk. The gap snapped closed, and the scar disappeared before my eyes. I caressed the tree with my hand and something within it stirred. The dryad moved forward; the floor around him groaned as he pulled impossibly large roots from the ground, splitting open the earth and causing a rush of water to burble to the surface. He strode across the room, leaving a stream bed in his wake, picked up the throne in his arms, crushed it to himself, then sank into the ground. The castle shook as he disappeared, and the stream that had risen divided and flowed around the dais, pooling in the wide groove that ran the perimeter and disappearing through the back wall.

The ground shook again, and power flowed through me. The castle was greeting me—welcoming me. And...thanking me?

The dais split open again, and an enormous egg-shaped stone rose to the surface. It was at least twelve feet tall and maybe six feet wide. It settled into place. Cracks ran along its surface, then the stone split open and fell away, melting into nothing.

A dark throne—glittering and black—was in the middle of the dais now, and a figure stood behind it holding a crown. From the gasps of awe, Jörð's appearance was an unexpected development.

"The throne disappeared when your last king was murdered," Jörð said, her voice ringing out over the throne room, and probably throughout the entire city. "And with it, any chance of one person being the rightful ruler of the Dark Sidhe. Now, it has returned to signal the true queen, the one who will unite the Dark and Light, has returned. Take your place, Dragon Queen."

I crossed the stream and walked past the two stairs to the dais, followed by Florence who was again bearing the orb and scepter. Jörð held out the crown. I hesitated for less than a second, before accepting it. The black and silver metals twisted and wove around each other creating a delicate pattern of flying dragons studded with black, fiery opals that echoed the appearance of the throne. I placed it on my head over the top of my silver and emerald crown. The two crowns snapped together with a chime that vibrated the throne room. The birds—phoenixes, I could see now—of the Light crown twisted around the dragons of the Dark crown until it was impossible to see where one crown ended and the other began.

A feeling of rightness washed over me, and after that, power. I could feel every creature of power in both the Light and Dark realms —no longer divided. It didn't push me to my knees like it had when I'd accepted the Light crown from Jörð, but I swayed on my feet as waves of pain and dizziness washed over me. Once I had my balance again, I turned around to greet my subjects for the first time. Florence handed me the orb and scepter, and when I held them, all the pieces fell into place. The barrier between realms fell as I bridged the Light and Dark.

Someone flung open the door to a balcony to the courtyard below, and Connor called out, "I present to you Eleanor, Dragon Queen, World Breaker, Destroyer and Creator, and now your Twilight Queen. Long may she reign!"

I walked forward, still drunk with the power flowing through me as the lands started healing the scar that had torn them apart. I stepped onto the balcony and looked out over the sea of faces chanting my name.

I'd done it. I was the Dragon Queen, and the Dark Throne was mine.

EPILOGUE

My private sitting room was not nearly as private as I would've liked. Currently, in addition to the ubiquitous servants and guards, it played host to the King Consort —the only person I really wanted around at the moment...we'd had precious little time alone together when I wasn't exhausted after a long day of queening, my chief advisors Connor, Acantha, Tanwen, Florence, and Alanna, Eithne, who so far hadn't taken any of my hints that she should hustle on back to the Southern Keep to keep an eye on things, Aeldress who was slightly more welcome, Clement who mostly skulked around for no reason I could discern, Inneacht who was trying way too hard to be my mom, leaving me feeling guilty when I couldn't get myself to reciprocate her eagerness to create a mother-daughter connection, and Petrina who was getting more and more restless as time went by.

It'd been three months since my coronation, and I was finally getting a chance to keep some promises I'd made. The dungeons had been emptied and mostly sealed up. I left a couple in case any Finn-type characters surfaced to cause trouble. But when we'd liberated the prisoners—most of whom were from Earth—we also found enough treasure to satisfy my dragon soul and make a dwarf blush.

Florence had met with all the freed witches of both halves of my new realm over the protests of those who'd been relying on kidnap victims to shore up their power. About two-thirds were determined to return to earth. The other third weren't interested in starting over in a world they didn't remember and that had no one left to remember them.

I picked over the treasure Medb had been hoarding and divided it into two even piles. Half was split evenly between the freed witches, regardless of whether they were staying or going. The other half was earmarked for the witches in Oregon to whom I'd promised reparations for the continued kidnapping and mistreatment of witches at the hands of my people. It wasn't enough. There was no such thing as enough. But it was, I hoped, a start.

I was dragging things out. I knew that once I finished this, once I'd passed my first few decrees to create a more equal and equitable world, that my friends would scatter, and we might never again be together. I was determined to have one more solstice before everything changed, and I had to stop pretending the adventure didn't have to end.

Midsummer was about to roll around again—the anniversary of my first encounter with Hedge, the first time the magic flowed through me, and the day I found out who I was—or at least who I'd started out as. After solstice, I'd be able to say goodbye.

THE SUN WAS RISING, lighting up the smaller receiving room I preferred to the hugely ostentatious throne room. Midsummer was over and the sun was heralding in the beginning of our journey towards the darkness of winter. And the darkness of my heart.

"You're gorgeous when you pout," Raj said. He leaned forward and nipped at my lower lip. "Your Majesty," he added.

I rolled my eyes at him. He was delightfully mussed—we'd celebrated Midsummer well—but still ridiculously beautiful. "It's disgusting how good you always look," I said.

"I am not going to miss this at all," Florence interrupted, striding into the room. "Everyone's waiting in the courtyard, are you coming?"

"If I must," I said, feeling my pout returning. Hand in hand with Raj, I followed her out into the sun-drenched courtyard. Jack had shown up a few days earlier after a one-year absence and announced his presence by braying loudly outside Isaac's window before dawn the morning after the full moon.

Now the giant jackass was laden down with the contents of the secret treasury that Florence was escorting—along with the witches who were returning—back to Oregon. She was going to help the witches get settled, aid them in finding covens who would take them in, help them heal, and not exploit them. And then she'd promised to return, even if she couldn't tell me when.

"I hate this," I said, grabbing Florence and pulling her in for a fierce hug. "How will I do this without you?"

"The way you do everything. With strength. With stubbornness. And with heart. I'll miss you so much, Eleanor. Thank you for taking me on this journey."

"Don't forget to come back. I don't want to have to tear the world apart tracking you down."

"I'll be back. Try not to break any more worlds without me."

The tears that had been threatening all morning spilled down my cheeks, and I turned my attention to the other group of people in the courtyard. Before I could say goodbye to anyone else, though, movement in the corner of my eye drew my attention. I turned away from my friends and towards the wall that surrounded the palace. It was... different. More leafy green and less inky stone.

"Hedge Antilles?" I gasped. A twelve-foot laurel hedge had displaced the castle walls and a feeling of rightness descended over me. Hedge, more than Finn, had been how my adventure truly started, and it was fitting he was here at the end. I sent a silent request to slow down the growth before he Sleeping Beautied me in and turned back to my friends.

"Petrina, I appreciate everything you've done for me so much. I'm glad you came when Raj asked for help. You've been a good friend, and I'll miss you. There will always be a place for you here."

"It's been fun," she said. "But I have responsibilities. I've been gone too long already. Besides, if I don't take over Eastern Europe, who's going to give Marie a run for her money?"

"Send me an invitation when you're being crowned Queen of the World," I said.

"Of course, Mom," she said, bumping me gently before pulling me into a hug. She stepped back, then hugged Raj. "Come visit me," she commanded.

"Maybe next year," Raj said. "I'll miss you, but you don't need me checking in too often. Take over Europe on your own, then call."

Petrina stepped back, then turned to Florence. I didn't know where they were, just that they weren't in the same place. The way they looked at each other broke my heart, but I didn't know how to force two people desperately in love with each other to just get over themselves and kiss and make up. All I could do was cross my fingers they'd come to their senses before their paths diverged once they crossed back to Earth.

"I wanted to say goodbye, too," Isaac said.

"I might have had to chase you back to Europe if you hadn't," I teased. He was holding Inge, who was almost big enough to walk now.

I brushed her cheek with one finger. "Goodbye, little cousin," I said. "Learn lots and get big and strong. Someday, this will all be yours."

She smiled up at me and held out her arms. I leaned in and gave her a hug, then pulled Isaac in. "If you ever need anything…"

"I'll let you know. I promise." He pulled back, and even though I knew things would never be the same between us, it didn't stop a pang of hurt from surfacing.

I let him go and stepped back, taking Raj's hand again.

"Goodbye, daughter," Inneacht said. "I hope someday we'll meet again, but for now, Inge will need a Fae around to guide her as she grows."

"We'll have time together again," I said. "But Inge will need you more than I do. Be the mother to her you never got to be for me."

She touched my face gently, then walked away.

Florence and Inneacht, fueled by the power of the witches accompanying them, raised the gate. The first of the witches walked through, then Jack and Petrina, followed by Inneacht. At last, only Florence and Isaac were on this side. It was all I could do to hold myself back from rushing forward for one last hug.

I held up my hand in farewell. Isaac and Florence walked together through the gate. Inge peeked back at us over Isaac's shoulder and waved.

"Bye!" she called. The gate snapped shut behind them, and I buried my face in Raj's shoulder. When I'd cried myself out, he dried my tears on his sleeve.

"Goodbyes are seldom forever when you're fabulous and nearly immortal. As long as we're together, my sweet, the adventure will never be over. And now that we're alone, relatively speaking, there are some adventures I'd like to have with you...how many bedrooms do you think this place has?"

I laughed, grabbed his hand, and pulled him towards the palace. "I don't have anything else on my agenda today... Race you to the third-floor guest quarters? It's definitely time to scandalize the neighbors."

The End

I'D BE ETERNALLY grateful if you left a review for The Dark Throne! Love it, hate it, somewhere in between...every review is appreciated.

If you want to keep up with new releases, exclusive previews, and my newsletter serials, you can sign up to receive my monthly-ish Cissell's Epistles—they're chock-full of cat pictures and writing news.

NOT IN THE CARDS
ORACLE BAY BOOK 1

Welcome to Oracle Bay, the town where the local psychics were already expecting you!

Oracle Bay has always attracted the preternaturally clairvoyant. When anyone with seers' blood in their veins steps foot in this quaint coastal town, their powers awaken. They receive a visit from the Psychics Union, and shenanigans ensue.

Sandy Franklin is on the run from her old life and her almost-ex-husband. Lured to Oracle Bay by a too-cheap-to-be-believable apartment with attached tarot reader shop, she has found new friends and a job she didn't know was possible. Hiding from her past while building a new future.

When Vincent, the handsome stranger who owns most of Main Street, announces he's selling Oracle Bay to stave off personal problems, Sandy and the other resident psychics devise a plan to save the town using their divination skills and a little old-fashioned sleuthing.

The one thing Sandy couldn't predict was how hard she'd fall for the one man who could crush Oracle Bay and her hopes for a new life without blinking an eye... Will Sandy get a second chance at true love with the man whose past might be even more dangerous than her own?

. . .

TAKE A TRIP TO ORACLE BAY. Come for the scenic Pacific Northwest, stay for the paranormal romance in these (mostly) standalone novels.

Once Sandy has you hooked, check out the rest of the psychics in Oracle Bay.

RAISING A DEMON
EDEN VALLEY BOOK 1

E velyn Addams stood in front of the mirror with her eyes
closed. She could see every part of herself clearly. Long, lithe
legs tapering to a slim waist. High, firm breasts big enough
to hold up a strapless dress and small enough to let her buy cute bras
at Target. Long, dark brown hair, smooth dewy, pale skin, and a face
unlined, unmarked, and perfectly plucked.

"Moooooooommm! Where are you?"

Evie sighed and opened her eyes. The reflection that greeted her
held only a passing resemblance to the image she'd conjured up in her
mind. She opened the bathroom door and stepped out into the hall of
the too-large farmhouse she'd moved into when her parents had
retired to Hawaii.

"I'm in the bathroom, demon child!" she yelled back.

"Ugh. You're gross," Liliana said.

"Did you need something? Help with your homework? A chore to
do? Or did you just want to come bask in my beauty?"

"Whatever, Momster. I just need more screen time."

"Lily, you've had more than enough screen time today. Go outside.
Play. Be free! It's a gorgeous day and you need to get some fresh air."

Lily heaved a sigh and fixed her mother with a glare. "You'd better be nicer to me when I'm ten."

"Not a chance, child," Evie said. "As soon as you hit those double digits, it's the Cinderella life for you. I'll have you scrubbing the hearth every morning before dawn, doing the laundry by hand, and sewing all your own clothes."

"You do that, and I'll bring in field mice to help out," Lily said. "And not just mice. Rats. Big ones. And tarantulas. They're great at sewing."

Evie laughed. "You're the worst."

Lily laughed and threw her arms around her mother. "You love me."

"From here to the ends of the universe and back," Evie agreed, dropping a kiss on her daughter's head which was just a few inches below hers now. They were already sharing shoes, and it wouldn't be too much longer before her daughter's height surpassed Evie's. "Now go play. Grandma and Grandpa will be here tomorrow to help you celebrate your birthday, so it's your last chance to play without senior citizens trailing you around the lake yelling at you to be careful."

Lily rolled her eyes. "Even when I'm ten?"

"Until you're fifty, probably," Evie said. "Stay out of the lake, though."

"I know, *Mom*," Lily said. "The lake is dangerous, even for strong swimmers, and I'm never to go in without adult supervision." She mimicked Evie's voice so well that Evie blinked in surprise before laughing.

"Exactly. I'm so glad you've listened to at least one thing I've said in the last almost ten years."

"Whatever. I'll go out. Cerberus needs a walk anyway." Lily whistled shrilly. "C'mon, boy! Get in here. It's walksies time!"

Lily stood, staring expectantly up the stairs towards her room, then petted the air in front of her in three different places. "Someday, someone will invent a better leash," she assured the imaginary three-headed dog, then opened the door, ushered Cerberus outside, and ran off.

Evie shook her head and walked towards the door. She started to close it but paused when she saw Lily make a stop in the garage. Evie closed the door and watched through the small window as Lily came back out of the garage with her backpack stuffed to the gills with something Evie couldn't make out. Lily looked around furtively, then jogged towards the small stand of trees at the edge of the property.

Evie slipped out of the house and followed. She normally trusted Lily; her daughter had a good head on her shoulders, and although she liked a good prank, she'd been a pretty decent child—so far. Things hadn't always been easy. It's tough being the daughter of a single mom, especially in a town like Eden Valley where everyone knows everything about everyone...and when they don't have the details, they make them up. But Lily was bright, happy, and relatively well-adjusted.

Lily had been the best and most challenging thing that'd ever happened to her. The challenges were often enough to make her want to tear her hair out and were responsible for most of the lines on her face and at least eighty-five percent of the gray hairs scattered on her head. But Lily had never been a troublemaker, which made her surreptitious raiding of the garage even more out of character.

EVIE HEADED towards the "witch's clearing" that she and her friends had made when they were Lily's age. It was nothing more than a small area in the middle of the wooded area abutting the property where no trees or bushes grew. Evie and her best friends Beverly and Vivian had spent endless summer days cleaning up the space and decorating it with items swiped from their doll houses, matchbox car sets, and Lego builds until they had a small village overseen by a terrifying but benevolent witch.

When she was too old for magical dollhouses, Evie had redecorated with repurposed deck furniture and an old tent, making a reading nook, and later, a place to sneak a couple beers. It was where she'd sworn a blood oath with Viv and Bev to stay sisters forever, where she'd lost her virginity, where she'd come to cry after finding Jeremy in bed with Brandy, Evie's former boss, and where she'd hidden away from the world when all she had was a positive pregnancy test and a broken heart.

Lily had found the spot the summer before and had dragged her best friends—Kevin and Shelby—to fix it up. It's where her daughter hid when she was scared or overwhelmed, when she was angry with her mom, and when she needed privacy—something that'd been more and more common the closer she got to ten.

Evie paused, the clearing just out of sight. Lily was speaking, and Evie didn't want to interrupt in case something innocuous was going down, and Lily'd just been grabbing snacks for an impromptu meeting of the top secret "no grown-ups allowed" best friends club.

Instead of giggles and the sound of junk food wrappers, she heard Lily chanting.

"Daemon esta subjetive volunteer me. And ligandum eros partier eros coram me."

Evie tilted her head in confusion as Lily repeated herself. It sounded vaguely like Latin, but not like anything she remembered studying during her one semester of Latin at the community college. She crept forward, careful not to disturb her daughter, and peered into the clearing.

Lily was sitting in the middle of the clearing, a Ouija board in front of her, birthday candles stuck into the ground at regular intervals, and rock salt Evie scattered on the sidewalks when it was icy poured in a circle around the candles. An old can of spray paint Evie had once used to mark the underground utilities in her yard was on its side a little way outside of the circle. Inside the salt was a large box of matches and a pile of spent matches on Lily's right side and a dusty bottle of wine on her left. Evie peered at the wine, but it was unopened—which was maybe not the most worrisome thing in the clearing, but the easiest fear to dismiss.

Evie stopped trying to be silent and walked towards her daughter. Lily was cross-legged in the circle, palms together in front of her chest, and staring intently at a huge, ornately bound book open on her lap. Her iPad was on top of the book, open to a website with a banner image that looked eerily familiar.

Was that…Sam and Dean?

Lily repeated the incantation, this time with impatience threading through her voice. Evie stood back, hands on her hips, and waited to be noticed.

After a third attempt with no apparent results—Evie wasn't sure what she was waiting for—Lily set her iPad on the Ouija board with the utmost care, then slammed the book shut and yelled, "Fucking fine! I'll wait."

Evie was so startled by Lily's cursing—more so than by her ritual—that she burst out laughing. Lily spun around in the dirt and stared up at her mom. Her eyes widened into an expression Evie knew only too well—there were about to be tears. Maybe an elaborate explanation about how none of this was technically against the rules. A denial of any culpability. A touch of blame-shifting to whoever had given her the book. And an absolution of any lingering guilt.

"Mommy," Lily said through newly formed tears. "I'm so sorry. I was trying to make Cerberus real so you could see him. It really hurts my feelings when you call him an imaginary dog and look at me like I'm lying to you. Even if he was imaginary, I don't think that's a very kind way to treat your daughter, is it? And I didn't do anything you've ever told me not to. I just found this old Ouija board and the paint and wine in the garage—they weren't being used. I'll buy new birthday candles from my allowance, I promise. It's Kevin's book, not mine. It was his idea to see if I could make Cerberus real. And no one was supposed to hear me say the f-word. You only heard it because you snuck up on me, something I'm not supposed to do to you, and you were spying. I have a right to privacy, and you broke your promise."

Evie was impressed. "That's some top-notch blame shifting, Lily-bear. I don't care about the swearing—as long as you save your curse words for when there aren't any other grownups around, especially at school. I'd rather you learn what the words mean and how to use them—and *when* to use them. But let me ask you this…if you thought you were so blameless and not doing anything wrong, why are you trying so hard to talk me into it?"

Lily stood up and brushed off her backside, then scuffed a break into the salt circle and walked towards her mother. "Mo-om, I'm sorry." She tipped her head back—although she didn't have to tip very much—and pointed her big, mournful, puppy dog eyes at her mother.

Evie looked around Lily and saw the painted pentagram on the ground where Lily'd been sitting. "Turn around, monster," she said.

Lily turned and Evie took a step back. Sure enough, fluorescent pink paint adorned the back of Lily's jeans. She sighed. This kid went through more clothing than seemed humanly possible.

"Next time, wait until the paint is dry before sitting in it," she advised. "Now clean up your mess—and give me that wine. I'm gonna need that after today."

"Yes, Mama," Lily said. She fetched the wine and her iPad and handed them to Evie. "I suppose you're taking away my screen time?"

Evie looked at the wine trying to remember where it'd come from and why it was in the garage. Oh. *Oh.* This was the last bottle of wedding wine that was supposed to be opened on hers and Jeremy's tenth anniversary—eleven years ago. Unfortunately, she'd spent that day in a lawyer's office signing divorce papers instead. Her chest tightened for a moment, as it always did when she thought about her divorce, and she turned her attention to the iPad before the tears pricking at the corners of her eyes had a chance to fall.

A photo of Sam and Dean Winchester was the first thing she noticed. Before she even had time to wonder what her daughter was doing with photos from a ten-year-old show that she was too young to watch, the rest of the page caught her eye. A list of incantations used on the show to summon demons.

"Were you... Were you trying to summon a demon based on something from an old TV show?" Evie asked, not even sure she wanted the answer. "And how do you know about *Supernatural* anyway?"

Lily stared at the ground. "I didn't understand the words in the book—they're written all swirly. But I know that there are demons on the show, so I Googled it. And you watch the reruns all the time after I go to bed."

"Keywords: after you go to bed."

Lily shifted back and forth on her feet. "Sometimes I sit on the stairs and watch with you when I can't sleep. It's relaxing."

Evie closed her eyes and counted to ten. Then twenty. "An adult horror show about killing monsters is relaxing?"

"It's not as relaxing as when you watch true crime, but it makes me feel close to you. And I like monsters."

Evie shook her head. "I've totally ruined you. Not even ten years old and ruined for life."

Lily looked up at her mom through her ridiculously long eyelashes to gauge the seriousness of her mother's words. "Are you joking with me?"

Evie smiled. "Yes, monster. I'm joking. I'm going to take the wine, your iPad, and Kevin's book and head back to the house. I want you to clean up the rest of your mess—and that means toss the candles and put the Ouija board, salt, and paint back where you found them, then come into the house so we can have a chat about demon summoning."

"Yes, Mama," Lily said. "Do I have to put the salt I poured out back in the bag?"

"Not right now, baby girl," Evie said. "See you at the house." She grabbed the book and walked back through the woods. Inside, she made herself some tea and sat at the kitchen table to wait for her kid. Discussions about demon summoning hadn't been in the parenting handbook. Who did you even call for this? It was harmless—probably. A little amusing. Slightly concerning that Lily went for the dark arts to make her imaginary three-headed hellhound corporeal instead of writing to Santa or God or something. She exhaled forcefully and took another sip of tea. Maybe it was a mistake not attending church. Any church. Or maybe the real mistake was allowing her to read anything she wanted up to and including all the mythology books she was currently obsessed with.

Evie looked at the book Kevin had given Lily. It was huge—at least a foot tall and almost as wide. It was bound with cracked, black leather and the gold embossed title was illegible from age and wear. She opened it up and a sheet of paper with Lily's scrawly handwriting slipped out.

Wish List for Demon
1. Mama to see Cerberus and buy him food
2. Meet my dad
3. Mama to be happy more

Evie tipped her head back and inhaled deeply. So much being said in fewer than two dozen words. She hadn't realized Lily even thought about her dad that much. Or Evie's happiness. Lily had asked about her dad a couple times when she was just starting kindergarten but seemed to accept Evie's explanation and didn't bring it up again. Damn it.

She turned her attention back to the pages of the book. Whatever language it was written in, it wasn't English. Or even Latin. Nothing Evie recognized. It looked like a hybrid of Arabic, Ogham script, and Egyptian hieroglyphics. She paged through, not surprised that Lily had given up on reading the sophisticated wingdings when something grabbed her attention. A page with only one "word" on it. She'd seen that before but couldn't remember where. She closed her eyes and tried to concentrate on the image.

It hit her. Luc—her summer fling and Lily's father—had this tattooed on his left shoulder blade. She'd asked him about it all those years ago, but he'd shrugged it off as a family symbol, then rolled over, pulling her on top of him, and drove all questions about his tattoos out of her mind.

Come visit Eden Valley—home to a new paranormal women's fiction trilogy chock full of everything any typical woman in their 40s experiences: single parenting, second chance romance, supernatural shoplifting, and the sassiest ten-year-old demon child this side of Hades.

Raising a Demon is the first in a new trilogy from USA Today Bestselling Author Amy Cissell. You can preorder now for the June 22, 2021 release!

ACKNOWLEDGMENTS

I have been writing Eleanor Morgan for the last seven and a half years and there are so many people who need to be thanked (or blamed).

From the beginning, my dad pushed me to be a writer, encouraged me in my creativity, and friended me on NaNo so we could write together. I hate that he died before he got to see my name in print, but without him, Eleanor wouldn't exist.

Christopher—my first reader, my editor, my proofreader, format-ter, and—maybe not least—partner. You held my hand when I published The Cardinal Gate 4 years ago, and you've listened to every single "ugh...this is the worst thing I've ever written" since.

Cat bugged me repeatedly and frequently until I sent her a draft of Cardinal Gate. Her love for Raj & Florence kept me going...and her threats of bodily injury should either character be harmed in the writing of these books.

Even the ex-husband gets a mention. He helped me name some of my characters and gave me so much time and energy to write the first couple drafts of books 1 & 2.

My ARC readers and Amyzonians—you all are the bees' knees. Thank you for reading, reviewing, and sending me so many supportive messages.

Last and certainly least: the cats. As is my custom, I'll acknowledge them in order of likability as of this writing (January 2021). Number one cat, always and forever: Darwin (RIP, age 15). He was my bff (best furry friend) for so long and saying goodbye in September 2020 was so hard. He had a good life and so much love and I will miss him forever. I will be retiring #1 in his memory.

Number two cat: Frank the Tank (age 6). The only reason you're not #1 is only because there no longer is a #1. You, sir, are a great cuddle, the most handsome of all cats, and the least assholish.

Number three cat: Mr. Sterling (age 13). I feel like you're barfing slightly less often, but you did run out of the house and into the street in front of a truck, giving me a near heart-attack and a hundred new grey hairs. The only reason you're not lower on the list is because Last Cat is just the worst.

Number six hundred & sixty-sixth cat: Rupurrt Giles (age 3). You are an enthusiastic asshole with nearly boundless energy, and you have broken a lot of shit. You're why we can't have nice things. Also, your new hatred of my child's feet and ankles is using up a lot of bandaids. Please stop eating plastic & breaking shit—for the love of Zeus! (as Liana would say)

ABOUT THE AUTHOR

Amy Cissell is a USA Today Bestselling Author of urban fantasy and paranormal romance novels. She lives in Portland, OR with her husband, her haunted house-obsessed daughter, their three cats, and the murder of crows she's conspiring to turn into her vengeful army.

When she's not working or writing, she's sleeping because that's all she has time to do! There are few things Amy loves more than a well-timed pun, a good book, a glass of wine, and time at the Oregon Coast.

Although she reads anything and everything, her first love is fantasy. Eleven-year-old Amy discovered fantasy when she 'borrowed' her father's copy of The Hobbit and an enduring love affair (mostly with dragons) was born.

Amy is the author of the Eleanor Morgan and Oracle Bay series. Visit Amy online at www.amycissell.com and sign up for her newsletter.

facebook.com/acissellwrites
twitter.com/acissellwrites
instagram.com/acissellwrites
bookbub.com/authors/amy-cissell
goodreads.com/acissellwrites

ALSO BY AMY CISSELL

The Oracle Bay Novels

Not in the Cards (October 2018)

First Hand Knowledge (November 2018)

Belle of the Ball (December 2019)

Hell and High Water (2021)

Tempest in a Teapot (2022)

The Oracle Bay World Novellas

Wing and a Prayer (January 2019)

Eden Valley

Raising A Demon (June 2021)

The Eleanor Morgan Novels

The Cardinal Gate (February 2017)

The Waning Moon (June 2017)

The Ruby Blade (October 2017)

The Broken World (March 2018)

The Lost Child (June 2019)

The Iron River (May 2020)

The Dark Throne (February 2021)

The Eleanor Morgan World Novellas

The Throneless King (March 2020)

Made in United States
Troutdale, OR
03/09/2024

18317401R00202